Jennifer Mills is the author of the novels *The Airways* (Picador 2021), *Dyschronia* (Picador, 2018), *Gone* (UQP, 2011) and *The Diamond Anchor* (UQP, 2009) and a collection of short stories, *The Rest is Weight* (UQP, 2012). In 2019 *Dyschronia* was shortlisted for the Miles Franklin Literary Award, the Adelaide Festival Awards for Literature and the Aurealis Awards for science fiction. Mills' fiction, essays and criticism have been widely published, including in *Best Australian Stories, Best Australian Essays*, the *Guardian, Lithub, Meanjin, Overland, The Saturday Paper*, the *Sydney Morning Herald, Sydney Review of Books*, and the *Washington Post*.

Also by Jennifer Mills

The Diamond Anchor
Gone
The Rest is Weight
Dyschronia
The Airways

Salvage

JENNIFER MILLS

PICADOR
Pan Macmillan Australia

Pan Macmillan acknowledges the Traditional Custodians of Country throughout Australia and their connections to lands, waters and communities. We pay our respect to Elders past and present and extend that respect to all Aboriginal and Torres Strait Islander peoples today. We honour more than sixty thousand years of storytelling, art and culture.

This is a work of fiction. Characters, institutions and organisations mentioned in this novel are either the product of the author's imagination or, if real, used fictiously without any intent to describe actual conduct.

First published 2025 in Picador by Pan Macmillan Australia Pty Ltd
1 Market Street, Sydney, New South Wales, Australia, 2000

Copyright © Jennifer Mills 2025

The moral right of the author to be identified as the author of this work has been asserted.

All rights reserved. No part of this book may be reproduced or transmitted by any person or entity (including Google, Amazon or similar organisations), in any form or by any means, electronic or mechanical, including photocopying, recording, scanning or by any information storage and retrieval system, without prior permission in writing from the publisher.

 A catalogue record for this book is available from the National Library of Australia

Typeset in 11.85/17 pt Adobe Garamond Pro by Post Pre-press Group

Printed by IVE

Quote on pages 325, 395 from 'A Litany for Survival', *The Collected Poems of Audre Lorde* © 1997 by Audre Lorde, used with permission.

The author and the publisher have made every effort to contact copyright holders for material used in this book. Any person or organisation that may have been overlooked should contact the publisher.

 The paper in this book is FSC® certified. FSC® promotes environmentally responsible, socially beneficial and economically viable management of the world's forests.

To be cared for is the invisible substructure of autonomy.

— Anne Boyer, *The Undying*

The way to see how beautiful the earth is, is to see it as the moon. The way to see how beautiful life is, is from the vantage point of death.

— Ursula K Le Guin, *The Dispossessed*

Salvage

1

NOVEMBER

Everything you carry bears the weight of what you're leaving. Jude has always travelled light, and this time she takes nothing with her, only an insulated mug of hot coffee. It's dark when she climbs into the truck. There's no-one in the street; even the dogs are still asleep. Her heart's hammering, though she hasn't touched the coffee yet. She sets it in its holder in the centre console, turns the key. The old engine, last of the diesels, coughs to life and takes a couple of gasps of the cold air. Windows misted up, frost clinging to the glass. The wipers squeak, but don't do much. That's probably why she doesn't see them.

Another hammering, against the passenger-side door. It isn't locked – there's no point around here – so she sits and waits for the handle's click. The door swings open. Ali's face is a blur in the gap.

'We're coming with you.' He mounts the metal steps with implacable grace. Behind him, she can see grey light emerging over a darker grey sea. A few stars linger on. She hasn't slept enough for patience.

'No, you're not,' she says.

Ali nods, climbs into the passenger seat and sits there.

'For crying out loud,' Jude says, letting her eyes roll back a little too harshly. 'Go home.'

He leans out only to gesture at the others. In the dim light she can see two figures: Solare and the teenage Tik, who have become inseparable over the last couple of months. She's almost grateful to hear Tik chattering excitedly, to see Sol moving calmly behind them.

Lying awake at two or three that morning, she had thought they might try this. With insomnia's ruthlessness, she decided to refuse. Celeste is her problem: the risk should be hers alone. But now that they're here, the decision doesn't seem to be hers at all.

'You're being ridiculous,' Jude tells Ali, as he folds his arms.

'You may thank me later,' he says, but when he tucks his long hair behind an ear his grin carries traces of anxiety. He looks away, climbs over into the back. Sol follows with a nod, and Tik springs up behind her. Jude's about to bark at them for not closing the door when another face appears, round, solemn and pale.

'No fucking way,' Jude says. Her voice sticks in her throat. She stares ahead at the condensation dripping down the windscreen. The world appears in foggy streaks, looking like it slept as badly as she did. This whole situation is Nora's fault. But what would be the point in telling her again?

Jude's breath goes in and out, hot and loud as the engine.

In the mirror, Ali's face is serene.

'Jude, we need her,' Solare says, clasping Jude's shoulder in one strong hand, bangles shimmering. Jude doesn't need any of them, but she doesn't have time to argue with Nora, to get tangled up with her exasperating goodness. Her shoulder turns to concrete, and the hand moves away.

'I can explain,' Nora says, avoiding Jude's eye.

The low growl that comes out of Jude surprises her. Maybe

the motor hides it, because Nora's expression doesn't change. There's a little hurt in that face, a little hope, always a sweetness. Jude clears her throat against the ache in her ribcage, blows warm air into her hands. The smell of oil makes her hungry.

'Come on, we're wasting time,' she says at last. 'But you get in the back. I need a navigator up here.' She makes eye contact with Ali in the mirror in time to see a glimmer of triumph cross his face and vanish.

The harbour is a steely colour, flat like the day they found her. Pulled her out of that machine, dragged her back into the world.

Should have let her drown.

Ali wriggles over to make room for Nora, then climbs through to the front, wipes the windscreen with a sleeve and stretches out a leg. He makes a small sound like he's going to speak, but Jude lifts a hand.

'Not a word,' she says, tapping the lid of her coffee. 'Not a word until I finish this.'

The truck creeps through Northport. Jude takes the corners with practised ease, passes the Common and the belltower, the old hotel. On the edge of the town – or village, since so few buildings are occupied – she pauses at the entrance to the highway, foot on the brake. There are no other vehicles, but she winds the window down to look anyway. Ali does the same.

Across the highway there's a weedy field. A reclaimed farmhouse, a patch of forest behind it, the white nubs of deer tails disappearing. A garden full with cabbages, ruined land beyond. So much effort, just for these small patches.

The cold air clears the windscreen mist into the corners, and she lets it, at least until Tik says they're freezing their tits off. Jude and Ali wind the windows up in time with each other, the old chrome cranks resistant, sticky as memory.

Better care in the Alliance, Jude tells herself. Real hospitals, well supplied. They'll know how to care for her sister – if she's still alive. Jude understands this, but that doesn't make it right. Nora and her colleagues traded Celeste for their own safety, for a few crates of supplies. She said the Alliance gave them no choice, but there's always a choice.

And now Nora won't even look at her.

Jude stares longingly at the mountains to the left. They hover in the sun's glow, seeming smaller and closer than they really are. There's no snow yet, the grey stone tinted faintly orange. Pleated lines as delicate as hair. Forget glacial melt, floods and rockfalls: the truck yearns for those winding roads. The wheel wants to turn in her hands.

'Okay,' she says, and swings it the other way, towards hostile territory.

'Can I talk yet?' Nora leans forward, softening her voice.

Jude feels the skin on that side of her body go warm, and shoots her a look in the mirror, trying to keep the heat out of her face.

'After I've finished my coffee, I said.' She lifts the cup to her mouth. Five hours to the border with the Alliance, maybe six if the road's bad. Jude takes the tiniest sip and puts it back in the holder. She might be able to make it last the whole way.

Ali's foot taps against the floor: a nervous habit of his, the bad limb talking. It's four years since they escaped the camp and crossed the Alliance together, heading for the Freelands. She remembers silent towns, treeless streets, rows of identical boxy townhouses. Ali quiet in his own thoughts, or asleep across the back. That anxious leg, his trust. The pass on the dashboard gave them three days, but she did it in twenty-four hours.

Tik is muttering restless questions about this river, that empty factory. In a better mood, Jude would jump in, share details. Sol's never travelled this way, as far as Jude knows, but she has – or invents – most of the answers. She's quick to belong.

Even Tik falls silent after a while. The further east they travel, the more broken the landscape appears. Villages sinking into wasted ground. Old orchards and rice fields where nothing will grow, not even moss. Just plains of grey stone or mud salted by rising seas, blackened by poison. It had seemed easy at first, becoming a Freelander. Anyone could – that was the point. Stay in the present; do the work. But then there was Celeste, and it turned out to be so fragile, this version of her life as paper-thin as all the others.

Jude steals a glance at her passengers. Tik's leaning their head against Nora's arm, and Sol's looking out the window, absently twisting a lock of the teenager's hair in her hand. Nora's face is cast down, her eyes hidden.

Three months ago, Jude didn't have a sister. Now she has another chance.

She has spent most of her life in flight, and outrun nothing.

Jude blinks, winds the window down a crack. The chill air burns her eyes. She will leave them at the border; Sol can drive the truck back. Things will be simpler when she's on her own. Belonging nowhere, carrying nothing.

She pulls her coffee from the holder, takes a long drink.

2
STATION

Before sight, there is a sense of a figure, or figures, withdrawing. Celeste is aware of a dull ache at the nape of her neck, a lingering memory of pain. Then the mask lifts, the air hisses.

When she sits up, the lights rise gently. She sees no-one, only the instruments that tend to her as she sleeps. They are indistinct, already retracting into the soft upholstery, their little lights pulsing with a fuzzy awareness. She turns to examine the bulbous form that covered her face, vision still blurry. When she puts the back of her hand to it, it is warm. Grey, like layers of smoky glass, or a screen. She pulls away slowly and the mask folds itself into a recess in the wall. Her hand feels soft, her wrist moves with a thought, but there's a shadow feeling to the body at first. It's keeping part of itself in reserve.

The bed cups her. She finds the dip in one side and drops her legs over it, lets her feet find purchase. Her knees are there, modest in a pale linen, warm to touch. There are places to put her hands, to brace herself to rise, and so she does, carefully, not trusting that her legs will hold her weight, surprised when they do. The walls are close. One wall, in fact. Grey and curved. The room is softly padded, like a cocoon. There is no door.

She looks back at the place she has left, and the bed is already rising, the indentation vanishing. This is the Station, she remembers, and can't help smiling. Only the Station watches her expression. She has this soft space all to herself. She pauses to admire its tidy luxury. Her eyes have adjusted; six curved rungs have appeared in the wall, six lights gleaming. She climbs at the edge of consciousness, an uncanny sensation in her arms and legs. At the top, she finds the outline of a hatch.

When she touches it, she feels vibrations. Things are whirring above. Judith is here somewhere. The thought runs sharply through her like a cold breath. Maybe she will be awake too.

We did it. The whisper pricks her throat. Moisture is a starburst. She blinks it back.

A small oval of black glass to one side. When she holds her hand there, the hatch slides open. She climbs another rung, pokes her head into a long corridor that slopes upward in both directions. There are other hatches in sight in the distance. Trapdoors, set into the floor that is also a wall. This is part of the uncanniness, maybe, the effort of orientation. She remembers her training: the mind will adjust. It dissolves like a message in a dream.

Beside her own trapdoor, there is a shallow recess where a pair of slippers waits. She sits on the edge and reaches for them. Pale grey, a grip pattern on the base. The inside lined with fine synthetic sheepskin. When she puts them on, they fit perfectly.

There are goose pimples on her arm, but it isn't cold. She isn't hungry or thirsty; her body doesn't seem to need anything. It's quieter than she expected, more comfortable. When she stands, the lights dim in the room beneath her, rise in the corridor that curves ahead. The slippers are slightly sticky on the floor. This is the uncanniness, too: her body moves easily because gravity is lower than she is used to. There is whirring at the hub. The Station spins.

A thrill runs up her skin from knees to chest. They made it. They are out.

The next trapdoor is a short distance ahead, maybe a minute's walk. The light's dim, but from here it looks identical to her own. Judith is in one of these rooms. She takes a step, and the lights come on ahead of her. When she glances back, they light up in that direction instead. A little laugh escapes her, crackling in the thin air. She walks on, wonderfully light on her feet, the slippers sticking to the floor. She pauses halfway to the trapdoor, listening.

Whirr, hum. Above and below. The Station protects them.

Judith? The name in her mouth, little more than a breath.

There is a click, and the hatch ahead springs open. Lights come up in that part of the corridor, emerge from the room below. She notices the colours shifting, as if reflected from water. So comforting. He has thought of everything.

A pang of uncertainty, and she steps forward.

A head pops out of the door, and then a person. She feels her lungs deflate. The person is too tall and slender to be Judith. They sit, find their slippers, stand. Turn away, then towards her, observing the lights. The same movements. The same off-white pyjamas, the same slippers. A dark face, hair curled close. They are squinting back at her.

Hello, Celeste says.

I think we're the first ones awake. Are we?

The voice is croaky, but the warm seriousness of it brings her whole personality back. Celeste takes a moment to remember the name. Carolyn Something-Something. Before the launch she had a quiet charisma. Wellness, cosmetics, an empire of confidence. Now she is a doubtful shape in a corridor, gesturing.

We should walk, Carolyn offers. *My eyes.*

Celeste moves closer. She can smell the chemical scent of the instruments on this woman, and now recognises the same scent on herself. The air seems cleansed of lesser human odours. It will have been two months. She remembers that they are meant to be woken in pairs, staggered and randomised to prevent friction. To prevent conflict. Psychological experts were consulted. This must be why they haven't paired her with Judith the first time out. The Station takes care of everything.

Yes, Celeste croaks. *For the exercise*. It's important to set a routine. Her training swims to the surface, flickers, disappears.

Carolyn sighs, and they set off together. Celeste tries to keep pace with her at first but though she feels strong, she tires quickly. She is smaller, lighter here. The floor curves, so each step is a little uphill, but it also rises to meet her, which feels strange. Her mind keeps expecting flatness, Earth gravity. She has to concentrate on what her legs are doing. Celeste finds it is easier to walk if she doesn't look at her feet.

It isn't a large circuit. They come back to their own hatches before Celeste remembers to count the other ones. Her vision is crisp again, but her thoughts are murky, clouded up like churned sea water. She pauses by her hatch, looking down at the empty recess, then at her slippers. She has a feeling she has forgotten something important. The feeling sits low in her belly.

Sleep well? Carolyn asks.

It isn't possible to have forgotten anything, because every detail has been planned, tailored to them; everything here is necessary, and sufficient for their comfort. In fact, she remembers, everything's perfect. When Celeste doesn't answer, Carolyn gives her a quick, tight smile, and she returns it. They carry on walking.

They are on their third round when Carolyn pauses at a hatch. *Yes*, she says, *that's right.*

Carolyn crouches and lowers her palm to the black glass oval. This trapdoor is different. It has no recess, no slippers. There is an image beside it: two black dots inside a horizontal pill shape, silver, hardly bigger than Carolyn's hand. Her movements are smooth, the confidence returning to her body. Celeste scratches her arm. The small door slides away. The interior does not light up.

After you, Carolyn says.

Not entirely dark, Celeste sees, her eyes adjusting. There are little points of light down there, inside a circle as large as their bodies, larger. Steady, unblinking points of light.

She remembers this room. The model of this room, before. The strange word they had for it: *cupola*. A term from architecture, signifying a dome. In the model they stood underneath, looking up. But this shape bends out and down like a bowl below them. A submerged mirror. She finds the rungs and lowers herself down into the dark in her sticky slippers. Carolyn's tall warmth above and just behind her. An indrawn breath.

When they are both standing on the rim of the bowl, Celeste reaches out to steady herself against the wall, and the other woman grips her hand. The points of light below are steady stars. Here is the Moon, radiant between their feet, its textures on display. And there, away to the left, the same size or maybe smaller, hovers another body, swathed in cloud skin, instantly recognisable. It looks just like the pictures. Just like the Earth emoji used to on her phone.

It's almost full, she thinks, and then another little laugh escapes her throat. The Sun and the Earth in a relationship of light, without her. They are out. Free. When she looks up, she can see Carolyn's teeth gleaming, her broad grin directed at the stars.

Fuck, says Carolyn. *We actually made it.* She squeezes Celeste's hand. The squeeze is not so strong, but it hurts her fingers. Still, she does not pull away.

Carolyn's other hand has not let go of the ladder. Her face is an outline in the moonlight, the earthlight, but Celeste can see her tears glistening, can feel her own welling up. She pulls her hand from Carolyn's. Judith should be here for this. They stand there for a long moment, watching the bodies below them move across the bowl. No, the wheel is spinning. A miniature version of an Earthly bias. Celeste wants to stop, she is dizzy with looking and placing herself. But she can't take her eyes off the universe, not until the Earth has passed beneath them and moved out of sight.

A light buzz or trill inside her head, at the base of the skull. She puts her hand there, feels the skin prickle. She should go back to her room. She's about to articulate this urge when Carolyn lifts her hand to her hair and says, *We should go back to our rooms.*

They stay a moment longer, looking down at the bowl of stars. The fullest cup. The feeling low in her belly. She is not hungry, except for this: the view is a meal or a medicine that will sustain them when they return to sleep. Looking away makes her head spin. She waits for the dizziness to subside before climbing up after Carolyn, returning to the corridor. They walk side by side in silence, keeping a little distance, then descend to their waiting rooms without speaking. No words seem worthy of what they have seen. The wonder all their own.

3

AUGUST

She woke early that morning from the usual dream: spinning, fire, a hurtling descent. Her skin cold with sweat, her chest empty. Jude let her eyes fall open. Counted until she slowed her breath. The dull ceiling of her little room. Still here, then.

It was growing light when she walked down to the harbour, the cracked concrete a dim grey underfoot. Jude had parked the truck where she always did, on its own in the open space beside the coastguard; as always, she was pleased to see it remained there. The sun already had some heat: it shone grey-white on the water's surface, two equally relentless forces. Bits of the old harbour wall poked through the glare, just visible at low tide. Two ragged gulls ran tilting from the shallows. The new harbour was already going under. The sea was a hungry animal; it would take and take, if you let it.

Jude glanced at her watch. She was up too early. They would not be ready.

She walked west along the harbour, water lapping against the wall. The stuff that washed up here was mostly what other places let pass: old timber, bits of smashed-up ships, and plastic, always plastic. Northport was a backwater, even for the Freelands. There were larger salvage stations further down the Gulf, with better equipment, more people. Still, much of what they found could be made useful. Plastic could be crushed and processed to make furniture and insulation, or to patch the roads. Even bad wood could be burned. The one thing they had plenty of was scrap. Never enough people to pull the scrap out of the water, tag and file it, stash it in the storage sheds, put it all to use.

Any boats that made it this far were usually wrecked, and the people weren't much better. Sun-damaged, brittle, injured. They were fewer each year. The group she was taking today arrived a fortnight ago; they were the first arrivals in many weeks, and had come by land from the south. It was the usual story: their boat fell apart before it could reach safety, and they swam to shore. Walked until they were picked up by a vehicle, brought here. People shifted around out on the water like so much driftwood, ending up anywhere that would take them. Well, it was her story too.

She glanced back at the truck. Still there. Across the street behind it stood the small clinic, a low white building with a red cross glowing over the door. All the new arrivals had received their clearance, vaccinations and what have you. Sorted for use, like materials. The Freelands were efficient, in their way.

It was still too early. She continued out to the end of the harbour where the barge waited empty, then turned. There was no-one else out walking at this hour, but the light was on in the coastguard building. Hamish and Karim would already be on shift. She waved at the salt-crusted window, though she wasn't sure they'd see her at this distance, and began walking back. The building had been a seafood restaurant before the war; it still had a few rusted letters fixed to the wall on this side, *R NT* dangling below a dim mural of a cartoon lobster. Salt and bird shit striped the faded paint. Above that, wide glass faced the water, pretty views repurposed. The lower half of the building stepped down into the waves. Those were the best tables once: out in the open, close to the water. Wealthy tourists would have eaten seafood there, the crisp scent of mountain wine lifted by the sea breeze. Now the terrace was a set of shallow pools where children liked to swim, protected by the crumbling wall. The pools looked clean today, the water relatively still. No lobsters in a generation. One of the kids claimed they'd seen an octopus last month. The currents spun strange patterns, and what they brought was unpredictable.

Jude had tried a coastguard shift once, and hadn't liked it. Nothing bad had happened; it was more the nothing happening that got to her. She'd been distracted by the thought of what might be out there, of everything that had sunk to the bottom. The Gulf was a graveyard, awash with half-forgotten trauma. Even now there was something unsettling about the water.

A lively movement on land caught Jude's eye: a hooded crow was hopping around on one of the storm-surge cement blocks, picking at a kelpy tangle. She wandered closer until she could make out what it was. Not seaweed but an old green fishing net, caught in something electrical: it might have been a drone or a toy. The crow was pulling wires from it, taking it apart, like it worked in the salvage sheds.

'Hey, crow.' The bird looked up. Its eye was curious and calm. It hopped sideways, making room for her observance.

Wires tangled up with net, a messy web. The machine part wasn't a shape she recognised. It looked to have broken away from a bigger structure: the frame was thickly reinforced, a little melted-looking. Maybe the Alliance drones were getting heavier.

Maybe it was space junk, a piece of some defunct satellite. She stopped.

The dream repeats: the Station falling, the pieces burning up. The metal heats white when it touches atmosphere. The rim of the air like a solid object. Her bones glow and disintegrate. In the sea, the hiss of shrapnel, ashes.

The crow hopped back, lifted its wings.

These were old visions. Familiar company. She blinked through the scene, backing slowly away from the bird and its object, waiting for her eyes to clear. It was better to let the frames play all the way through, to wait until the image settled. Impossible to stop it otherwise.

The church bell began, the images flickered and dissolved. From the Common it was much too loud, but it sounded gentle from here. Eight chimes. No time for self-pity. Returning to the truck, Jude opened the back, lowered the benches and secured them in place, checked the fastenings twice. Behind her, the crow went calmly back to work. On her boots, a rim of salt was drying.

She climbed into the driver's seat, flipped the sign on the dashboard from *Back in Five!* to *OPEN*, and started the engine. The old girl chugged to life, filling her lungs with its odours: today's batch smelled vaguely of popcorn. Despite its emissions, she preferred the diesel motor, which ran mainly on waste oil from the kitchen, processed and filtered in a shed near the creek. The second motor, electric, she'd installed in her second year here; she didn't trust it. The batteries were old, didn't hold a charge for long, and it wasn't strong enough to get a full load up some of those mountain roads. Jude pulled a sleeve over the heel of her hand and ran it tenderly across the inside of the windscreen. Electric was all right for backup, but diesel was the truck's spirit.

Some people – mostly Ali – had accused her of nostalgia for the old polluting engine. And she was attached to the truck: it was a survivor, a twentieth-century workhorse, older than she was. Ten reliable tonnes, the dented cab a red that had lost its gloss, the trailer a scruffy white, strong enough to haul whatever was needed: food, materials, people. She'd built the two long fold-down benches inside herself, from salvaged timber. Took good care of both the motors. There were few vehicles like it, and nothing else in Northport that could handle so much heavy lifting. It made Jude useful.

She started the engine, satisfied with the healthy growl, and checked her instruments. The tank was full. The batteries were charged, the roof panels receiving morning sunlight. The GPS was broken, but it had been for months; there was no point replacing it. She knew the roads she needed to know, and when she didn't, the F-net's crowd-sourced maps were more reliable than busted old satellites anyway.

She shivered, pulled away from the harbour and headed uphill to the Common. The former school stood firm on its rocky perch, its back to the sea. Safe from the water for a few more decades. Its murals were cheerful, the garden alongside thriving. Though it wasn't at its centre, the Common was the main building in Northport. Most of the old village was clustered around the hill to the east. Newer structures clung decrepit and empty to the coast below. Glass-fronted holiday apartments stood in chest-deep water, their windows salt-crusted. The older houses had survived earthquakes, floods, wars, but they were small and cramped. Behind them, a once grand hotel, an eighteenth-century folly, provided extra accommodation. Scaffolding advanced along the wall they were repairing. Washing hung from the upper windows, a dozen tents were pitched here and there in the grounds. Building was proceeding quickly by necessity. In a few months it would be too cold to live outside.

Her passengers were tumbling out of the Common now, clutching their kits. Everyone wore the odd fashions found in the store: a mix of the discarded and the handmade, mismatched but comfortable. Ali's brightly patterned shirt was a couple of sizes too big, his hair loose and swirling in his face. She could see from his movements that his leg was good today, his mood happy. When he looked up at her, crow's feet formed around his eyes.

She checked her watch. They were only a tiny bit late – early by Freeland standards. If they left soon, she and Ali should be back by afternoon. The days were still long. She could enjoy the gentler evening sunshine, maybe even go for a swim if the water looked clean. If the heat wasn't too much.

Jude could feel it through the windscreen already, was anxious to escape the worst of it. She resisted the urge to hurry everyone along.

The system was mostly reliable. Villages put their requests on the F-net; when new people arrived, they were assigned a place that would suit their needs. The F-net's algorithms were smart about a lot of things, but Freelanders were maddeningly devoted to democratic participation, so every decision had to be run through a committee. Even if they mostly just signed off on the F's decisions, people liked to feel they had a say, and had it at great length. Iterative democracy, Ali called it. There'd been a meeting about this group, the details of the assignment gone over, weighing up what everybody wanted. The right decision would have been arrived at. Jude hadn't been at this meeting, because Jude never went to the meetings.

This was a matter of taste, rather than principle. A person could appreciate the value of consensus decision-making without having to engage in it for hours at a time. Jude did her bit, kept her head down. That was enough for her.

Driving was simple. She only had to hit Accept on the F to assign herself the task. In theory, anyone could do any work they wanted here; in practice, people had preferences and skills and favoured tools. In theory, no-one owned anything either, but it was understood the truck was Jude's.

She watched in the rear-view mirror as they piled their gear into the back. Their faces were familiar. She'd spoken to a few of them when crossing paths in the laundry or the kitchen. Most had already lost that frightened, defiant look they'd had on arriving. A few were laughing now at something Ali said. Jude watched an older woman refuse a young person's offer of assistance with her bag, lifting herself up the step into the trailer.

Ali was in his element: taking his time speaking to each of them, enjoying himself. Jude couldn't hear a word over the engine, but she saw the motions of quick translation in his body.

Orson should be a good match for these people: a village of thirty or forty, in high country, for a long time in need of skilled shepherds and builders. Far from town, but this group wouldn't want to see the water again in a hurry. They were a mismatched bunch, of various ages, but united. Nothing like a near-death experience to bond people quickly.

Her pulse ran restlessly. Too much coffee this morning, maybe. The sour of it still sitting in her mouth. Jude hadn't been to Orson in over a year. There were few populated towns along the winding road into the Ouai Valley. The valleys tended to be unstable in geology, weather, and political affiliation. Most people referred to them collectively – unimaginative place names were an unfortunate side effect of the Freelands' polyglot population – but in reality, each valley had its own distinctive culture. Though technically Freelanders, Valley people were often only haphazardly involved in decision-making: bad F-net access, or just disinterest. They tended to consider themselves a little apart from Freelander business, and the troubled relationship between Valley and Port was a favourite subject in the bar at the Common.

Privately, Jude thought it came down to the roads. If it was hard to travel, it was hard to participate, so most Valley people had developed a take-it-or-leave-it attitude. They had their own cultures, let their eccentricities flourish like the moulds on their weird artisanal cheeses. She could see the Valley side of things. The Freelands had a tendency towards regulation that she found distasteful. Northport was bearable, but further south, in larger towns and in the lone Freelander city of Portosacre, there were rumours about the next Assembly: secret meetings, binding rules, enforcement. If Valley people didn't want to get caught up in it, then good luck to them. Each to their own.

She was getting ready to honk the truck's obnoxiously loud horn when at last Ali concluded his storytelling and hoisted himself up to join her. There was space in the cab for three more bodies. Jude was glad no-one climbed in behind him. She wasn't in the mood for chit-chat.

'You finished with your captive audience there?'

'That new medic's really nice,' he said, ignoring the tease. 'I can see why everyone raves about her.'

Jude glanced in the mirror. A squat woman, dark hair, pale, was stepping back from the trailer, waving brightly. The new doc had moved up from Portosacre a few weeks ago. Jude was yet to speak with her, but had heard only praise.

'You should ask her about the insomnia maybe,' Ali said, pulling his seatbelt. When he turned, the lurid shirt fluttered its yellows and oranges at her.

Jude shrugged. 'What's the point? There was nothing the last seven medics could do about it.'

He raised his palms at her in mock self-defence.

'Did you ping the village again?' she asked, reaching into the seat pocket for her cap. She had sent the transport confirmation through to Orson at six that morning, but there hadn't been a response.

'Yep,' Ali said, swiping his phone. As a translator, he carried a rare personal device. He muttered at it, shook his head. The range in the Ouai Valley was poor. If they didn't get an answer now, they might not hear anything until they arrived.

'We're going anyway, though, right?' Jude asked. The arrangement with Orson had been finalised two weeks ago. The confirmation of arrival was just a formality. Network failure was the most obvious explanation. Access was so patchy in the valleys that people called it the Off-net.

'Course.' Ali refreshed the phone again, then gave up and slid it into the console.

There was no point worrying about it now. No reason to be anxious. Jude tugged the black cap down low, felt the comfortable texture of the wheel beneath her hands, the strength of the engine.

But even when they were moving, she couldn't shake the feeling. The sun glaring in the mirror. The heat like something in pursuit.

4

BEFORE

There should be an image, a trace scent or texture, some memory of first care, but if it's in her head she can't find it. Jude is three when they take her from the hospital, and she doesn't remember a thing. A faulty memory can be a mercy, even a point of pride. The world falls away around her, and she survives.

She remembers what they tell her: how lucky she is to be given this gift of a fresh start, to be snatched from the clutches of poverty, rescued from a doomed life and elevated to one of promise. To this immense privilege – they gesture at Sovereign House, the luxury compound to which she has been delivered – and an existence that could never have been dreamed of for her, before.

The story is the same, whether it's told by the family or their numerous staff. It is not told all at once, but in fragments: neglect, followed by salvation. Expectations are subtly expressed: a remark here, a raised eyebrow there, a dusting and grooming.

She does not doubt them for a moment. She is careful; she is always close enough to happy. Everything she needs is given to her. It's impossible to question their affection. Only to wonder if she'll ever deserve it.

Most of this is not part of her conscious awareness: it's more like something she breathes in, day by day. The air at Sovereign

House is triple-filtered, stripped of all toxins and hostilities. The desert outside the compound might sing with heat or rage with dust and storms, but it can't get in.

The gardens around the house stretch out, a green, irrigated enclosure. Beyond the green, the earth is stony or silken with dust. Tiny, unlikely flowers break through it. Around the compound, a high fence, and beyond it, more arid land, more saltbush, the country unchanging. Only this side of the fence is safe.

Jude is supposed to grow like the garden, but she grows like the desert: stealthy, tough, in shadow. Out there, she is both safe and out of the way. She walks most days, sometimes followed at a distance by a member of staff. She listens out for parrots, spies wallabies against the rocks. She captures insects, cradles lizards, digs grubs from the roots of bushes, fascinated by their cool white flesh. Jude returns these living things to earth.

One day, she finds a scrap of silver-yellow fabric hanging from the fence. When she bends down to inspect it, she sees the translucent scales of a snakeskin stuck to a protruding wire. The little reptile has used this hook to peel away its outer layer, then slithered off, naked and free.

She pulls the fragile-looking scrap away, surprised how strong it is, how it holds its shape. A creature too small to be held by the fence that surrounds her, too strong for its own skin. She looks at the pattern of scales, gridded like a net. She looks up at the fence, observes the echo of its high, tight chain-link. Her gaze follows the razor wire that spirals along the top to a post. A camera swivels lazily towards her. She ducks her head.

Security is important: intruders must be kept out. The house behind her is huge, safe, protective. The Princes love her as their own. She puts her hand to the wire, traces the links with one nervous finger. The net vibrates around her, tuned to the wind.

She carries the skin back to the house, folded between two cupped hands. Almost expects it to have flaked away by the time she gets there, but it's unharmed. She slips it into a paper bag and then into the drawer where she keeps her collection. Wipes sweaty palms on her jeans, peers down.

There isn't much in the drawer. A few stones, acacia pods, a twist of mulga root. Six cicada shells. A doll she doesn't remember being given – it is old plastic, worn dull, and the eyes are stuck open. Pale blue irises and corn-silk hair. It looks a bit like Celeste.

At the back there is a set of cufflinks that she stole from JB's things. He's never noticed them missing, or never said anything if he did; he must have dozens the same. They are gold, with the Prince Industries logo: an arrow entering a curve of earth, a sun-like crown above it.

This collection might map her existence. Because she came with nothing, came from nothing, everything that's hers is theirs. So everything that's hers is also stolen, with its own history first. She pushes the cufflinks into the corner, fingers a chunk of dirty white quartz. Lines up a few feathers, a few small bones. Bits of nature don't belong to anyone, so these are safer. Bird things don't care if she doesn't remember. The doll, though. The doll was Celeste's. She closes the drawer.

*

In the years that JB is officially her father, he is at the centre. The house changes its energy around him. When he is there, which is rarely, he fills doorways, heads tables. He strides down corridors, laughing robustly. The staff turn subtly towards him, waking like plants to sun.

Jude glimpses him through windows, watches his back in the car; he takes the front passenger side, makes a point of sitting up there with Spence. James Barton Prince is a public figure, the centre of an empire. He goes by JB with the family, brings himself down to their scale. Spence calls him Sir.

When he is not there, everything goes still and quiet. The house listens for the sound of his voice returning. Jude listens too, lying stiffly in her little room. She has always had trouble sleeping.

She sees a little more of Elisabeth, the third and smallest wife. The wives, Celeste complains, have gotten smaller each time, possibly for emphasis. Younger, too. There are ten years between Jude and Celeste, but only nine between Celeste and Elisabeth. The third wife is often away, in their city apartment or beach house, places Jude has never seen.

Jude is not starved of affection. There are always people around, dozens of them: looking after her, playing with her, trying to teach her something, watching over her. Sometimes they bring their kids to work, and she plays politely with them, though she's happier on her own. There are the au pairs, a series of interchangeable German or Swedish girls from an agency. They are always kind, and always replaced. The au pairs go off, having saved enough to live the lives they always meant to, somewhere else.

There are two brothers, sons of the first wife, Emily – cancer, very sad, a long time ago, there is a foundation. The brothers haven't lived at Sovereign House for years; they come and go, their hands in the business, jostling for their inheritance. Just a little hair-ruffling for Jude and a few stiff questions about school. When she spends time with the family, it is mostly Celeste.

Celeste is the daughter of the second wife, Astrid, who started a new family and her own business in America, thanks to the spoils of a long divorce. She has the mezzanine, a sprawling territory with its own bathroom and a separate study and a walk-in wardrobe almost the same size as the study. Celeste is sharp, fine-featured, with the pale blonde hair of girls in magazines. She is polite, clever, and can sing. Her skin is clear, the white of the good bond paper of her many framed certificates: achievements, donations, performances. No-one can fault Celeste; she does everything perfectly.

*

Jude is one of Celeste's projects. Hair brushed, lipstick clumsily applied, the-third-wife-Elisabeth's shoes, and she is pushed towards a mirror. Jude isn't sure why the image of herself in this get-up makes her want to cry, but she does, spoiling everything.

Celeste pats her on the back and calls her *baby Judith, pet*.

Family photographs are formal affairs, conducted annually. In them Jude is always propped up in front of her sister, those thin, pale arms wrapped round her like a harness. She knows she does not match the family, or the flounces in the dress. Her disobedient brown hair casts an ugly shadow. She makes Celeste look paler, blonder, more perfect.

They are inseparable. Everyone says so. She follows Celeste around, waits for her warm side to shine. Sometimes Celeste gets sick of it, and shuts her in the wardrobe. Locks the door, so Jude has to sit on the carpet, feet aching in the wrong shoes.

She doesn't mind. The wardrobe is bigger than her own room, and she can play alone. If she makes a sound, Celeste yells through the door: 'Judith! Don't you dare cry.'

All of this is for her own good. She has to learn how to be.

Her sister is too old for dolls, too young for children. The-third-wife-Elisabeth has no children of her own and not much interest in either of them. Celeste is kind to take her on. She likes having a sidekick.

'It's you and me against the world,' Celeste says.

*

After she turns six, Jude is driven each morning to the day school, bundled into the back by one of the au pairs. It is hard to make friends with other children. They are in awe of her last name, too careful, and she is not used to them.

She is proud of her important sister. Wants to appear with her at the school gates, but Spence drops them off at separate entrances. The car ride always makes her sick. Sometimes Jude has to stop to vomit on the side of the road. Sometimes she doesn't make it.

Celeste gets out first at the school, and Spence often turns to look at Jude when she has gone, checking her face carefully before he drives to her side of the huge red-brick castle. Wipes ready in the glovebox. She looks her best for him, manages a smile to match his care. Those few seconds are her safest, the cool evaporating from her skin.

At school, it doesn't matter if the things she thinks to say come out too formal, too cold. She has no reason to be sad or filled with doubt, to feel her body waver in the heat. She is lucky; she is safe. She has power, even if it's not her own.

She must learn to manage. Soon, her sister will finish high school and Jude will be on her own.

Celeste goes away, too: skiing, sailing, France. Occasionally, at the weekend, she has visitors: the other fine-boned daughters of their small establishment, her classmates from the exclusive school. They call Jude in so they can look at her. She stands obediently before them, her back against the wall.

'She doesn't look like you,' says one of the friends.

'Oh, she's a rescue,' Celeste replies. She hasn't looked up from her screen.

'Is she always so,' another girl says, waving a hand in the air. Jude straightens uncertainly.

'Yes,' Celeste replies. 'I'm working on her.'

'You should do something with her hair,' yet another proposes. Jude lifts a hand to her skull, protective, and the girls titter.

'She won't brush it out,' Celeste complains. 'Hopeless. Go away now, Judith, pet,' she waves.

Later, when they are gone, she will be summoned back into the bedroom, held in an embrace, and told that she is loved.

Celeste sighs. 'You know how it is.'

Jude doesn't know. She wasn't born to this. She listens, picks up details, trying to work out what she is supposed to do, what she is worth to them. She learns to pay attention.

That's how she finds out about Endurance, about the disaster there. Not all at once, but in fragments. A poisoned town. People got sick and died. An accident, of course. The project had to be abandoned. The site remediated, at great expense. Reports were managed, difficulties kept out of the courts.

They don't talk about it much. *A shame*, they say: not in a way that means shame exactly but in the way that Elisabeth might say, on the phone or to her assistant, that she isn't available to attend an event. *A shame* can mean nothing at all.

The flaw adheres to the lost. To the people who stayed, who should have tried harder. Better not to know about her parents, all the ways they let her down.

The more Jude pays attention, the less sure she is about the meaning of anything, even her name. She doesn't feel like a Judith, or a Prince. When she's sad, even her sadness seems to fit her badly, like it's their invention. It's hard to miss what you don't remember.

She's lucky.

On one of her walks she finds a wounded corella, long-beaked, flock lost. She wraps it in her jumper, carries it to the kitchen. The cook finds a box, and Jude watches over. It's dead in an hour, maggots boiling in its broken shoulder. Celeste won't look; someone gets rid of it.

'You can't save everything,' she says.

5

AUGUST

The landscape was wearing its full summer splendour. It was an illusion: rows of trees beside the road screened grey fields in the distance. Still, the hills gave an impression of abundance. Birds shot from the branches, their peace disturbed. Olives gave way to stone fruit, then walnuts, chestnuts, pines. Sheep and goats grazed. Even the roads were not so bad; there was not enough traffic to destroy them.

Jude had missed the mountains, hadn't realised how much; now they seemed to welcome her back. She almost said so to Ali, but there was no need. His eyes were fixed on the peaks ahead, his expression enough.

Soon the Fort appeared in the distance, a squarish monolith emerging from its hillside host. A stark medieval structure with few windows, it had been taken over by an artists' collective. Caravans and tents were gathered in the meadow behind it, solar panels were propped on the roof, and one side of the old stone wall was covered in an abstract mural. A pink creature was emerging from a high window, waving a monstrous inflatable tentacle.

'Is that new?' Jude asked, nodding towards it.

'Nearly finished,' Ali said. 'They're having a party in the autumn. Aiming for Halloween.'

Jude's sense of being welcome wavered. She was an interloper in this hemisphere, still felt disconnected from its seasons. And large gatherings made her nervous.

'They've worked quickly,' she said.

Ali looked at her. 'It's been two years.'

'Really?' Jude flushed.

He smiled. 'You lose time like other people lose their glasses.'

'Busy years.'

When they came here, four years ago, there'd been more work than they could handle. Dozens of people in need arriving each week. It had seemed as though demand was always going to increase. Meetings went on about sustainable population, food production, land reclamation, the problems of overwork. Jude wondered about a second truck. Then the new arrivals slowed to a trickle.

Northport wasn't the most popular destination in the Freelands. It was damp, with few entertainments, and the high country around it was dangerous. Most people chose the more densely populated towns to the south, the settlements around Portosacre where the work was more varied and the housing better, and there were more likely to be others who spoke one of their languages.

But it wasn't just Northport; the pattern was similar all over the Freelands. A decade after the war, the border disputes on either side were slowly being settled. To the north, the Alliance had been reinforcing its territorial boundaries with several adjoining countries. The sea to the south was increasingly patrolled, the airspace overhead surveilled by drones. Squeezed between these nervous powers and the water, the Freelands was becoming hard to access. Jude tried not to pay attention to such things, but she had a sense that the looseness that distinguished the postwar period was tightening, a new order closing in.

She hadn't been anywhere except on local supply runs for weeks. There were never many other vehicles on the road, but the emptiness today seemed eerie. Technically, the Freelands *was* empty. Most residents had been evacuated during the war, or killed. The Alliance didn't want to be responsible for the clean-up and rebuilding, or for settling a growing population of stateless people, so Freelanders were left alone. On paper, none of them existed; there was no country here, only uninhabitable land. For now, they could make their own rules, but it was hard to know how long any of it would last.

The Fort shrank away, and there was the turn-off to the Ouai Valley – in red spray paint, someone had written *OUAI NOT?* beneath the name. Most jokes lost something in translation, but people couldn't help themselves. Jude glanced at Ali, who held the phone out the window, pulled it in and shook his head: still no signal.

Empty villages looked down from precipitous rocks, old hydroelectric infrastructure hanging loose. Decrepit churches were turning back into piles of stones. Past the turn, branches reached out to scratch the truck's sides. The road was dotted with fallen rocks, and narrowed in precarious sections. As the gradient increased, the truck lurched on some of the hairpin bends. Jude could hear unsettled voices from the back, but didn't want to stop until she could find a safe place to pull over. Orson was another forty kilometres away, more than an hour at this rate. She clutched the wheel.

To her left, the hillside was a fresh spill of grey rubble. On the slope to her right, a few small trees were already springing up.

She glimpsed the half-wild goats that thrived in this harsh pasture, bending their heavy horns to earth.

The road was clear of debris for a section, then it grew steeper, folding into another set of hairpin bends. At the first turn there was an old grotto, white paint peeling. The statue inside was dirty, the saint's hands broken off and crumbled at its feet. The dread Jude had felt as the day began returned, reknotted.

She slowed the truck to a creep, then stopped. The road was blocked by several large boulders.

Rockfalls were common enough in the valleys. Glacial melt was an advance of stone and floodwater as much as a retreat of ice. Repairing anti-avalanche nets was specialist work, difficult and dangerous for small communities. In the defrosting landscape, dams often broke, rivers ran high and violent. Chunks of mountain could break away, swallow whole towns.

These rocks were evenly spaced. Painted yellow, and marked with black crosses. It took Jude a moment to realise they were not tombs but barricades. It was almost satisfying when the dread found its justification in something tangible.

She got down from the cab and walked the area, wanting to make sure she could turn the truck around. The air was cool. Might as well let everybody out to stretch their legs. Behind the trailer, Ali was already helping people down. A single bird piped and went still. There was good hunting in these forests. Valley people liked to travel armed.

The rocks had a childish quality, like a *Keep Out* notice on a cubby house. Most were too big to move by hand. Moss grew on their shaded sides, and wildflowers were springing from the gravel, colours mocking the yellow paint.

Something nagged at the edge of her perception. Jude listened, but there was no sound but the forest. Nothing moved that she could see. She went to check on her passengers, encouraging people to stay close with a scoop of her arm. Ali chatted with the eldest, a sharp-boned woman, grey hair tightly curled against her scalp, eyes darting nervously. The eyes fixed on something behind Jude and widened. Jude turned to see a man emerging from the shaded trees beyond the stones.

Her nostrils flared at the cigarillo he was smoking. The man wore a faded blue plaid shirt beneath a khaki puffer vest. He was bulky, but not tall. His shirtsleeves were rolled up, exposing tattooed arms, and his expression was hidden beneath a black baseball cap. Instinctively, she moved closer to the truck.

When he lifted his head, she saw a grey moustache, blue eyes. He smiled. Not a smile Jude liked, but at least it was fleeting. He leaned against the fender before speaking.

'Where are you folks headed?' His voice was softer than his face suggested. He spoke English with an unplaceable accent.

'Orson,' she said, 'but what's with the barricade? You fixing this bloody road?' Jude cursed her mouth. She'd been aiming for comradely, masculine, not hostile.

The man regarded her.

'What you want in Orson?' he asked warily.

'Resettlement,' said Jude. 'All organised.' She indicated the people behind her, felt them draw closer to each other.

He stared past her at the group, his chin rising.

'First I heard of it.'

Orson was not much further up the valley, but it was possible that this guy was a lone traveller or hunter, out of F range in an abandoned lodge for the summer. You came across survivalists in the valleys from time to time. They didn't usually like to interact.

'The request was accepted weeks ago. We messaged this morning to say we were on our way from Northport.' She glanced at Ali, who looked up from his phone, shook his head.

'Hold up. Let's take a look at this situation,' the man said, warming up. 'How many of 'em have you got back there?'

'Eleven,' she said calmly. Eleven *people*, she almost said, but could not trust her voice for neutral emphasis. There was a cross among the tattoos, she saw, ornate, covering most of a forearm.

'On what authority?'

It was a meaningless question in the Freelands.

'Eleven, you say?' Voice raised, he walked past her and peered at the canvas side of the truck. She could smell his sweat, alcohol, smoke and stale tobacco. He faced her with an expression of incredulity that he must have rehearsed.

'Nobody asked you to bring 'em here.'

'That's not true,' said Jude. 'The request –'

'We're full,' he said, so loud that a bird shied from the undergrowth nearby.

Jude took a step back. Tried to hide her flinching. Too late: not enough to calm him.

'Yeah, you back off, *lady*.' He moved closer, waved his hand at her for emphasis. He was too close, but she stood her ground.

'You want to watch yourself,' she said, prickling. Getting called *lady* always pissed her off. It happened rarely; most Freelanders weren't this rude. Ali appeared beside her, hands in his pockets, a reassuring shape. She waited for the anger to subside but didn't bother trying to conceal it.

'Look, the request our end has been open for months,' she said.

'Almost a year,' Ali added.

'Well, it's closed now,' the man said.

'Are you sure?'

'I'm *from* Orson.' His chest swelled a little, the furrow shifted. He moved until he stood between them and the makeshift barricade. Jude caught a hint of uncertainty in his expression. How long did that *from* indicate? A year? Five? Almost everyone in the Freelands was from somewhere else.

'If the F request was cancelled, we would have been notified,' Ali said. He was better at feigning patience than she was.

'That's your rule, is it?' the man said.

'Not my rule. Just the way it's done.' Jude looked behind her, ensuring their passengers were all in sight. No-one else emerged from the trees, at least.

'And you say you're free,' the man spat, gesturing at the road. He sucked on his pungent cigarillo. The Freelands wasn't home to him, she realised. It was down there somewhere, a foreign place with foreign regulations.

Jude studied the barricade. It should be possible to move a few of the smaller rocks by hand, squeeze the truck through. Easier if she reversed a bit and used the winch. But there was no point driving through to Orson if they weren't going to be welcome.

'Let me try to get a signal.' Ali sighed, lifting his phone. Jude saw the man's confidence falter for a moment. He'd put the cigarillo back in his mouth and was staring at Ali. Jude's hands were sweating. She thought of the goats on the rocky hillside, butting horns. It was important to show calm.

Ali had perched on a tree stump, frowning into his phone. He was quietly discussing something with the older woman from the group of arrivals. She moved to speak with the others, was quickly out of sight.

The man watched her go, and Jude took the chance to study him. He was familiar. Fiftyish, with an ex-military demeanour. Yes, she had seen him in town last summer, working on the sports centre. They'd nailed roofing in the same team for three days, sweating in the heat. She remembered a strong but aloof guy, sure of his work.

'I know you,' she said, making her voice light. 'You were down in Northport in the summer. We fixed that roof together.' She pulled at the sleeves of her flannelette shirt. 'You're a hard worker,' she added, touching her cap, disgusted at herself.

He grinned. 'What do they pay you for driving, huh?' he asked. 'More than for roofing, is it? Because we got nothing.'

'We got the roof fixed,' she said. 'Food and shelter. We all get the same.'

'I can feed and shelter myself. What good is your little club-house to me, up here?'

He had a point. From here, the decisions of the Assemblies probably seemed arbitrary, unrepresentative. Hell, they seemed that way to Jude half the time, but she couldn't come up with a better way to run things.

She turned away, but Ali had walked up the slope in search of F reception. As soon as he saw her movement, he came back, scrolling through the message feed.

'There's still no response.'

It would be up to them to negotiate. That was how it always was. If a trade could be made, some compromise reached, they had to make it work on their own.

If you can help, help – that was one of the key Freelands principles. Of course, it wasn't how things worked in reality. In the valleys, that promise of mutual benefit was hazy and optimistic.

The man sneered at Ali, probably jealous of his device. Jude knew that look as well as she knew that *lady*. Knew Ali would rise above it, while she let it get to her.

'We could maybe take *some* of them,' the man said. 'Depends what you'd be offering in exchange.'

He toed the ground.

Jude could hear voices in the truck behind them, low and anxious: the passengers had already climbed back inside. They were attuned to threats, and probably used to waiting for decisions to be made about them.

'Well?'

Jude and Ali glanced at each other. She should cut the man some slack and negotiate. Things were fragile here. Peace was always cobbled together. It took work to hold it, endless compromise.

'Fuck it,' she said. 'Let's go.' She caught the man's shocked look before she climbed back into the truck.

Once Ali had settled beside her, Jude leaned out, pulled the door closed, yanked the wheel and forced the truck into a three-point turn. The man jumped back under the trees to get out of their way, then he recovered himself, shoved his hands in his pockets, glared through the smoke as if he'd won.

Maybe he had. He could go back and tell his people that he'd turned them away. They might cheer him, tell him how strong he was, and he'd feel safe and useful for a day or two. The next time they came this way there would be better barricades, more men to guard them. One day, a fence and an army.

'That went well,' said Ali. In the corner of her eye, she could see he was smiling.

'Yeah,' she said. 'Back to wherever the hell we came from, I guess.' Her voice was barely shaking.

The fuel gauge was low, so she switched to electric for the downhill run. She drove slowly on the hairpins, past the old saint with the broken hands. Someone should have left flowers, at least. She would remember the saint for next time, if there was a next time. The map in her head was already changed.

When they were back in range, Ali looked for other options. There was always a backup plan or three.

'There's Roana,' he said, reading off the screen. Jude glanced at the sun, high in the sky now. She liked it up there, and the drive would be pleasant; it was a gentler valley. But it would take all day, and more fuel. And anyway, it wasn't up to her. There would have to be another bloody meeting first.

Her shoulders aching, Jude pulled over at an open space by the river, just before the Fort. There was a shelter with a few benches, an old trough, water running from a mountain spring. She splashed the chill water on her face, wanting to feel the burn of it. Teenagers braved an old stone bridge, tossing sticks into the water below. Ali talked the adults through their options. The older woman was watchful, nodded without argument. She turned from him, called to the young ones and closed her own circle.

The discussion wasn't long. Ali sent a message back to Northport. No-one had to wait for an answer. The Common was always open, anyone welcome.

It felt like going backwards. But the sun warmed away some of Jude's chill. One of the teenagers seemed to have a theatrical bent, and made the bridge his stage: he did a comical imitation of the man from Orson, folding his arms and bulking his long slender body into a stouter shape, puffing on an imaginary cigarillo.

Salvage

The dread ought to have left her as they drove out of the valley, but it clung on, unsatisfied. Approaching the turn-off, she thought she heard the buzz of another engine in the distance. An Alliance drone, probably. When she blinked, the familiar shuttered images briefly returned: white heat, disintegration, the fall.

6

BEFORE

It's Jude's fault they are left behind. The one time she was taken up in the helicopter, she was violently sick on the upholstery. So JB, Elisabeth, the two brothers and the handsome guest climb aboard without them. It will be boring anyway, Celeste assures her. They are only going to visit one of the open-cut mines that dot this landscape, that transformed a sheep-and-cattle station into a fortune in a few generations.

Celeste doesn't have to stay back with her; they have staff for that. But she insists it's her job to take care of little Judith, and she'll look after her.

'You are an angel,' Elisabeth says, kissing the air beside Celeste's face.

When she is gone, Celeste mimics this gesture perfectly.

JB doesn't say goodbye: he is deep in conversation with the stranger. The brothers flank him, complete the square. Jude registers a pattern repeating. Her sister's arm around her, they wave at the glass as the party walks out to the helicopter pad, a flattened hill no higher than the compound.

As soon as they're gone, Jude slips out into the garden. She likes to find the edge of the irrigated part, where the landscaping stops and the desert takes off its disguise. She is happiest there, in the wide strip of earth that grows how it likes.

She squats in the dust, her back to the high fence, and watches. Shadows move too slowly to be seen. Sovereign House is a half-buried rectangle, sunken gardens hidden in its folds. It looks as though it has grown out from the rock, a natural and permanent feature.

There is a soft *whoosh* behind her, and she turns to see two wallabies staring over clumps of grass on the other side of the chain-link. The razor wire buzzes overhead; it's windy now, and the air carries a strange heat. She ducks away from the camera. The animals' ears swivel and assess the wind, their nostrils alert to its meaning.

In sudden unison, the wallabies lift their heads and bound away.

She decides to follow the fence around until she hears the helicopter return. Maybe she'll find another snakeskin.

Jude walks until her feet hurt. She doesn't hear an engine. When she looks up, she is almost back to the start. Hungry and thirsty, she heads for the compound. The helipad is on the other side; maybe they landed already. People are always telling her she's distracted. *Pay attention, Judith. Listen.*

She slinks back in through the fire-escape doors, makes her way up the concrete stairwell. And there is Celeste, furious and frightened, surrounded by a blur of uniforms. Black marks ribbon down her face.

Jude's stomach knots, her hunger vanishes.

'Where have you been?'

Her sister's face is transformed: imperfect, vulnerable. Her voice is different, too.

Suddenly, everyone in the room is talking. It takes Jude a long time to understand that there has been an accident. They explain it to her again, more slowly. The helicopter has fallen out of the sky. Something went wrong. The wind pushed it into a hill, and there was a fire.

'She's afraid of flying,' Celeste tells the uniforms. There are too many of them, more have poured in, so the kitchen is a forest of black and blue. Jude wants to defend herself: it's sickness, she can't help it. But it isn't clear who's in charge, or who might listen. She waits for a chance to speak. Someone hands her a peanut-butter sandwich, a glass of milk. A door swings open and Spence comes in. He folds himself down to her height, pushes the hair from her forehead with a calloused thumb. She can feel each grain of dust stuck to her skin. A phone on the counter is ringing over and over. Dirt cracks in her teeth. She is lifted, carried from the room. The sandwich is still in her hand, one bite out of it she doesn't remember tasting. Then there's a strange sound trailing her down the hall, like a wild dingo. Celeste is howling.

*

There are people in the house all the time, holding meetings, assigning and reassigning tasks. There are a lot of lawyers. The board appear and disappear, in person and on screen. Executives move quietly through the corridors. A caretaker period is declared. More lawyers. More screens. There are the funerals, family and state, and then it is just the two of them, plus about thirty essential household staff: kitchen, cleaning, security, advisors, Spence.

Celeste is in and out of meetings, in and out of bed. She doesn't eat. Her perfection reseals: it is a strong surface. Jude is not permitted to wander around the grounds on her own anymore, it's not safe, so she goes down to the garage and bothers Spence. He's undemanding, familiar. Doesn't hassle Jude about going back to school.

The new au pair, Fiona, has been vetted thoroughly by the security company that the board has engaged to watch over them – a security company that is wholly owned by Prince Industries. Fiona isn't European; she's a country girl, little and bird-boned but very strong, from a station up near Geraldton. An honest family, the lawyers say, which is different from a good one.

She's the same age as Celeste, but they aren't friends. The three of them eat together sometimes, and it's so awkward that time seems to stop completely. When Celeste mentions the accident, Fiona's face changes. There's a strange clench in it, like she's in pain.

Jude asks her about it eventually.

'That was no accident,' Fiona says. 'They don't tell you much, do they.'

'What do you mean?'

'Nothing,' Fiona says. 'I read, that's all.'

Jude knows how to pick up clues, to follow a trail. She types quietly; she scans search results. She confirms the facts of the incident: surprising, fatal, unsolved. Then she finds the theories. Sabotage. Eco-terrorists, or a corporate rival. Revenge for the Prospect River disaster.

They don't tell you much.

She hardly ever thinks about her first family, her birth family. She knows what happened to them, in theory; nobody has hidden these facts from her. But nobody has been direct about it either, and it's hard to ask. She doesn't know their names, or what kind of people they were, what they loved, why they worked out at Endurance, accepted the dangers of being there, made a life in the tailings, had a child.

When she looks it up online, reads the forums and the old newspaper reports, it's obvious that the place was doomed from the beginning. A spill was inevitable. But the mine's operation was essential to the state's economy, its revenue unimpeachable. The warnings were put aside. And there was an inquiry, and it found that Prince Industries did nothing illegal, ticked all the environmental boxes, demonstrated corporate responsibility, did more than was required.

It seems to Jude that there are two stories. Two versions of reality that happened, side by side.

In one reality, accidents happen. In the other, there are culprits.

In one reality, Jude is lucky. Safe.

In the other, things fall apart without warning.

Worlds change in a heartbeat. One day, Fiona's gone.

The compound felt too big before the accident. Now, its vast monochrome rectangles, long corridors and panoramic windows seem to go on forever. It's always been possible for Jude to disappear inside its architecture, find a room, a corner, even a storage cupboard where she won't be found for hours. Lately she disappears even when she's not trying.

After things settle down, after the meetings and the reshuffle and the confusion, when it's just her and Celeste and the remaining staff, the compound's emptiness becomes profound. She sometimes climbs into one of the cars with a book, stretches out on the back seat, comforted by enclosure. In the garage she is well hidden. Eventually, Spence will knock on the window, lean down to give her a little wave. 'Just checking you're alive,' he'll say. That is a comfort too.

*

At ten, she is an avid but undiscriminating reader. She gets through what is available in the house: boxes of sci-fi comics that the brothers left behind, Celeste's old school texts – Austen, Shakespeare – and teenage magazines. Then she reads whatever the algorithm on her device recommends, whatever else she's curious about.

Sometimes Spence will bring her books from outside. Tintin. Philip Pullman. The Earthsea books, in a huge brick with tiny print that she has to hold close to her face. Her favourites are second-hand. She traces the names of strangers written on the first blank page, the prints of something spilled. Books remember their readers. She leaves her own marks, with only vague thoughts of a future.

The staff keep the house clean; inside, careful order reigns. Celeste manages, or is managed, pretty well. But the landscape around the house is not a priority. Before, it was irrigated to an eerie green. Now the desert is creeping towards them, feral cactus rivalling grasses, spiked and grey-green, its surprising flowers sprawling in the dirt. Jude prefers this new, unkempt version, with a bit of everything growing, and spends as much time out there as she can. She soon learns that, while she isn't supposed to leave the house, no-one will come looking for her.

There is only one landscaper left. Jude watches him from the fire escape, door propped open, or perched on a nearby boulder, legs dangling. The light softens outward from the house, encircled by stone and the limits of her vision. Some days, the fence glimmers; others, it fades away in the haze.

The energy demands of the compound are enormous. It is closed off in sections. Windows are shuttered, wings secured. Gradually, Celeste narrows the building to a central spine. Instructs Spence to sell off most of the cars. Whittles away at the staff, at everyone's budgets. She folds herself into the isolation. Spence says maybe this is her way of expressing grief. Or maybe there isn't the money.

Jude wonders if her rescue was temporary.

Sometimes she imagines the compound is a kind of starship. The building hurtles through space, jettisoning dead weight. Boardroom, ballroom, bedrooms: closed doors. Or it is a ruin. The infinity pool transforms into a haven for weeds and algae, swamp hens and frogs. It begins to evaporate, its little ecosystem turning hostile. The building has commenced its abandonment. Jude wanders its dim rooms, pretending she's the last survivor.

When she comes across Celeste on a sofa in a corner, her face lit up by a screen, or in the kitchen with an untouched bowl in front of her, it doesn't break the spell: Celeste is a character in her game. Too thin, hardly eating, a body suspended between worlds.

It isn't loss, or not just loss, that changes her sister. There's some other desire in her, an older, darker, more unspeakable thing. She's like Sovereign House, with its closed-off rooms. Maybe the hunger comes from the house itself, or from the rocks beneath. It's like a wound that refuses to heal.

One night, Jude wakes in the middle of a tremor. It's gone before she's fully awake. A quake beneath, too small to dislodge anything, hard to believe until it's confirmed. When Spence explains plate tectonics, she nods, half listening. Understands it as the friction between two kinds of grief.

He tells her Celeste will get well. She is getting help; people come to the house and help her. The best help available.

'And she loves you,' he says, as if that counts for anything.

7

STATION

The second time she wakes, she stays in place. Lies still in the blur of light and waits. When her vision improves, she takes a moment to examine her cocoon more closely. There are few labels or markings. She can see inlets, outlets: air, water, nutrients and waste. She doesn't know how it all works; doesn't need to know. The Station takes care of everything. The mask is warm to the touch, its surface shining. The retracting bed has an undulating texture that ripples like an animal beneath her. Her heart rate feels slow, but she has no watch to count it. She is aware of the effort of waking. Not struggle, exactly; more a reluctance in the body, a fog she has to climb through. It's mildly euphoric, like the after-effects of drinking or a high-altitude hike. Was it like this last time?

She finds the rungs, climbs to the ceiling, reaches for the black oval. The hatch opens to her palm. The corridor above is just as it was before: the recess, the lights, the other trapdoors in the distance. She crawls out, pulls the slippers on. There is the gentle tearing sound of other footsteps. Judith. Yes. Her sister was just here.

Celeste?

A slight lisp brings the whole man to mind. It is the eager voice of André Weiland, inheritor of precious stones. Of the twelve, he had been the most nervous in the weeks before they left. Though she would never have shown it, his anxious manner had irritated her. He is walking quickly towards her now, his slippers scraping. She climbs to a standing position; her head takes a moment to clear. They are face to face. Same height. His eyes too close to hers. Same as her own, almost, the palest blue.

So? How are you feeling?

She turns, begins to walk. She wants to go straight to the room with the cupola, to see the Earth pass far below, but she isn't sure she wants to go there with him. Despite the low gravity, his feet thump along beside hers. The corridor is narrow and her body skirts the wall. He gained weight for this, thought it would help. She has kept her slenderness. *There is less space than you think*, she will tell Judith.

Dreaming, he says. *It is wonderful. Is it not?*

I suppose, she says. Certainly, she wants to go back to sleep as soon as possible. The other world hovers, patient and complete. But she doesn't remember her dreams. And this is essential, the walking and the conversation both: a regimen of physical and mental exercise to cover what the machines cannot. The Station dispenses care precisely. But they can't fully extract themselves from a need for human company.

Her vision's not right; lights spread and burst as they come on in the distance. This time, her memory of the layout is clearer, her understanding of her purpose more accurate. If she concentrates, she thinks she will be able to remember everybody on the list. There is André beside her, and Carolyn Leighton-Westley, who was with her on the first walk. There is Judith, and of course there is Nick Fry; without Nick she would not be here, nothing would be here. They arrive at the observation hatch before she can think of another name. She will count her way around the rim: there should be twelve trapdoors. She doesn't want to ask André what he remembers, in case he answers.

Here, he says. Celeste crouches and puts her wrist to the silver pill shape, the two dots like blank eyes. The hatch opens. She lets him go first, waits longer than she has to, looking out along the curved corridor. In both directions, darkness.

When she gets down, he is crouched over the glass bowl. His shape blocks a section of the view. There is little room to move in this space, and the floor around the edge is narrow. It feels like the interior of an enormous eye, an eye that gazes ceaselessly. He rises and stands across from her, his head bent, and she hears that he is speaking.

What excited me the most in the beginning was the idea of going home again, André is saying, his breath struggling to keep up with his voice. *The wonder of it, you know. The triumph! But now we are here, and I am most excited to be here, just – experiencing this. Isn't it so?* When he lifts his face, his features glow with starlight.

Celeste hasn't thought about it. Going home. How small it seems. She listens as kindly as she can.

They do have things in common. His family murdered by terrorists, a revolutionary mob, his country destroyed by its own delusions. Left him with the wealth that couldn't be seized, his nightmares, and a sense of purpose. To make something meaningful. To make history from what remained. He liked to speak in those terms. He made it all seem ordinary.

You know, I can't remember arriving, he says.

Irritated, she looks down, but she can't see the Earth, just the Moon sliding past beneath them. Not beneath: ahead. It is always ahead, they follow its orbit, it only passes because the Station is rotating. The Moon looks smaller than it did from Earth, though it is the same distance from here as it was from there. She struggles to hold all these positions in her mind. It is confusing to visualise the relation of objects with no real floor, no anchor. Celeste lifts one foot and lets it fall, then does the same with the other. Her body still has substance, but the fall is hesitant, the floor submits. The Earth is still the centre.

And you? What did you want the most?

What she wants is not to be in this conversation. When it's Judith beside her, wondering at this experience, she might answer. When it's their turn, they will laugh about the others. It doesn't matter if the Station listens, judges them. They are family; they understand each other. The other people are just passengers.

I couldn't say, she says, with a chill precision that pleases her. She steps aside, making room for him to exit first. While he climbs, she takes a moment to look down at the stars between her feet, arranged in unfamiliar patterns. There is no end to them, only a limit to what she can see.

Four months must have gone by already. The next time, it will be six. A year will pass quickly this way, taking brief breaths of company between long rests. She should make use of this time, should concentrate. Remember her purpose. She climbs the ladder. André is waiting for her in the corridor.

Who else have you seen? she asks him.

André stops walking for a moment. He lifts his face to the blank, curved ceiling.

Ah. Arvind, he says. His voice is still breathy. *And then* – he scratches his cheek; one eye squints closed, like he's sighting something in the distance. But when she looks, the distance ahead is just blacked-out corridor, one hatch-light visible. The curves play perspective games.

He shakes his shaggy head. *And then you, Celeste.*

No word of Judith, then.

She should mention this, ask questions, but she is tired now. She needs to return to her place in the wheel. To close her eyes and let the Station take over, let it knead and care for her. Sleep will restore the balance. She will see her sister soon.

When they arrive at her hatch, she is glad to watch André shuffle off towards his own trapdoor, pale pyjamas fading into darkness. She waits until he's out of sight, then kicks off her slippers, opens her hatch, descends. She has forgotten to count the doors, but it doesn't matter. There's time. The lights come on in her room, and she's grateful for its simplicity, the way it does everything perfectly. She is in the Station's hold.

Before she lies down, she sits a moment with her legs crossed, tries to focus. The pale linen soft and loosely woven. In the low gravity, memories float apart. Her thoughts don't quite adhere. Sleep is the most important thing. Next time, Judith will be waiting. There is nothing to plan, nothing to organise. Her only work is rest.

Sleep is soft. Under the body, instruments play. The ground moves with a forest's sprung decay.

8

AUGUST

'This is weird,' said Ali, scrolling through the day's newsfeed. The contents were often boring: work requests or offers of resources, notifications of obscure committee decisions. Jude rarely bothered to read them. If there was anything interesting happening, someone would tell her eventually. She waited for Ali to summarise.

'Something odd washed up at the port today.'

Jude's throat prickled. 'Oh?'

He frowned, reading back over the post. 'Unidentified – whatever that means.'

It could mean anything. A vessel, a vehicle. A human, living or dead. Animal, cargo or scrap. Each of those had its own four-letter code, though.

'When was this?' Jude asked, keeping her voice light.

'This morning,' he said. 'Not long after we left, looks like.'

She remembered the crow with its wire puzzle. Weird stuff washed up all the time; there was no reason it should interest her.

'Are you okay?' Ali's expression was slightly alarmed. Jude realised she had let her foot sink on the accelerator, let the truck gather too much speed. She lifted it again.

'Fine,' she said, as calmly as she could. Her ankle was cramping. 'Just keen to get back, is all.'

He watched her for a minute, but said no more.

*

It was late afternoon when they finally pulled up in front of the Common. Jude got out and helped the passengers unload their cramped bodies and kits. Back to the beginning, back to the same beds they had left that morning. Freddie from the kitchen came out to help, and was treated to the boy's impersonation of the man from Orson with new embellishments. It should be like this, just a funny anecdote, but Jude couldn't relax. Freddie was trying to catch her eye, so she found the gauge in her pocket and bent to check the tyre pressure.

Ali found her crouching by the driver's side door.

'You hiding?' he asked. His shadow was long on the ground beside her.

Her boots were scuffed. The left one was developing a hole in the toe. She should take better care of them.

'No.'

He waited, but she didn't move.

'Not coming inside, then?'

She put her hands on her knees and rose stiffly, tilted her chin towards the harbour. 'I'm going to refuel,' she said. 'Charge the battery.'

'You look like shit,' Ali said. His eyes were shaded, but his voice was gentle. 'You need some help?'

Jude shook her head. 'Nah. Go be social.' She could hear the others heading inside, the back of the trailer being latched. She stood and yanked the door open, pulled herself up and settled behind the wheel. The sun was in her eyes. It was still warm, but getting late. She needed to hurry.

Jude started the motor, then frowned at her hands, bent the fingers admonishingly. There was no need for them to be shaking.

*

She coasted down to the harbour and parked the truck neatly, perpendicular to the shed, not that it mattered. The concrete dock was a blank expanse, empty of other vehicles. Even the crow had found something better to do.

They must have pushed or rolled or winched it into the shed already. The barge stood empty at the far end, and the water was a gently churning green. She knocked on the coastguard door, sweat gathered at her sides. From above, the faded lobster regarded her inscrutably.

No-one answered the door. Karim and Hamish usually shared the long day, sleeping in shifts; there was always someone there. She turned the handle, stuck her head in. The desk was deserted, the soft lights of the monitors the only movement. She went round to the shed.

It was locked. It was never locked. Jude hammered on the tin before she could stop herself. She heard voices through the door, then footsteps. Hamish opened it, his sandy hair ruffled, squinting a little without his glasses. His expression was urgent, almost frightened.

'Jude,' he said. He sounded surprised to see her.

'I heard you found something.'

He hesitated, glanced into the dark shed.

'You better come in.' He checked the harbour behind her, then pulled the heavy door closed with a bang. At first she could hardly see anything. Hamish slid the bolt and Jude followed him, her sight adjusting. A light in the rear was trained on something half the size of the truck, suspended over the cement floor. The sheds had been used for boat repair before the war, and the old hoist was still operational. She saw at once that this was no boat.

Her body turned cold.

'They're not responding.' Karim's voice was muffled; she couldn't see him.

There was another figure, a squat shadow, holding a torch up to the part of the machine that had been wrenched open. Karim's movements were visible in the opening. She heard him grunt. Light glittered in the pool of salt water below the hoist.

'Keep trying,' the figure said, their voice calm. 'We need as much of it as you can get.'

'What's happening?' Jude whispered.

'There's someone in there,' Hamish murmured. 'Come.' He touched the back of her shoulder, then walked away from her, towards the light. She saw him reaching for the opening, a kind of awe in his torchlit face.

She stumbled closer, almost tripped over something. A stretcher.

The medic looked up at her, expectant.

'Take the other side,' she said.

Jude barely heard her. Inside the machine, a jumble of tubes and wires, dim shapes refusing to make sense.

'Careful,' someone was saying.

'Watch it.' The voice too close.

The medic's softer tone, then: 'Careful. That's it. That one too, if you can.'

In the opening, objects were shifting. Jude caught sight of

a form, a memory. A chill flashed through her like a fish. The medic moved quickly. The stretcher lifted.

'Give us a hand.' Her voice stronger, impatient now.

Jude heard the words as if through water. She started to say that she couldn't help, was no use here, but her body was already moving. Her hands reached for one end of the stretcher, ready to take the weight.

'Lift them gently.' The medic's focus was entirely on the task. Jude was two arms, a pair of hands. In the tangle of tubes and wires, there was some kind of casing. Rounded, clouded. One end slid out onto the stretcher. It wasn't as heavy as Jude expected. Karim's upper body emerged behind it, crouched, tugging out whatever connections he could manage. 'This one?' he asked, and a braid of wires moved in the dark.

'Just bring it all.' The voice was growing strained. Jude's body shifted automatically as the whole object slid into their care. The stretcher seemed flimsy, shamefully low-tech. Through the casing near her hands she could see two shapes that might have been feet. Barely more than bones. Was she taking enough weight? It was much too light to be a body. It was plastic, maybe.

'Let's get them to the clinic,' the medic said, her voice clear and strong again.

There was a tug. Jude's hand slipped, her mind skidded, but her body caught the load.

*

The dusk light almost blinded them. Karim walked behind her, struggling with salvaged machine parts. In front, the medic was walking backwards, focused on the plastic shell, pausing to check her path or attend to details as they went. It was a short journey to the clinic, a couple of hundred metres at most, but progress was slow and careful. At some point Hamish appeared beside her, taking half the weight.

She glanced down. Saw nothing living. Wires, cushioning. A net fallen around the mask. No: white hair, dry and thin. She could not see a face. It might be a doll, its plastic eyes closed. She closed her own a moment, wanted to be sick.

At the doors, she let Hamish take over. Holding her stomach, Jude stepped out of the way and let them struggle past her, watched the clinic doors slide closed and shut her out. The others made no sign that they had noticed her fall away. She was another set of hands, that was all. This object had nothing to do with her. But stars fell in her mind's eye. Bodies burned.

She crouched until the nausea passed, then watched the movement through the glass. They disappeared into the back of the clinic, moved quickly out of sight. A lingering scent of oranges, cinnamon, and sanitiser floated away on the breeze. Jude inhaled deeply. Then she stood, wiped her hands on her jeans, and walked calmly back to the truck. She climbed in behind the wheel, put her head down against the hard round shape of it, and did not move again for a long time.

9

BEFORE

Jude blinks awake in the strange room. She has her own suite. Like the rest of the place, it's all cool concrete, grey tones, artificial light. There are two flat screens and three game consoles in the drawer with the remotes. She can order anything she wants on the tablet by the bed without having to speak to a single person. There are no windows. She would have liked to be able to see the stars.

She does wish there was something else alive in here: a potted plant would do, but the one in the corner is plastic. She lies down with her head on the carpet, wriggles until she finds a spider under the enormous sofa, in the corner where a steel leg protrudes. It has caught a beetle and is busy wrapping it in silk. The beetle hangs and writhes for a while, but its legs soon go still. Up close, she can see the individual threads in its tiny shroud.

The door clicks open without a knock. A shadow falls across her legs.

'What's wrong with you? You're not even dressed.'

'Am so,' Jude says, rolling onto her back. She is wearing the T-shirt and jeans she wore yesterday, and not the dress her sister made her bring. Celeste is in a backless gown, forest green, a favourite. Heels like blades. She is beautiful.

She frowns from a height. 'I guess that will have to do,' she says. 'Shoes, though.'

Jude scrambles up and pulls on sneakers, follows her sister into the corridor, laces trailing. Turning to fix them into tight bows, Celeste hisses: 'Judith. Don't ruin this.' But when they get to the presentation room she's all kindness, a soft hand guiding Jude to a seat beside her in the front row. Celeste sits up attentively, though there's nothing urgent happening. There's just the chatter of strangers behind them, the usual milling of people in suits.

Celeste insists that Jude has met Nick Fry before, but she can't picture him. He is a friend of the family, whatever that means. He came to the house more than once, when their father – Celeste's father – was still alive. Jude hasn't told anyone, but she struggles to picture JB as well. It's a couple of years since the accident. She's almost a teenager, can already feel the past disintegrating behind her.

When he appears in the blue light of the presentation room, everyone applauds. Now that Jude sees him, he's familiar. His skin looks soft and glistening, like he's used a filter. Makeup, maybe. Dark hair that seems to sparkle. He touches his assistants' arms as he goes, parts groups of people like curtains.

He's not handsome or tall or even interesting-looking, but Celeste's eyes light up at the sight of him. When the applause stops, her hands stay together, palm to palm, and she sighs deeply. For once, she seems happy.

Jude doesn't get what all the fuss is about.

Going to space is supposed to be exciting; so far, it's just a lot of boring speeches. Even in the front row, Jude can't see what Fry's eyes are doing. Under these lights, they're like blank circles. One of his assistants sees her staring, grins: the over-friendly type. There are several of them standing near the edges of the platform, all young and feminine and impeccably groomed. Jude looks at her knees, fidgets with a hole in her jeans. Her shoes feel tight.

The talk goes on and on. Space, rockets, whatever. This is comic-book stuff, and it's hard to take any of it seriously. She tries to sit still and act sensible. Tries to have the kind of gravity people expect from Princes, but it doesn't come naturally. Of course it doesn't.

Sitting there, Jude can still feel the texture of the carpet against the side of her face, the scratch of it against her ribs through the T-shirt. She thinks of the spider wrapping its prey, remembers she hasn't eaten breakfast. Celeste is always forgetting about meals. At Sovereign House, they have kitchen staff to remind them. Her stomach growls, and Celeste's hand moves to her leg, shushing her even though she can't help it.

Jude tunes in and out, letting her thoughts spin in their private cocoon. Fry's voice is steady, almost flat. He doesn't seem that excited about the Endeavour either. It's so far into the future that maybe it doesn't feel real. Or maybe he just seems dull against the screen that flashes behind him, its bright animations and booming music.

She twists in her seat, scans the room. There are about thirty adults, half of them staff; the other half are potential investors like Celeste. There are no other children. Most of the investors are men. In the row behind her, one notices her looking and leans forward. He has a friendly face, with warm brown eyes set above broad cheekbones. A soft grey jacket, wool, with a tiny

Star Trek pin on the lapel. He winks at her, and she turns back to face the stage.

'Don't scowl,' Celeste whispers, the cautioning hand squeezing her leg. 'Pay attention.' She doesn't take her gaze away from Fry. Jude tries, but it doesn't make much sense to her. She notices he doesn't call them investors, he calls them partners, as if this is one big complicated family. It makes her stomach flip. Maybe she's just hungry.

After the talk, Jude goes straight for the snack table. She's sure no-one will care if she eats before she's invited, but she hesitates over the unfamiliar spread. A waiter appears beside her, materialised by her confusion. She reaches for the first thing she recognises: a green leaf, raw and curled. 'Oh. That's more for decoration,' the waiter says. 'Here.' A napkin appears, then a tiny grey orb that she thought was moulded plastic. Hesitantly, she sinks her teeth into the orb. It turns out to be sweet and chewy, filled with black sesame paste.

'Thanks,' she murmurs, her mouth full, her body awake.

On the video wall behind the catering table, a model Station spins. Doll people blink in fresh-made gravity. A radiant blonde unclips her harness, pivots to a darker man beside her. They bring their hands together, joyful, the way Celeste did a moment ago. It's like an ad for a car or a holiday, except there's no sunny day out the window, just stars zooming past so fast they make little lines in the darkness. Beside her, the waiter watches the video loop, his neat face almost expressionless.

Jude has to ask. 'Will you go?'

The neat face turns. 'Can't think of anything worse,' he whispers. Jude isn't sure if he's joking, but she can't help liking him. 'You?'

She tries doing something ambiguous with her mouth, something that could answer either way. It's a knack of Celeste's she's been practising, and it fails.

'Don't like the flavour?'

She swallows. 'No, it's good.' Lets her whole smile out, then feels it collapse, wilting fast in this artificial light. She's too embarrassed to speak.

'Don't worry, sweetheart,' the waiter says, bending down to her. 'None of this is ever going to happen.'

She's briefly shocked, then relief floods through like sugar. He sparkles, and questions stir in her throat, but he has to stand up and attend to the important guests. Other investors are crowding behind them, chatter rising in volume, density.

If it won't happen, she doesn't need to be afraid. Doesn't need to think about how far away the Station will be, hundreds of thousands of kilometres from dirt, rocks, birds, clouds. Doesn't have to wonder which of these people she might be stuck with for company. What they will eat up there, in a place with no spiders.

She can hear Celeste's shimmering laughter. She can't ruin this for her, not now.

There she is across the table, getting close to Fry, somehow looking up at him although she's taller, especially in those shoes. She's probably forgotten Jude is here, but Jude adjusts her posture nonetheless. Later, maybe, when they are alone, Celeste will sit with her for a moment, take the shoes off and say they are killing her, and they will be close again. She will be better, and this trip will have been worth it.

For now, she works. Dials her charm up to maximum: the face, the laugh, the voice, throwing everything she has at this man.

Jude hopes that no-one else can see her desperation, the shadow of grief in her protruding spine.

Fry cracks a smile at something Celeste has said. He closes his eyes when he does it, like there's not enough room in his face for that much feeling.

The room is loud with conversation. Most of the partners already know each other. 'It's a small world,' a man bellows, his hand on Celeste's bare back. Jude wants to object. The drive took hours. But he means *their* world, the one for people like him and Celeste.

Jude chews her pastry, reaches for another. They will be stuck here for hours, possibly days. She finds a corner, sinks to the floor. On the opposite wall, through the milling group that contains her sister, the video loop plays on. Jude watches the model passengers beam at each other, lift their hands in wonder.

*

The drive home seems to take twice as long. Spence in the front, the night all around them, stars and stars and satellites. Her sister rides behind him in silence, scrolling on her phone. Eventually she stretches out and falls asleep. Jude stares out the back windscreen. The desert moves past darkly, showing only slight features like rocks or small trees, like it's facing away from them.

'I wouldn't worry so much,' Spence says. Jude touches her face, wishes she was better at hiding her feelings. It's something Celeste is so good at. Her sleeping body is a slight paleness on the black leather upholstery.

'I'm not worried,' she whispers.

'It will probably never get off the ground,' he says. She can't tell if he's just trying to ease her nerves. 'Most of these guys don't amount to much in the end. You'll see.'

'It's her dream,' she says. Celeste is breathing evenly, half her face hidden in her silky blonde hair. She looks peaceful.

'And she needs it, for now. So let's just play along,' he says. His brown eyes in the rear-view mirror, glancing from her to Celeste. Jude nods. It's not the first time he's given her this advice.

He sighs, flicks at something on the GPS screen, and it zooms out. The desert road extends. It would have been quicker to fly, but Jude won't get on a plane. The earth scrolls past them, trees and rocks at eye height, tyres attached to road, the dirt within reach.

*

The investigation is so thorough that it ends up taking years. The helicopter was too small to need a flight recorder. They analyse the crash site, the remains, the maintenance logs; they go back to the manufacturers. The findings, when at last they come, are deflating. There was no mechanical fault, no terrorist attack, no sabotage. Pilot error, gusty winds. Just an accident. Nothing to fear.

Of course, fear doesn't work that way.

Jude didn't see it, but she can't stop seeing the explosion: the helicopter slipping from the sky and slamming into the side of the hill. It falls slowly at first, resigned to gravity. She watches its nose crunching into the earth, its tail breaking away. Counts to three before it bursts into flames, feels the heat on her face. By the time the rescuers reach it, there is only a shell, broken blades, the bones of people turned to ashes.

The frightening part is not dying like that. It's the moments before it: the knowledge that the machine has failed you, that gravity has won, as you hurtle back towards the ground where you belong. The thought that there's nothing you can do, and if there is, you're not doing it.

There is no *way* she is going to space.

*

When Jude can't sleep, she walks outside, puts her hand into the red soil, feeling for the rotation. Even at night, the earth is as warm as an animal. Without this mass beneath her, she is nothing. The planet gives her substance, wants nothing in return.

The gardens are mostly dead. The drought that has lasted seven years suddenly breaks in summer, and the rain slides across the dry ground and floods the place. Rivers appear where before there were only lines of trees. There are suddenly wetlands around the compound, and an absurd number of frogs; they materialise in the garage, settle in her boots. She knows about the climate crisis. Prince was one of the largest emitters, for over half a century. All that wealth has come at a cost. There is talk of reparations. No wonder the rich are nervous these days, prone to escape plans and conspiracy theories.

But they aren't rich, Celeste tells her, not anymore. The company is being broken up and sold off in pieces. Jude reads the reports herself, written like obituaries. A juggernaut of coal, steel, gas, and in later years hydrogen and carbon-capture projects that never quite work, Prince Industries is now a set of stranded assets, shedding value by the day. Other companies have managed the transition, with varying degrees of public pressure, state subsidy and shareholder intervention, but Prince misjudged: it has missed the boat.

No-one says it explicitly, but they all imply that Celeste is out of her depth. Even helped by the board and a web of advisors, she can't manage without her father's experience, her brothers' business sense. She's too young, too emotional. Jude knows this isn't fair, on principle. But she also knows her sister. Celeste *is* fragile, her moods unpredictable. Something inside her has cracked, and it's taking all her strength to keep the surface smooth.

When the floods evaporate, everything stinks. Jude finds blackened frog skins stretched out on the soil. Birds and insects take care of each other's remains. The winter is windy, full of storms, over too soon. By September, there are fires all along the west coast. The sky is blanketed by smoke. Hundreds of people die in their homes or in their cars, trying to get away. Countless animals. The sunsets are incredible. At thirteen Jude learns about shifting baselines, new normals, everything people should have done sooner.

A cyclone makes landfall six hundred kilometres further south than cyclones should. Her sister orders additional security, patrolling of the fences, as if this is any use against the wind. The compound sits through dust storms, rainstorms, hailstones the size of fists.

Celeste's moods come and go, but her belief in the project persists. Celeste is at her desk, in meetings, Fry's on-screen face reflected on her framed certificates. Spence and the waiter are wrong. At some point, the whim tips into an obsession. The Endeavour rises slowly, like the temperature. It's nothing; it will never happen. And then one day, it's too late.

10

AUGUST

She tried to get through the hall without speaking to anyone, but the Common was full of people, and all of them seemed to be discussing the capsule. Freddie stopped her by the exit, their look a question. Jude raised a hand before they could speak.

'Can't stop,' she said. 'Need sleep.'

They stepped back as she pushed past, struggling through the noise.

The driver's room was neat, sparse, calming. Jude stood with her back to the door and breathed slowly. Then she took the headphones from the bedside table, picked up the F-net screen and swiped seven notifications away. She called up the music library, put on an old favourite, reliably, deafeningly loud.

Half an hour later, still awake, she read the messages. Three were from Ali, checking in. Two were irrelevant committee updates, the kind that got sent out to everyone. Another informed all residents to avoid the sheds and the clinic because of a medical emergency, no specifics. The last was a work request: Roana had agreed to house the new arrivals right away. They could leave as soon as they liked.

Jude hit accept, scheduled the job for first thing the next morning, and rolled onto her side.

She must have slept, because the usual dreams had no trouble finding her. Falling dreams, and burning. She woke with an ache in her body as though she had been fighting. One ear was crushed against the headphones. The music had turned itself off. There was a note under the door from Ali, which she prodded with a toe. The F already told her he'd accepted the job. There'd be a quick meeting this morning to confirm, but if she waited until nine, she would miss it. When she lay back down, she closed her eyes for a moment, but only saw stars.

Jude swore and pulled her boots on. She still had to refuel the truck.

The damned medic must have been watching out the clinic door; she met her at a brisk walk.

'Jude, isn't it?' Her expression seemed harried above the face mask, and Jude relented. Probably this woman hadn't slept much either. The eyes were intelligent and penetrating, a muddy green. Jude did not like medics as a rule, and this one looked her in the eye for longer than was comfortable. She grunted, reached up and opened the driver's door.

'Nora,' the medic said. She held her hand out, too close to ignore. The hand was smaller than her own, a warm but firm presence. Jude felt some of the resistance leave her body. Nora was a bit shorter than she was. With one boot on the metal step it was easy enough to look past her grey-black hair at the road behind her, to shift her weight towards the day's journey.

'Thanks for your help yesterday.'

'I didn't do anything.'

The medic's expression was ambiguous. 'Do you have time for a quick chat?'

Jude shook her head. 'Got to move. Refuel.' She waved a

hand at the truck, could not seem to speak in full sentences. Didn't owe this person her politeness, anyway.

'I wonder . . . I need someone in the clinic,' she said. 'Just until we –'

'Sorry. Already committed.' Jude raised a hand.

'That's a shame. You were such a help yesterday.' Nora's shoulders fell slightly, but her gaze was clear and direct.

'Not a nurse. Just a driver,' said Jude. Her chest was tight.

'That's not the kind of help I mean,' Nora said. She reached a hand towards Jude's arm, but obviously thought better of it; the hand moved away before it made contact.

Jude looked up into the waiting cab, but did not climb the steps. Over at the clinic, a feeble barrier of yellow tape had been placed outside the door.

'The feed said to stay away,' she said.

'Well, in general –' the medic started. She glanced at the tape. 'That's why I'm asking you. You've already been close to her.'

Jude froze, but just for a moment. 'Can't,' she said, then cleared her throat and added: 'Don't like hospitals.'

'Me neither.' Nora's eyes softened above the mask.

Jude caught a playfulness there, a spark of humour. Something lit up the inside of her skull like a struck match, but she snuffed it.

The church bell rang twice. Half-past eight. She had to get going, get coffee.

'Sorry,' Jude said, 'I can't,' and climbed behind the wheel.

*

She only had to manoeuvre the truck around to the side of the shed, tap one of the drums of biodiesel, find the funnel and unroll the hose, stick the funnel into the tank. But she forgot the funnel, then forgot to turn the valve. Those green, murky, interfering eyes were watching her, putting her off.

Finally, the hose was rolled, the cap replaced. She checked three times, retightened. Emerging from the shed, Jude saw that there was no-one watching after all. Nora must have gone back to work, given up on her. Jude wiped her hands on her jeans. That should be the end of it. By the time she got back from Roana, it would be over.

Not her job, anyway. Nothing to do with her.

Painted across one wall of the clinic, in neat red and white letters, was the Freelands principle: *If you can help, help.* But it wasn't a rule. You could choose the kind of help you were good at, capable of, and forget the rest.

*

They were on the road soon enough, Ali beside her. The silence between them had become uneasy. Jude pretended she had to concentrate, though at first they were driving over the same ground as they had the day before. They passed the same sparkling river, same chestnut trees, same sheep. Familiarity made the journey quicker, but it also gave her room to think. That was the last thing she needed.

To get the medic out of her head, she replayed the conversation with the man from Orson. She always thought of things she should have said much later. There was a phrase for this in French; Ali had told her once but she'd forgotten it.

She swung to the right at a junction, her mind filled with yellow boulders, black crosses. It was maddening. If Valley people wanted autonomy, insisted that they were not beholden to outsiders, didn't that make them Freelanders through and through? But people could always find reasons to fence themselves off. Vulnerability masquerading as logic. Humans were by and large a lost cause, Jude thought, easily overwhelmed by emotions. You had to trust your instincts, know when it was pointless to intervene.

Ahead, she could see the hydroelectric plant looming, which meant they were almost at Cuoretto. The old truck stop there was still a truck stop, though it carried little in the way of fuel. It had been fixed up after the war and was now a hub for the people working on the hydro restoration. There would almost certainly be coffee.

Jude pulled up beside the disused bowsers. Ali gave her a questioning look but said nothing.

She climbed down without a word and went to open the back of the truck.

'Taking a break,' she explained, gesturing at the building. No-one moved. Their eyes were wary, tired. The woman with the grey curls glared. 'It's okay,' Jude added, a little impatiently. 'Safe.'

'Okay, okay,' said one of the teenagers, loping past her and out into the sun. He muttered something to the rest of them, and they began to shift.

Grey curls climbed out last, ignored Jude, beckoned Ali over, bangles dancing on her wrist. Jude couldn't understand what they were saying, but the tone sounded sharp. Ali listened patiently, made an eating gesture with his hand. Grey curls turned to calm two noisy teenagers who had interrupted them, switching languages – her third or fourth, Jude guessed, and stood aside in monolingual embarrassment. She had no head for words, and in all her years of working on the ships, living in the camp and here in the Freelands, she had picked up only a few greetings, a few exotic swears.

A young man walked over to Ali and began to speak with him. Slow, hesitant; Jude could get the gist of it from body language. They had left in a hurry this morning, and people were frightened. Would the next village be any better? Could they be trusted? Jude had been in his position herself, knew the feeling, but there wasn't much she could do about it. She tapped her foot impatiently, then closed up the truck and headed for the roadhouse.

Cuoretto wasn't much of a town, just a place where two roads met, and beside them two small rivers. There had been a rest stop here for thousands of years; she'd walked to the ruins of the ancient town on the outskirts a few times, stretching her legs, and imagined weary travellers stopping for water, bread. How many countries had been invented on this ground, how many wars had it seen? Two gruff-looking men passed her on their way out of the truck stop, each carrying a large pumpkin. Both men smiled broadly. Jude nodded back, let her mind clear, and realised she was hungry.

The truck stop had a homely air. Cleaned up and refurbished by the community, it was something between the original roadhouse and a small Common. The big room was filled with mismatched tables, plastic chairs, and the sweet smell of roasted vegetables. A woman in a headscarf welcomed her with a warm greeting. Jude barely paused before heading into the kitchen to see if they had anything resembling coffee.

She recognised the cook, a pre-war local in a red beanie,

with a kind, round face and a wonky grin. They didn't share much language, but at her one-word request he poured her a cup from a pot on the stove. It was watery and barely warm, but it would do. She inhaled gratefully, refused the honey jar he pushed her way.

The kitchen was better restored than the dining area. An ancient wood-burning stove stood at its centre, cold now.

The bench looked clean, but the old man wiped it down while she drank her coffee silently. Another woman came in, took a large pot from the electric stove, clicked her teeth and went back out again. As soon as Jude emptied her cup, the old man took a bottle from a shelf behind him, unscrewed the lid and offered it to her. She sniffed. Some kind of homemade bitters, rich with mountain herbs. Jude shook her head.

In the bits of languages they had in common, they began to chat cautiously about the difficulty of supplies. Coffee was grown not far from here, a hybrid variety, but sugar was a problem; the honey came from his own bees, hives out in a field somewhere near the ancient town. Jude asked about the journey to Roana, hoping to be reassured.

He lowered his voice. 'Road is okay. Mountains unhappy.'

Older Valley people often spoke like this: as though the land was animate. If she stayed up here long enough, drank enough of that homemade bitters, she'd probably start talking about rocks and trees like they were people too. Jude thanked him, washed her cup and left it on the sink to drain.

In the dining room, her passengers had gathered at the largest of the tables. People were ladling out soup, passing plates piled high with corn bread. She watched a moment, then took a seat near Ali, who made room for her without pausing his story.

He was telling their hosts about Orson, about the barricade. Jude listened to his smooth voice, adding nothing.

The next table over bore the weight of a dozen enormous pumpkins. Along the wall behind it there was a shelf with many more, several dusty wine flagons, a small wooden horse that looked hand-carved, antique coffee-makers in various shapes and sizes.

The Freelands way had felt like scarcity to her at first. No-one really owned anything, and there was never the excess of choice there had been in her early life, or the multiplication of waste. Jude had worked in enough kitchens to understand the relationship between wealth and wastage; she'd seen enough scarcity in the camp. The Freelands were, in general, a relief of making-do.

She sometimes thought of the luxury rooms on those ships. Of soft sheets and anonymity. It was so simple to arrange all the small things in your favour, if you had money. Life was still like that for people across the border, on the ships. The rich ones, anyway. The rest had to work.

Jude grabbed an empty jug, filled it from a mosaic-tiled sink, then circled the room, topping up glasses, avoiding the occasional glances or words of gratitude. She set the jug down, took Ali's bowl and her own, began to stack.

'Sit,' Ali said. 'Eat something.'

She frowned. 'We should get going.'

'Everyone's hungry,' he said. 'We had an early start.'

Jude heard the judgement in his voice and let it pass. 'Better to get there in daylight,' she said.

'There's no hurry, though, is there? Let them settle.'

Jude saw she was being unfair. She carried the pile of dishes to the kitchen, scolding herself for being short with her friend.

She would never not be grateful for his presence in the truck with her, the blur of those first few days. Driving over the border at dawn, desperately sleep-deprived. His extravagant snoring. Reaching out to wake him, to tell him they were here, hands shaking in the silence. She wouldn't have made it without him. She would have lost her nerve.

'Roana's organised a welcome party,' Ali said, appearing beside her with another stack of dishes. 'They keep messaging.' She pushed the kitchen door open for him with a shoulder.

'All the more reason to get going,' she said, but her voice held a note of apology.

Ali sighed, his elbow against hers. She left him shaking his head in the kitchen, went to speak with their hosts.

'Do you need anything from up in the valley?'

'Oh, no. Give our best to Wendi, though. And take her some of those.' The head-scarfed woman pointed to the pile of pumpkins. Jude lifted one. It must have weighed ten kilos. Early for the season, but the seasons were haywire. There had been plenty of rain.

'Perhaps you can bring us some firewood, if they can spare it,' the other said, handing a second pumpkin to Ali, who'd returned from the kitchen. 'Are you sure you can't take more of these?'

'Maybe on the way back,' he said, through gritted teeth.

'Yes, stop by again, and take some for Northport. We'll send down some dairy as well,' their host said. 'We have more cream than we can safely handle.' She patted her round belly and grinned.

'Sorry about Orson,' said the other. 'We've tried to keep in touch, but no-one's been that way for a while now.'

'Not so many travellers these days,' the first said, 'but we make the best of it.' She piled a smaller pumpkin on top of Jude's load.

When they struggled back out with their haul, the woman with the grey curls opened the door for them. 'Thanks, Solare,' Ali said. She nodded seriously. There was something about her, Jude noted, a maternal or even grandmotherly authority. A slight gesture from her hand brought one of the teenagers over, and he lifted the weight from Jude's arms. Everyone else was already waiting out by the truck.

Jude felt a hand on her elbow.

'This other place – this Ro-hanna – will be safe for them?'

Jude hesitated. In Solare's position, she would want an honest answer.

'As safe as anywhere can be,' she answered finally. 'We trust them.'

Solare accepted this, decisive and cool. She made another hand sign. At the door of the truck, the young man was watching carefully. Kid, Jude corrected: he looked no more than fifteen. He should be at school, free to choose his future.

Jude felt the woman's arm withdraw. Her thoughts swam in darkness. It was only later that she noticed that Solare had said *them*, and not *us*.

*

'Are you going to tell me what's going on?' When Ali finally spoke, it was gently. Still, Jude expelled an exasperated breath.

'Nothing's going on.'

'Jude. You've been acting weird since yesterday. Since that pod thing.'

'Nothing to do with me,' she said sharply.

'What is it, anyway? Some kind of submersible?'

'I don't know any more about it than you do.'

His eyes were dark, undaunted. 'I thought you were there.'

Jude waited.

'Karim said there was a survivor.'

The turn-off to Roana was lined with chestnut trees. Fields were giving way to stone.

'He said the life support was so complicated, he'd never seen anything like it. Over-engineered.'

She turned towards her window, not trusting her face to hold its neutrality. There was no privacy in the Freelands. For that, you had to come up here.

Sections of the loose stone walls had crumbled under the weight of the trees above them: olives, figs, pomegranates were rotting away. This was farmland that had been terraced cleverly in the past, though much of it was abandoned now.

'I wonder who they are,' Ali went on. The innocent tone did not seem feigned. He was her closest friend here by a long shot, but there was still so much he did not know.

'I told you, I didn't see anything. Anyway, it's the clinic's problem.'

Jude knew she sounded gruff. There was a pause in which Ali didn't say any of the things she thought he might. She slowed as branches reached across to scratch the truck.

'Did you talk to her?' he asked eventually.

'Who?'

'The new medic,' he said. 'Nora.'

Jude glared at him. 'Ali, please. Give it a rest.'

'What?' He was grinning at her, pleased he'd found a crack. 'She's *nice*.'

'I'll get around to it,' she said, and watched the road. These walls needed to be rebuilt, the trees cut back. They should get a work party out here. She would add it to the F, if she remembered. Could use a few days out in the open herself, the honest work of heaving stone. Put some hardness back into her muscle. Feel useful, and not have to talk to anyone.

'I keep thinking about that Orson guy,' she said.

Ali settled back in his seat. 'Maybe it's religion,' he said.

Jude remembered the saint's hands, lying unrepaired. The man's tattooed cross. There were pockets of faith in the valleys, but she didn't think this was about religion. No, it would be simpler than that. Something immediate and material. It was difficult to unlearn habits of scarcity and competition and possession. Sure, resources were limited: not enough vehicles, not enough tech. But it was foolish to close yourself off when people were what you needed most. People to repair buildings, fix walls, prune orchards. People to harvest what food they could grow, and cook it, and carry it to tables, and clean up. To turn soil and filter water, plant and pull and cut, restore this place to some kind of health. It was long work, difficult. It needed care and time.

Her hands felt rough and dry against the wheel. Useful hands, with strength in them. Good for some things. Honest work had been enough for her, for a while. It should be enough for her still.

11

BEFORE

Judith, dinner, the house system says. Jude refuses to answer, but it's a protest nobody notices, not even the house. She folds her manual and slides it on top of the crate of tools. Pushes herself up from the chair in Spence's office, kicks it so it rolls away. He is in the garage, polishing one of the remaining cars. Celeste doesn't go anywhere these days. She barely leaves her room.

If Jude doesn't go and eat there will be more reminders, and eventually an alarm. The house will know where to find her. So she sings out, 'See you,' trusting Spence will hear her, runs up the stairs and into the grey light of the compound's ground floor. She can feel the heat coming through the glass passageway that separates the outer hall from the inner. Highest temperatures in a hundred years, they're saying. Outside, the kangaroo grass is bleached and flattened. The spinifex that crept in under the fence is turning grey. Even the sunken courtyard garden is mostly dead. She glimpses stumps of cycads, brown ferns hanging over them like veils.

Trees sag in the heat. The lumps in the shade below them could be wallabies; it's hard to tell. In the evening she will go out there, take the animals some water, and find them unmoving, stinking of death.

The meal is served by a stern young woman from the agency they've been using since Celeste let the regular kitchen staff go. Absurdly, there are shellfish: linguine alle vongole, hundreds of kilometres from the sea. The oceans are boiling, fish stocks collapsing; millions of people are starving because of it. Jude reads the newsfeeds. She knows Celeste does, too, though they don't discuss it much.

Jude watches her sister carefully. She is eating, for once; more often she just sits there, staring into space or moving things around on her plate. Tonight she actually seems to enjoy it.

'They grew in tanks,' she says, 'no heavy metals. I made sure they were tested.'

'It's not that,' Jude says. The mussels are disturbing in other ways: somehow both alive and not. When she picks out a forkful of pasta, they release a rich liquid. Jude has no appetite for them, but she doesn't want to give Celeste any excuses to talk about what they will miss when they leave. To say that up there, they will be lighter, no matter what they eat.

She is featherweight already, fine-boned and fragile. Jude is a stocky opposite. Not tall: at fourteen, her body only wants to grow broader. Spence says she will be strong, with good stamina.

'You don't like it,' Celeste says, crestfallen.

'No, it's good,' Jude says, ashamed by her ingratitude. The table is so long that she has to stand up to reach the salt, and garlicky steam flushes her skin.

Jude is unpleasantly aware of her body inside the oversized black T-shirt she's been wearing for three days now. The laundry is piling up in a corner of her room. She wishes her sister would notice things like this. No-one has come to deal with it, though someone will eventually. Someone from the agency.

'How's school?' Celeste asks. She is talking tonight. Another positive sign.

Jude shrugs, her mouth full of pasta. It's not as if the tutors can do anything if she misses their online meetings. She lets their messages – encouragement, frustration – pile up like the laundry. Most days, she hangs around in the garage, occasionally giving a cursory look at a screen to keep Spence off her back. She doesn't see the point of learning that stuff. There's no fixing things out there.

'Good,' she says.

Celeste isn't listening. She's staring into her plate like it's a mirror.

The windows are silted up from all the dust storms. The country looks like a planet in her comic books. Things are changing faster than anyone predicted.

Half Jude's meal has gone without her tasting it. She pushes the plate away.

'Can I ask you something?'

Celeste looks up, torn from her reverie. 'Sure.' She smiles perfectly.

'Is the town still there?' Jude is surprised she has let this question out of her mouth. It has been living in there, coiled like a brown snake under a rock.

There's maybe a microsecond before Celeste controls her expression. 'I think everyone was rehoused, moved to the city.' Everyone who survived, she means. 'There can't be much left. It's been closed for what, seven, eight years?'

'Ten.' She should know that. But Jude won't start a fight.

'Hmm,' Celeste says. She reaches for the sparkling water. Someone appears from the shadows to pour it for her. Jude waits for them to withdraw.

'Can we go see it?'

'Why?' Celeste narrows her eyes, as she does at any suggestion of an outing. There are always protesters camped outside the compound, though Spence says they are harmless. The police are supposed to clear them away.

Jude holds her gaze.

The air stills. She's messed this up, mistimed it.

But Celeste looks back at her calmly, her face relaxed to blankness. 'Okay,' she says. A leaf – baby, organic, greenhouse-grown and thrice-washed – disappears into her neat mouth.

'Really?'

Celeste swallows, pats her mouth with a folded square of linen. 'It might help,' she says. 'You know. Closure?' Her expression is kind, almost generous.

Jude waits for the quid pro quo, but nothing comes. She will be in her sister's debt again, but decides it's worth it.

'Can we go tomorrow?' Jude hears the hope in her voice, the need, and cowers from it.

Celeste shakes her head. 'Leave it with me,' she says.

*

Of course, they have to wait for cooler weather. Jude feels like she is holding her breath, not wanting to pester. A mood might blow across Celeste, send her spiralling into a days-long sulk. And maybe it's a bad idea, and the trip will tip her delicate balance. But when the day finally arrives, Celeste is up and dressed early, firing instructions at staff.

In the garage, they find Spence whistling cheerfully, but he's silent when he drives them up the ramp into daylight, as formal as ever behind the wheel. The morning is all golden ochres and rounded boulders. A spill of finches in the distance as they leave the gates. Gradients of pale sky.

Not far past their perimeter, they see the protest camp. *REPARATIONS*, says a huge banner draped across the few measly tents. A torn flag whips against its dead-tree flagpole. There are no signs of life, but it's still early.

'We must do something about those people,' Celeste says, without much force. She sighs. 'They're just never satisfied.' Spence catches Jude's eye in the mirror, but doesn't speak. The camp vanishes behind them without trouble. After that, Jude watches the dry country flash past, a blur of grass and dust and rocks, and wonders what it's like to care so much about something that you will brave the deadly heat and the police, give up weeks of your life. Celeste sits up, watching out the window, sharing an occasional grin with Jude. On the seat between them, a basket holds sandwiches, fruit salad, cake. Celeste is wonderful when she is like this, even if it's all surface. It will do her good to leave the compound. Maybe Jude's got something right for once.

Asphalt for half an hour beyond the camp, then the wheels crunch over gravel. It's well graded – they own this road – but barely used these days. The car makes anxious noises. Spence glances back at Jude, taps a long finger on the dashboard, shifts in his seat. She begins to wonder if she should be nervous.

Celeste turns to her.

'You know, this is not going to be easy,' she says.

Spence pretends he isn't listening, but Jude can sense his approval. He's coached her for this conversation.

'I know,' she says.

'You were *so lucky*.' Celeste rests a hand on Jude's knee. The hand is bones, mostly; cold even through the denim.

Jude shifts in her seat, aware of her skin against the fabric, of her face making the appropriate expression automatically. She is grateful to be saved.

There is no fence around the site, just a huge white sign with *Prospect River Exclusion Zone, No Public Access, Road Closed*, and a whole lot of smaller text about permits and departments that Jude doesn't have time to read because they drive past without stopping. Someone has spray-painted a symbol on the back of the sign, a jagged rune she doesn't recognise. The track in is much worse than the road: corrugated, edges crumbling. Spence loses some of his composure, talks to the car as he negotiates ditches. When it gets too sandy, they have to stop.

'We'll walk from here,' Celeste says, extending a leg as if she's getting out in traffic.

On either side, wallaby and motorcycle tracks peter out into the scrub. Jude has memorised the map. They are roughly north-west of the compound, hours from the city, and the nearest real town is a hundred kilometres away. Still, she's not prepared for how quiet it is out here.

It looks like the rest of the desert. Worn red rocks in tumbled piles, fine red earth. A few trees clawing into sky. No birds in the trees. In all directions the horizon is a smudge of heat.

She wants her heart to swell with recognition: a homecoming. She wants her body to remember something, but it just feels hot and sweaty. The landscape doesn't move her as she'd hoped. It all feels insubstantial, her tread barely touching the sand.

Jude walks towards the loose row of trees. Spence told her not to go near water. This turns out to be easy, as the river has dried up completely. A few red gums hang on, branches greying. Animal bones – she hopes that's what they are – lie tangled in their roots.

She follows the dry creek to the few remnant buildings, breath shallow, steps careful. Jude isn't sure how toxic this place still is. Prince Industries claimed they spent millions to restore the landscape around the mine, but she can't tell from here if that's true.

She is grateful there is evidence of human habitation, even if it's only a few remnant buildings. Complete repair would be erasure, wouldn't it? She finds what was once the main street, now an oddly rectangular stretch of ground. Recognises the facade of a mechanic's garage, concrete castellations, the ghost of a sign. The houses appear, gestures of steel and stone. Which of these yards did she play in, under which roof did she sleep and cry? They said her parents neglected her, but maybe they were just young, or sick. Got work here and didn't understand the risks.

Jude is aware of Celeste walking a few metres behind her, of Spence leaning in the shade of a corrugated-iron veranda. Broken glass glitters at his feet. She moves back towards the river and inhales the air. Maybe a dead kangaroo somewhere, an old spill of petrol, stale fire. That, or the dust, scours the inside of her nostrils, burns her throat. If her body recognises anything, it's danger.

Upstream, maybe thirty ks away, the mine site. A burst dam, the tailings turned to floodwater. Somewhere between there and Sovereign House – home, Jude has to admit – is the site of the helicopter crash. Twin disasters, bracketing her life. She bends to the soft shale and spiky grass at her feet, finds decaying plastic, a rusted bolt. Nearby, a car chassis lies butchered in the flat.

She was expecting more: unwashed dishes, fallen chairs. But sick people have time to pack. They took away whatever was valuable or meaningful. Others have come through since and taken the rest: windows, roofing iron, copper. She can see where thieves have smashed out render to get to the pipes.

Jude wanders to a structure in a field: a few brick walls, a cracked cement slab, a collapsed shed beside it. This must have been the school. There are the remains of a small fire, and the interior walls have been sprayed with messages.

A lizard swivels its head at her presence before waddling with surprising velocity around the corner of a wall. She touches the brick, feels its absorbed heat and language. The scrawls too layered and too worn down to read. In the dirt there is a gleam of something silver, something others must have missed. She bends to lift the treasured evidence, but it is only a piece of flaking stone, glittering with minerals. She pockets it anyway.

Light-headed, she steps back into the sun. Her feet are loose on the ground, attached to nothing. She pauses over a few rocks in a clumsy line: maybe there was a garden once. She glances back at the roof tin, burst open like an acacia pod. It all feels hostile, like no-one should ever have lived here. But people looked after this land for thousands of years before she was born. She struggles to think about that much time, that much persistence.

If there are wounds here, people brought them.

Maybe Celeste is right. You have to leave before disaster gets you. There's no chance after it arrives.

*

Celeste and Spence are waiting in the shade beside the car. When Jude nears, Spence disappears into the driver's seat. She inhales her sister's scent, incongruously perfumed.

'I'm sorry,' Celeste says. She never apologises. Isn't really, now. She bends to speak, though she isn't much taller. 'I know it's sad,' she says, 'but just think – you got away. And you didn't just survive. You made it to a much better place.'

Jude's face takes on its habitual shape, but her limbs fill with a furious heat. She wants the dust to enter her lungs, she wants to step into bad water.

'You were so small,' Celeste says. Jude feels a hand on her shoulder apply a gentle pressure, slight but emphatic. She submits to an embrace.

When she releases her, Celeste's eyes glitter like the stone in Jude's pocket. False gold, and distant stars. All the pity has left her face.

'Okay, Judith,' she says. 'You've seen it. So it's time to go.'

12

STATION

The next time she wakes, Hui is waiting by the hatch. He sits cross-legged on the floor beside her slipper recess. She's disappointed it's not Judith, but she's glad it's him. Hui is rare metals, Inner Mongolia, likeable. A talker, but not like André.

Here we are, he says. *The Station.* He spreads his hands. She nods, because he seems to want confirmation. It's easier when they are walking side by side, at a pace just brisk enough to warm the body. She remembers to count the hatches at their feet.

Have you seen the astronauts? he asks. *The engineers. I can't seem to find them. Last time . . .* His head moves in a kind of orbit, scanning the walls. His conversation is slow and considered, if a little one-sided. She tries to think about what he's asked, to find an answer, and loses count.

She stops. His arm is raised towards the ceiling, towards the hub. It is close, but not within her arm's reach. Smooth, unpadded. Hui is taller, and his fingertips brush the surface. She doesn't remember anything about engineers.

Is it the light that's poor, or her vision? There is a mark there: she hasn't seen it before. Hui seems to know what he is looking for, presses his fingers to the shape; it opens. The ladder he pulls down extends towards them and he has to step back. He stumbles, slowly rights himself.

No resistance, he says, covering his mouth. *Yes. I remember this. Or something like it.*

His uncertainty flickers, as comforting as a status light on a machine. Stars twinkle somewhere out of sight. Peripheries are fragile. There is the hole the ladder came from, and a circle beside that the size of a hatch. A third thing, a small black oval set into the ceiling, a sensor. None of it was here before. *What's up there?*

The bridge, he says. He climbs the first two rungs of the ladder. It is made from fastened sections of plastic and aluminium that look like they would not take his weight on Earth. When he lifts a hand to the sensor panel, she holds her breath, but nothing happens.

You try, he says.

Sleep sits in her mouth like thirst. She waits for him to move away, then steps up, the ladder cool under her hands. The sensor doesn't respond to her palm, her wrist, the back of her hand, her thumb, or to any of her fingers. She presses the surface hard. Repeats the sequence, like a loop in a dream. She knows there will be nothing there.

It won't open, she says. There is no bridge. There are no engineers, no captain. He is confusing this with *Star Trek*.

Hm, Hui says. He reaches out a hand to help her down. She doesn't take it.

It's not meant for us, she says. It seems the kindest way to say it. She pictures the shape that holds them, circles them, closed to interference. At the centre of the wheel there is a bank of machines, gently idling. Lights flickering in her mind's eye, and no people. They are cocooned around the rim, cupped and padded. He has forgotten. She wonders if she should be afraid. Of him, of anything.

Maja says they have to stay separate, he says. *I wanted to be sure.* He pushes the ladder back into its hollow, and the ceiling closes over the space. Now that she knows it's there, the hatch is obvious. Like Maja's name on the list, and Hui's. What you can and can't see.

They walk for a time, not speaking. Hui is restless, arms unable to settle behind his back, swinging by his sides. His stride is longer than hers; she has to hurry to keep up. He scans the ceiling, the blank walls, the floor. He stops at the observation hatch, but she shakes her head and they move on. A few doors past it he pauses again, scuffs at a symbol in the floor with his slippered toe: a green circle with an arrow inside. Celeste is certain she has never seen this sign before, but at the same time, it is familiar. Has the Station been changing shape while she was asleep? No, it wouldn't do that. It is designed to care for them. They are its purpose.

Hm, he says again. There is a sensor beside the green symbol. He does not bend to touch it.

Celeste doesn't bend either. She remains composed. Hui is frozen, but he doesn't look frightened; she examines his face in detail, the round health of his cheeks, the perfect hairline, a neat mark below it from the mask. He is listening for something, or just stuck. Then he turns away. They move on without speaking.

At his own hatch, he stops and touches the wall, feeling its texture. He seems loosened, his height bent over. She thinks of a slip of paper standing on its edge. He sighs and dusts the hand against his thigh, though there can't be any dust in here. Out here. Can there?

I wanted this so much, he says. *I don't want to sleep through it.* He sounds like he is going to cry. He has not taken off his slippers, and the linen leaves a gap above his ankles. She thinks of a hospital ward. He is an oversized child, at the mercy of something incurable.

Celeste is exhausted. She is looking forward to returning to her bed. Next time, she'll remember everything better. The Station will make more sense. Judith will be awake. Jude will always be with her: they will always look out for each other. She will remember to check the ceilings, count the trapdoors, keep her bearings. Everything is taken care of.

Well, goodnight, he says, and bends a knee to wake his hatch.

The room beneath lights up. It strikes her that there is nothing personal about it. No pictures, no trinkets, no clothes of his own. A sad purity.

If night means anything up here, he says. Grinning up at her from his hole in the floor, his face is charming: the boy is not sick after all, only playing. Descending barefoot into rest. The cure is a prize he knows he deserves. She watches the hatch close over him. The floor is sealed.

She hurries to her own room. Three doors down. No, night means nothing up here. Up and down, here and there, in and out, round and round, none of it means anything. Still, we must go on. She bends to the hatch, and language scatters at her feet. Where she's going, she won't need to speak. Feet first into the padded room, she lands on the soft bed, crosses her legs, and lifts her face to watch the hatch slide closed overhead. The little lights beside her bed flicker, waiting. They will dim when she does.

Her room is the same. Empty, purified. She doesn't need mementoes.

She closes her eyes a moment, picturing Judith asleep in her room, an exact copy of this one. She will be afraid, alone like this. She will have questions when they see each other. Celeste should prepare herself. This heaviness at the back of her skull. She is too tired to think.

She forces herself to sit up a moment longer. If not Judith, then it will be Nick. Yes, he will meet her at the door. Familiar company. After all these years, he is like family.

Nick is easier to think about. She tries to go back to the beginning, to the first conversation. He surprised her; he sounded nervous. Called to give his personal condolences. Of course she knew him. JB had dealt with him for years, had mocked and envied him. He was still new then, a real up-and-comer. Not yet the richest man in the southern hemisphere, but only because JB was still alive.

First, he was sorry, genuinely sorry, a great man – and what a blow to lose them all at once like that. He couldn't imagine. She must be bereft. She looked out over the grounds, half listening. The heat wrinkled everything in sight: the trees, the fence, the desert beyond. It was all dying. Judith was a small figure leaning over what was left of the pool, a long stick in her hand. They still had each other. The image on the screen was sharper than the world. Nick Fry had delicate features, a marsupial intensity. *A peace offering*, he said. Celeste hadn't known she was at war.

The promises came first. He would release her from her father's obligations. He would tear up the agreement, return whatever funds he hadn't spent, recoup what he could from other investors. It wouldn't be fair to hold her to the project, given what she had lost. *The project*, Celeste said.

Yes, the Endeavour. She waited for him to explain.

On the other hand, he went on, if there was still an interest, if she wanted to pursue this chance, there would be a place for her. Dozens who would take that opportunity. So it was her decision.

A place. A safe place, somewhere. That was the offer.

She was in a good position, he continued, strong. JB had got in early, right at the start, and the project was well underway, of course she knew all this –

She bit her lip so she would not ask. Drew breath and counted. Said she didn't have the details in front of her, and could he send them through again. She was only twenty, so brave, all her training coming into play. She is proud of that person now. *She got us where we are, Jude. Safe.*

He paused a long time, the small eyes watching. Then he sighed. *I'll come out there*, he said, *if you don't mind. Or we can meet somewhere else – somewhere neutral.* She thought of him in the house, of Judith, of the security issues since the accident. *Somewhere else*, she said.

Yes, it was a war. Like surviving a bombing: you learn to seek shelter, to wait it out. The senses keep on ringing. Even here, her head aches. Time is in patches. She does not remember arriving, but she remembers this.

She lets herself fall back against the bed, and the soft lining welcomes her. Machines beneath the fabric wait to tune her body while she sleeps. The Station will manipulate her muscle, a million miniature electric shocks per minute. This cocoon keeps her alive. Keeps her in condition, mental, physical. Hui said he didn't want to sleep, but sleep is essential, maybe the most important part. It's how they will survive. How they will find each other.

She closes her eyes, and the mask descends. Beyond her body, a bed of endless stars. All she has to do is rest.

13

AUGUST

A few kilometres from Roana, the road was blocked by a fallen tree. They would have to walk the rest of the way. Jude groaned, but it was perfunctory; nature was intervening, and as she stepped down from the cab into the cooler air, she only felt a small surge of relief.

Jude loved this country, so different from the place she'd come from. The mountains were wide shadows broken by narrow bands of light. The peaks to either side were snowless and grey, but the forest that lined the valley was a mix of living tones, and it smelled damp and rich.

One of the teenagers – Topo, they called him – had found the sack truck strapped to the inside of the trailer and was piling pumpkins on top. She reached for a couple of ratchet straps, passed them to him and began collecting their kit bags. By the time she returned to the trolley he was tilting it against his knee, the load secured.

'Thank you,' she said when she caught his eye. 'Good job.'

He nodded, barely a flicker of a smile, but she felt the pride in him gleaming. The kind of kid that would be sent on ahead by his parents. Maybe they were not alive to send him. She resisted an urge to take the trolley from his hands, and instead walked quickly ahead, alone, trying not to think about anything at all.

It wasn't her; it couldn't be. No-one had survived Endeavour Station. That body belonged to a stranger. By now it would be laid out in the little morgue behind the clinic, ready for the field across the stream where they buried the unknowns, their graves marked with blank white stones. The medics kept records: tattoos, teeth, DNA. Many were never identified. But plenty of strangers visited that field, mourning their own lost dead.

'Jude!'

The rattling of the pumpkin trolley behind her, the laughter and voices, came to her as though from a great distance. Ali was striding ahead of the group, jogging to catch her. She unclenched her fingers, inhaled deeply. Had been marching, fists tight by her sides, mind elsewhere. The smell of salt, of wet metal. She reached for the wall by the road, put her head against the cold stone.

'Are you okay?' Ali asked when he reached her.

'It's nothing,' she said. 'Dizzy, that's all.'

'You need a good night's sleep,' Ali said. 'It's getting late. We'll stay in Roana tonight, hey?'

It would be dark walking back to the truck. Darker still, driving. And what waited for her back at the harbour?

'Yeah, maybe.'

'And then will you go and see the medic when we get back?'

Jude turned from his touch and rotated her shoulders, working against the stiffness. 'Leave it, Ali. Please.'

Something in her voice made him pull away. Other voices bustled close behind them.

Jude lifted her chest.

'Almost there,' she called out brightly.

The village had a welcoming air. No-one was in the narrow street, but there were lights on in some of the windows, and Jude could smell woodsmoke and garlic cooking. It struck her that the Freelands – even just the valleys – could contain both Orson and Roana, both welcome and refusal. But then, most countries had the same inconsistencies.

Topo had persisted with the trolley, and was pushing it across the flatter stones that lined the road on one side, forming a slanted footpath. Jude could hear Ali and Solare among the adults bringing up the rear, speaking what sounded like Arabic, laughing.

The river was only a creek up here, but it was set far below the road in a deep, stony gully. It must flow full and furious at times, but for now the water was gentle and clear, the smooth stone visible beneath. A narrow bridge across it, sparser buildings on the other side, then meadow. A pile of logs lay seasoning in a clearing, a mild-looking donkey munching the grass beside them. Vegetable patches, fenced with sticks. A small herd of healthy-looking goats ran across their yard to investigate, and Jude stopped with the youngsters to watch, standing a little apart as her human companions bleated sociably in return. The Ro Valley had been spared the worst of the war, was of no strategic value. She inhaled the clarifying air, heard cowbells in the distance, calling. A person might have room to move up here. Take refuge in these deep green shadows. A person could disappear.

Artemis ran down the road to greet them, which made the goats stand to attention, and some of the passengers flinch. Jude bent to touch her ears. Topo had moved quickly, put his body and the trolley between the dog and the younger ones, was watching her carefully. Artemis pressed her nose into Jude's leg, but Gloria must have called her; she turned her velvet ears, then her head, and trotted back to the village. Jude's back ached when she stood. Too much driving in two days.

Ali quietly caught up with her. She was glad he would be in front to greet their hosts, to reassure their guests. The convent's lights were on, its main chimney smoking. The facade of the old place was properly quarried, rendered white. When Jude was last here, six months ago, the walls were plain; now painted animals peered out from the arches. A single high attic window lifted, then closed. She thought of snipers, drones. There was no violence here, no threat. The road beyond narrowed before petering into long-abandoned ski fields, dried-up glacial lakes and hiking trails. Full of tourists before the snow retreated, before the war. A couple of hundred people these days, dotted through the valley. A need for hundreds more.

In the tiny piazza in front of the convent, an orange cat watched sleepily. Ali rapped on the wooden doors. The curtains were drawn. A voice boomed somewhere, then Artemis barked. The cat didn't flinch, but Jude felt the others shifting in the space behind her, sensed their nervous movements.

Be grateful you were saved.

'Wendi,' Ali cheered, and the two hugged long and warmly. Then she caught Jude in an unexpected embrace. The hair under her knitted hat was witchy: long, blonde-grey and unrestrained. She let Jude's stiffness go and beamed at everyone. A teacher, an artist, an organiser, she might have been a convent leader six hundred years ago, the way she herded everyone inside. This building had a long history of refuge, she was already explaining; Ali's simultaneous translation was lost in the noisy interior.

There were twenty or so people there to welcome them in the convent's small common room. Languages were quickly tested, found. Wendi was telling Ali that these were the first arrivals in months, that houses were ready, just needed painting. Jude looked for an exit, saw a familiar face inside, nodded before turning away. There was nowhere you could disappear completely.

Gloria didn't seem bothered by her presence. She was busy making introductions, finding company for the children. The young ones quickly formed a pack and ran outside in search of the cat. Jude found a quiet corner.

The valleys could be difficult. Medical help was far away. Resources were fewer, social visits rare. Instability and risk: avalanches, storms, floods. Exhausting workloads, loneliness. In this warm room, with the tables laid and the noise of welcome, the bonds of shared community felt more perilous than any of that. Her mountain fantasy flaked softly down around her like snow. It would be suffocating, a place like this. Jude couldn't stay longer than a day.

Gloria brought her a glass of mulled wine, Artemis at heel. 'You could have told me you were coming,' she said. The dog's snout pressed against Jude's calves, sniffing. Jude put a palm down to greet her again, then closed both hands around the warm wine and felt her cheeks flush. 'Last-minute thing,' she said. 'Didn't have time.' In truth, she hadn't thought of it.

'You're staying the night,' Gloria began: an unspoken invitation. Jude felt the flicker of an old attraction, let it pass. She looked at her boots until Gloria touched her lightly on the arm, and walked away.

There was a small shelf beside the table. Jude pulled out a

book and began to flick through recipes, though she hardly ever cooked anymore and registered nothing from its pages. The drink made her feel maudlin, so she pushed it aside. A meal was announced, but Jude had no appetite. She got up to go to bed while the others were occupied, leaving her half-empty cup behind.

Ali watched her leave. The smaller the community, the greater the surveillance.

Jude felt the darkness yawn behind her, the junk past crashing to earth. The crow pulled wires from its prize. There was a crumpling in her body. A few more steps: hold on. She kept her eyes on the ground.

'All right?' Solare was in her way.

Jude forced a smile. 'Just tired,' she said, and pushed past without another word.

The corridor was hung with simple decorations, a few colourful paintings. The upstairs rooms were small and plain, one or two beds in each. At some point the old convent had been a hostel for tourists; during the war, a refuge again. They were still fixing up the building. A staircase folded down from the attic. She smelled pine shavings, linseed oil. Honest work.

Jude knew her way. The room was peaceful, neutral. The walls were decorated with plain textiles, and a faded towel was folded neatly on the single bed. A rough basket in one corner held extra blankets. She closed the door behind her and inhaled: a lived-in cleanliness, a little dust. She kicked off her boots and crossed to the window. There was a fountain in the courtyard below. A vegetable garden, staked beds of yellowing tomatoes, corn, beans, an abundance of herbs. In one corner, a statue of a saint stood dressed in a denim jacket and straw hat. Its praying hands intact, she noted. Above the courtyard, tiled roof, a rectangle of sky. The endless stars.

She was not trapped here. She could walk out right now, get in the truck, drive to Portosacre. Plenty of work down there. Or she could disappear into the valley, hide away in some narrow fold of earth.

Jude closed the window, pulled the heavy curtain across and sat on the bed. She shrugged off her jacket, stretched out. Her body felt heavy enough to sink through the mattress, the floor below, the mountain. To sleep, you had to trust the earth to take your weight.

14

BEFORE

Jude is on her own in the back of the car; unlike the drive to Prospect River, there is no picnic on the seat beside her. Celeste is fidgeting up front. For days, she has been knotted with excitement. Fry has invited them back for another meeting, a private one. They have passed the first stage, secured their places, moved to the next level of the process. They will be saved, Celeste keeps saying. Her hands twist restlessly; her head turns too quickly, looking left and right.

Jude hasn't eaten, and she feels as hollow as a dried-up pig melon. The grounds around Sovereign House are full of them now, edging in from the fence line, leaving their fruits out rudely in the sun. When you kick one, it bursts and scatters seeds.

They have to slow down to pass the camp. This time, there are a lot of people around. Jude glimpses some of the banners:

Always was
River killer
Land back

And *REPARATIONS*, looking worse for wear.

She tugs the long sleeves of her T-shirt over her wrists. The EV is smooth and almost soundless, quiet enough that she can hear the people outside calling to each other. A group of them rush towards the car, hurling accusations. Their faces, sweaty, pained, dirty, appear too close to the glass. A sickness rises in Jude's chest.

'I can't believe these people,' Celeste is saying. 'What good are the police, I ask you.'

Spence only murmurs in response. He catches Jude's eye in the rear-view mirror, but keeps his expression neutral. There have been raids of the camp, Jude knows, but the protesters keep coming. Celeste says it's political. The minister wants to seem sympathetic. They could send their own private security out here, but you have to consider the optics.

Jude can feel the heat, despite the air conditioning. She touches her fingers to the handle, leaves them there. Spence's eye shifts in the mirror, his expression softening. He's trying to tell her something. She chooses to believe it is *go*.

She hasn't planned this. Her body just knows. She can't make it to the base, can't sit and listen to Fry talk about his secret space rockets, can't watch Celeste fawn and grovel again. She can't give her sister what she needs, can't make her well, can't pull her back from this precipice.

She moves her thumb over the release. Her other hand against her pocket, the shape of a glittering stone. She is fourteen years old, and full of certainties; she believes she can get free.

Spence slows the car. The group of protesters is too close to the road. They bang on the windows, faces hungry and sad.

'What now,' Celeste says, from far away.

Jude unclicks her seatbelt with one hand, opens the door a crack with the other. Nothing beeps. The ground blurs past below, black asphalt rolling away, a streak of red dirt beside it. Celeste doesn't seem to notice. Time is very slow. The voices outside are clearer, without the defence of glass. She falls out onto the earth.

Jude tumbles to the ground, bruising, other bodies all around her. Her name is tiny, turns to dust. Hands grab her by the arms and legs. A sharp thumb in the soft upper ribs, a mouthful of metallic earth. Someone pulls at her, she thinks; someone else calls out *Stop*, but to stop them, or to stop her, she doesn't know. She is yanked away, into and then far from the shouting. The first taste of liberty, and she has no power at all. She is just a body in the dirt.

'Let them through!' someone yells. Jude's sight blurs. The car is nowhere. She is on her feet, pushed into a tent, led out again. She is surrounded by faces, noises, strangers.

'Clean her up,' a voice says.

A cloth is wiping the dust from her face. The cloth is scratchy, damp. Around her, voices are raised, emotions swirling. Slowly, she becomes aware of individuals, sentences, meaning. They are talking about a ransom. A bargain. She blinks her vision clear.

'It's abduction. They'll crucify us. She's just a child.' Decisions are being made without her. There is too much shouting.

Jude gets to her feet and waits for a break in the sound, her body trembling. Does she have a right to speak in this place, among strangers? There are no staff here to carry out her wishes. No-one stops talking to make room for her voice. For a moment she feels she has disappeared. Then a young man hands her a bottle of water, takes her by the elbow, makes her sit down again.

'You're okay. You fell,' he tells her. He smells of sweat and spices.

Her knee is badly grazed.

'I didn't *fall*,' she answers, but he's already moving away.

'She's just a kid,' someone is saying, 'she's scared.'

'I'm not,' Jude objects, but the voice isn't right. Isn't hers. It's hoarse, too high, and shaken. Two women near her begin to sing, a low keening in a language she doesn't recognise, soft and aspirated. The song flows into her body like water. She breathes, refuses feeling. Her heart has been thumping much too fast, but now it slows. She has no idea what she is doing.

'It's a risk to the whole camp.'

'This is bigger than the camp, Ade.'

'Is it?'

'We don't have time to argue,' the woman says. 'We have to take her back.'

Silence. And then all eyes are on her.

Jude sits up in her chair.

'I'm not going back,' she says.

She is not, has not been, afraid; the adrenaline has been coursing through her body, hiding hunger, making her fierce. Later, as it slips away, it will leave a lump in her throat like she's been crying. But at this moment, she's invincible. She has crossed over, walked away. The Endeavour, her sister's plans: all that is finished.

She thinks it's that easy.

'Come with me.' A woman bends to her, copper curls falling across her face.

Jude scrambles to her feet and follows her into a tent. A medic lifts her onto a bench, cleans up her cuts and bruises, looks in her eyes and ears. He's nice enough, tries to make small talk, but Jude's injuries are hurting. She wants her body back. Wants to get away. Outside, they are talking about where they will take her. Where will be safe. Voices low; it's hard to hear them.

When she doesn't respond, the medic gives up talking, gets on with the disinfectant.

It's hard to tell who's in charge here, how decisions get made. Five people file back into the tent and start to ask her questions. Wanting to know if something has happened, if someone hurt her. She wants to slide down from the bench, but the medic isn't finished with her. It feels like an interrogation. She tries to sit straight and tall. Information is her weapon.

'I can help you,' she says. She stretches out one leg so she can reach into a pocket of her jeans, digs out her phone. This is power. When the world finds out, there will be consequences. They will be stopped.

There's a small conference. Someone holds a hand out, and she puts her phone in his palm. He holds it face down, at arm's length. Doesn't even look at the screen. 'They can track you with this,' he says. 'They can track all of us.'

'I have evidence,' she says, reaching for it.

'We have to smash it.' The young man pulls away, sniffing.

'I don't think we can keep her,' the medic says.

'She's what, fifteen? She can decide.'

Jude doesn't correct them. She's not certain of her legal status. In this state, she has read, ten-year-olds can go to prison.

'It's kidnapping,' another says, and stomps out of the tent.

'It's her decision.'

By the time the medic has finished, there are only two other people left: the friendly one with the copper curls and another skinny one, younger.

'We can help you, but only if you're sure that's what you want.' At least these two speak to her directly.

Jude nods firmly. 'I'm sure,' she says. She won't go back to Sovereign House. Never.

The one with curls has a friendly face. Up close, the copper's streaked with grey.

'You can't keep her here,' the medic says. 'I've said I'm not prepared to do that.' He raises gloved hands, begins to peel them.

Curls nods. 'Listen. Put this on, and come with me, quickly.' She hands Jude a black hoodie, red and yellow pattern on the back. Jude slips it over her head. It's way too big. The medic tugs a beanie over her ears.

'Take care,' he says. 'Now, go with Holly.'

Holly leads Jude into the crowd, keeps her close. No sign of the black car, the police, but there's a helicopter overhead. Jude hopes it is too far away to see her.

'Hood up, come on. Not safe.'

'They'll know it's me,' Jude says, burying her head in the heat of it.

'I don't think it matters,' Holly says. Her voice is compassionate. 'I'll take you to my place. It should be safe for a day or so, and then we'll see.'

Jude's throat is filling with moisture. The build-up of dust. 'Just let me show you,' she says, 'my phone,' but her voice is hoarse and the woman doesn't respond. She opens the side of a white van, waves Jude in.

'Later,' she says, squeezing a shoulder.

Jude doesn't hesitate. She crawls into the corner, lets Holly pull an old blanket over her. The helicopter roars by, fades. If they catch her, it will look like an abduction. Maybe it is.

They have to wait until it's dark. There's a roadblock, so

Holly drives the dirt road around the back way, through the community. She chats the whole way, her voice like a GPS narrating where she's going – *Turning left up here*, or *Bit bumpy* – so Jude can brace herself. Her body aches, especially her ribs and the knees where they are scraped raw; she can feel the scabs forming when she reaches her hand down. There's a lot of dust in the blanket, and it gets in her ears, her nostrils, her eyes. She keeps them closed. Maybe she dozes.

Eventually they hit asphalt, and the van stops rattling. The quiet wakes her. Holly says she can sit up if she wants: they're almost there. She puts her head up, looks out the window.

Something feels strange. It takes her a minute. No motion sickness.

Night. The outer suburbs of the city, or a large town. If it's the city, this is not a part of it she recognises. Near her old school, where Spence used to drive her when she was little, the houses always seemed too close together. Here they are even more tightly packed, and much smaller. Each with its little yard around like a moat, and a low fence anyone could step right over. Most of the yards have cars or caravans. Some have tents. A dog barks, shows its teeth. Jude pulls her face back from the glass.

'You're my niece over from Sydney, if anyone asks,' Holly says, 'but probably no-one will. People in this neighbourhood don't call the cops.'

'Why not?' Jude imagines it's political. A word from the minister.

'There was a shooting last year. A boy your age. We prefer to work things out between us.'

They pass a woman smoking in a small fenced cement yard,

her hair wrapped up, watching the van. Miniature houses with junk in their yards, busted sofas, broken prams. Metal sculptures, overgrown gardens. Someone's Christmas lights, though Christmas has been over for months.

Holly parks in front of a red-brick box, helps her climb through to the front. She says it will look less suspicious for her to get out that way, but Jude gets the sense that no-one around here will care.

'Oh, she's a softie. Are you okay with dogs? She's been unwell – she's getting old, I guess. Sorry, you probably don't need to know all this. Are you hungry?'

Jude stares at the giant white animal in front of the brick box and feels her skin prickle. A tall, pale woman with straight black hair emerges, stands in front of the open door, arms folded. She looks like a furious ghost.

'That's Rachel,' says Holly. 'And this is Rosa.' Rosa's tail moves cautiously, her mournful eyes fixed on Jude.

'I have the kettle on already,' Rachel says, and then she hugs Holly and growls into her curls, in a quiet voice, 'This is a bad idea.'

Jude pretends she doesn't hear. She waits for them to let her inside.

The house is small and grim, and smells of damp and dog. There is already a cot unfolded in a corner of the little lounge room. Colourful blankets. None of the furniture matches.

Rachel looks her over carefully. 'Are you okay with she/her pronouns?'

No-one has ever asked Jude this. 'I guess,' she murmurs.

They bring her tea and a plate of biscuits, homemade, that fall apart in her hands. The tea is much too sweet, but the biscuits aren't sweet enough, so it evens out. Inside the hoodie, she feels herself disappearing. She gets through half the plate before they speak to her again.

Holly sits opposite her. Rachel stands, mug in hand, a look of calculation. 'So,' she says. 'You mentioned information?'

Jude digs in her pocket for her phone, and remembers she doesn't have it. There were photos on it, evidence of the Endeavour. They will just have to take her word. But once they know, once the plan is out in the open, it will all be over.

'They're leaving,' she says. Her mouth is dry, her voice too small. The stone in her pocket weighs a tonne. She puts her hand there, to feel the texture of it. The flaking shine. 'Leaving Earth,' she adds. It's a shock to say it out loud. It should shock these women, too.

They only exchange a look that Jude can't read. At their feet, the dog starts whining.

15

AUGUST

Voices in the hallway, children playing. Still groggy from brief, restless sleep, Jude took a moment to remember where she was. Then she was pulling her boots on, ready to leave.

Downstairs, she made coffee and watched the other early risers. Wendi's son had grown tall, was stalking around on long, unsteady legs. A younger child followed him, and he bent to watch her crawl beneath the tables. When the little one's laughter started to turn, he scooped her up and took her to a corner, began to show her objects: stones, seedpods, the soft nest of a small bird. Jude looked away.

Ali had left his phone charging on the counter. She picked it up, only to check the time. Too early to get going. Jude scrolled the newsfeed, reading back through posts she usually ignored: requests for materials, work groups, deliveries. She wasn't looking for the message, but stopped when she found it. *Unidentified vessel. No life signs.* It hadn't been updated.

Her hands closed around the case. She could still feel the weight of the stretcher, that awful lightness against her palm.

The children were laughing, the sound valley-sweetened. Jude dropped the phone on the counter and went to get some air.

In morning light, Roana looked like a village out of a fairytale. Surrounded on all sides by rocky slopes, the central stretch of trees and river seemed greener than was natural, whatever nature meant these days. Goat bleats filtered through the narrow lanes, stone walls leaning in at angles. For hundreds of years, maybe thousands, these houses had been assembled from whatever the mountains let fall. Flat slate for roof tiles, whole tree trunks for beams. Northport sometimes looked depressed by its air of salvage, but Roana seemed at home in it.

Pacing the lanes kept her warm, but the coffee went cold quickly. Eventually she heard Ali clearing his throat behind her. He was watching from the convent door, wrapped in one of Wendi's handmade blankets. The orange cat appeared beside him, stepped slowly across his feet.

'How long have you been standing there?'

He watched the cat saunter away. 'You can relax, you know. There's no hurry.'

'I don't like to leave the truck,' she said. She joined him by the door, reached for his coffee, took a sip. The morning had grown bright around her, stars and satellites hidden in the pale sky. No drones. Still, she felt observed.

'No-one's going to do her any harm,' he said. 'Not here.'

She blinked, but he was only talking about the truck.

He nodded at the rest of his coffee, watched her drink it.

'We'll go as soon as you're ready,' she said. She could talk more when they were on the road, just the two of them.

'Come in and eat something first. The kids are making breakfast.'

Jude must have looked sceptical.

'There's more coffee,' he added, already halfway through the door.

She could not linger in the chaos of the kitchen, so took a slice of bread and butter, went outside again. The loaf had berries and nuts baked into it, and the butter they made here was salty and slightly sour. She sat on the step.

The sun was casting some warmth by the time Ali showed his face again.

'Sure you're all right out here?'

'I can always go without you,' she told him.

He rolled his eyes. 'Wendi's lending us bikes.'

She appeared from a lane beside the convent as if conjured, wheeling three bicycles: two in one hand, one in the other. She leaned them against each other, then reached for Jude's empty cup.

'A few of us will walk down later and collect them,' she said.

'Really?'

'I used to ride up to the pass every weekend, if you can believe it.' She turned, not waiting for an answer.

Jude called out, confused.

'Wait – why three of them?'

'Solare's going with you,' she said.

Jude had no right to be annoyed. Solare was free to make up her own mind.

Ali stepped over to inspect the bikes, pulled the largest and most garish one forward and tested the brakes with his hands.

'You'll like her, Jude. She's actually nice.'

'Sure,' Jude said.

'Also, she speaks six languages, including two I don't. If she can help with translation, I'll have more time to write.'

Ali was always saying things like that. Always working on his stories, taking notes. Picking out details as they happened, or as he happened upon them. Sifting through water-damaged papers, filing odd items he'd unearthed from the sheds, conducting interviews in a corner of the Common. His approach was totally unsystematic. Even if a Freelands history could ever be written, she knew he would never finish it. It wasn't exactly a pointless project, more an infinite one, which amounted to the same thing.

Solare was in the doorway, saving her from speaking. 'I can come?'

'Of course,' Jude said. 'Your decision. But aren't you better off up here?'

'They're safe. I want to help others,' Solare said. 'I have this much life left.' She raised her hands to the width of her chest, palms facing. Jude wondered how she knew.

'Come, don't come,' she said. 'Up to you. But we have to go *now*.'

She pulled the worst-looking bike towards her, leaving the light racer for Solare. As the older woman finished her farewells, Wendi passed Ali a backpack stuffed with walnuts. Gloria walked over, looked Jude in the eye, pressed a small packet of herbs into her hands and patted them closed without speaking. Then they were gone.

There was too much wind to think. For long moments, she forgot the weight of the stretcher, the capsule, Nora, *No life signs.* In a couple of places they had to dismount and pick their way over potholes, Solare taking a confident lead. In full daylight, the landscape looked less idyllic. Most of the country was overgrown, uncared for. The roads were temporary solutions of sand and crushed rock that would wash away in heavy rain.

At an abandoned municipal building, they stopped to drink from a spring tapped centuries ago. It was ice-cold, the flavour of stone, and fortifying.

The truck was waiting where she'd left it. They dismounted, wheeled the bikes under a prominent tree where they'd be easily seen and protected from the weather. Jude scanned the branches; a pair of robins hopped in and out of view, ochre chests flashing.

Ali threw the walnuts into the back of the cab, and Solare climbed in after them.

'Okay back there?' Jude was startled by the woman's grin in response; it changed her face completely. This was an adventure for her, a release from obligations. Jude could not help smiling back.

Jude started the engine. Ali yawned, tied his hair back into a loose ponytail, and closed his eyes. With any luck he would sleep the whole way and ask no questions.

Jude squinted against the sun as the road wound through little abandoned villages, past boarded-up shops and ghostly churches. The land along the river was overgrown in some patches, grey in others. The country was recovering too slowly. You could bring a thousand people here, ten thousand, and it wouldn't be enough.

At a bend in the road, the morning light hit the valley sideways, picking out the walls of distant villages, exposed cliffs, the folded hills below. She heard Solare inhale. Roads and rivers converged ahead, Cuoretto's hydro plant rising from the junction like a castle. The valley seemed beautiful again. Not ruin: possibility.

*

'It looks like someone survived,' Ali said. He hadn't slept long; they were only at the junction.

'Hm?' Jude was watching her side mirror, flashes of wall and overgrowth. She swallowed.

'That vessel yesterday. The clinic has to close, says there's a risk to the survivor. So, there must be a survivor.'

Solare leaned forward, asked something. Ali replied and showed her the screen.

Jude shifted in her seat. Her knee was aching, back stiff. She needed to stop driving, stretch her legs.

Ali turned to her. 'You saw them, didn't you?'

'Didn't see anything.' She remembered the relief she'd felt when the stretcher was taken from her hands. Nora would take care of it. That was the clinic's job.

Solare and Ali conferred a moment. After a pause, he translated for Jude's benefit. 'She was asking if it was someone like her. A new arrival. She wants to help.'

A true Freelander, Jude thought bitterly.

'I said I didn't know the details,' he said slowly, watching her. 'Something bothering you?'

'Just tired,' she said, rolling a shoulder. 'Slept badly.' She hated the way he could read her. She couldn't speak now, in front of a stranger.

Ali nodded carefully. 'You need to see that medic,' he said.

'Well, I can't today, can I?' said Jude. 'The clinic's closed.' A cold little triumph, but it was true. She wouldn't have to go anywhere near the place. When they got back to Northport, she would make a plan. If she had to leave – if it was Celeste – she would do so quickly and decisively. *Survivor.* It couldn't be her. It wasn't possible.

16

BEFORE

In the morning they bring her tea and toast, ask whether she takes sugar, how she slept. Jude gives one-word answers. They are dancing around the reason she's here. She pokes at the cold toast on her plate. The tea tastes like damp cardboard. Outside are the crowded sounds of cars, people, birds. Little kids playing in the street. Must be strange to live so close together like this.

'Would you like cereal instead, love?' Holly asks.

Jude sets her cup down. She has no appetite, and not much patience.

'We have to tell people.' The world should know about the Endeavour, what Fry is planning. When people find out they will stop them.

The women don't answer for ages. They don't even look at her. Rosa is shuffling under the table, paws close. Jude picks up a triangle of Vegemite toast, holds it down near her knee until she feels the animal's mouth tug it gently away from her.

Rachel has her back to them now, moving stuff around on the counter. Holly speaks in a low voice.

'People know,' she says.

'But I have evidence,' Jude says.

'It doesn't matter, love.' Holly tucks her curls into the yellow scarf she's wrapped around her head. The endearment puts distance between them, puts Jude in her place. They don't want her here. She's no use, only a burden. The dog's nose is wet, demanding, pressing into her palm.

'We need to move her.' Rachel gestures at Jude with the dirty dishcloth, tosses it on the sink, then stalks out of the room.

*

In the back of the same van, not hidden this time. The scratchy blanket is folded into a square. Jude perches on a plastic stool beside it. Both women sit in front, Rachel driving. They speak too low for Jude to hear much. She tunes in to the engine instead, the calming clank and rattle of the van on rough roads. Jude is dressed as a boy, in an oversized hoodie and jeans. They've cut her hair shorter, combed the fringe over her eyes. Still, it's not so far from her usual style that she wouldn't be recognised if someone was looking for her. She keeps the hood up, tucks her hands into the sleeves, and tries to trust these people.

If they're stopped, Holly will say she has a fever and they're going to the hospital. They all have surgical masks on already. She says the police will back away from sickness, and no-one will be surprised there wasn't an ambulance. Apparently there are shortages everywhere, especially in their part of town. Buses, fuel, electricity, water. Jude's embarrassed to learn this. She didn't know it was so bad, so close to home. Didn't understand how safe she's been until now, or how naive.

They will drop her off at the gates of a hospital on the other side of the city. She will sit in the emergency waiting room, near the door if she can, try to look like she's sick. If she's shaking, if her hands are cold with adrenaline, it will only make it more convincing. She'll have to keep her head down, face hidden in the grey fleece. Someone from 'the movement' will meet her there. Then a long drive interstate. Across the border, she can change her look, her name, her background. Maybe someone will find a use for what she knows. In Jude's head, maps of the continent unfurl.

Holly is humming softly. A pink crystal hangs from the mirror, a parrot feather tied below.

Celeste thinks all these people are terrorists. By now, she will be at the launch site, watching Fry speak about the future. She believes him when he says they will be safe up there, safe from people like this, with their cold toast and their kindness. Jude folds her arms in front of her chest, keeps her eyes down, tries to push her sister's thoughts out of her head.

A red and white sign glows through the trees. Rachel stops on a corner where the streetlights are broken. They hug Jude tightly, one after the other. Holly's cheeks are wet with tears. It hasn't even been a whole day, and Jude's brought them nothing but risk.

She walks stiffly down the road towards the entrance, doesn't look back. They will be happy when she's out of the way.

The hospital looks like a haunted house. The dark brick walls are old and grimy. Inside, Emergency is a fluorescent glare. Lino crackles underfoot. Faded posters sag on the walls. Dozens of people are waiting: old people, kids, people on crutches. A pregnant woman in a wheelchair smiles as she passes, half her teeth gone. No-one's at the desk, no-one acknowledges her entrance. It's a good place to hide, but it's lucky she doesn't actually need a doctor. At Sovereign House, doctors come to them. Psychologists, therapists, assorted specialists. Celeste burns through them. Jude has read about the hospital system, the breakdowns, the staffing crisis; she knows it in theory. Here, collapse is no longer theoretical.

Jude won't think about Celeste. She sanitises her hands and takes a plastic seat at one end of a half-empty row. Nearby, an old man makes a low growling noise. Her palms feel papery, her body insubstantial. Down the hall, someone screams. Jude hunches, her face cold. She wishes she'd eaten breakfast.

Barely half an hour later, the staffer finds her. She doesn't need to look up. She knows him by the way his shadow looms. He sits in the chair beside her and says her name in a voice that's firm but gentle, and then it's over. The maps retract. In a way she's relieved, though she hates to admit it. This is a rescue.

At least they didn't send Spence.

*

Hilal usually works security. Looks like it, even out of uniform. He's young, around Celeste's age, and the suit seems stiff on him. He asks her to come with him, his voice gentle, but it isn't really a question. The waiting room falls silent. People are watching. The old man is still growling when Hilal walks her out, one hand on her shoulder.

'You're not hurt,' Hilal observes, phone in hand. Jude straightens. He takes a picture of her, then sends a message, confirming her collection like she's a package. The car seat is smooth and comfortable after the back of the van.

Someone was always going to come for her. There's no escaping. Not the way Celeste thinks, and not like this.

People already know about the Endeavour. They know what Fry's planning, and they don't care. According to Holly and Rachel, some people even admire him for it. She's been so stupid. Jude shuts her eyes and tries to sleep, but it's too quiet. Nausea chews at her belly like a worm. She leans back to watch the sky out the window. Stars, and the steady slide of satellites. A slender moon hangs like a blade in their midst, lightly corroded. There are mining companies on it; Prince missed their chance. Jude stretches her legs out on the leather interior, feels the texture of the car negotiating the gravel road, the touch of earth beneath it like a ghost.

They wake her in the underground car park. The first thing she sees is Spence's face, wrinkled up with disappointment. Is that because she left, or because she failed to get away? She will ask later, if she gets the chance. For now, it is easier to submit to the interrogation.

'It isn't an interrogation,' Celeste corrects. 'It's just a few questions, and then you can go to bed.' She, Spence, and another security man, someone higher up than Hilal, sit her down at the grand table in what used to be JB's office and has become her sister's. There is a schematic drawing of Endeavour Station on the wall behind them. It's been there for ages, right where anyone can see it.

They ask her where she's been, what she's said to outsiders. She doesn't give Holly or Rachel's names, but other than that, she tells the truth. She watches Spence's face for signs he might be on her side, but it's blankly professional now.

'I'm just disappointed,' Celeste is saying. She's so pleased with herself, running through her little script.

Jude can't bear it.

'I'm tired,' she complains. She really is exhausted. Her body feels heavier than ever, gravity burrowed deep in her bones, knees and bruised elbows aching. She might sleep for years.

Can almost understand the attraction of the Station. Her eyes trace its elegant, circular design. Up there, they'll be able to rest. Protected from choices, consequences.

'The camp's cleaned up, by the way.'

'What do you mean?'

Celeste is smiling dreamily. 'The police minister gave the order this morning. She will not negotiate with terrorists.'

Jude stares into her lap. Shame runs through her, quick as a grassfire.

'Bit of a struggle, apparently, but I don't think anyone was too badly hurt. They had to use tear gas. Quite a few arrested.'

Jude thinks of the medic in his tent, of all the people who helped her. Celeste's complaints about the government's inaction. All she has done is given her sister the excuse she was waiting for.

She will always be living inside some architecture of Celeste's, without the wit or cunning to see it until it's too late. She's trapped, no matter what she does.

But it's not herself she feels sorry for. It's her sister, seated behind this great black desk that dwarfs her slender figure, in front of her drawing of the Station, pretending to be in control. Celeste is as much a prisoner as Jude is, but she doesn't even know it.

17

AUGUST

Hamish waved Jude inside the coastguard building, rummaged around for his reading glasses, looked over the mail she handed him. They'd stopped long enough at Cuoretto on the way back to have more pumpkins pressed upon them, a box of herbal tinctures for the clinic and a couple of letters for Hamish, one so weathered it might have been posted before the war. The desk was cluttered with instruments that measured water currents, temperature and pressure, radar, coming storms. Other screens showed various newsfeeds: storm damage, bombing, world politics. Jude watched them scroll past without reading.

When Hamish asked her something, she murmured a stiff response.

'You right?'

'Of course,' she said.

'I was saying, that's where it came up,' he said, pointing along her line of sight.

Outside, the light was beginning to fade. The sea was turbid, a purplish-brown; the clouds above were turning to matching bruises.

'Don't know how long it was in the water. Some kind of tracking scrambler. But nothing ate it, so I guess it wasn't out there *that* long.' It wasn't clear if he was joking.

'Weird,' she said.

'*Deeply* weird,' Hamish agreed, rubbing his hands together. 'Nothing about it registered on our instruments, and certainly nothing that suggested life. It looked unusual, though, so we went out with the barge and brought it in. Honestly, we thought it was an empty shell until we got it open. None of our sensors told us. Thought it might be something from the war. Strong stuff, whatever it's made from.'

'Built to last,' Karim chimed in, not hiding his admiration. They must have already told this story a number of times.

'Took a few hours to crack it, and then the sensors went off, so we rang across to Nora.'

Jude let the pause drift out, watching the waves.

'And then you were here,' Karim said.

'That's right – you saw her. The state she was in.' Hamish was looking at Jude carefully.

'Alive,' Jude said. Her voice seemed to come from some distance.

'Only just, apparently. Nora will tell you all about it when you head over.'

'The clinic's closed.' Her arms folded across her chest. Fingers cold against her ribcage, doubled bars. 'Too dangerous.'

'Oh, but you have to go over there. Didn't you get a message? She's been trying to reach you all day.'

Jude wiped her nose on a sleeve. 'Where is it? I'd like to see it.' She didn't even know what to call it.

'Still in the shed,' Karim said. 'Sealed off now, though. Nobody's supposed to go near that, either.'

'Oh.' Jude was dimly aware that there must have been a meeting. Rules had been laid out, boundaries drawn.

'Too late for us, though.' Hamish was delighted. 'Come check it out.'

He took the shed key from the desk without waiting for an answer, and Jude followed. As in a dream, her body seemed to move without her will. She would look again, and reality would assert itself. This would all make sense. It would only be a lifeboat from a ship, an old submersible. It couldn't be the Station, because the Station was gone. Lost years ago. It was just her insomnia. The mind played tricks.

The air shot goose pimples into her sleeves as Hamish fumbled with the padlock. Someone had taped a handwritten sign beside it: *HAZARD – KEEP OUT* on white cardboard, marked by grubby thumbprints.

He hit a switch, and a light came on deep in the salvage shed's interior. Jude followed him, picking her way past timber and steel and other materials piled up in the dark. A proper look would put this to rest. Just another piece of scrap, that was all it was.

But when she reached the vessel, she knew it immediately.

The capsule seemed smaller up close, more fragile. The metal was blackened in places, crusted white in others. She touched it, expecting warmth, but it had none. Its texture was slightly pitted, like an emu's egg.

'Magic, huh,' Hamish said. 'Probably tough enough to survive a nuclear blast.'

Glitter crumbled under her fingers. She lifted tiny crystals to her mouth: sea salt. Space left no traces.

In the original drawings, in the videos and simulations, these capsules were like small pimples attached to the Station's wheel:

three tiny additions to a much bigger structure. Standing beside it now, she sensed the immensity of the project, its scale and ambition, and felt diminished. A child.

But these were familiar materials, domestic almost. She could see inside the wall where they'd cut it open, less than a metre thick. The outer layers were composed of tiny pipes, like a wasp's nest. And what was left of the equipment inside looked like any pile of disembowelled, out-of-date computers. The place where the body had been was cushioned by ordinary foam.

The body. She took in a rush of air, tasted salt and damp timber. The smell of other humans in the room, their stale breath. Seaweed and decay. The smell of Earth, held in its bubble of atmosphere.

The Station had failed. There were no survivors. That was history, a known fact.

'Jude?'

From the pain in her knee, she understood that she was kneeling. Her head down. The taste of acid in her throat.

They were gone. She had known it in her bones, had read about it. Fry had tried to sell the Station, but no-one wanted the cost of retrieving it from space. It was broken apart remotely, the parts set adrift. What was left of the Station had fallen into the atmosphere, burnt to ash. The bodies inside, long dead, were given a bright cremation. They were shooting stars.

'Are you all right?' Hamish's voice was gentle.

She put her hands on the salted ground, rose to her feet. 'I have to go.'

*

The clinic looked deserted through the sliding doors. Jude was just deciding to leave when they opened. The medic was standing to the side, one hand on a green button.

'I thought you'd never get here,' she said. 'How was the drive? Come in, come in.'

Jude cleared her throat, and found she could not speak.

Nora was quick movements, a smell of oranges and cinnamon. A compact body, strong. No white coat, just a light brown jacket. Jude was sweating, grimly aware she needed a shower.

Inside the clinic, a central desk dominated. A privacy wall separated the two small wards to one side from the entrance. In the back, a broad glass window looked into another room.

Nora's hair, more salt than pepper, was cropped close to her skull at the back. A delicate tattoo behind her right ear. Jude tried to look unruffled, eyes flicking towards the glass. She would see the body, and it wouldn't be her. Then she could go.

When Nora turned, her eyes were a deep greenish-brown. 'You got my messages, then,' she said.

'I was driving.' Jude's voice was uneven. The medic stood too close. She tucked her hands against her ribs, felt her body's solidity. 'I was in the mountains.' She took a small step back.

'I know.' There was a moment's quiet, then Nora seemed to come to some decision. When she spoke again, it was more gently. 'Well. You're here now. That's good.'

Jude followed Nora to the desk, accepted a flimsy face mask, glad of the chance to hide her expression. Her cheeks felt warm. The medic squirted sanitiser into her hands, then examined Jude again up close, resting a hip against the desk. This time Jude had to look away. She saw a clock in the corner, a whiteboard.

A poster with a diagram of the heart, its parts coloured blood-red and sky-blue. The pane of glass, no movement behind it.

'It's good of you to come,' Nora said. There had been a mistake, but Jude didn't interrupt. Nora was already launching into an explanation. 'We have to keep her contacts to an absolute minimum. And since you're already one of them, I'd like to requisition you. Temporarily, of course.'

'Her contacts,' Jude said, voice papery behind the mask. She could taste the bitterness on her own breath. The medic nodded at her, and looked past the white divider at a glass wall. Jude could see light, machinery, movement. She could hear something humming.

'It's not normal, I know. To be honest, I was about to give up on you, do a callout on the F – obviously I can't second you here against your will.' A flicker of a smile. 'But the risk of introducing someone new is too high. So I'm glad you made it.' She screwed up her nose and her face made a brief transformation to innocence, then became serious again, eyes scanning with professional scrutiny. 'No symptoms?'

Jude shook her head.

'You've been here a few years, right? Had all your shots?' She had produced a piece of paper and a pen, was scratching brief notes.

'Four. You can look it up,' Jude said. It was all on the F. She had come in here to get whatever tests and vaccination upgrades the F-net reminded her about, if only because it would keep sending her notifications until she did. But she tended to avoid the clinic otherwise.

'I like to double-check.' Nora paused, and handed Jude the paper. Then she disappeared behind a door.

Jude glanced at the form. A long list of questions about her medical history, allergies and vaccinations. The words swam. She could hear Nora conferring with another person behind the door.

She could walk outside right now, get in the truck and drive.

'You can bring it back tomorrow,' Nora said when she returned.

'Tomorrow?'

'I'll be honest with you, we don't know if she'll make it through the night. We don't know much at all, actually. Who she is, where she's been. The important thing is to minimise the risk of infection.'

Jude must have looked worried.

'The risk is to her life, not yours. Her immunity will be very poor. She's been hooked up to a complicated life-support system, and we don't know how long she was in there. We're adapting what we can to our systems here, but we don't understand all of it. We don't understand *most* of it at this point.'

'She's alive,' Jude said.

'For now, yes. In a bad way, lots of muscle atrophy, poor organ function. But I'm optimistic.'

'Can I see her?' Jude managed.

'Only through the glass, today. You won't see much. But go ahead.'

She followed the medic into the rectangle of light. In the room, the translucent shell was diminished by a web of tubes and wires. Inside the case, packaged in it, was the shape of a body. Suggestions of feet and arms and pale hair. She was too thin. The hands were swollen. The face obscured, distorted, by a tube. The body was still, but the monitors were moving: life, maybe.

Jude felt her own chest hollowing. She was waiting for a stab of recognition, of joy, anger, anything. But she was empty.

'I can't,' Jude muttered. The form fluttered to the floor beside her.

'You're tired,' Nora said, bending to collect it. 'I know it's a lot to take in. Get some sleep. Bring this back tomorrow morning. We'll sort you out with PPE and everything then.'

Jude was hardly listening.

The medic folded the page, slipped it into the pocket of Jude's shirt. A corner dug through layers, into skin.

'And keep your contacts to a minimum. Her immunity – she's very vulnerable. Better to be over-cautious, until we know more.'

*

She got through the Common without speaking to anyone, but at the top of the stairs Ali was coming out of the shower in a burgundy robe, towelling his hair. He turned when he saw her, but Jude raised a palm.

'Don't,' she said. 'I'm supposed to stay away from you.' She backed towards the door of her room. 'From everyone.'

'Who is she?'

'I couldn't say, Ali.'

'I heard she was hooked up to some kind of machine,' he said.

'Ali, please. I'm exhausted.' She heard the meanness in her voice, and regretted it.

'Okay, well, let's hope for everyone's sake you get a good night's sleep.' The space in the hallway echoed with his soft footfalls, then the click of his door.

When Jude closed the door of her room, her mind seemed

Salvage

dull. She undressed, left things lying where they fell. This room wasn't even hers. Why hadn't she taken a proper housing allocation, fixed something up in the hotel or one of the empty buildings on the hill? She wasn't social like Ali. Why hadn't she found some privacy?

It would only take her ten minutes to pack. Headphones by the bed, a coat on a hook behind the door, a few books that belonged to the library downstairs anyway. She could take her things and go right now, never have to explain her past.

Her body was leaden. Whatever happened, sleep had to come first.

She stretched out and closed her eyes.

It was always worse if she thought about how much she needed it. But when she tried to think about anything else, her mind went blank. Just a rush of stars.

After an age she got up again, felt for the square of paper still folded into her shirt pocket, flicked on the light beside the bed. She knelt on the floor, spread the form out on the wooden crate she used as a bedside table. The first few questions were about her family history: she skipped those. Wrote what she knew about her own allergies, vaccines and immunisations. What she remembered.

All the while, she was making calculations. A few hours' sleep would be enough. She would pack a bag, leave before anyone else was up. She would fill the truck, choose a road. South, maybe. She thought vaguely of Portosacre, the few people she knew there.

At the bottom of the page, there was a final blank line above her signature: *Relationship to patient*. Jude began to make a mark, then scratched it out. She covered the curve with a small black square. Beside it, she carefully printed *None*.

18

STATION

Jude is in the sandy creek bed, picking her way across patches of glare and shade. Appearing, disappearing. The wrecks of houses stand between them. Heat shimmer makes her seem unfixed, an image drawn into the landscape, or swimming up through it. The image wavers.

Jude is in the garage. She is stretched out on a bench seat, engrossed in her phone. Probably reading. It's hard to tell: the vision is grainy, leached of colour.

Jude is seated across from her. Celeste feels the slip of warm mussels in her mouth, savours the salt of them. Her sister watches through the steam. Her face is clouded.

She opens her eyes, waits for the fuzz to clear. Her mouth is dry, the little tube retracting. Heart in her chest like a sparrow. When she feels for it there, her ribs are close to the skin. She likes the order. Blinks again. Her vision is taking too long. She scrambles up, scales the rungs. Jude will be waiting.

When she pokes her head out of the hatch, she can see

just well enough to know there is no-one there. The fuzz is uniform. No presence but the Station itself.

She puts her slippers on and waits for clarity, leaning against the wall. Jude must have overslept. She can feel the wheel spinning around her, a dull ache in the back of her head. She has been dragged back here from a long way away, a good place, sleep. She has not left the Station. The Station knows what is best.

She pushes her body away from the wall and into the corridor. Walks the way the lights show. The more distant lights are still splayed; the wheel curves up ahead of her. It takes an uncertain amount of long time to walk it. All this corridor, all these lights. She circles back to her own room without seeing a soul.

I wanted this, Hui said. Safety. A wheel, spinning away in the dark. She has weight, she remembers, because of the spinning. A salt taste lingers in her mouth, a memory of softness. There is a small sore in the back of her cheek where she must have bitten her own flesh in a dream. They don't eat: the Station feeds them while they sleep.

This ache in the back of her skull. She walks on, takes a second circuit. She will find her. Count the doors. A sister's work is to keep hold, to repair.

First her own, then Carolyn's, then the one with the green arrow. Two more, then the observation room. Progress seems slow. She bends to open the hatch, looks inside but doesn't climb down. No moon. The stars are pinpoints, they do not flicker, they get no rest. Night means nothing here, and is eternal. Jude is still asleep.

When she stands, they are in the car. A desert road, familiar. The journey is important. The patch of earth ahead, and Jude stretched out across the seat, looking up through the back windscreen at the stars. Just a child.

She leaves without her. Takes Spence, leaves early in the morning. It is only meant to be a meeting to get the details of an agreement that she hasn't made and will withdraw from. There is no risk in it. Nick is already too much; he is quick with a gesture. He sends flowers: white roses, and lilies for her loss. There is an address, gold lettering embossed on thick card, like an invitation to a wedding. Two hours, give or take. He says he will send a driver, but she insists on her own. Leaves the flowers on the counter, cold and unspoiled.

Celeste knows how to behave. Not angry, not hungry. A white jacket, grey linen dress, to show that she is in grief's shadow but not its clutches. Simple diamond studs: she is still rich enough to be casual about it. She is entitled to her name. All that still matters. The world and her position in it.

Dressing, she sees that she might fortify. Find some way to protect what's left. If something can be managed, maybe they can stay. The empire is falling. She knows it, donning armour. Their small disaster chiming in a symphony. What they have is what is left: the compound, a few loyal staff, each other. Safety falls away. She reasons with herself, and all the time the charge in her is pulsing, it already knows: this, this is your chance.

Welcome, he says, like he owns the place. A restaurant on the shore of an inlet, wind in their hair, secluded, nobody there but the two of them and whoever's in the kitchen. The chef acting as waiter, kind but unobtrusive – like this is a date, when it's clearly a business meeting. Nick's security team concealed somewhere nearby. Celeste checks her irritation, her posture, resists the mirror. She heard her father say to his sons a thousand times: never let them see you flinch. She'll say this to Judith when she sees her, when they circle this corridor side by side.

But when she opens her eyes, she sees no-one. Nick's presence vanishes like an image on water. She scrunches her toes in the slippers, her heart fluttering too quickly, vision still blurry. What this is doing to her body, this separation. All this sleep. It will be worth it. It will restore her.

She closes her eyes. Rest a moment. Here are the drivers in their tinted cars beneath native fig trees ripe with birds, the sound of the wind in the leaves. The briny water stained by melaleucas. Nothing moves in it that she can see. There is the smell of everything living, of rotting leaves. There is nothing here.

This place should be underwater, he says. *I like it so much I built a levee.* When he waves, she looks. Across the inlet, the hot smudge of horizon. *Would you like wine?* She orders a glass of pinot gris, Elisabeth's preference, and barely touches it. It tastes like salt. The meal is plant-based, biodynamic, subtly exquisite, tiny.

Two security men appear by the door during the main course, disappear. The heat is making her drowsy. Water laps beneath the deck. He is staring at her: it makes her uncomfortable in ways she knows not to reveal. She picks at a puree of native yam garnished with pickled seaweed, and decides to cut through.

What do you want from me?

He dabs his lip with a napkin, makes a solemn face. *Your trust*, he says. She smiles automatically.

You think you can escape, she says, waving the wine waiter away from her half-full glass as if she does this all the time. She can still taste the salt in her mouth.

It isn't about escape, he says. *It's about being ready. One day we will found a new society. A new Earth. Sooner than you think. Right now, this is the most important work we can do. Make preparations.*

It is hard to tell his age. She guesses mid-thirties. More future than past, all the promise of his winnings, and still he has the anaemic look of someone who spends long hours in front of screens. A boy who plays games. His artifice of muscle will slide off in a week. She looks out over the still lagoon. A new Earth.

Have you given up on this one?

Oh, I've run the odds, he says. A fly lands on his hair, but he doesn't brush it away. He seems detached from his body, enviably indifferent to skin.

Things are changing quickly, she says.

He nods. *We have to stay one step ahead. This planet, it's always been our greatest limitation.* He gestures at the lagoon, the bird that cuts the space just above the water, skimming without touching, then raises his palm to the atmosphere. The sky has the warm grey colour of smoke, though she can't smell it. The horizon is a long way away. She wants to go home, back to the fences and walls and glass and screens and filtered air of Sovereign House, her faltering enclosure. Of course it is already lost. The shell is breaking. The whole of Earth is not enough for him, and she can't keep one building.

When she opens her eyes, she is already here. Lights flicker in the empty corridor. She blinks back.

Home. The depth of the ocean. The stars beneath her feet.

He is talking about his travels, diving to shipwrecks off the coast of Portugal. Four-hundred-year-old spices in their jars. The laden vessels that bear the weight of trade routes, old wealth tracked from Asia to Europe. He speaks about this history with awe, a childish excitement in the movement of goods from place to place. Periphery to centre. It's something he has in common with her father, that essential innocence. His eyes gleam like wattle seeds. *Exploration is in our nature*, he says. *Even the oceans are limits.* He casts his gaze into a water glass, a sad god condescending. *And we will lose them, anyway. Sooner than you think.*

You will die, she says.

He smiles. *If you must die, make it spectacular.* He might be laughing at her, at death. He looks up, with a stage actor's timing: *What if it's your destiny? To look back at all this, and see a ruin.* The glass swirls. The water beside them ripples, hot and empty. Something in her ripples, too.

Options are shutting down, like the rooms closed off at home. Sovereign House is sinking into the desert. The clamour of protest crunches at her hull. The numbered days fall out like teeth. There is nowhere safe from loss. Not even the ground beneath her feet, which should be underwater. It will all be ruins.

She reaches out a hand to steady herself against the wall. The little lights are comforting. She can only see so far ahead, but the corridor is endless. Under her feet, unceasing stars. She can't walk another circuit. Her head hurts: it must be the spin of the Station that causes this dizziness. So tired. Her own hatch, somewhere along here. Empty. Must be. Next time, she –

There is a breath in the corridor, and she turns quickly to see the shape of a person stumbling towards her, hand outstretched to balance against the wall. At first she thinks they are struggling in the low gravity, but their movements are too jagged. Her heart leaps towards them, suddenly awake. *Judith*, she says, and steps into the centre of the corridor. Her back aches. She has been leaning – slumped – against the wall.

It isn't Judith. It's a tall woman, broad-shouldered. What is her name? The empress of a Swedish retail chain. Athletic type. Clumsy, now. She trips in her slippers.

Maja?

The woman catches herself and looks up, face shadowed. She slides along in slow motion. *I thought I was alone*, she says. Her expression is confused, the eyes unfocused. Her shoulders are not so strong. *My wife*, she says, and topples forward.

It's me, Celeste. Are you hurt? She reaches, stops the woman's fall. The weight that leans against her hand is lighter than it should be.

She was just here, Maja says. *I can't see. A migraine, I think.* Maja is murmuring at the floor, in her ear. One hand against the back of her neck. The other touching Celeste's waist. A golden fall of hair against her. *I thought – my wife.*

You're okay, Celeste says, *it's fine, I'm here. It's time to go back and rest.* Yes, time to sleep. She pushes away, has been awake too long. She waits for the other woman to steady herself. Even stooping, Maja is tall beside her. *I am sorry. I thought –* her eyes are stars away. Celeste waits for her to finish, but the thread has slipped out of her grasp.

Let me take you back, she says. *You should be asleep.*

A hand waves at the air, the face clouds, and Maja accepts an arm.

They pad together down the corridor, weaving a little, until they reach a hatch with an empty slipper recess. No other identifying features. Celeste stoops to the sensor, helps Maja to her knees. The woman's head seems loose on her neck, like a sleepwalker's. Celeste lifts the slippers from her feet, moves her feet onto the ladder. Murmurs of complaint, assent, gratitude.

Sleep preserves them. Keeps them alive. The Station does the work of care. She herself is very drowsy.

She watches Maja descend into the bed below. Soft grey, lights pulsing. The dark mask gleams in one wall. The woman is folded up, her golden hair planted like the eye of a rose. Before she opens out, before the mask can move, the hatch slides closed and the image is gone. Celeste pauses, but there is nothing else for her to do. If there's something wrong with Maja, the Station will take care of it. She is so tired. She must go to her own room.

She glances back once or twice, but the corridor behind her is dark. Distant objects disappear from sight. She completes the circuit, falling more than walking. When she reaches her own hatch, it is easy to push off the slippers and bend to the sensor. She has forgotten to finish counting the doors again. She has remembered something else, though. Maja was a widow.

Twelve, she knows this: yes, she must have counted them. Nick is here. Jude. Celeste descends to her bed, closes her eyes and waits for the mask. The Station is enough. It is her world. All that she knows, all that she remembers. It closes over her. Its hold is limitless.

19

NOVEMBER

'Can I speak?'

Nora's voice is warm against her neck. Jude shifts, reaches for her coffee.

'What for?' If she wasn't fumbling the cup she might have succeeded in holding the anger out of her voice. It's empty, anyway. She shoves it back into the holder.

Nora sinks back. The springs in the seat creak sulkily. 'I didn't know,' she says. 'I wouldn't have let them take her if I knew.'

Easy to say that now. Sol and Tik are asleep, or pretending to be. Ali has turned to the window. Jude checks the side mirrors, sees the road unspooling into the mountains behind them, undulating and branching into the valleys.

'You couldn't have stopped them,' Jude says. The Alliance wants Celeste. She's worth a lot to them, or the thing in her head is. If the Freelands hadn't given her up, the Alliance would have taken her by force. They were badly defended here. No match at all.

'I should have tried.'

'Don't worry about it,' Jude hears herself say. 'Too late, anyway.' It comes out kinder than she intends. Her anger has boiled down to syrup, thick and sweet in her throat.

There's a silence lasting half a kilometre.

'It's a lot to tell,' Nora says. Her voice is husky.

'It doesn't matter,' Jude says, avoiding the mirror.

Ali turns to her, eyes steady. Jude shifts in her seat. All this attention, it's throwing her off. She needs to focus on the days ahead, make a plan. She has to get across the border, find Celeste, find a way to get her out of there. Her thoughts are jagged, shimmering. Out where? There is nowhere left to go. Celeste knew this. No safe place on Earth.

'We'll find her,' Nora says.

Jude wants to argue, but then Tik makes a gentle sound in their sleep and she stops herself. When she leaves the others at the border, she will explain it all as calmly as she can. This is her risk, her history. Her debt to pay.

'Don't talk,' she says. 'I need to focus.'

The road is flat and clear and straight here, and the fields to either side don't demand attention. Jude lets the truck accelerate, bracing herself against the wheel. The road's vibrations are like music in her hands, every stone and crack a numbing rhythm. If she drives fast enough, she can't tell the difference between good country and ruin.

The border is close now. There are signs on this part of the road, names from an old world not completely torn down. She remembers the fence: high steel mesh, imposing white buildings like airport hangars on the other side, cartoonish surveillance towers. Probably no-one even up there. It's a performance, designed to intimidate. She needs to be unruffled, pretend fearlessness, forget that they could kill her. It will be easier once she's on her own.

What weakness made her let them come this far? The last

thing she needs is these people clinging to her; all she's doing is putting them at risk.

A concrete warehouse looms and retreats on her left. Beyond it, a small caravan rusts away beside a brick structure that could be forty or four hundred years old; it's being pulled back into the earth by a great mound of ivy. On this side, passports are meaningless, controls non-existent. On the other side there is a functioning state with police, military, laws. Decisions will be made about Celeste, about her. She can be disappeared in an instant.

Jude keeps her eyes on the white line in the middle of the road. All she has to do is watch the short space ahead of her. Narrow her focus right down, sharpen it like a knife. Here is the truck's familiar need. The scent of it, fried grit and smoke and vinegar. She thinks about her hands and feet and attention, the way she fits into the seat. Eventually, she stops thinking about anything else.

She startles when Ali says 'Look,' but instead of barking at him, she follows his gaze up through the windscreen. Jude expects another surveillance drone, but the line in the sky is curving, graceful. Geese, or maybe cranes. She can hear their honking through the open window. The formation shifts and ripples, but it holds.

'They leave later every year,' he says, and sits back. The birds disappear behind the trees, fleeing a diminished winter. She hopes they have a good place to land.

20

AUGUST

Waking, she was only a small thought in the dark. A heart, engine-steady, then warmth and breath. Still alive, then; still here. Jude opened her eyes, threw off the blanket. A piece of paper fluttered to the floor.

She saw a broken hulk, a glistening pool of shadow.

The facts returned with force. The survivor. Her pale limbs, glimpsed between machinery. The possibilities.

With any luck, she will be dead by now.

Even if she lived, if she woke, she might not remember who she was, what had happened to her. She might not recognise Jude at all.

Jude didn't have to go down there and find out. Didn't have to be dragged back into Celeste's orbit. She had grieved already, had processed the loss, was even glad of it. It had set her free. If she moved quickly, she could stay that way. A clean existence, no attachments.

She would not bother with breakfast. Hunger wasn't strength but it could trick you, put some distance between you and your thoughts. Sometimes that was enough to get going. Coffee first, and then she was definitely leaving.

At the window, the grey fade-in of daylight was just perceptible. Jude dressed quickly, picking up the form from the floor and shoving it into her shirt pocket. Something rustled beside it, and she pulled out the packet of herbs from Gloria, turned it over, dropped it into the crate. She grabbed the headphones, put them down again. There was nothing in this room that she needed.

The corridor was empty, Ali's door closed; she made it downstairs without interacting with anyone. There were a few people eating and chatting quietly in the Common, some kids poring over the guts of an old F-net terminal in one corner, a bearded man dusting the piano. There was coffee already brewed in the kitchen, weaker than she would have liked, but supplies were low. When she checked, there was a note on the board; someone would have logged it in the system already. She poured herself a cup and drank it standing. The pumpkins had been piled on the counter, one cut open to a gaudy orange, the air sweet with seeds and ripeness. A day wasn't long enough for anything to rot.

Jude swallowed the dregs, washed the mug and left.

It was warm out, a salty breeze coming in over the water. In morning light, the town was a tumble of colours spilling down the rocks, falling knee-deep into the sea. Pink edges on the distant clouds, dissolving into pastel sky. It might be beautiful weather, might turn hostile with heat. By the time the wind decided, she'd be gone.

The truck stood where she'd parked it, almost cheerful in this light. She made a beeline for the old beast, climbed up into the driver's seat, stretched her arms in front of her and saw the glint of glass in the passenger footwell. The tinctures from Cuoretto. One fist thumped against the wheel.

It would only take a minute.

Jude climbed down, the small box balanced in one hand, the heel of the other throbbing.

The clinic had been a motorcycle shop before the war, serving rich holidaymakers touring the coast, but the original windows had broken long ago and were bricked up. The sliding doors faced the water, reflecting morning light. The tape was gone, but up close, a paper note gummed to the inside of the glass said RISK OF INFECTION. PLEASE KNOCK. She put her forearm up beside it, leaned close. The facility was sealed; there was no-one in sight. She would leave the box on the ground and go.

But here was Nora, bustling towards her, bright with welcome. Jude stepped back and let her arm fall. The medic waved, pressed the button on the wall. The doors slid open, letting out a mixed scent: pine, alcohol, oranges. Jude's throat constricted.

'Jude, I'm so glad you're here – how are you? She's doing a little better this morning,' Nora's voice leapt up, her dark eyes excited. 'I've never seen anything like it. Come in, come in. I've got to keep this closed.' She glanced out, rushed Jude inside with a touch of her arm, fingers brushing her skin above the elbow. Before Jude could think, she had locked them both in and was thrusting a paper mask into her hand.

Jude hoisted the box under the other arm, had her excuses ready, but there was no space to begin them. Nora moved more swiftly than her shape suggested she might, like a wren hopping in undergrowth, chattering without pause. Jude could only follow.

'It's touch and go, of course, but this gear. We were just saying how amazing – this is Ramon, by the way. Ramon, Jude's coming in to help us out for a few days.' A tall man with a long face raised a hand, barely looked up from his screen. He seemed to find his colleague's energy amusing. Jude nodded a greeting and followed Nora to the other side of the desk, where she was still talking, shifting papers and equipment. Numb, Jude watched her soft hands move lightly over the surface. Finally she saw the logic of the cleared space, put the box down, donned the mask in her hand.

Nora was looking at her expectantly. She must have asked a question. Whoever had made that coffee should be brought to justice.

'Did you bring your form?' Nora repeated.

'Here,' Jude said, pulling it from her pocket. She held it out, still folded, warm from her body. 'I didn't finish it,' she said. 'I can't. I haven't –' Beyond the doors, the water was shimmering. She might dive in and swim away. It seemed as likely as any other exit, now.

'It doesn't matter. Any info helps at this point. I have your vaccination records, but if it's okay we might take a blood sample, check you for a range of pathogens. A simple flu could kill her, maybe a cold; we just don't know. She's stronger than she looks – incredible, honestly. It shouldn't be possible.'

'She's still alive,' Jude said. She bent her head, concealing an untrustworthy expression.

'So far. Sit down, roll up your sleeve for me?'

Jude fumbled with a button, tugged up a sleeve, sank into the chair indicated, submitted. Nora hummed a short tune, rummaged in a drawer beside her until she found her kit.

'We're flying blind here, so being extra cautious. I've never dealt with torpor before, but I've read some of the studies. Officially, research stopped years ago. Too dangerous.'

'Torpor?' The word felt foreign in her mouth, her mind too slow to connect it to meaning.

'There were a few fringe experiments, before the war.' She caught Jude's confusion, shifted her register slightly. 'It's similar to hibernation. In torpor, the metabolism is slowed right down, meaning all the systems: breath, heartbeat, digestion, glands. Some animals do it naturally, a way to survive a bad season. Or it can be a trauma response. I've seen something similar in children, but never induced like this. So we're not sure – we have to be extremely careful with her.'

Nora held out a hand, and Jude placed her wrist in its soft nest, felt it withdraw, wrap her upper arm, then the sharp prick of the needle going in and withdrawing. She tried not to show a reaction, but even with the mask she was exposed.

'All done.' Nora pressed a swab onto the red dot that was emerging from her inner elbow. Jude looked down at the hands. Less calloused than her own, the nails trimmed neatly. The medic's touch was gentle, confident. Left a trace sensation on her skin.

'I'm fine,' Jude said. Her heart was steady. She slowed her breathing.

'Tell one of us if you're feeling off.' Nora passed the blood sample to Ramon. He taped something to it, slid it into a compartment in a grey box on the desk, and flicked a few switches.

'That's probably not going to be the only blood you see in here,' he said drily.

'Sorry,' Jude said. Her cheeks felt cold. 'I won't be – I mean, I'm not actually –'

The man lifted an eyebrow and turned his back. Nora laid a hand on her wrist, and Jude's mind went blank.

'Nonsense, you'll be fine. You've been careful? No crowded parties last night, no rash behaviour?' Nora's grin implied something illicit. If she was trying to put Jude at ease, it wasn't working. In close range, her face shifted again, became serious.

'She's been in extreme isolation for an extended period. She won't have been exposed to much, so her body's vulnerable to diseases; on top of that, torpor has suppressed her immune system. She should be in a proper ICU, fully isolated, with round-the-clock observation, but we just don't have the resources, obviously. Full PPE when we go in. I'll show you the procedure. Come and see her while we wait for your results.'

'Twenty-seven minutes,' Ramon read from his screen.

'I'm not staying,' Jude began again, but Nora was already crossing the room. Words were blurring. Maybe the blood test would rule her out, save her from language. They stopped at the glass pane that separated the back room from the rest of the clinic. Jude forced herself to look through it, to focus.

She had been in hospitals, clinics, the wards and morgues on ships, countless first-aid tents. But at first, Jude felt the kind of bafflement that Ali claimed to feel when he looked at an engine. Then her eye began to pick out known components: tubes, wires, screens. Gradually, in spite of herself, Jude made out the shape of a human being in the centre.

Her body lay netted in these gadgets, systems that both contained and seemed to be a part of it. The shock of the tube down her throat. She wasn't moving. At the base of the narrow bed, Jude could make out a pair of feet, partly covered by a cotton sheet. The ankles may once have been shapely, delicate; now they were bruised and swollen.

'There's sleeping beauty,' Nora said, her voice hushed.

'Sleep,' Jude murmured. Sleep was a fairytale, a gift. This body was not sleeping. It was suspended between worlds, caught halfway to death. Jude's throat constricted. Distantly, she was glad she hadn't eaten.

'Something like it, anyway. Hard to say what's going on in her head.'

'What's wrong with her legs?'

Nora seemed pleased to be asked. 'Pressure. The blood learns to compensate for low gravity, and redistributes itself around the body. So it's having to learn to live with it again.'

'With gravity,' Jude repeated.

Nora nodded. 'The capsule seems to have eased her transition. We don't know how long she's been under. Months, at least.'

'I don't understand.' Jude looked across at Nora. She'd never been very good at guessing people's thoughts.

If Nora had been about to speculate, she changed her mind. 'It's impossible to know what the effects are going to be. If she does wake, we don't know how much she will remember, if her mind will work at all. There's a reason they banned this practice. You're right: it isn't sleep, not really.'

'There's so much stuff.' Jude waved a hand, knowing she sounded less than smart, but it was true. So much stuff, and so little person. The bloodless, doll-coloured arms lay beside the hard lump of her body. The equipment all looked suctioned to her, alien.

On the wall above the body, two monitors displayed soft waves, as gentle as the harbour that morning. The breath – was it breath? – was so slow it was hard to watch. This calm was the machine's doing. Hard to see what indicated that her mind was working.

'I'm hoping we can take that tube away today,' Nora said. 'Her body's coming back online remarkably quickly.'

Jude waited for feeling, but there was only cool air.

'I thought we might lose her overnight,' Nora said. Her breath left a little mark on the glass. 'She's tougher than she looks, this one.'

Nora cared whether this stranger lived or died. That was an expertise as complex as the tech, and just as alien. Jude did not have the stomach for this, didn't have the instinct or the training. Her coldness would be obvious to Nora soon enough.

The medic was already on the move again, donning protective gear. 'I'll run you through the basics. Frock first.' She donned a ghost-like gown, a simple face mask, gloves, talking all the while. 'We have to get this stuff from the Alliance, at a cost. Supposed to be disposable, but we don't have that luxury. We wash.' She touched an open bin with one surgical-booted foot, misted the air with something from a glass dispenser, then walked through the spray as it fell. It smelled of the distillery. Finally she pulled the hood up. Just the eyes now, grey-green and clear. Then a plastic visor. A Halloween astronaut, shining through the costume.

'I'm not,' Jude began again.

'You'll be all right. Back in a minute,' said Nora's shape.

She disappeared through a door, entered the scene behind the glass. Jude rested a hand on its fine timber frame and glanced down. Here at last was something she recognised. She had helped to find this window, driven it down from the mountains a couple of years ago. Prised it out of some rich person's abandoned chalet. They'd collected some pretty nice furniture, a generator, fuel, two quadbikes, crates and crates of good wine.

The snow had retreated years ago; the house had been empty since before the war. Gold taps in the bathroom, a luxury habitat for spiders. An ancient *For sale* sign on the gate. They'd boarded it up to keep animals out.

That house was probably still empty, still secured. She could go there if she wanted. Half a day's drive, then a long walk down a broken road, blocked by fallen stones. She could clean the place up and make it comfortable. Disappear for a while.

And then what?

Nora's body drew the eye. Her back to Jude, shoulders round beneath the gown, tending to her patient like a bee to a flower. She was near the head, moving something. Jude watched as she lifted a layer away. Pale hair wisped to the side, and there was the top third of a face. The slightly pinched thoroughbred brow.

She had known, of course, but now it was undeniable: Celeste had survived. And all Jude felt was an absence, a barren landscape expanding in her chest. She was right there, on the other side of the glass, but she might have been light years away.

21

BEFORE

The summer after Jude's failed escape, the storms are epic. Hail the size of her fists slams into the compound, piles up against the walls. She watches as lightning runs out across the open country, throwing the world into sharp relief. She is wrapped in a cashmere blanket, a hot chocolate in her hands. Flinching at thunder from behind security glass.

When the storm has passed, she takes her cup to the kitchen. There's a bottle of sparkling water open on the counter, a bottle of pills beside it. Celeste takes them so she can sleep. Jude tips a couple out into her hand, remembers the cameras will see her, pours them back.

Security has increased since she returned. Sovereign House sends chirpy reminders when she's heading outside: *Remember to stay within the safe area!* Cameras are in every room, in every corridor. She isn't sure if anyone watches the footage, or if it's all just processed by the house system. Hours and hours of her existence, fed into an algorithm.

Celeste hasn't mentioned the upgrades. Doesn't talk about her escape attempt, or even about the Endeavour much. Jude would like to believe that she has dropped her plans, come to her senses. But it's more likely that she's just shutting Jude out.

She moves around in an airy calm. It's impossible to talk to her when she's like this.

But in many ways it's a relief to be home. Jude's room is clean, the bed is soft, the temperature is carefully controlled. She doesn't have to sleep on dusty spare mattresses, or ride in vans, or eat strange food, or trust people. She thinks of the people in that hospital every day, and the protesters in the camp. She knows how lucky she is to be here. Knows her luck comes at a cost.

*

There are no more tutors. Less contact with the outside world. But Spence still lets her sit and read in the cool cement basement. He's on his own, and doesn't have much of a fleet left to guard. A couple of EVs and the last of JB's vintage collection. He won't let Jude near the newer vehicles – too many computers – but eventually he lets her tinker with the old Jag. She loses hours with the engine, absorbed in mechanical work. It's a relief to have something logical to focus on, something that can be fixed.

'I worry about her too,' he says, reading her thoughts.

Jude extracts a tiny spanner from the box resting near her hip, leans in.

After a minute, he clears his throat.

'I guess you've tried talking to her.'

Jude shrugs. 'Sort of.'

'Grief takes time. But there is a world out there,' he says. 'You both need to find a way to live in it.'

Jude can't explain how it feels. She is coming undone from the world, the few fragile connections she has dissolving around her. Soon she'll be floating in space. Celeste is the strongest thread that

Salvage

attaches her to life, and vice versa. She leans her small hand into a gap to reach a bolt on the manifold that Spence can't get to.

'How come you don't leave?' He has always seemed like part of Sovereign House, a permanent fixture.

'This is a good job,' he says, stretching.

Jude flushes. She's made a mistake, reminded them both of his position. He lives here in the basement, in a small apartment, so he's always available at a moment's notice. But this is not his home.

'Do you have family?' She's never considered this.

He glances at the camera in the corner, a spare alternator cradled in his arms. 'I used to have some people left up north. A brother kept in touch for a few years. But I was pretty young when I left home. Sixteen.'

'You can't go back and visit?'

His face shifts, and she sees the shape of his skull in shadow. He has turned his back to the camera. The house system is recording the entire exchange: capturing her tone, her questions. It won't catch the way his expression collapses. Or the way that it performs that demolition in reverse, recomposes itself into its well-practised elegance.

'The island's gone,' he says, and reaches for the wrench.

Jude watches his hands.

'They took you in,' she says.

He nods. Reaches for the fault.

'Like me.'

He shakes his head. 'No, no. I work here, love. I was never family.'

*

Jude walks beyond the traces of landscaping out to the boundary, now encircled by a second, higher fence, cameras at every post. Out there among the red rocks, facts and statistics and reports fall away, even the sense of being watched. There is only sun and air and water. Lizard, feather, roo print, bone. The planet is in trouble, but the earth here is steady. Takes her weight as if it's nothing. It is nothing. Her sneakers hardly leave a mark.

She puts her eye to the diamond in the wire. Steps back on a loose stone, stumbles into a feral succulent half as tall as she is. The gardens have gone so wild that she can't even call them gardens anymore.

The earth isn't steady at all; she's just used to its moods. The storms have dried up, and for weeks, the air has made a smoky shroud around the compound. The fires are the worst since three summers ago, when they were the worst in decades.

There is no getting away from it. She shouldn't be out here, breathing this hostile air.

Just as she thinks this, her phone pings. It's the house system, telling her to come inside. Jude's not sure what bothers her more: the interruption or the way her thoughts were moulded by it, even before it reached her. She stalks back through the grounds, enters air-conditioned safety, clutching the device in quiet fury.

She would smash it against a rock if it didn't offer access to news of the world. On screen, Jude sees some version of the reality she must prepare for. Homes destroyed, animals burning. Children in gas masks rowing small boats away from shore. Outside, the sun dangles like an old coin on a string.

When Celeste appears, she swipes the emergency from her screen. Does her best to rearrange her face. It always seems to overcome her anger, this impulse to protect her sister. Impulse, or duty.

'Everything okay?'

'Great,' Jude says, the smoke a faint trace in her clothes.

'Great!' Celeste stands grinning in the doorway, the empty air heavy between them. Her eyes are too bright, her smile too wide. She looks past Jude, though there's only the blank wall behind her.

It's obvious that her sister isn't well, under the surface shine. Jude wants to help her, knows she should try, but everything she does feels wrong. She needs to be strong, to be the thread that tethers her to life, that holds her in this world.

Jude looks down at her screen and waits, knowing she will let Celeste down again, that her sister will sigh with disappointment and leave her alone. 'Come on,' she says instead. 'We're going out.'

*

'That's better,' Celeste says, turning her by the waist with one hand. She wrinkles her nose, sniffs, examines Jude in the mirror. 'The hair will have to do.' Jude is taller now, but she will never match her sister. She pushes her shoulders back, makes her expression blank.

Jude knows that no-one will notice a thing about her. She doesn't mind. It's a good sign that Celeste wants to leave the compound, be in the world again.

'Where are we going, anyway?' she asks.

Celeste is looking at her own reflection. Mascara in one expert swoop. She hands the stick to Jude, who puts it in its bottle, sets it on the stone ledge below the mirror. She has applied none of the products Celeste has passed to her, just lined them up in a row like soldiers, but today her sister isn't annoyed about it. There's a fragile calm between them. Jude tidies the arrangement, settling herself in its small order.

'You'll see.'

Jude checks her sister's expression in the glass, and the bottles rattle under her fingers. Even though no-one's mentioned it for months, she knows exactly what Celeste's talking about.

If she wanted, she could break this mirror with her fist.

Celeste touches a thumb to the end of one eyebrow, makes an imperceptible adjustment, her slender fingers fanned. Then she softens her face and shapes her mouth like she does for photographs. She was trained for this. She has worked so hard.

When their eyes meet in the mirror, Celeste's happiness seems real. Jude feels the connection between them draw tight, the thread knotted to her ribs. She can't pull away.

22

AUGUST

Nora moved around and between the equipment like a skilled musician at a complex instrument. Jude started when Ramon appeared beside her.

'Incredible, isn't it?'

When she looked up, he added, 'Amazing system.'

'I guess,' she said, and turned back to the glass.

'You're all clear, by the way,' he said. 'Flying colours.'

'Thanks.'

She supposed she had to tell them now. When she glanced at him, all his attention was on the monitors inside the room. Jude didn't know how to begin, but she did know how to handle gearheads. 'How's it all work?' she asked, and let him tell her.

As he spoke, she went on watching Nora's hands move, calm, expressive. Nora would be the one to tell, she decided. She would wait for her to emerge.

'And all that came out of the capsule?' She prompted Ramon when he paused, though she was only half listening.

'Some of it,' he said. 'Most of the monitors are ours, and adaptors – I was up all night trying to hook the systems together.' He had a slight lisp, an accent she placed somewhere east of the Alliance. His voice was quiet, but full of pride. 'We had to improvise.'

'Advanced technology, I guess.' It would have been state-of-the-art at the time.

'Oh no, it's mostly old shit. And we are used to working with old shit around here.' When he grinned, his mouth was wide. Jude caught sight of a silver tooth.

'The Alliance, they would know what to do with all this. Big hospitals, big teams, proper equipment.' He looked sad, then shook his head against it. 'Well. It works, that's the important part. It's keeping her alive.'

'How long will she be like this?' It was easier to talk side by side, facing the glass.

'Depends. If she wakes up . . .'

Behind them, the printer rattled. Ramon left her side to attend to it, returned with a piece of paper. When he handed it over, Jude saw a roll of numbers and letters that meant nothing to her. The printer was old shit too, and had left a white streak through the text like a scar.

'You've been lucky,' he said, and she understood: this was a transcript of her body, a history of the illnesses she'd had and recovered from. She'd been measured, documented. She handed the paper to him without speaking.

A door closed, and Nora took the report in one gloved hand, looked it over, murmured happily, then passed it back to her colleague, snapping her gloves off at the same time. Ramon went back to his screen, and Jude watched Nora remove more protective covering.

'Are you feeling okay?' Nora's gaze was an examination.

Jude pinched the mask over her nose. The elastic was making her ears burn. Now would be the time to speak, but her throat felt dry.

'Sorry,' she said. 'I'm not . . .'

'Talkative,' Nora observed, head on a tilt.

Jude felt her face warm, but mercifully, Nora had already turned away. Her mind must be a clarity of priorities. One in which Jude barely registered.

'You know, you haven't asked me who she is, or where she came from. That's all everyone else wants to know.'

'Oh.'

'So, we do have an idea, but it's a bit far-fetched. You might think I'm crackers.'

Jude looked at the linoleum between her feet. A grey marbled pattern, very scratched. Needed replacing. This was something she knew how to do: scraping back and sanding, applying adhesive, laying out a fresh surface.

'Do you remember the Endeavour?'

The bulk of the work would be moving all the furniture. They had rolls of lino, easily enough to cover this room. There would be some in the shed at the harbour, she thought, and then she could see the capsule lurking back there, its shadow obliterating all else.

The silence seemed heavy and long.

'Heard of it,' she managed at last.

'I wondered if you might, being from that part of the world.' Nora's glance was quick but sharp.

Jude took a small step back from the glass.

'The accent,' Nora said.

'Can't get rid of it.' Jude's throat caught.

Murky eyes smiled above the mask. 'You'd hardly notice. Only I had an Australian girlfriend, years ago.'

Jude blinked as some part of her filed this fact away. She had no courage to speak, but she found she lacked the will to lie. 'I knew about it,' she said finally. 'Everyone did. I thought they all died up there.'

'That was the finding. There was an inquiry. I think the guy went into hiding.'

'Fry,' Jude answered automatically. 'Nicholas Fry.' She'd tried not to follow the investigation, kept busy on the ships. But she'd never been able to avoid the news completely. He'd disappeared after it all went to shit. She had done her best to do the same.

'That's the one. If this is part of it, it won't be hard to identify her. Find her people, if she has any. Some of them had no-one left, which makes it – well, I won't say understandable. But you had to feel for them, in a way. The poor, rich fools.'

Jude needed to get outside; she couldn't breathe in here. She looked out through the glass doors. The day was growing bright, the truck waiting. She should have been on the road by now, on her way somewhere else.

'You can leave, you know,' Nora said. 'We're not going to keep you here against your will.' The judgement in her words was light, but Jude felt it sink her.

'She might not wake up. Ramon said.'

'We still have to ID her. Inform the family, if we can find them,' Nora said, glancing at her colleague. He was typing something into the F terminal. A moment later, he held up a small screen.

'Here,' Ramon said. He rolled out on his chair, made room for them. On the cracked device, a video was loading. They stood behind him, one at each side, and he pressed the tiny triangle with a knuckle. Jude watched, even though she knew what was coming. She could have played this footage in her head.

She'd replayed it a hundred times, a thousand, in her mind's eye. In caravans and cabins, tents and ships, in sleepless hours.

First, a slideshow of still photographs. Celeste in her Endeavour uniform, looking like a young Olympic hopeful. All of them assembled in a group photo, grins as white as the sky. The suits are covered in advertising logos, more sponsors than a sports team. This was the early days: exclusive subscriber content, lots of media. As time went on, the company logos fell away, the uniforms faded to white. The videos got sparser, crisper.

'That's her,' Ramon said, finger to the screen. He clicked up the volume. It was hard to tell them apart in their gear, but Celeste was easy to pick out if you knew her. She was shorter than most of the others. Younger, too. Her pale hair whipped around her face in close-up, a helmet in her hands. 'Among them, Australian resource heiress Celeste Prince,' the voiceover said, its eager tone sounding fifty years out of date. 'To many, a vision of the country's future in a time of global insecurity.'

Ramon froze the video on a close-up of Celeste's exultant face. Her makeup was perfect, as usual. Her eyes like two white suns. Jude's stomach fell. Time was collapsing. She should be there, standing with her.

'Yeah, that's her.' Nora was writing the name down.

'I can't do this.' Jude wasn't sure she had spoken.

For a moment nobody reacted, then Nora turned to her. Her voice was low and grave.

'Listen to me. It doesn't matter who she is, or what she's done. She still deserves our care.'

*

Minutes later, Jude was disappearing into the protective gear. She would never remember the procedure on her own. Nora leaned in to straighten the suit. 'Sorry,' she said, and reached an arm around Jude's neck to fix the collar.

Jude shook her head, felt Nora's breath against her ear, could not speak. Nora was gesturing towards a chair; Jude sat and received hand sanitiser, gloves, little overshoes, an alarmingly brief set of instructions.

'Don't touch the mask with your hands. Don't touch anything unless you have to. Ring the buzzer if you notice anything, even if it seems like nothing. It's better to wake us if you're unsure.' Nora handed her a plastic visor, scratched but fairly new. Jude slipped the band over her head like a leash.

'I won't be any use in there,' she said at last. 'I mean, I'm just a driver.'

Nora's eyes were kind. 'That's bullshit,' she said. 'It's a skill like any other. Anyone can learn it.'

Easy for her to say; she was obviously good at all this. Jude folded the visor down and pulled the hood over her hair. The medic's hands were tugging it over her ears, shifting the mask against her until it fitted.

'Don't know what you want me to do.' Jude's voice was muffled by the gear.

Nora let a little frustration show.

'Sit with her.' She lifted a spray bottle. 'Watch. Stay awake.'

'That's it?'

'Talk to her, if you can. It's supposed to help. The voice, the human company.'

Then Nora was clouding her with antibacterial spray, and for a few seconds, Jude had to stop breathing. She would play along, get this woman off her back. Soon, none of it would matter. If that body was really Celeste, she was too far gone to survive.

When she entered the room, Jude made herself inhale. The scent in the room was all wrong. Machine, chemical, a hint of salt. Nothing familiar, nothing human.

She closed the door behind her, stood with her back to it. Her heart felt small in her chest. There was a chair, plastic, set close to the bed. She pulled it further out, sat, and glanced at the window. The medic was watching her, mask around her neck. Nodding encouragement.

Jude realised that she was holding her arms tight against her sides. She made her shoulders drop, tried to force her posture into a shape that would look more natural, and made it more awkward still. Here were the machines, the monitors, the tubes and wires. The ceiling. The glass. Eventually, there was nowhere to look except at the body.

A mask covered the face, distorted by the tube that brought it air. The skin at the neck had a pale, unblemished quality. She thought of the white flesh of witchetty grubs, dug up from desert sand with a stick and held in the palm. As cool as the earth, hardly moving, but you knew they were alive. She closed her hand around the memory.

It was obvious that she would die. This body could do nothing by itself, was entirely dependent on these mechanical interventions. The artificial breaths were unpleasant to listen to, too quiet and too slow. She touched her own throat, reassured by muscle, heartbeat.

Up close, the equipment did not look so sophisticated. Ramon was right, it was mostly old shit, and that too was a measure of time's collapse: it was long ago, and it persisted. She tried to interpret some of the components. There was a beeping rhythm on one monitor, about half as slow as her own heart. Then a row of numbers, graphs. Easier to study those than trace any semblance of life.

Nora was still watching. Jude inched herself forward.

'Hello,' she said. Her voice was just a whisper. Nothing happened. She lifted her hands.

These hands, much younger, holding an injured corella. Carrying it back to the compound, its broken wing hanging loose. Its desperate, grey-ringed eye. Someone, not Celeste, had told her how to care for it. Must have been one of the kitchen staff. A box in the pantry, a towel, water. Warmth. Antiseptic. Don't leave it alone: animals are comforted by voices. It had died under her watch, its pain decanted into a last soft croak, the wrinkled eye gone distant. She'd forgotten its existence until now.

'You can't save everything,' Celeste had said.

Jude sank back into the chair, the plastic cold and hard against her. She studied the pipes that brought Celeste air and eased her heart and smoothed her restful metabolism and kept her sleeping, safe. Was this presence life? For all they knew, this body was just a shell, the conscious mind shrivelled away like a parched snail. Maybe she would not live long enough to wake. It was a grim thing to hope for.

The room was humming. There was the red button, the one Nora had told her to press if anything changed. Here were power outlets, gas pipes. Below the hum there was the beat of her own heart, the steadiness of her internal machinery, its natural pace and heat. The blood was tight in her hands as she pressed them between her thighs and the hard plastic seat.

They are comforted by voices. It's supposed to help. But she was just a child. Her voice, that chance, was gone.

23

BEFORE

Jude sleeps most of the way, and when she wakes she doesn't sit up, only watches the night roll past overhead. The desert sky is crowded. They have left the smoke behind them. She used to like the stars, the way they put things in perspective. Now the clouded galaxy is taunting.

Then the stars fade, and there are the bright lights of the entrance to the facility. It's a former military site, rezoned for private use, some deal of Fry's. The gates have been reinforced; the fence is intimidatingly high. Armed guards wave them through. A few minutes later, Spence turns down a looping drive and pulls up at a new building.

The staff wear crisp uniforms like this is any old hotel, and lift the small bags onto a trolley. The welcome feels cold, a little rushed. The staff aren't much older than Jude is, but they're as formal with her as they are with Celeste. Fry doesn't come down. There are a few other guests in the lobby, but Jude doesn't see anyone she recognises from last time. It's been a couple of years: she barely recognises anything. It has grown, as Fry's wealth has grown. There's an indoor pool now, a solitary figure swimming laps as they pass on the way to the elevator. They only spend a few minutes in their rooms; Celeste doesn't want to miss a thing.

The observation tower uses a separate elevator. It looks out over a vast patch of dusty country, cleared of trees and saltbush and whatever else once lived there. The launch pad and scaffold stand in the centre of this barren field. The rocket looks smaller than Jude imagined, but it's too far away to tell how big it is, and maybe this is part of the theatre of it, the disruption of ordinary scale.

Most of the other investors are already gathered, facing the glass; they turn to acknowledge the new arrivals. Celeste knows some of them, greets them warmly. That blonde woman must be the swimmer; her hair is still damp. She fidgets with the ring on her hand. A cheerful man with a South African accent, keen to talk. Maybe twenty people. Jude stands back and watches the way they interact as a group, like a small flock of mismatched birds: the focus shifting between them, not quite friends and not quite competition.

The glass-walled deck takes up most of the top floor of the building. No videos this time. Instead there are actual models of parts of the Station, perched on white stages around the room. There is a tiny sleeping chamber like half an avocado, the outside hard, the inside softly padded. A man has climbed inside it and is yawning theatrically, resting his elbows on the rim. And here is one of the capsules that will take them there, that are meant to bring them home again. It's also upholstered inside, but not as soft. It smells like a new car. Instead of seats, there are three vertical chambers arranged around a central pillar, glittering with instruments. When Jude climbs in, it feels like a game, though it doesn't do anything, even when she puts her hands on the control panel.

The touchscreens are just screens. It is only a display, it can't think, but she senses its will moving against her own. There's not enough air in the capsule. She needs to get out.

Before she can move, a man and a woman poke their heads into the capsule, hardly noticing her. They're thin, pale, blue-eyed, middle-aged; they could be brother and sister. The woman exclaims delightedly, like she's looking at an expensive painting or a cleverly redesigned apartment. 'So small, though,' she adds, running a hand along one of the panels as though checking a mantelpiece for dust.

'Not much of a footprint, compared to the bunker,' the man adds gruffly. They step back, lean against the outer husk to speak. Jude will have to wait, or slip out between them. She decides to stay where she is, stay invisible.

'My new installation's a two-thousand-square-metre *castle*. Four hundred acres of forest, fully patrolled. Total reinforcement. No-one's getting in there when it hits.' They can't be siblings; he's trying too hard.

'Trouble is, you have to trust your security teams,' the woman says. 'I sold mine while the market was hot. They're just not worth as much these days. Those places depend entirely on recruitment. Staffing's a nightmare. Simply too many variables.' She waves airily, indicating the trouble other people pose.

'A lot of it's automated,' the man says, blustering. 'I'm just keeping my options open.'

'Yes, of course,' she says. 'We all have options. I'm not committed here, but this is so *fun*. Come and try the simulation.'

Jude climbs out of the capsule, pushing against the control panel for purchase. She notices the staff everywhere in the room, waiting on the assembled partners, invisible to them, and a small bubble of shame bursts inside her. There is always someone there, making their meals, cleaning up, driving them around. The launch is going to need dozens of technicians, engineers, people to check their work, fix their mistakes. Even when the Station is in place, it will still need people on the ground. If they run out of something they need, other people will have to bring it to them, or run the robots that do the job. How far can this dependence reach? They will be three hundred thousand kilometres from Earth, and three hundred thousand kilometres from the lunar bases, and maybe neither one will be in the mood to offer assistance if something goes wrong. The Station doesn't solve the problem of survival; it stretches it to breaking point.

Jude's throat is dry. She looks for her sister. If she can explain, find the right words, then maybe Celeste will see that it's impossible.

The backs of the partners are lined up, their eyes glued to the view. The countdown has begun, the test launch is about to happen. Celeste is standing between two men, her slight figure silhouetted against the sky beyond. Jude can tell that she is holding her breath.

For the first time, the launch goes perfectly. Nothing explodes in flames. By the time Celeste sees her, the rocket is gone, the partners turning to clink their glasses and laugh. The waiters have opened more champagne. Jude's in the way of the celebrations.

A few minutes later, the launch is supposed to land neatly back on its pad. When it reappears, the descending rocket has a slight wobble to it. Jude feels it in her stomach. One part of the base hits the ground, and then the whole thing topples and crumples like a cheap toy. By this point, hardly anyone is watching.

'Still a few details to get right,' Fry says, making his entrance. The partners burst into nervous applause. 'No point saving the stuff,' he jokes, leaning over to get his glass filled by the nearest variable.

There is laughter all around him, like breaking glass. Investors cluster, and Celeste stays close to the centre. Whenever Jude looks for her, she is at his elbow, making herself available, helping him to work his way around the room. He doesn't address her, but if she's gone from his side for more than a minute he starts to look around with a slightly helpless expression.

With a flash of understanding, Jude sees he isn't good at this. He needs all the props, the theatre of it. He needs someone beside him to laugh at his jokes, nod when he speaks, make him look important. And at all this, Celeste is expert. She moves with calm confidence, happy with purpose. She has been rehearsing for this role her whole life.

They need each other. And at once Jude sees her mistake. She is not the thread that holds her sister in the world. This is.

24

STATION

This time she is sure it will be Judith. Her body is certain; she can feel it in her blood. She gets up quickly, climbing the rungs even before the mask folds itself away, moving as though pulled by an invisible rope. When she opens the hatch above her, she is surprised by how dark it is. Celeste remembers sunlight. Can still feel it on her skin. She pauses at the hatch, confused a moment, wavering between that dream and this. Particles move in the air in the corridor, and a voice comes into her head from nowhere.

No, she says. Her head hurts. She stills herself, waits for her eyes to adjust. She got up too quickly, that's all. She reaches for her slippers, sits on the floor to pull them on, and closes her eyes.

At the restaurant by the lake, the sky is growing dark. There are cumulus clouds on the horizon, moving fast. The cool change can be felt behind the wind. Celeste tries to picture the atmosphere surrounding them, but she sees a shaken paperweight, the glitter swirling. Thunderstorms always give her a headache.

I'm sorry we're unable to continue the agreement, she says. She told herself she would not apologise, but there it is, lying on the table between the crumpled napkin and her uneaten dessert. She folds her hands in her lap and holds her gaze steady. Controls her tone. She can still extract herself. *The reality is that our circumstances have changed*, she says. *Given the absence of a contract. I appreciate your understanding.* It is, she thinks, a good attempt. It would be her father's move: invoke a reality in which she would benefit, even if it's one in which she has ceased to believe.

I think we better leave our options open, he says. *Let's take some time to consider. Everything's still in development. There's no rush.* He might be laughing at her.

I can give you three months, she says. *We need to see details. The accountants will have to go over it.*

The accountants. He smiles, as though she had spoken of elves. He's right: they couldn't save the company, could barely save the house. Well, you can't save everything. He folds his napkin and places it on the table. Moves it until he is satisfied with the angle. Lines up the knife, fork, spoon. Takes pleasure in it, just as Jude would. A briefly ordered world.

Your father was a decent man, though not a visionary, he says. *A pragmatist. He believed in this project, in his own way.* An admonishing finger has lifted from the plate, but he restrains himself from raising it, avoids attempting the paternal mode, and she's grateful for that. *He believed in my work*, he says.

My father is dead. She lets a little pleasure into her voice. That, at last, catches him off guard. Yes, she is glad of it. His death removed her limitations, even as it introduced many fresh obstacles. She is a kind of pragmatist too.

That's just what I mean. You are –

Celeste doesn't want to be described. *We'll speak again*, she says. She pushes her chair back. The breeze is chilly now, catches her hair. He reaches across the table. She steels herself, but his hand is aiming for her abandoned dessert, lifting the plate onto his own.

A sweet tooth, he says. For a moment, his greed is undisguised. The ice is soup, a glacial pool. Antarctica is breaking apart, time running out. She wavers.

The Station wavers. A visible future, where a version of herself is waiting. Where Judith is waiting.

These places, she says.

Place. He addresses the melted ice cream, dispatching it with pleased efficiency into his boyish mouth.

Excuse me? Celeste goes still.

He secured one berth. That was the agreement. He watches her face, the appetite resurfacing.

One. In her lap, fingers knot.

A second launch, when we are up and running – in the long term, families –

Don't, she says.

When Nick raises his palms to her, she is shaken. But Celeste has always known how to steady herself. When she does, she sees his teeth emerge, that appetite showing. He's seen something he likes in her. Something he could enjoy.

Well, she sees something too. That soft mouth, open to a spoon. *I can't go*, she says. *I couldn't leave my sister.*

He completes the movement. Swallows before speaking, like there's all the time in the world. *So bring her. We'll find a way.* And he turns in his seat to catch the waiter's eye, though they are the only ones there. It is her choice. Her moment.

And then Celeste is awake in the corridor, standing, and there is breath on her skin, a hot voice at her neck. The smell of decay and disinfectant.

The others are all asleep, he says. It is an American voice, round and not unfriendly. The businessman from Chicago; she has forgotten his name. It sounds like a question, but it isn't. She glares at him.

Calvin, he says, *remember?* His face used to be round too, but now it's angular. *Hey. Are you okay?*

Judith, she says. Then: *Sorry. Celeste.* She lifts her fingers to her chest. It's hollow. There was no storm, no ice cream. No hunger.

The angles soften. *Hey, it's all right*, he says. *We are eight months in, I think. You've been asleep a long time. It's disorienting.*

Instead of responding, she shuffles until she rests her back against the wall. Blind spots to either side, a darkness where her mind stops conjuring. He's been asleep just as long, and knows no better.

It gets hard to feel the difference, he says. *Wait a minute. Look at me.* He steps in front of her.

The hand beside his thigh is twitching. Thumb touching fingers, a shadow flickering against the pale fabric. She remembers him now. The social-network guy, what was it called, something ridiculous. But he's different, more drawn. The skin darker around the eyes that peer out to address her directly.

We're on the Station, he says. *Lagrange point five.*

I know, she says, although just now she wasn't certain.

We have to remind each other, or we lose . . . touch. Contact with the real. There are eight of us, I think.

His doubt reassures her. She shakes her head. *Twelve. Twelve doors.* This part feels more certain. The map in her head clearly matches her surroundings, the map on the wall of her office. It's obvious.

He looks confused, then something dawns on him. *Yes, I see*, he says. He clears his throat. *But some of these doors – I'll show you.*

And the astronauts, she says, remembering Hui. *The bridge.* She raises a finger to point at the ceiling, then gives him a confident smile. She knows more about the Station than Calvin does. She knows its secrets.

He looks startled, almost recoiling. He seems about to argue, then changes his mind. *Come on*, he says. *We don't have much time.*

They have more time than the world. She follows him, stops when he stops at the first hatch they come to. Calvin kneels down, inhales, knocks loudly. The sound is muffled in here, or her ears are dull. They wait a moment. He tries again. Celeste wants to speak her sister's name, but something stops her.

No-one answers the knock. Judith is asleep in the car. Asleep in her room. In another room, somewhere on the Station. This door is Carolyn's. Celeste remembers everything perfectly. Calvin stands, swallows, pushes at Carolyn's slippers with a foot. He seems to have forgotten his purpose.

Let's keep going, she says. *It's not her turn.* They are supposed to keep moving. The exercise. Keep separate. No friction. She pushes him in the back of the upper arm. It is unpleasant to touch him; he is all bone.

Two at a time, she says. *It is the rule. Avoids conflict.*

Not just conflict, he says. His mouth is serious. He doesn't explain. At the next hatch along, he stops again. There is the green circle with an arrow inside. Yes, she remembers this. Some of the rooms are not rooms; some of them are exits.

Three pods, he says. *I think it's worth considering.* He whispers to himself, like he is reciting a list.

What is?

When to use them.

She laughs. The voice crackles like a bad old line on a satellite phone. Like helicopter radio. Like any dead tech, like nothing on Earth.

I'm serious. He is grinning back at her, but it's skeletal. That distant rattle in the neck.

It's safe here, she says. This is the capsule. The way they arrived. She does not remember arriving, but she knows.

But that's . . . He trails off, looking into the darkness. *We're not supposed to be stuck out here forever.*

She yawns. Exhaustion is dripping down her spine, flooding her bones with unnatural heaviness. She registers pain in her body, but it's hard to place. *I'm going back to bed*, she says. She is certain this will help.

Okay, says Calvin. *I'll walk with you.* For a moment they both stand there. She can't think which direction she is supposed to take. Then she remembers that it doesn't matter. The Station is a wheel. It circles, it returns. So she chooses the way she is already facing. Despite his offer, Calvin doesn't follow.

Hey, the voice calls out behind her. *Who's Judith?*

25

AUGUST

When Nora appeared at her side, Jude stirred from a state close to sleep, taking in the room around her: Celeste's unmoving body, the steady hum of the machines. She stood and followed the medic out into the clinic.

'She's still with us,' Nora said. 'How did you go?'

Jude lifted her visor, caught the glare in the sky beyond the doors. Her legs ached, and her back was stiff. She stretched awkwardly.

'Could use a different chair,' she said.

'You're coming back, then.' The medic grinned.

Nora walked her to the exit, stood beside the glass doors, hand at the release button. There was a blast of heat, the smell and noise of the sea. Jude swallowed, stepped out into the light.

'We'll see you back here in the morning,' Nora called. 'Go for a walk, eat something. Get some sleep, if you can.'

Jude was already halfway to the truck, its shadow a black mark on the earth.

'Jude!' The voice was urgent. Jude should have known that Nora would want more: a commitment. She steeled herself, ready to disappoint. But when she turned, the medic was smiling.

'Thank you,' Nora said, and let the doors slide closed.

*

The truck was waiting, but she still needed fuel. The morning felt like weeks ago. She crossed over to the sheds, found the steel doors locked. The thought of having to speak to another human being was exhausting. When no-one answered her knock at the coastguard door, she was relieved.

Jude slipped into the Common kitchen unnoticed, drank cold coffee straight from the pot. The siesta hours lent the space an eerie quiet.

In her room, the driver's room, Jude sniffed the air, shook out the blankets. Her body smelled of the clinic: disinfectant and sanitiser, plastic and PPE. A dog barked outside, and she went to close the window. Down in the street two children chased the prancing animal, laughing and calling to it. The air was sticky; the sky felt close enough to touch with a hand.

She lay down, kicked her boots off, closed her eyes, but it was no use.

She needed to move. Go for a walk, like Nora said. Jude sat up, undressed, pulled on swimming shorts and a singlet, straightened her shoulders, avoided the mirror. A swim would clear her head, help her sleep. Then she could focus, pack, think about where to go.

She reached the back gate, took the concrete stairs that descended into water at high tide. The bottom steps were slippery now, the handrail rusted. She had to swing herself around an olive tree to get to the start of the rocky track. She followed it along the coast, walking over plastic, driftwood, tracing the edges of a rising tide.

The water in the bay was calm. It wasn't much of a bay, just a gap in the rocks where the waves shallowed over a curve of pebbles. The path broke away. No-one else was there. She leaned down to feel the water with her hand, the sea's uncanny warmth, then waded in and duck-dived as soon as she was knee-deep. There was a sunken city out there, taken by the water thousands of years ago. Earthquake, maybe. She didn't know what civilisation it belonged to; maybe no-one did anymore. When it was clear you could catch glimpses of the place. Bits of wall and tile, an outline of a room. An echo of the rubble on land, a future waiting.

She dived again and again, her hands brushing rocks and sand, staying under until her lungs began to ache, then swimming up, washed blank. She climbed out, stood dripping on the rock. The heat would dry her in a few minutes.

She had been no great swimmer before nearly drowning. She had pushed herself to strength since coming here. Now the muscle in her arms, her back, her neck and shoulders welcomed the work of it. The body could become a life raft, a preserve against loss.

She followed the track back to the Common and hurried in beneath the olive tree. The tide was just below its roots now. Two steps at a time to the back door, up the stairs, into the shower. Ali's door was open, his room empty. He'd be working downstairs. Jude dressed in fresh clothes, hung her wet gear out the window. She braved the mirror, met her own gaze. She was capable, she told herself. Mostly she was hungry.

Downstairs, a few dishes had already been prepared. She brewed more coffee, served herself a plate, and took a seat alone by the wall. She ate methodically, head down. Roast tomatoes, pasta, wild herbs. Someone was mucking around on the piano in the corner, a flat tune threading through the voices of parents and children. She let the sounds wash past her until she heard a familiar laugh. Ali was sitting at the bar, notebook open on his lap, Karim and Hamish perched beside him.

The coffee tasted sour. Jude eased herself out of the chair, took her dishes, but could not help pausing on the way to the kitchen.

'Like an alien egg,' Hamish was saying.

Of course they were talking about the capsule. What else was there to discuss?

'You would think humans would have learned by now not to go near the alien eggs,' Ali said, turning slightly to acknowledge Jude and beckoning her into their circle. She was standing too close to pretend she hadn't seen.

'Doesn't sound like you have met many humans,' Karim said.

'We didn't know she was alive in there,' Hamish went on. 'As soon as we did, we called for the doc.' He glanced at Jude.

'Can you describe the smell?' Ali's hand moved fast against the paper.

'I can't, really,' Hamish said, shaking his shaggy head. 'Like stale rooms.'

'An old smell,' Karim added. 'Like a grave.'

'It smelled like death?' Ali frowned.

'No, I don't know how to explain,' Karim said. 'It was like a tomb closed up for many years.' His hands closed doors against his chest.

Hamish raised an eyebrow, regarded Jude. 'So, who is she?'

Jude waited, but nobody else answered. The dishes rattled in her hands. She excused herself and carried them into the kitchen, hoping the conversation would move on.

When she came out again, Hamish was leaning against

the bar, one hand raised. 'The committee,' he was saying, 'or whoever was there this morning. Giorgio.'

There were no official leaders, but Giorgio was one of those people who was involved in everything.

'They want to keep it secret?' Ali was still in interviewer mode.

'Not exactly. It's too late for that. But the shed's locked until we know what we're dealing with. They want to see if she's going to live. Who she belongs to, what she might be worth. If anyone wants her back, then we can trade her, maybe. At least trade some of that gear. I mean, if it's true, then she would have to be rich. They all were.'

'You were at the clinic, Jude.' Ali turned to her. 'What do you think?'

Jude was watching Hamish; the words 'trade her' caught in her mind like thorns. 'Who decided to lock the shed?'

He glanced at Karim. 'The meeting, I guess.'

'But I need to get in there. I need fuel.' She bristled under Ali's look. He'd know there were no trips scheduled.

'Can't be helped,' said Hamish. 'You'll have to bring it up at a meeting.'

It was too noisy in the Common. The air was closing in.

'But what does Nora say? Who is she? Will she live?' Ali would not let it go.

There was a pause while they waited for Jude to speak. She looked down at her empty palm and closed her fist.

'I don't have the answers,' she said.

She hadn't ever lied to Ali. She couldn't start now. Later, when they were alone, she would find a way to explain it. To unpick the complicated stitches that attached her to that story.

Until then, there was nothing to connect them. She could stay here, live the life she'd made for herself. She could still be free.

Ali was studying her.

'You look tired,' he said calmly. 'You should get some sleep.'

She shook her head. 'I know,' she said.

*

In the morning, Jude made her way downstairs. Solare was curled in an armchair by the bookshelf, reading a long procedural document in a binder: minutes of old meetings, useless stuff. She looked up when Jude passed and reached out a hand to stop her.

'How does it work, the clinic?'

Jude shrugged. She'd managed three hours, maybe four, of sleep. Coffee waited just through that door. 'Not my thing,' she said.

Solare frowned. Her gaze was steady.

'I could help,' she said.

Someone like this, someone with a conscience. That's who they needed in the clinic. Jude would suggest it to Nora. She nodded and moved past.

Nora. On impulse, she filled a second cup while pouring, pocketed a small envelope of sugar, took both cups with her. Outside, the morning was still cool. There was a slow football game in progress in the street: one languid child absorbed in his footwork, the others calling, 'Here, here!' Two women cycled through the middle of it, bells ringing. She didn't want to leave this place unless she had to.

*

Salvage

Nora shook her head at the coffee. 'Thanks, but I don't drink it.'

Jude put the second cup down on the desk, bending to hide her embarrassment. 'How do you live?' she asked.

'I don't like to create a dependency. Not when you can't rely on the supply.'

Jude prickled, implicated. 'I'll drink both,' she said. This wasn't going well. The first cup was almost cold. She drank it down, leaning against the desk. Nora was busy with her charts, seemed rested, clear. Jude wondered where she slept.

'She's still with us,' Nora said. 'Breathing on her own, with oxygen.' When she looked up, the seaweed in her eyes was adrift.

This was the moment to say something. Jude swallowed, turned the empty cup, the patterns in the glaze like a half-formed language. Such intricate, accidental detail.

'You can go straight in,' said Nora.

The clinic doors opened and another nurse entered, someone Jude didn't know. He greeted Nora warmly, and the two were instantly absorbed in technical conversation, the easy calm of experts.

Jude examined herself in the chalet window while she donned the PPE. Would anyone recognise her? There was little resemblance to the person she had been back then. Just a kid. Her hair was cropped close, grey in patches. Time had marked her skin. No, no-one would make the connection, unless Celeste did. And she would not be capable.

She pushed open the door. Celeste looked much the same. If she was doing better, Jude couldn't see any evidence of it. The breathing tube was gone, an oxygen mask in place. The plastic chair had been swapped out for an office-style one with a softer seat. Jude pulled it away from the bed, sat, and felt it swivel underneath her.

Through the mask, the expression on her sister's face was milder, blank. Whittled down to neutrality. As Jude watched, the chest rose slightly, sank again, with the machine's even, inhuman rhythm. She could see the ribs, the concave places at the throat. Just bones.

It would be easy to lift the mask. Detach the body from its supports. A terrible urge, and yet it filled her with hope.

'Hello,' she ventured instead.

The machine beep pressed on, undisturbed. Nora had made that up, about the talking. Just wanted to give her something to do.

Jude glanced at the glass, but there was no-one watching. She could say or do anything in here, and no-one would hear it.

'Celeste,' she said. The name was sharp in her mouth.

26

BEFORE

'Wait till you see it,' Celeste says. She reaches for the platter of fresh fruit that appears on their kitchen table every morning. Her hand hovers over the intricate arrangement.

'Why would I want to?' Jude kicks the table leg with one sneaker. 'It's going to be the same as last time.' She mimes the way the rocket toppled on re-entry, her hand crumpling against the tablecloth. 'I hate those people.'

'I have a good feeling about this one.' Celeste ignores the second statement, answers the first. She is talking to her like she's a child. Unstable. Hypocrisy, when it's her own moods that flash bright and burn dark. Jude watches as she extracts a piece of dragon fruit, peels the purple skin away with one fingernail, places it delicately on the edge of her plate, and sets the fruit on her tongue. Her eyes close. She swallows.

'Enjoy it,' she says, and opens them.

Jude pokes at the platter, ruins the pattern.

'It's not the same,' Celeste says after a pause. 'It's down to the shortlist now. It's getting *real*.'

Jude eats a single, perfect strawberry, pushes her plate away. The Station is out there, or parts of it: it has taken up its position at Lagrange point five, as far away as the Moon. It's being assembled by its own huge robot arms. But it's still not real.

Celeste talks to Fry all the time. Their meetings, as she calls them, go on late into the night. And when she's not talking to him, she talks about him. The gift he has. Like how he won the Lagrange point, even with all these competitors. It's not so clever. He just had more money than anyone else.

Private space missions are flourishing. There are bases on the moon, mines on asteroids, luxury observatory-resorts circling in near-Earth orbit. Leaving orbit is harder, more expensive. Fry seems to think this Lagrange point is the key. A stepping stone to somewhere. But it's not even a place, just a point relative to the Earth and Moon, the third corner of a triangle spinning.

Real is the body, the air they breathe, the gravity that holds them to the Earth. Real is the compound, the soil, the temper of the atmosphere. It has been stormy this week, the wind hurtling through like a vengeful spirit, throwing down trees and power lines. Real is its rage.

Celeste's look is sharp. 'Eat something, Judith. We might not be enjoying fruit like this next year.'

Jude hides her expression in a slice of mango. A year is optimistic, but it is clear that the Endeavour is far more than a whim. There will be a successful launch eventually, and Jude is supposed to be on it.

'Don't call me that,' she mutters. Celeste only uses her childhood name to put her in her place. Jude puts the half-eaten fruit back on her plate, makes a pursed shape with her mouth. 'Well, we won't be able to eat like this forever, either way,' she says.

The money will run out, but that's not all. Pineapple is impossible since the cyclone. Even mango is becoming hard to get. The abundance they once took for granted, the availability of anything and everything, is shrinking away, bit by bit.

Celeste believes the world is ending.

She's not well. Not coping.

When the floods reached them here, Celeste stayed in bed for three weeks, refused to eat. But outside the compound, the land recovered in its own way. Maybe the world they knew is ending, but another is blooming. Why can't Celeste see it?

Over coffee, Jude watches her sister's face. She's always careful to look nice, even for breakfast. This takes a lot of work. On the inside, it's not calm or pretty. She falls into black holes, needs to be pulled out. Needs Jude's help and her protection. At sixteen, Jude tells herself that she will stay with her as long as she can. Do what she can to keep her safe.

'Okay. We'll go,' she says, swallowing the coffee.

Celeste beams. She hears a promise, and why not? The Endeavour is the one thing that brings her joy. She is dancing on her feet as she stands and turns.

'Let's watch it again,' she says.

Jude follows her into the projection room. Celeste's eyes glitter with reflected screen light as she starts the latest video. She whispers the words of the voiceover like a prayer, already ascending.

On screen, the Station rotates. A wheel shape: four spokes, and each joint swollen like a knuckle. The centre is empty. A broad array fanned out beside it catches the sun. Celeste grips Jude's wrist, trapping it against the black upholstery. Around the rim, their sleeping quarters are distributed. In each knuckle, the capsules they'll arrive in, the same ones in which they will return to Earth.

Jude's not sure that Celeste is planning on returning.

There must be a way to convince her not to go. It's Jude's

responsibility to find it. They are each other's only family: Celeste is all she has left.

Music fills the room. The video sticks to the public narrative: Endeavour Station as research, an honourable experiment, a step closer to the stars. The furthest away from Earth humans have ever lived. They will prove it's possible for a year, two years.

But it's more than that. This planet is dying. They will stay out there while the wind rages, while the world burns. They will sleep through the worst. Celeste is counting on it. Maybe Earth will get its shit together; maybe they'll find another planet they can get to. Either way, they'll be out of it. Adrift in the Moon's wake. Safe, for as long as it takes.

The thought of it makes Jude feel seasick.

It's a fantasy, she reminds herself, struggling under her sister's grip. It will never happen. There are no other planets near enough or safe enough, and this one isn't dying. No-one can really sleep that long, even with the augmentations Fry has promised. The Endeavour is just a dream. What matters is that it keeps her sister happy for now, gives her a future she can believe in.

On screen, the wheel spins gracefully. The credits scroll, and music soars: 'The Blue Danube'. At least Fry has a sense of humour.

'Wonderful,' Jude says. Forcing all the kindness she can muster.

'And that's us,' Celeste whispers. 'We'll make history.'

Jude waits until the grip is loosened, pulls her hand out from below, and bends the wrist. She doesn't want to be made into history.

Celeste grins. 'Imagine, all that space and quiet. A perfect world, fully contained, just for you and me.'

You, me, and all those other people. Twelve, including Fry himself. The list has been diminishing, the closer the Endeavour gets.

'He wants us all there for this presentation,' Celeste is saying.

'Why?' Jude swipes the controls, brings back the light.

'Not sure.' There is the dark beneath the glow, a glimpse of something terrible. In the sudden clarity of LED, she is much too thin, her paleness marked by shadows. Maybe the end of the world begins inside a person, spreads out through their skin.

'Some kind of announcement.'

Jude sinks into her chair, stares at the blank screen where she and her sister appear as ghostly shapes.

'I know it's a lot,' Celeste says. 'But it's our only chance.'

That night, Jude goes outside to look at the stars like she used to. The wonder they once held has turned hostile. She lifts her gaze to contemplate the vastness, to feel the humbling, forgiving scale of the universe, and sees the satellites racing between them, crossing through each constellation's meaning. She thinks of what it will be like to stand there and look down on her home planet, and all she feels is nausea.

A moment later, Jude is on her hands and knees, palms against the dirt. She finds herself examining the smallest details. Grasses sprout like fine hairs, lizard tracks dot the sand between the rocks. Quartz glimmers in that sand, and ancient shells from a long-gone sea. So much complexity that she can't see, even at the smallest scale. So much time.

It can't be too late. She is just getting started.

She wants to understand her sister's logic. But the more she thinks about it, the more afraid she is. The thin layer of atmosphere that protects them here is already so fragile. Up there, in a tiny pocket of enclosed space, they will not be safe. They will be at the mercy of one man and his fortune. The Station has no dirt or trees, no horizon, and no exit. All their food and water, even the air they breathe, will have to be brought with them. It is only a smaller cage.

Jude's feet are numb from scrunching her toes into the sand. When she goes back inside, her steps leave traces of red dust on the black-tiled hall. The cameras follow her everywhere she goes; when the dust is swept away, there is always a recording.

27

AUGUST

Jude didn't hear the door to the back room open. She started when Nora cleared her throat.

'I have a couple of arrivals in,' she said. 'Teenagers. A little beaten up.'

'There was a boat?' Jude hadn't heard anything about a rescue.

Nora shook her head. 'They got a ride some of the way here, then managed to walk about ten kilometres. One of them on what looks like a broken foot.' She grimaced and reached to tuck a lock of hair behind her ear. When she didn't quite succeed, Jude caught herself wanting to complete the movement for her.

Ten kilometres? Jude fought back a clumsy fury. If she'd been out there driving, she would have passed them. Helped them. She was no use to anyone shut up in here, sitting on her numb hands. The day was slipping away; she should have left by now. She tried to stand, but Nora stopped her with a gesture.

'No, stay. I'll be busy with them for the next few hours, that's all. Just hit that buzzer if you need me or Ramon. If she responds, or . . . anything else happens.'

Jude followed her gaze, but the monitors looked unchanged.

'Hm,' Nora said. Then she turned and left the room.

Jude studied the monitors for a moment longer, none

the wiser. She examined the cool, taut planes of the face. Celeste, too, seemed unchanged.

She thought of the man from Orson, of the old laws of welcome that applied. Had applied to her, when she came to the Freelands. Nora's words echoed that principle: *Doesn't matter who she is. She still deserves our care.* Jude was ashamed. If Celeste had been a stranger, she would not have hesitated to do whatever was needed.

Jude had arrived with one friend and a stolen truck. Not much in the way of a story. She had only what Ali knew of her past: the camp, and what little she'd told him about the rest. For a long time that lightness had felt liberating, a kind of protection.

She'd always been vague about where she was from. Working on the ships, and before that in the north of what had once been Australia, it had been easy enough. People let her be, so long as she did her work. If they asked too much, she moved on.

Jude counted on her hands. Almost a decade since she sat on the bonnet of a dead car among termite mounds, waiting for a light to appear in the sky. That was the last time she'd come close to telling anyone.

Celeste had been gone that long. Lost, mourned, and then forgotten.

But she was here. And if she lived, she would be the only person who had known Jude as a child. Not just known: Celeste had moulded her, shaped her, tried to make her fit. Celeste was the first person she'd wanted to please, the first she'd truly cared for. They were each other's histories. It frightened her, she realised, to think that bond might reach her here.

Jude cleared her throat. An eyelid could have twitched.

She waited, silent. Nothing more.

Out in the clinic, she heard furniture scrape against the floor. Voices rose and fell, too muffled to understand. Celeste might have been carved from stone.

'I thought,' Jude began again, then stopped, already tangled in the wrack of detail. She cleared her throat, glancing from the face to the monitors.

Not a flicker.

It was strange to watch over someone you had once known. To have the intimacy of this long looking, after so long apart. A kind of vigil with the body, like some people still held with their dead.

She wasn't dead, though. Not yet.

Ramon's unexpectedly hearty laughter.

She pulled the chair closer to the bed, so close that she could smell the staleness of her sister's body. Scent was supposed to connect you to memory, but this was as distant as ice. The atmosphere around the bed was thinning. Again she felt the temptation to lift the oxygen mask, to sever the connection.

Then something was beeping. A small green light flashed. She reached for the buzzer, stopped. The moment opened.

Jude stood, her legs stiff. The chalet window showed her shabby clothes and poor posture, her eyes shadowed. In the wrap of protective gear, her flannel shirt was damp with sweat. She should not be here.

She pushed at the door. Tossed the coat and the rest of the gear into the box by the window, kicking off the stupid little shoe covers. She could not be expected to do this. Talk was useless. A voice could not bring a person back from the dead. She hadn't been able to keep her here the first time, had never been able to change her sister's mind. Jude had tried to tell them she wasn't up to this; they should have listened. It was better to get away before she did any more harm.

A groan, then more laughter. Shadows moving behind curtains; Ramon seeing to the broken foot.

The doors slid closed behind her with cool indifference. Late-afternoon sun reached out across the water. The sea churned, burning in reflected light. Scrap pushed up at its fingertips, over and over, presented like a gift. So much of what was made by humans stuck around, but it was always the wrong stuff that lasted.

The buzzing sound was not just in her head. She squinted into the sky until she could make it out: the insect mark of a drone in the air above the harbour. Jude stared until it rose and disappeared, uncomfortable to be observed. That hadn't changed.

Jude touched the fender as she passed the truck. She could get halfway to Portosacre on the battery, but would have to stop and wait for it to charge. It was smarter to refuel now, though she would need to be quick. She hurried for the shed.

The padlock gleamed in its hasp. She grasped it, let it drop, and swore under her breath. She had forgotten about the decisions of committees that had nothing to do with her, yet could impose restrictions on her movements.

Jude walked around to the coastguard door and knocked. The painted lobster looked down on her as she waited. Movement inside, and footsteps, then the door opened a crack and Karim peered out, dazed. He looked like he'd just woken up.

'Sorry,' he said.

'Need to get into the shed,' Jude said, shifting her weight from one foot to the other, trying not to sound breathless.

He paused, glanced past her, then ushered her inside.

Jude was glad to find he was alone on his shift. Hamish would ask questions, but Karim was taciturn, especially if you got him on his own. He went to the desk, looked out at the water, his expression troubled.

'Night shift's late,' he said. ''Nother meeting.'

Jude sniffed. 'You see that drone?'

'Alliance,' he said. 'Not one of ours. Not quiet, either. They want us to know they're watching.'

She looked out beside him, waited. It was awkward, the way a simple lock could change a relationship. She scuffed her boot against the table leg.

'Look. I just need to fill the truck.'

'Yeah, I'm not supposed to,' Karim said. He looked over at the row of hooks screwed into the noticeboard.

'I'll be quick,' she said. 'I won't touch anything.'

'They said no-one . . . but I guess you're okay. I mean, if it's just for diesel, I'm sure it's fine.' He leaned an elbow on the comms panel, reached for a small silver key. Instead of handing it over, he walked out with her. He was jumpy, looking over his shoulder. It couldn't just be the drone; Alliance surveillance was regular enough.

Jude waited until he had removed the padlock. She tried to make it sound casual.

'Who put that on there, anyway?'

Karim dropped the lock into his breast pocket. The shirt sank with its weight, made him look lopsided. 'They don't want people messing with the capsule. In case it's dangerous, they said.' He didn't sound convinced.

'It's just a wreck,' Jude said.

Karim shrugged. 'Might be worth something to somebody.' He fished the padlock out and held it to her. She took it before he could change his mind.

'Put it back on when you're finished,' he said. 'I'm going up to eat.'

She left the door open a crack, letting in just enough light to find the switch, but it was dead. Still, that wasn't unusual. She waited, let her eyes adjust. The shed walls were lined with stacks of timber, sheets of glass, crates filled with tools and parts and other materials, everything sorted into categories. Most of what was in here had washed up in the harbour, but some of it was brought down in her truck from ruined buildings nearby; she had moved a lot of this junk with her own hands.

There were other sheds like this, at least one in every town. Not even the F-net would know what was in all of them. Freelanders were such hoarders.

The fuel was in thirty-litre barrels, against the wall in a neat row. She always knew how much was there without having to think about it; there were few other diesel engines in Northport, and nothing that was driven as often as her truck.

The sack truck waited in the dark beside the barrels. Jude touched its handles, confirmed her mental estimate, tilted the trolley towards her. She would take two barrels out, use one to fill the tank and strap the other into the trailer. That would be enough to get her anywhere in the Freelands. For a day or so, no-one would notice she was gone.

Salvage

That thought should have been more comforting.

She let the sack truck fall back to a standing position and walked into the dark.

The capsule was on the far side, by the harbour doors. They hadn't moved it. The puddle beneath had dried to a crust and now glistened in the light that entered through the gaps in the doors, through holes in the roof like dim, close stars. The harbour-side doors were closed and chained. A sliver of sea in the gap. She could hear the water sloshing steadily against the stones. It was easy to forget that it was rising.

The capsule gaped where they had cut into it. It was a hulking shadow, blistered with burn marks. Parts of its surface looked melted, either from their tools or from the atmosphere, the heat of re-entry; the Earth had resisted her return.

Inside, the gear had been gutted; most of that stuff was in the clinic with Celeste. It seemed different to the model Jude had once climbed inside, but she recognised the same structure: three slots and a central pillar. Each slot was a tiny space, barely enough for a body. What had happened to the others?

Jude put her hand against the cut edge, just above her head. The shell was a couple of metres thick, both fragile and over-engineered. The space inside was still smaller. Celeste must have been pressed into it like a bird in its egg.

Karim's hands, the closing of a tomb.

She had to put her knees into the shell to hoist herself up. Reaching into the little cave, she felt its surface. Not smooth, or strong. Some lightweight material, improbably domestic. No smell of car upholstery.

Fry had made it all seem state-of-the-art, like something from the future, but this had lost all illusion of luxury. The capsule was a grey, banged-together vehicle, as beaten-up as the truck. Not much better than any other scrap in this shed.

Jude crawled right in and touched the thin panels. No future, no magic, only the material that held: these woven straps, the hollow tube, the shape where Celeste's body had fitted. She slid her body into the hole where her sister had been, and then she was in space, her arms reaching for the sides, the walls too close. To want the stars, to reach for them, and be given this. And yet it had been enough to keep Celeste alive.

Jude closed her eyes, felt herself falling.

She was not as tall as her sister, but broader now; her hips didn't fit easily in the narrow space. The straps that had held Celeste in place were broken where they'd cut her free.

Jude filled the cell, felt the pressure of the padding around her body. Felt the earth slip away. In her chest, she could sense the drop and shake of the atmosphere. There would be resistance on exit, a rattling heat as she hurtled through. Then the soft fall outward, her own weight lifting away. The nightmare in reverse. A few days in transit, maybe awake, maybe asleep, maybe a third state between. Then the Station's arm extending to catch her, bring her to its mouth.

Jude would not go. Couldn't stop her. The weight of those twin failures would always live in her body. It would always confine the air.

Footsteps, confident at first. A subtle change in the light. Jude blinked, disoriented. Lifted her head. No room to sit up, barely enough to breathe. How long had she been lying here? The footsteps petered out.

'They want better images,' a voice was saying. 'Confirmation.'

Salvage

She recognised Giorgio, from the committee. Some other voices, maybe Helena and Ailin, and Jacopo, the engineer who looked after the barge. Jude remembered where she was, and that she was not supposed to be there. Her heartbeat rapid, breath constrained. The small space claustrophobic.

A sound of metal falling and they stopped. 'Shit. It's so dark in here,' Ailin complained. While they scrabbled, Jude rolled onto her side as quietly as she could. There wasn't enough room to turn around without making a sound. She would have to slide out feet first, right in front of them.

'Help me move this.' Karim was with them. She stiffened, waited. The lock was in her pocket.

'I must have dropped it somewhere,' he added. The meeting must be over; he must know she was still in here.

'They told us not to let anyone interfere with it,' Giorgio was saying. 'They want it in one piece.' She noticed the anxiety in his voice, out of character for him. The unnamed 'they'.

'Bit late for that,' Helena muttered.

'They know there's damage. That's not our fault.' Karim again, defensive. 'We had to get her out.'

Someone wanted this capsule preserved. It must be Portosacre. Maybe they wanted to study it, see what they could learn from it. But Freelanders had no interest in space, did they? There must be other applications. Ways of sustaining life in harsh conditions, maybe.

She lifted her head, and a loose wire poked her in the cheek. The capsule was ripped to shreds inside, surely useless. When they found her, she would tell them she was only curious.

Metres away, something heavy was knocked to the ground.

'Look, it's dangerous stumbling around in the dark.'

Karim's voice was higher than usual; he was feigning a cheery manner.

She would have to tell him later how false he sounded, how grateful she was. If she was still here.

'I have a better light in the office. Come and we'll find it. You won't get good images in this.'

More murmurs – impatience, complaint – but the steps retreated. Finally, the scrape of metal door against concrete slab, and silence.

Jude wriggled out of the capsule, shuffled her body close to the edge and slid down onto the concrete. She filled her lungs, let in the sea air, its churning scent of living and dying.

The vertical felt strange for a moment, her legs learning the return to gravity. She must have been asleep a while. She would only have a minute or two to disappear.

She moved carefully across the shed, took the lock from her pocket, dropped it on the ground by the door and kicked it into the dark. The barrels of biodiesel stood right where she had left them, but there was no time for that. She had missed her chance.

Pulling the door open just enough to slide out, she hesitated. It was almost dark. If she went up to the Common now, she would be seen. There was no going back to the clinic.

Jude walked briskly across to the truck, climbed up and closed the door, crawled into the back seat and lay down. Ali would laugh if he saw her like this, a grown person hiding like a child, but she needed to think.

Lying down wasn't helping; her head was spinning. She clawed at the back of the driver's seat, pulled herself up and peered out the windscreen.

Salvage

They were filing out of the coastguard door. First Giorgio, striding; then Helena and Jacopo, carrying a crate between them. Karim with a huge lamp over his shoulder, Ailin with the camera. They looked like they were off to make a film.

One by one, they disappeared into the shed. She rested her head against the back of the driver's seat, waited for the dizziness to settle.

A knock at the window woke her, maybe minutes, maybe hours later. It was dark outside. The voice that followed the knock was muffled, and for a moment she thought she was still in the capsule, hiding. Then Jude saw Nora's face through the glass, screwed up with concern. She leaned across to pop the handle, aware of the stale air, the scent of her breath and her body.

'Needed a minute,' she said. She should have been kilometres away by now, but she had to go and look at the capsule, had to see inside it, had to let herself be dragged backwards through time and space.

'I thought you weren't coming back.'

Jude climbed into the driver's seat, the medic's face round in the opposite door. It was deep night behind her, no moon. She wanted to start the truck and go, but something in Nora's expression made her pause.

'You might as well get in,' Jude said.

Nora climbed nimbly up onto the passenger seat and pulled the door closed. 'Nice place you got.'

Jude felt the medic's scrutiny, her quiet humour. Nora's eyes were calm on the surface, lively underneath, like water. Like water, they glistened in the dark. She should be furious at Jude for disappearing, but she looked secretly delighted.

'What is it?' Jude asked.
Nora smiled, wholly trusting.
'She's awake.'

28

BEFORE

In an ordinary family, there would be a moment where a line was crossed. A conflict to drive the two apart: a screaming argument, a scene. Years later, when she knows a bit more about the world, Jude understands that's how it usually works. But hers has never been an ordinary family. The Princes are a business and an empire, a life raft and a trap.

Jude paces the hallway at night. When she can't sleep, she could walk forever, just placing one foot in front of the other. At the end of this corridor there is a picture window where she often pauses. She likes to imagine herself stepping out of the compound gates and walking away. She imagines she will leave like that: on foot, empty-handed, completely free.

But tonight, she doesn't pause. She keeps going, pushes at a door, walks down the fire stairs.

The garage is dark. She only turns the office light on for a moment, finds the keys on the desk, the remotes for the garage door and the gates.

It isn't stealing if the keys are in her pocket. It's her car, because it's the one she's worked on the most: an old Jaguar composed largely of spare parts. Spence calls it the Jag of Theseus.

It will be Spence who notices it's gone, she's gone. It's his friendship she will be sorry to lose. He's asleep in his apartment right now. Just through that door. She could knock, say a few words into the dark.

He would lose his job.

Jude hasn't forgotten that look he gave her the first time, when she tumbled out of the car and into the dirt. She won't forget the books, the conversations. He's been teaching her to drive, showing her the exits. Has given her chance after chance to escape.

She takes only one thing with her. A stone in her pocket, the weight of a life. Her car is already facing the exit, and it starts first go. The warmth of its scent surrounds her. Old leather, faded luxury, hard work.

Security cameras will record her departure, like they've recorded every other moment of her life. Alarms will sound somewhere, but alarms, like fences, are designed to prevent people from getting in, not out.

The road out of the compound is empty. No-one ever comes or goes. Jude travels slowly at first, but then it's out of sight behind her and the engine hungers for momentum. She passes the old protest site with a pang. There's no trace of it now. Celeste's fault, she reminds herself.

Jude glances often at the rear-view mirror, checking for the lights she thinks might follow, but there aren't any. She begins to relax behind the wheel, to feel the car grow happier with heat. She pays attention to the road, the patch that's visible in headlights: a few hundred metres of solid ground ahead. Sometimes the eyes of an animal flash at the roadside, lit up as if with their own interior beams, but mostly there's just the dark. Nothing in her way. Her calm spreads outwards, an abundance unearned.

By the time she reaches the outskirts of the city, the sun is coming up. She's tired, mouth dry, head sore. She drives past suburban developments, abandoned mid-construction. She spots a few tents in the vacant frames, tarps thrown over unfinished rooms. The older houses are worse than she remembers. Many look empty: no doors, broken windows. Signs hang from gates, some angry, most just hungry. A woman struggles with a pram, glares over as she passes. Instead of a child, the pram holds a plastic container full of something that looks like water.

Jude leans over the wheel and tries to concentrate. Aims for the cluster of tall buildings up ahead. One of these blue glass spikes used to be Prince Tower, but she can't pick which one now.

Closer in, the suburbs get a little more orderly. A few shops and security posts, fuel and recharge stations. She stops at the first second-hand dealership she comes to and waits in the driveway for it to open, engine running. Then she lets the nice old man who waves her in the gate rip her off. Nothing matters except gaining distance.

'No relation,' she says, when he frowns at her paperwork. He pouts at the car, shakes his head over the engine. Decides to act like he believes her.

She tucks her ID back into her wallet, but she'll need to get rid of it. It's not a crime to flee, she's no longer a minor, but she needs to let go of the weight of that name, the questions it raises.

There's a bus stop across the street but she walks on to the next one, refreshing her phone, waiting for the money to appear in her personal account. When she reaches the shelter there's a cracked seat, a bag of garbage sitting under it that smells like shit. She will have to get rid of the phone as well. She stands with her face in the band of shade, feels the heat building.

After half an hour a man appears, glances at the device in her hand. She shoves it into her pocket with the stone, lets him appraise her face instead.

'No bus,' he informs her, lisping. When he steps close, she smells staleness, smoke. He doesn't have many teeth. 'Dun't stop here. You hafta walk down to main road, thaway. Three-four time a day, is all.'

She nods, waits for him to leave.

He squints at her. 'You gotnything to eat?'

'No, sorry,' she pats her pockets, pretending to check, aware of the phone at her hip and the few thousand dollars now sitting in her account.

'Here,' he says, and pulls a paper bag out of his coat pocket, hands it to her. 'You be right.' He walks away before she has time to unwrap it. A single bread roll. The shock of the gift. Sweat trickles down her skin.

She follows the track worn in the weeds, picking her way through prickles and faded rubbish. The path doesn't look right to her, but after a few minutes it descends to the highway. There's a little shelter down there, one other person waiting with a few laden shopping bags. She pulls the hood up over her head and joins them. An old woman grunts and looks past her.

Celeste will be awake by this hour, sitting in front of her breakfast. Maybe she's going over the timeline while she eats her perfect, unblemished fruit. Still years away, but it's her obsession: the upcoming training schedules, the tests and preparations, the augment she's been promised. Maybe she thinks Jude is sleeping in. Maybe she doesn't think about her at all.

Across the street there's another housing development, this one still just a field. Every so often a surveyor's stake interrupts the ground, tape flapping, but the weeds are high. *SAFEHAVEN*, says the billboard with its optimistic family. It has torn at the bottom, leaving a white patch in which someone has sprayed *REFUSE!* in wonky black letters. In the dusty grass behind it, a few kangaroos are grazing indifferently.

She stands by the gutter, shades her eyes from the sun. Behind her, the woman is muttering to herself. Jude turns, nervous. The shopping bags hold blankets, clothes. The woman smiles generously.

'Not long now, love,' she says.

Jude looks out for the silent black security car. The phone will tell them where she is. Celeste can find her without much trouble. It won't take long.

But the bus pulls up first, and she helps the woman with her bags. The driver waves them both on without a ticket. Jude clutches her stale bread roll, throat too dry to eat it.

'Thanks, love,' the old woman says from three rows in front of her. Her leg is sticking out into the aisle, swollen shiny. Jude looks away.

Across the aisle, a man asleep in his hoodie, face hidden, tattooed forearm exposed. Behind her, a woman with a baby in her lap and a little kid squeezed beside her, staring out the window, eyes too wide, face too pale. Jude's carsick too. She looks out with him at the unfamiliar world, the one where all these people live. The one they say it's now too late to save.

29

STATION

Judith is in the corridor. She is learning to run, she is only four, her strides are confident but clumsy. A misstep and the small figure slips on the polished granite, lands face down. There is a pause the length of a breath before Celeste reaches her. The wail starts up, and Celeste grips her small warm body, lifts it. The weight in her hands. This is a trick the world has played on her; this is her secret. Even on her worst days, her sister's need ties her to life.

They're in the car again, restless starlight overhead. Earth spins faster than they move, a thousand miles an hour, but she can't feel it. When her sister is asleep, she is so silent that Celeste could almost forget she is there. She twists in her seat to watch the small figure, waits to see the breath move in her body. The trust that lets her sink so deep. Spence at the wheel. Nick waiting. She knows they will be safe.

When the hatch opens, Calvin is peering down at her, his face close. It's not supposed to be him again. He's messed up the system, or she has messed up time. Her sight is getting worse, her head full of doubt. She has to trust the others, use their eyes.

Come with me, he says. The Station circles. There is nowhere else to go.

Celeste accepts a hand to help her rise, feels weakness and uncertainty in his grip even as he pulls her to her feet. His image emerges from the fog. A sadness to it, but he turns away before she can reach him. She follows him to the next hatch. He bends to one knee, palms the sensor. This is a looping memory, a fault in the pattern. It has happened before.

The hatch opens with a hiss, and Carolyn's dark head emerges. Her hair seems thinner. When she lifts her face, her cheekbones are so prominent that Celeste puts a hand to her own to feel for a comparison. She has always been slender, always felt the bone close to the surface. Carolyn gets to her feet, moving carefully, and Calvin shimmers in and out as she looks from one grin to the other. They seem much older than she is, much older than before. How long has it been?

There have never been three at the same time. It shouldn't be possible. Something is wrong. She should tell Nick. The Station will wake him. And then there will be four.

Where is Nick? Panic starts in the chest, spreads forward and down through her arms, but it doesn't take over her thoughts. She feels distant from it, from the others, from her own body. They are safe here, of course they are. Jude is sleeping through it all.

Quickly, Calvin says. *There isn't time.* They hurry to the next trapdoor. She follows, does not want to be alone. Another passenger is waiting there, she knows him, his whole profile comes to mind: Arvind, telecommunications, an SUV filled with explosives, his wife and son.

Maja's dead, Arvind says as he climbs. *It isn't working. We're starting to lose them.*

The engineers, Celeste says, gesturing up. *The, the astronauts. They'll know.* She studies the ceilings, but can make out no marks. Have the lights in here changed?

Carolyn's hand is on her shoulder. She shakes her head. *Celeste. There's no-one there. It's just the Station.*

Then it's a dream, like all the others.

There isn't time to explain, Arvind says. They look at each other, then at the corridor behind them, curving away into the dark. When she looks back, Arvind has begun to walk away. She watches him diminish into fog. The others follow. When she wakes, it will all return to normal. The loop will reset. The lights will come on ahead and drop away behind them. Jude will be here beside her. Two at a time, no more. The wheel spins like a clock; it can't stop. The gravity works perfectly. In the distance, Arvind descends into a hole in the ground, which isn't the ground, and nothing changes.

She catches up to the others. The three of them kneel beside the hole and look down. Their heads are almost touching at the centre. The room below is different. More primitive-looking, less comfortable. Wires, tubes detached from the wall. Three hollow spaces stacked like batteries around a central column. Is this how they arrived? It looks so small.

Celeste, says Carolyn. She draws back, makes a little room. Her palm descends above the hole. At first Celeste doesn't understand.

Judith, says Celeste.

Carolyn, says Carolyn, shaking her head, touching her collarbone. She hasn't understood either. This happens in dreams. Identities are slippery. People transform.

Go on down, says Calvin, pointing into the hole. *There's not much time. We're getting sick. We're losing contact.*

His hand is on her back. She pulls away, but she is smiling. *No, thank you*, she says. Gracious, as is her habit, even in dreams. It is a ridiculous suggestion. If they leave the Station they will die. Someone is dead already, maybe. But it doesn't matter. It isn't her. Where is Jude? Safe, asleep. No-one should be allowed to wake her.

Beside her, Carolyn is folding herself into the gap.

Look, Calvin says. *See this?* He points to the circle, the green arrow beside her knee. His breath is close to her face. It's warm and smells of rotten broccoli. She knows it's a dream, because they don't eat here. Celeste looks down into the hole, the space beneath their feet, a room laced with wires. *The capsule, remember? All you have to do is get in. The Station will calculate the way.*

But we have to go now, Carolyn says. She has lowered herself into the space next to Arvind, and looks up like a grub peering out from its cocoon.

Celeste shakes her head. *I can't leave my sister.* Then laughter bubbles up from her mouth like a gas. Doesn't sound right. It hurts her chest. They are making a mistake. There is no rescue, no escape, because those things have already happened. This is safety, here. She does not want to go back.

A look passes between the others, and then Celeste is lying down. It doesn't stop the laughter from moving through her, nauseating her. She's dimly aware of voices, sharp and heated, close by. She picks out words: *mind, oxygen, contact, time.* Time in patches. She is home at Sovereign House. The corridor is bigger. The windows broken, coated in dust. All that is over; Jude is gone. When she lifts her head, the others have gone too. The hatch is closed. The little green arrow is dark.

Celeste rolls onto her side, lets her head rest against the hatch. She closes her eyes and waits. Thinks of them floating away in their tiny capsule, three seeds in a shell. The thought already has the quality of a dream. She doesn't hear them leave, doesn't feel anything through the floor. The Station continues to spin.

She must go back to sleep. Jude will be waiting.

30

AUGUST

Ramon was standing at the chalet window, tablet in hand, expression serious. Jude stopped with him as Nora went in. She could hear the muted whispering of the teenagers in their room.

They watched as Nora tended to the body, moving or dismantling the structures that held Celeste's head in place. The head was limp beneath the medic's hand. Some fluid was leaking to the side. For a moment, Jude thought she must have misunderstood: that Celeste was gone, that it was over. Old grief swallowing.

But Nora had only lifted the oxygen mask away, moved the pillow. Celeste's face was still and grey, marked by the lines of the equipment. Ramon inhaled sharply – he'd been holding his breath; they both had. They watched as Nora reached a hand to the exposed face. Jude was moved by the gesture, its offer of solace. The medic leaned closer.

It was just a subtle motion in the mouth at first. Jude thought of an electrical impulse, the sluggish movements of machinery set in train.

Ramon spoke softly, almost to himself.

'She's awake,' he said.

Celeste opened her eyes. For a second her expression seemed joyful, childlike. An illusion, maybe.

Jude moved automatically, began to don the gown and mask, the gloves and slippers. She struggled with the string of the gown, took off one glove and tied it, put the glove back on inside out, and looked up to see Nora was standing in front of her, watching.

'It's unbelievable, isn't it? I've never seen anything like it.'

Jude's hands were numb. She pulled the mask over her mouth.

Nora caught her gaze again.

'You can go in now,' she said.

Teenage voices rising, easy laughter. Jude was incapable of speech. Through the window, the skeletal face was still. Had never moved at all.

'Jude?'

Her breath was close inside the mask and visor. Not enough air. But she did as she was told, pushed open the door, felt the subtle shift in pressure as it swung shut behind her.

Celeste's eyes were closed again. Her breath was slow and shallow. Without the mask on she seemed asleep, even peaceful. Her mouth was neat and thin. There was nearly nothing to her.

Jude sat heavily in the chair, which hissed beneath her weight.

For a long time, the body did not stir again. Jude could feel Nora watching her through the glass. When she looked up, Ramon was there too: both medics observing with all the surface calm of their strange profession. Jude might be in a model scene, a diorama. The machine pinged its regular rhythm. She knew they waited for her to speak.

'Celeste,' she began. The name softened in her mouth. Jude stopped. What could she say?

The mouth moved faintly, and then the eyes opened. For a moment they seemed clouded and unable to focus, and then they were searching the room. This room, or another. They looked everywhere, not settling on anything. And then they found Jude. Celeste's mouth pursed slightly, as though disapproving. The eyes held something deeper, though. Something like horror.

'You're still here,' she whispered.

*

Jude found Ali alone in the Common, bent over the usual spread of open books. She pulled up a stool and helped herself to the toast abandoned at his elbow. He mouthed something to himself, then adjusted his glasses. They needed a clean. He needed a haircut.

'Hungry,' he observed, and she nodded, swallowing the last of his breakfast.

'You want a coffee?'

He shook his head, closed the page he had open in front of him, keeping his place with one finger. She twisted to read the spine. Galeano again.

'Tea?'

'Water.' Ali looked tired. It was not yet six; he would sometimes work all night, but maybe he had just woken early. She'd been surprised by the pink blush of dawn herself when she stepped through the sliding doors. The clinic had its own sense of time, untouched by the world's turning.

She went to the bar and filled a glass for him, then one for herself.

'Do they know who she is yet?' he asked as Jude slid the water towards him.

There was no point keeping it from him. She had to do it

quickly; could not endure the thought that he would find out after she left.

'Celeste Prince,' she said, and then, in a hoarser, quieter voice: 'Endeavour Station.'

He removed his finger from the book, slipped in a scrap of paper, folded his hands together in front of him and smiled, anticipating a joke.

'The space station?'

'You remember it,' she said, uncertain how to go on. How to introduce the connection. He knew that she had lost her family when she was young. Had been raised by another family, cold people. He thought she had no-one left, like him. It had been true enough at the time. Now she'd lost track of what she'd let slip. She'd been too comfortable here, she realised.

'Sad story.' The levity in his expression had fallen away.

Jude rotated the water glass, making wet circles. Her hand seemed only vaguely attached to her body. She could not look at Ali.

He was born in a city under siege, shrinking around him. It was wiped from the map in increments. He'd been away at university when it was finally turned to rubble. These books, these notes of his, were all he had. They made the past into a place he could access, a place that he could honour.

'But she survived?'

'She's sleeping. Torpor.' Jude made a neat pile of the books between them. Celeste had not spoken again. Jude had sat with her for hours, until Nora came in and told her to go and get some rest.

'So then she's some kind of billionaire?'

'Was.' Jude's eyes were heavy, her voice soft. The access of memory was a skill, like languages. She didn't have it. Too much was overgrown and tangled. The garden sprawled out to the horizon, all end and no beginning.

'Are you okay? You look exhausted.'

Cold water swirled around her. Voices called out in the dark. Jude, the wall of a ship behind her, being pulled into the deep. Her friend reaching from the surface, dragging her back to life.

When she heard the door swing open behind her, Jude turned gratefully away.

Solare crossed the room with youthful energy, a hand raised, teeth flashing. 'I just came from the clinic,' she began. And then paused, sensing a heavier conversation was in train.

Jude got up from her stool. Solare slipped into her place with ease.

'I'm going to bed, anyway,' Jude said.

'Wait. I need to speak with you.'

Jude hovered a moment, doomed.

'I just wanted to ask you how the requisitions work. For equipment, and so forth.' Solare had a formal way of speaking. Jude wondered vaguely if she was like this in all her languages, or only English. Ali had once told her that it was like having multiple personalities.

'Just put a request on the F-net and it will run the allocation. It works fine, most of the time. Why?'

'I was hoping to use the truck,' she said.

Jude felt herself stiffen. She caught Ali's expression in the corner of her eye. 'What for?'

'Those kids need supplies. Medicine. It won't be much. Just up to Cuoretto and back.'

'I can drive it,' Jude said, tapping her fingers on a book.

'You're a wreck,' Ali said gently.

'I'll go later.'

'Nora said she'll need you back there,' Solare went on. 'Don't worry – I can drive anything. I was a driver even before the war.'

'The truck, though.' Jude's skin felt hot.

'Trucks, tractors, school bus – whatever we had. Road trains. A tank, once.'

Ali raised his eyebrows, and she grinned. 'I can fly a chopper, too. Long story,' she said.

'You don't know the roads,' Jude said. It was not that the truck was hers: technically speaking, everything here was a community resource. It was just that in practice, she was the only person who drove it. She and Ali had arrived in that truck; she was the one who took care of it. People respected that relationship.

'I only need to go as far as Cuoretto. It's a good road. I've been down it twice now,' Solare said.

Jude was cornered. 'Fine,' she said. She pulled a key from her pocket, passed it over. The solar charge would easily last the distance to Cuoretto and back. Jude would sleep through the morning, and when the truck returned that afternoon she would fill it up and leave. 'Bring it back straight away.'

'Will you come, help me translate?' Solare said to Ali. He glanced at Jude, made a quick assessment. 'If it's just for the day,' he said, and to Jude: 'Get some sleep, my friend. We'll talk again when you're rested.'

31

BEFORE

After two hours of lurching through unfamiliar suburbs, they arrive at the city's central bus station. It looks like a giant silver crate dumped on a corner. People dressed for office work walk fast around her, looking at their phones. She fumbles for hers, checks to see the money from the car is there, then thinks about the payments being traced. There's a grimy-looking ATM in the station entrance. She walks across to the ticket counter and looks up at the timetable. An array of small towns, distant cities, names she does and doesn't know. In the waiting hall, people sit on their bags or on the few plastic chairs bolted into the floor in the centre. Jude feels clean, sharp, sleep-deprived, and completely alone.

Beside the ATM there is a young woman in a nest of blankets. The air conditioning is cool but there's a blast of heat every time the doors open. There are others sleeping inside the terminal, dozens of people once you start to see them. Jude's hands are shaking. She makes the maximum withdrawal possible. Her card will register her presence here. Maybe no-one's looking for her yet.

She books a ticket halfway across the country, the next long-distance coach to leave. She pays with cash. That leaves her with a few hundred. She goes back to the ATM, holds two fifty-dollar notes out to the woman in the doorway, who looks up and scowls, suspicious. 'I don't want charity,' she mutters, but she takes the cash and tucks it into her shirt, disappears back into her blankets.

The bus doesn't leave for a few hours. Jude goes over to the little cafe in the concourse, gets a donut and a coffee, a bottle of water, and less change than she expected. The cash feels flimsy, only thin plastic. Her life has been privileged, static; she hasn't travelled much, has rarely had to handle money. She has never known what anything is worth. How much she owes the Princes, the world. How much she will need to survive, how much she can afford to give away.

Jude has plenty of time on the bus to think about it. It will take twenty-two hours to get where she is going.

The coach exits the city via a motorway, quickly putting all the broken-down suburbs behind them. It makes silent stops at eerie roadhouses, lit green, each almost identical, like a recurring dream. Jude stays on board except when she needs to use the bathroom, keeps her hood raised. There are enough passengers that she doesn't feel conspicuous, but neither does she feel safe enough to sleep. She prepares stories about herself, but no-one asks who she is, where she is going. Most of the others have headphones on, an enviable ability to sleep.

Tiredness wins out eventually. She wakes with a jolt at the state border. A roadhouse, a concrete kangaroo, a queue of vehicles under bright lights.

There is a checkpoint. There are moans of complaint from people woken. After a while, a uniformed guard gets on the bus, walks up the aisle with her weapon slung across her chest. Jude's heart races, and she sinks down in her seat. There are whispers from the other passengers: *police, passports, territory.* A baby cries. But the guard doesn't ask anyone for identification, just looks around, has a few low words with the driver, plods away.

Long hours still to go. The baby cries itself past the point of exhaustion. Jude tries to read the news. While it has reception, her phone is all catastrophes: fires, floods and cyclones, broken treaties. Mostly, it's out of range. She switches it off, not knowing whether they can trace it anyway.

The city she is headed for begins as an expanse of salt pans and cement. When at last they get to its centre, it looks smaller and sadder than the place she left. The bus stop is just a car park beside a building that looks to have been abandoned and reoccupied, with hand-painted banners flying from the roof. The doorways are lined with sleeping bodies wrapped in blankets, like those fat caterpillars that march end to end in the desert.

Jude climbs down and finds a bathroom, washes her face, looks at herself in the harsh light and tries on a few tough expressions. As soon as she steps out again, a gaunt man approaches, asks her if she might give him a little money for some breakfast. He's polite, has an explanation, but she doesn't want to listen. She hands him all the cash she has and walks off.

It doesn't take her long to get rid of her remaining money. She finds a branch office, lines up for an hour to close her account, pays cash for a room in a small, grubby motel near the railway station that doesn't seem to have a name or care what hers is. She walks around with the rest of it in her pockets, tucking notes into folds of blankets, dropping them into paper cups. Eventually she sees a post office, writes the name of an organisation Holly mentioned on the front of an envelope, wraps the rest of her cash in a piece of paper, writes *SORRY* on the paper. Pushes it into the box before she can change her mind. Maybe the organisation doesn't even exist anymore.

The woman in the bank took her card, broke it into pieces. Jude does the same with her ID, drops the squares in the bin outside the post office. She finds a second-hand electronics shop staffed by a long-haired paranoia enthusiast, and trades in her phone for an ancient one that won't track her location. The man erases everything from her old phone while she watches.

'They can still find you if they want to. CCTV, facial recognition,' he says. Jude shrugs. She has a hundred dollars left, and a pocketful of coins that jangle when she walks. For the first time in her life there is nothing else that she can draw on, nothing to hold her if she falls. It's exhilarating, maybe, unless this cold, rushing feeling on her skin is fear.

She goes to the room, but she's too wired to sleep. Each time she closes her eyes she sees the highway out the bus window, the dark sky. The motel's window is jammed shut by an air conditioner that rattles loudly, shakes the frame. She turns it off, listens to the hum of the city below, drifts off for a minute. When she wakes, she is covered in sweat and mosquito bites. The street noise has a wild rhythm. She peers out the gap beside the air conditioner and sees the corner below is full of people in masks, waving flags and chanting.

Jude has an impulse to go out there and join them. Understand what they are celebrating, or fighting against. Maybe Holly and Rachel will be down there, or people like them.

But it feels good to be alone, with only her own needs to worry about. The world can end or save itself, for all she cares. She lies back on the stiff blanket, stretches her hands over her abdomen, feels softness, latent muscle. She didn't think it would be this easy.

The TV works when she flicks it on, but there's nothing about protests. Instead, there are images of military trucks moving up and down the central highway. A blonde woman frowns and says the violence is getting out of hand. The government promises to ensure the safety of all Australian citizens, and Jude can't understand why this sounds vaguely threatening.

Things are changing up north. The treaties have been falling through; there's a movement of people from south to north, north to south. The next story is about the latest bushfire. Whole towns lost. Damage measured in the many millions. Hundreds of people have had to flee their homes, the newsreader says. A man whose face is streaked with ash asks where people are supposed to go, and his voice sounds like smoke.

She could go anywhere. Cut loose, she is like a spore or seed waiting for a gust of wind to give her some direction. No demands and no connections. No Celeste to save.

'You're free,' she says aloud.

She thinks she understands what it means.

32

AUGUST

When the knock came, Jude stayed at the window. Ali would let himself in. The door creaked, she caught a scent of cinnamon and oranges, and the person waiting cleared their throat.

'Ali told me I would find you here,' said Nora.

Jude wanted to be annoyed, but Nora's expression stopped her. Away from the clinic, it had a worn look. The lines around her eyes were deep. Probably just a side effect of the profession, dealing with other people's grief.

She put a small bottle on the desk. 'Help you sleep,' she said. Then she looked around. The blankets awry, the little wooden chair, the crate, the boots tucked neatly under the bed beside it. Nora reserved judgement without entirely hiding it.

'This is where you live,' she said softly.

Jude felt as small and messy as the room. It was early afternoon now, and warm; she hadn't slept long, had passed out fully clothed that morning, had been sitting here trying to plan her exit, waiting for Solare to come back with the truck. She eyed the bottle, lifted and shook it. Pills. No label. Jude didn't remember telling Nora about the insomnia. She'd set Ali straight as soon as he was back.

Jude stood and shook out a pill without bothering to ask what it was. A glass of stale water on the floor by the bed, the scrappy curtain flapping at the window. She sank onto the bed, which creaked predictably.

'Valerian,' Nora said. 'Feverfew.'

Jude wanted to say that she didn't have a fever. She closed the pill in her fist. Beside her, the bed accepted Nora's weight with a creak.

'It's true what I said, you know. That anyone can do it. But that doesn't make it easy.'

Jude grunted, closed her eyes, said nothing. Although it was meant to be encouraging, the medic's voice had an edge in it.

'It's a lot to take on.'

There was her heartbeat under Jude's ribcage, steady as machinery. If she held still, Nora would leave. The thought had an animal logic. But when the weight began to lift, Jude found she didn't want her to go.

'Wait,' she said. The other woman turned. Knew her weakness, could scent it in her. It would be as obvious to her expert eye as the insomnia. Jude didn't want that to be her last impression.

'I'm not like you,' she said, and felt herself flush.

'I mean, I'm not a good person.' Exposed to the air, the words were flimsy. Only self-pity. 'It doesn't come naturally,' she added.

A frown appeared on Nora's face.

'That's not how it works,' she said finally. 'I don't do this because I'm good. I do it because it needs doing. Don't tell me care is in my nature. It's in no-one's nature, and in everyone's. We're *all* needed.'

Nora hadn't understood her meaning. This wasn't an abstract principle: it was personal. Jude had let her sister go, had left her to die out there. The need that should be met was long past.

'The Freelands doesn't owe her anything,' Jude said.

'It's not what we owe. It's what we're capable of giving.'

'Well, maybe I'm not capable.' The pill in Jude's fist was a stone.

Hurt flashed across Nora's face. When she spoke again, her voice was quieter.

'We've all thought that about ourselves at one time or another,' she said.

Jude reached for her boots. Pulled them closer.

Still, Nora didn't leave.

'It's not going to be forever,' she said.

'What do you mean?'

There was a little hesitation. 'It's only been a few days. She will get better. She needs strength now, continuity. And you're so calm with her. A solid presence.'

'You make me sound like a tree,' Jude said.

Nora smiled, and the room spun gently on its axis. The humour was back in her expression. 'Look, you don't have to come every day. I can't make you. But I can see you're good for her. Good company.'

It was hot in the room. Jude bent her head, began to tidy. Picked up the glass, set it on the crate.

'She asked for you,' said Nora.

Jude's hand went still.

'I didn't think she knew your name until she said it. We must be getting through to her.'

Her eyes were studying, merciless.

'Oh, and passionflower,' Nora said, 'I forgot.' She crossed

to the door, then paused to watch Jude's reaction, considering something.

'Get some rest,' was all she said.

The door clicked shut behind her.

33

STATION

The process is the same. The mask slides back, the instruments retract, the sleeping place folds away. The loop has reset. She climbs up to open the hatch, yawning. Her eyes are foggy, slow to adjust. This time it will be Jude's face she sees at the top of the ladder. It has to be.

Jude's face. So young and vulnerable. She is still just a child.

She fumbles with the sensor. Her hands feel clumsy. When the hatch finally opens, the waiting face is a blur.

Jun-Sang, he reminds her, after a long moment.

I know. Celeste, she says, scrambling up from her hole. She holds out a hand for assistance. Her body feels weak, the wrist like a twig in his hand. Jude's fine, safely asleep in one of these rooms. Her closeness is a lovely certainty. But it should be her turn.

Happy birthday, says Jun-Sang.

What?

It's been a year. You must have had one.

He looks pleased with himself. It's been the twelfth of January at some point, of course. But time doesn't mean anything here. Her age. The others all seemed older. In the dream they seemed much older. Something was wrong.

Thank you, she says, graciously. *And to you.* She counts through the meetings she remembers: Carolyn, André, Hui, Maja. The social-media guy, what was his name. Something uncomfortable about him, something out of place. And Maja is a snag in her thinking too, a knot she can't undo.

Maja wasn't well. It was just a migraine. The Station treats everything. By now she will have forgotten she was ever in pain. Sleep preserves them. Celeste is as certain of this as she is of her own name. There is an image of the woman standing tall and straight in the corridor, so clear she might as well be right in front of her. Then the lights flicker, and Jun-Sang's expression becomes crisp. It has lost its humour.

How did you sleep? she asks him.

He had a media company, she thinks, or several. Part game, part shopping mall, part virtual escape. Did well out of the catastrophes. He is supposed to look youthful, it's his brand, but his face is strained. That softness only a trick of the light.

I go to the forest, he says. *Ahopsan. It's so pure. Where do you go?*

The question makes no sense. There is nowhere to go, only round and round. She smiles politely, takes a step. It is time to walk the loop, as they must. Exercise and social stimulus. No more than two at a time, no friction. Nothing to get upset about. Lights come on ahead of her, just as they should. They turn off in her wake. Distant things are not visible. Easy to focus on the task. Reduce the universe. Three times around, then she can go back to sleep. Her eyes hurt. She can't remember if this is new. Or the tingling at the back of her neck.

He is taller and his stride quickly catches up to hers. The sound of their slippers in sync, pacing out a gentle rhythm: stuck, unstuck. The gravity still works perfectly.

Who have you seen? She tries to make the words light.

Oh, everyone, he says. *Arvind, André, Calvin, Carolyn, Hui.* He counts them off on one hand before switching to the other. But the second hand is forgetful. *Maja*, he says, and his shoulders fall. His voice is a whisper. *You.*

That isn't everyone, but she decides not to correct him: he is confused, that's all. They both need rest. The Station takes care of them. They walk on, the linen hanging loosely, the slippers stuck, unstuck.

Observation room, he says, pausing at the trapdoor with the two dots in the pill shape. Neither suggests descending. Celeste keeps moving. Her limbs are enjoying the work; she doesn't want to stop. She feels light on her feet, she must weigh very little, her body is changing. *Capsule*, he says, when they step over the arrow. It's really quite annoying, the way he names everything.

The arrow is grey. Three heads of hair down there. Three bodies, encased like batteries. But the trapdoor is closed, and the memory has a static quality, like the memory of a photograph. It must be something she recalls from their training. Jun-Sang grunts, an oddly old-man sound to emanate from the youthful face. He's older than she is, must be, looks it. The skin on his hand is loose. She looks at the arrow, the circle, both dark grey beside the darker oval.

She bends to the sensor, not thinking about it, but Jun-Sang takes her by the wrist and pulls. She is lifted to her feet. The hatch doesn't open. *That one's gone*, she says. She knows it only after she speaks. They seemed so afraid. She couldn't leave her sister. *Happy birthday*, she murmurs.

Come on, he says. *It doesn't matter.*

When she stands, she can feel the bones in her back scraping against each other. She remembers Calvin, the eyes pushed deep into his face. How thin they will look now, Calvin and the other two. Skeletons floating in space. The image is frayed at the edges. She can't see the stars. Jun-Sang is hurrying away, she can hear his ragged breathing, he will want to go back.

I don't want to sleep through it. Hui said that. But that was a dream. He was mistaken. There were never any astronauts.

There was never a bridge, only the blank ceiling. Death is on Earth, well out of reach. There was nothing to lose.

Here you are, Jun-Sang says. She looks. Here is her room, laid out below. Everything just as it was. A soft place, formed to fit her. A refuge.

There is Jude, standing out in the overgrown garden. So happy to see her.

Celeste descends.

34

NOVEMBER

The road widens, forks out into lanes that once held boom gates and checkpoints, then narrows again. Jude brakes at a high mesh fence. Guards stir from the shade on the other side. White buildings behind them, angled cubes like fallen blocks. A tower.

It's almost noon, the shadows concentrated. The guards saunter to attention, one on each side of the gate, cradling automatic weapons in their arms. Cameras on high posts all along the fence. Through its mesh, the road on the other side is well-maintained, freshly resurfaced. Jude reverses the truck, pulls over and sits there, engine still running.

One guard waves the other forward, speaks into a pocket radio. The border has been closed since the war. No-one crosses it, officially, but people find a way. She leaves the key in the ignition, unclips the seatbelt.

'Sol. You drive back.'

Ali reaches across her and switches the engine off. The silence is startling.

'Don't be an idiot,' he says.

'You can't go any further,' Jude says, keeping the shake from her voice. She opens the door, keeps her eyes on the ground. 'Too dangerous.'

Jude hears birdsong as she drops one foot down, then the other.

She glances in the mirror, paused at eye-height, glimpses Tik and Solare watching from the back, looking to Ali for their next move. Can't see Nora from this angle. She steps down, and her friends disappear in a gleam of fender. It's warm out here for nearly winter: the sun is hot on the back of her neck.

'Jude, stop,' Ali says.

He's crawled across to the driver's seat and is looking down at her, hair curtained. She has a sudden shiver of memory: half-drowned, climbing up from cold salt water. A burn of rope in her hands, his hands. Another chance.

She fills her lungs with air. Clear, strong; the taste of leaving. Her friends should be waking to an ordinary day: a shared breakfast, the F-net, conversation. They will go back, and it will all persist for them.

Instead, they are clambering out of the truck, bodies surrounding her.

'Wait,' Jude says. 'I'll go and speak to them first. Not so threatening.' Her voice catches in her throat. They cluster behind her. She hopes the guards will let her in quickly, make this easy, not shoot anybody. She feels about as threatening as a rabbit.

Legs too heavy in her boots. Sweat gathering at her sides in the denim jacket, but the padding steadies her. She makes a quick judgement and approaches the less intimidating-looking soldier. Younger. Black curls sticking out from under her cap, eyes alert, maybe even curious.

'Excuse me,' she says. 'I'm Jude –' and she pauses. Stumbles like a fool on her own name. Which history does she admit, which version? She has been Kite, Shearwater, Starling, none of them real.

The soldier does not wait.

'We know who you are. Come on through.' She nods over at her colleague, who taps a device on his chest. The fence rolls open. The only border now is the gate's track set into the concrete, a nothing she can step right over.

Jude looks back at the truck, at the others clustered there. In a moment she will wave, and the gate will roll closed between them.

'Don't worry – your, ah, friends can come in with you. Park the truck in here. My colleagues will take care of you all.' The older one has a low voice, a soft authority. His hands are open, nowhere near his weapon. He shoos her with them.

Jude walks back to the others, wondering how to make them leave. The four of them are standing shoulder to shoulder; their bodies form a soft wall. They are doing their best.

'We heard,' says Ali.

Nora moves closer, but Jude only shakes her head.

'They were waiting,' she says. 'Something's not right.'

'We'll figure it out,' says Nora.

Jude frowns, glances at the truck. 'It's too dangerous,' she says again.

Ali is rolling his eyes at her. 'You're not getting rid of us now.'

'You have to go back, Ali. This is –'

'This is not your call,' says Solare.

Tik is looking from one to the other.

Jude hears one of the border guards clear their throat.

'We choose,' Sol says.

Jude knows when she has lost.

'We leave the truck on our side,' she says. 'Walk in empty-handed.'

'Good,' says Ali. But he takes hers in his own, and squeezes.

As she steps across the line that divides this country from their own, Jude holds her breath, closes her eyes. When she opens them, nothing has changed. The road is smooth underfoot, the guards are watching. Her friends have flanked her, the shadows behind them slanted and merging. She keeps walking.

The towers loom. She hears the soldiers close the gate behind them, return to their places. There are two more soldiers out the front of the white cube, keeping their distance. Not in uniform like the first two, but a clean, official white. It's all choreographed; the scene has a feeling of déjà-vu. She looks back to see the gate closed behind them, shutting off a world. The truck looks so small parked there with nothing else around. Its little shadow pooled beneath it like an oil spill. Someone will make use of it. Nothing goes to waste long in the Freelands.

Jude turns to face the welcoming committee: well-groomed, serious. More soldiers, unmistakably. Even when they're in good suits, you can tell. She feels Sol stiffen, whether out of habit or mistrust. Glass and steel in ordered lines. Solar panels glinting from the roof. No trace of improvisation: everything efficient, built to order.

Alliance laws, Alliance rules and prejudices. They can throw them in detention, make them disappear.

A tall, broad-chested woman steps forward, the brass buttons on her jacket shining. She nods at each of them, bows her head a little longer before Jude.

'Joy Beckett,' she says, lifting her head and smiling warmly. 'Well, General Beckett, but Joy's fine. I won't shake your hands – health protocol – but please feel very welcome. We have a few quarantine processes to get through this side, and then the Health Minister wants to meet with you in a couple of days.

Until then, I'm your supremely over-qualified babysitter. Ask me anything.' She's fifty-odd, her skin a soft, warm brown, a sweetness in her face. Great teeth. Someone deferent appears beside her, squirts sanitiser into their hands.

'Couple of *days*?' Jude claps her hand to her mouth. What did she imagine, that Celeste would be waiting here, on the border, for rescue?

The others calmly accept the gel, wringing it in their hands. Each of them experienced in borderland patience. Nora puts a hand on her forearm, applies a tender pressure, and Jude inhales and introduces them all, leaving out her own name.

The General listens patiently. She already knows who they are. She introduces her colleague as Nguyen, and points out the entrance to the largest of the buildings. She is still smiling.

'If you'll follow me, we'll get you checked in,' the General says, and she turns for the wide glass doors. Despite her warmth, Joy doesn't suit her at all; it will be hard not to call her General.

The foyer has security scanners, but they walk right in. They follow the General across the marble floor to the lifts, Nguyen bringing up the rear. He's unarmed, but uniformed personnel stand at irregular intervals around the open space, long weapons slung around their shoulders.

Jude, Nora, Ali and Nguyen take one elevator while Tik, Solare and the General wait for the other. The arrangement seems casual, but it's clear they are being escorted. Jude can see a tremor in the young soldier's hand. Nora whispers some observation to Ali, and he makes an amused sound, though his expression is unchanged in the mirrored doors. The elevator moves fast, releases them into a long white corridor. When the other arrives, the General steps out first, wearing a distant, neutral expression that Tik will later describe as 'standby mode'. The warmth in her face reboots quickly.

'Let me show you to your rooms,' she says.

They are on the fourteenth floor. The cube didn't look this high from the outside; maybe it has underground levels. Jude needs to concentrate, be more aware of her surroundings. She used to be so vigilant.

'You're required to stay a minimum twenty-four hours here, for clearance purposes,' the General says, almost apologetic. 'Quarantine protocols, you know. Might be a little longer. Hungry? Thirsty?'

She doesn't give them time to answer.

'A medic will visit with you in the next hour.'

The door closes, and Jude is alone.

It's a shock how new the room is. How perfectly clean. There's a plate of fruit on the counter, including dragon fruit and mangosteen, a single perfect pomegranate. Jude hasn't seen a dragon fruit in years. She reaches for it but stops, thinking of her sister's delicate hands.

For all its polish, the room is small and simple. The bathroom is spotless, the bed perfectly made, the surveillance infrastructure discreetly concealed. She finds cameras in the bedhead, above the mirror, and in the light switch by the door. She nods at whoever's watching, though it's probably just an algorithm. Jude sits on the edge of the bed, falls back and tries to think.

There's another one, beside the light fitting in the ceiling.

After a minute she gets up with a jolt and tries the door, but it isn't locked. She sticks her head out, looks down the corridor. Halfway down, a moment later, Ali does the same thing. She waves when he sees her, then flips the hand palm-up to sign a question. He mirrors the movement. They watch each other for a moment, looking for signs of distress. Then each returns to their own cell.

It isn't a cell. It's a hotel room, like the luxury suites on the ships. Fresh towels by her hand, fresh flowers. She thought she would be banging on the gate, imprisoned. Instead, she's being treated with care.

Except it isn't care: it's theatre. The Alliance wants something.

They already have Celeste. Jude struggles to concentrate, to decode the games of power and control that underly this place. Such things have always confused her. Too much dissembling. The Freelands is frustrating, inefficient, but it's mostly honest.

She thinks of those days driving across the Alliance in the truck with Ali, not knowing what the future held. How her hands gripped the wheel. The pass they gave her. The bed is so soft, but she can't sit still.

She gets up to examine the screen that takes up most of one wall. There's another camera in the top of it, a subtle mark under black glass. That's five. She touches her hand to one side of the screen and it disappears, replaced by a window. The outside world is so bright that she steps back, blinking. The glass responds, dimming itself in increments. The room is reading her, adjusting itself, anticipating her needs.

She looks out over the view of the border station.

The truck is exactly where she left it. The two soldiers at their posts, the road empty. A few official-looking cars are parked on this side, identical white apart from the panels on their roofs and rear trays, glistening in the sun.

Jude puts her face to the glass and looks as far as she can into the Freelands. She can't see the mountains from here. She needs to think about her next move. Find out where they are keeping Celeste. Get there. Negotiate her release.

Nora will know how to talk to them.

She lies on the bed, closes her eyes. Doesn't quite sleep, but is startled when the doorbell rings. At first she's not sure if it's a phone or an alarm; she's not used to locks and buzzers. She gets up and cautiously opens the door. General Beckett, beaming, and a man in white with a small grey box in his hands.

'We'll have a meal brought to you shortly,' the General says. 'How are you finding things? These rooms are *very* spartan, I'm sorry.' She seems anxious to seem anxious to please.

'It's fine,' Jude says, and casts a curious look at the man behind her.

'This is my colleague Dragan,' the General says. 'He's just here to check you're not a health risk. I'm sure everybody's fine, but it's protocol.'

Jude begins to roll up her sleeve, but Dragan shakes his head. 'No need,' he says. He takes a glass tube from his box and waves it at her wrist, then her neck. The tube lights up and he presses it back into its soft nest of foam. On the inside lid of the box, a screen displays a marvel of statistics.

'Okay,' he says.

'That's it?'

'Well, it can't tell me everything,' he says, a little smugly. 'Just the main pathogen types, any imminent risks. You'll be cleared formally tomorrow.' The box snaps closed.

'There you go,' says the General.

Jude watches them head down the corridor. The skin on her wrist cools in the air-conditioned room, but her face is hot with shame. She thinks of the printout in the clinic. She didn't know the Freelands was so far behind.

Celeste will get the care she needs. That's what Nora thinks. They will take the thing out of her head, and she'll get better. For a moment she allows herself to believe it.

35

SEPTEMBER

The eyes flickered, letting out a glimpse of blue.

'I'm still here,' Jude said. She said this every day, and every day it was surprising. Almost three weeks now, and it had slipped away like a dream. Celeste had fleeting moments of lucidity, sometimes several in a day, but it was difficult to know where she was in time or space. Sometimes she seemed to think they were on the Station. At other times, she spoke as though she was still at Sovereign House, and Jude still a child.

She waited to see which version of Celeste she was dealing with.

'Your voice,' Celeste said. Hers was a series of creaks and whispers.

Jude didn't answer. She needed to be vigilant; all versions of Celeste were hazardous.

'You can't get sick,' Celeste declared, and set her mouth in a hard line. 'The tests.'

Nora had said it was best to play along, protect her from the shock of the real. The body was healing astonishingly quickly; the mind would catch up. Nora, Jude had learned, was a terrible optimist.

'You passed already,' Jude answered.

A smile crept into her sister's features, seemed to ripple and fade.

Jude looked up at the instruments, scanned the screens. She had learned how to read some of them: breathing, heartbeat, blood pressure. The body seemed to make more sense each day, while the mind continued to unravel. Jude supposed you had to be an optimist to do this. Nora was in the other room, attending a birth. Standing between life and death all day, acting like it was no big deal.

Celeste's gaze wouldn't settle. Her sight had been affected: Nora had said it might never recover. Sometimes, Jude allowed herself to believe that the confusion was purely visual, that if only she could see what was around her, the evidence, then reality would clear. There were moments she seemed to know Jude, or recognise one of the medics or nurses, but most of the time she was far away.

Jude kept her mask on, just in case.

Celeste turned on her side. Her hair had been rich and lustrous before she left. Now the back of her skull held thin wisps, like a woman twice her age. There was a small scar just above the nape of her neck, a raised white mark. Nora had said it looked like an old injury. They couldn't know what she had been through. What she had put herself through.

Jude reached for the back of her own head. There was a vulnerable valley there, a place where a hand might hold up the head of a newborn to protect its unset skull. She thought of the child coming into being in the other room, barely human, so in need.

Celeste's breathing was slow. It was easier when she was asleep: the body could be tended, cleaned and fed, observed. A vigil kept. Awake, she was out of reach.

When Ramon came in to move her and change her bedding,

Jude helped to lift the body that still weighed so little. She was getting used to touching her sister, but not the lightness of her, a suspension of gravity. Rolling her into position, he caught Jude's eye.

'They come and go,' he said, misunderstanding.

Beeping instruments filled the silence. Ramon moved around the room, checking everything was working, taking notes. Round-the-clock care took all they had. Celeste didn't understand what it was worth. She just took it.

'Close now,' he said cheerily. He meant the birth in the other room, and not the death in this. When Jude didn't answer, he excused himself and left.

Today, like every day for three weeks, she had meant to tell them. It was never the right time.

Ali should know first. If anyone here had a right to her story, it was him. She'd tried to fill in the blanks, some of them anyway, but he was hard to catch: either surrounded by people, or busy with his books, writing or translating. She couldn't do it today: he'd gone to Roana with Solare to check on the others, the folks she'd arrived with. They took the truck again, left her with this. An office chair in a locked ward, a person in fragments. A place where time moved in loops like the wires that fed these machines.

Before Celeste arrived, before the clinic, Jude was sure she had a life here. But it all fell away so quickly. Weighed so little, when she turned it in her hands.

*

When she woke again, Celeste was different. This version opened her eyes quickly, wide with fear.

Salvage

'Where's Jude?' Celeste said. Her expression shifted, changed again like light on water. Beneath these moods there was demand, a jagged constant.

'Still here,' Jude said.

'No, no. They're all gone,' Celeste said, letting her head fall back against the fresh pillow. It was already stained with her saliva.

'Not everyone,' said Jude.

A long silence in which the body went on with its processes, the mechanics whirred. Faintly, a woman could be heard screaming through the walls. Jude waited for sleep to take her back, waited what seemed like a long time. The screams subsided.

Celeste was watching her.

'You left,' she said.

An old ache rose beneath Jude's ribs. She swallowed it down, shifted her weight in the chair.

She had tried, for Nora's sake, but the reality was undeniable: Jude left. That was all she knew how to do. She'd left, walked calmly down to the garage of Sovereign House and driven away, and she kept leaving, city to city, ship to ship, one disaster to another. She would leave this too, break her promises, save herself.

Jude closed the door behind her, quietly removed her mask. It was flimsy, cheap. The fibres were softened from too many washes. A factory somewhere. Useful work.

Voices elsewhere in the clinic. A woman groaning, and Nora's generous laughter.

She crossed to the desk, opened the F. Scrolled through the feed.

Northport was becoming busy again. The summer heat

was fading, and people were starting to come down from the mountains. The Common filled each evening, crews working on the old hotel, trying to finish the apartments before the winter. A group had travelled south to attend the assembly in Portosacre; they got back yesterday, full of news and gossip. Excitement about the capsule seemed to have settled, people had moved on. Locks had quietly disappeared from the shed doors, and the clinic was no longer quarantined. People still kept their distance, though.

She skimmed the assembly updates, flicked across to the list of work requests. A callout for a roadworks crew. A few people were out sick, and they were looking for last-minute replacements. Leaving in less than an hour. Hard work in the open air, the kind of work that cleared your head.

She checked her watch. She could make it if she left quickly. Jude thumbed in her confirmation. She found a square of notepaper, scribbled a short message, then halted. It was pointless to apologise for something and then do it anyway. She crumpled the note and pocketed it as she walked out the sliding doors.

The morning was overcast, but the clouds were moving fast, patches of pale blue appearing over the sea, the water darkly churning. She was halfway to the Common when she stopped. She had left her jacket on the chair outside Celeste's room. She would have to go back.

Inside the clinic, the main desk was unattended. Nora was nowhere to be seen. The newborn was alive, already crying. Someone had picked up her jacket, folded it and placed it on the desk where she would see it.

36

BEFORE

Jude decides to leave when the water begins to come inside her ground-floor flat, making a wide dark curve in the carpet around the sliding doors. But when she steps out into the front yard, she sees the driveway is already under. She has no car, just the second-hand bicycle leaning against the wall outside. She doesn't even own gumboots. The river that was her street would be over the top of them anyway. She stands in the rain, unable to make a decision.

'Hey,' a voice calls. One of the women from the upstairs flats is leaning over the balcony. Two smaller faces peer around her, one just eyes and hat above the sill. 'Didn't you get the alerts? It's gonna get way higher than this.'

She knows the family by sight, though she's never spoken to them. It's a week-to-week rental, and people come and go a lot. Jude's only been here a few months. The landlord comes by on Mondays, but she's not been seen for a couple of weeks; probably she left town when the warnings started.

'Are you all right?'

The rain is soaking Jude, but she stays where she is. Water is already lapping at the soles of her elastic-sided work boots. She imagines they will be heavy if she swims, tug her down below the surface.

She looks up.

'Yeah, I'm all right. Are you?'

The woman's grin has gaps in it. She pushes a fist out, raises the thumb.

'You'll want to come up here out of it,' she says.

Jude glances behind her. A child's plastic suitcase sails down the street, clothing spilling from the unfixed zip. Then a traffic cone. A boarded-up house across the street has a hand's-breadth of fence left showing.

'You got food and water up there?'

'Some,' the woman says.

Jude doesn't move.

'Enough,' the woman adds.

'Okay,' Jude says, and goes inside to gather what she can.

There is not much to eat in her flat. The shop closed a few days ago. She grabs a bulk pack of noodles, a bottle of juice. A can of pineapple she doesn't remember buying. She tries to fill an empty bottle from the tap, but the water's off. Clothes, raincoat, lighter, knife. Jude's had practice, but she's still bad at packing things to save from catastrophe. She leaves a photo-booth strip of herself and a woman named Chris, a brief encounter from a previous existence that must have seemed important at the time. A discount voucher for takeaway pizza. Will she need a can opener? Jude shoves items in a shopping bag, and then another.

The carpet's squelching underfoot by the time she's ready. She makes sure all the power outlets are off, unplugs the kettle. On the kitchen sill there's a small chunk of stone, glinting with mica. She clicks her tongue against her teeth, picks up the stone and pockets it.

Salvage

The rain is coming down hard, as it has on and off for the last three days. She walks along the ramp to the concrete stairwell, keeping close to the wall, then tramps up to the upper balcony. It used to be shared between the four top flats, but they've built a half-wall between each of them, a double row of cinderblocks filled with plants, so she has to put her bags down to climb over. After the first one, she hears the family doing the same from the other side. She hands her bags over to the woman, laughing, and they shake hands through hardy landlord succulents. Jude is wet through, potting mix stuck to her shirt.

'Nikki,' the woman says. 'And this is Damon and Frankie – Frankie, get down! – and Lilah.'

'Jude,' says Jude.

'If it gets real bad we can get up on the roof from here,' she says, showing Jude the ladder on the balcony. The missing teeth give her a bit of a lisp.

'You didn't want to clear out?' Jude asks as she follows the woman into her tiny, chaotic flat.

Nikki gestures at her children. 'Try getting this lot out the door.'

Inside, the children examine Jude. They are assorted sizes, all skinny, and she can't remember which is which. Once they make up their minds about her, they go back to making cubbies out of couch cushions. One of them, possibly Frankie-get-down, climbs up the back of the couch and falls face first into the structure.

'This is fun for them,' Nikki says, and shakes her head. She looks out at the ladder. 'No clue. I used to climb up on the roof all the time when I was a kid. It's safe.' She's trying to convince herself.

'You've lived here a while?'

'It was Mum's place. She died.'

'I'm sorry,' Jude says, but Nikki only shrugs.

'Happens. She was here thirty years and it was never like this. Never.'

'I've only been here a few months,' says Jude.

'Oh.' She sounds disappointed. 'Where are you from?'

'The west,' says Jude.

'My father's from over Ceduna way,' Nikki says, eyes on the children. 'Mum was born in Adelaide, but we're not sure . . .'

'Not sure of what?'

The rain drowns the question. Nikki pulls closed the sliding door.

'I thought it was supposed to be a flippin' drought,' she says.

'Yep.' Jude retrieves a damp stuffed giraffe from the place by the door where the rain's been coming in and hands it over. Nikki props it on the kitchen table. The rain's so thunderous that for a while, there's no point speaking. Even the children fall silent, gazing out of their rebuilt cubby. Jude should have gone back for the bicycle, but it's too late now.

'Have you got a radio?' Nikki asks.

There's been no power for days. Jude's phone went flat last night, but she takes it out and looks at it anyway. She shakes her head.

'Just have to wait it out, then.' Nikki sits at the kitchen table for a moment, taps her fingers on the laminate. Then she's up again, moving round, collecting things. 'We'll get up on that roof, I guess,' she says. 'Wait for a boat or something. SES.'

'Maybe when it eases,' Jude says. But packing and preparing for the next step gives them something to do.

Salvage

The rain stops not long afterwards, but the water keeps rising. It hasn't reached the top storey, but Jude can see the level on the ground-floor flats opposite, and it's halfway up their doors. Her unit will be wrecked. She hadn't liked it much anyway. Hated that carpet. Was already thinking about moving on.

They get the children up first, all good climbers. Jude comes last. The roof's not flat but it's at a gentle angle, easy enough to push themselves along it until they can prop themselves in the space between the row of air conditioners and the solar panels. They make a flat space by shoving bags of clothing in the gaps, couple of blankets. It's safe enough.

A couple of months ago, this town had seemed like a fresh start. She didn't know anyone. The calm of the wide river, its big old trees; birds so loud in the mornings she could stop thinking for long minutes. But even before they started telling people to leave, it was obvious it wasn't going to last.

Of course she could have gone to the evacuation centre with her neighbours. They even knocked on her door and offered her a ride down there, but she told them she was right to walk. Eventually, they ask you for ID in those places.

Nikki's got the youngest child in her lap, a hand in their knotted hair. That ponytail needs redoing. Jude wonders why they've avoided the shelters, but doesn't ask. She's been managing to stay off the grid, mostly. She found the flat through a note in the supermarket. Gets around on that old bicycle, no licence needed. There are more living like this than most people imagine. Up north, they say it's even easier. Though it's not certain how long they'll tolerate freeloaders moving up, looking for a way to disappear.

The sky clears, but the water keeps rising.

'Come away from that edge,' Nikki calls out. The two older children are bored and have shuffled down the slope, stealthily sliding closer to the rim. They slide back up again.

'Your bums are wet,' Nikki observes. The children scowl at her, unashamed.

'I hope it doesn't get in our wardrobe,' says the girl.

'Pet spiders.' Nikki raises an eyebrow.

'Can't be more than this, can there?' Jude asks. The river had seemed so innocuous and gentle, days ago.

'Yeah, well. I thought it peaked this morning.' Nikki's the opposite: dead calm under the busy surface. A bit of shed goes past, opened like a tin. The old pub on the corner, long abandoned, has water up to its boarded-up windows, but the wonky old balconies are inexplicably intact. Houses beyond it stand in the water like islands. The top halves of trees emerging senselessly from the brown. No birds now; Jude wonders where they go.

Nikki sits close. The girl, Lilah, crawls up on the other side of her and perches just close enough to be in her space, the way a cat would. Jude doesn't look at her, but can see she is shivering. Nikki too. It isn't cold: might be fear. Jude pulls a blanket over her legs, and she tucks it round the child's.

'No-one's coming, are they,' Lilah says. She sounds worn out by life. She might be nine or ten.

At that age, they were still sending Jude to school. She'd been allowed to attend a camp on the coast before the accident. A storm came in from the ocean without warning, the wind tearing tents apart, turning the ground into a creek bed around them. They had all taken shelter in the homestead, huddled in fluorescent light, empty stone rooms amplifying voices. Spence drove for three hours to collect her. In the middle of nowhere, wipers thrashing. That feeling of rescue when she slid onto the warm upholstery.

Jude has learned how to do things since then. She can repair a bicycle, build a fire, make a raft, construct shelter, find food and water. She's kept moving, taught herself to be strong.

The girl's bare legs kick the blanket away.

The light is fading. 'No-one's coming,' Nikki confirms.

The child scrambles to her feet, using Jude for support.

'It's going down though. Look,' she says.

Across the way, plastic bags hang from the trees, half a metre above the water line. The pub's sills are visible, covered in brown mud.

The girl's bony hand still clutches her shoulder for balance. Jude has never trusted anyone this much.

'I'm climbing down,' says the other one, Damon. He stays where he is, looking at his mother's face.

'Wait a bit longer,' Nikki says. She leans her head back, sighing.

Jude leans too. There are stars out now, and the first few satellites. She shuts her eyes.

*

They climb down before dawn. The upstairs balcony is a tray of mud, but inside, the floor is dry. Jude pulls her boots off, spreads out the couch cushions, makes a nest of them. The kids settle like puppies, and she lies under the kitchen table, head on one soft corner.

When she wakes, Nikki has a gas camp stove set up on the counter, is making toast in a pan.

'Not your first blackout,' Jude says.

Frankie-get-down yawns in the mess of their kitchen. 'Find the sugar,' Nikki tells him, one leg nudging him in its direction.

Jude steels herself. She's overstayed.

Nikki flips the toast onto a plate.

'Not even my worst.' She smiles. 'You want coffee?'

'If you've got it.'

'How do you take it?'

'Black,' says Jude.

'Well, that's lucky.'

The boy returns with the bag of sugar, tilts it over his toast.

'Use a teaspoon,' his mother says, but he ignores her, folds the bread into his sleepy mouth and crunches crystals.

Nikki hands Jude a mug of strong instant. 'Thanks,' she says. 'It's really kind of you. Sorry if I'm in the way.'

The woman looks at her like she's said something incomprehensible.

'It's what people do,' she says.

They stare at each other over the coffee. There are limits to how much you can expect from strangers.

Jude puts her cup down. 'It didn't wreck your floor.'

'Yeah. I guess we'll manage.'

She pushes back her chair, looks around for her shoes. Will leave the food she came with. Take nothing, owe nothing.

'You can get a relief payment, you know,' Nikki says at the door. 'Or go to the shelter. There'll be help there. There's always charities, and that.'

Jude carries her boots across to the door, flanked by staring children. They'll be relieved when she's out of their way. She grips the frame and pulls her boots on, socks still damp.

'Thanks again,' she says.

'I'll have to go down there myself. They need dry clothes,' she says. 'Real food. There's no shame in it.'

Jude's already hopping over the balcony dividers.

'But you know. Suit yourself,' the woman mutters, and closes the door.

*

The SES shows up in the afternoon. By then the water's subsided so much that they can only reach the end of the driveway in the inflatable. Jude watches Nikki hand the children into the boat through branches, upended planters, a broken mailbox post. Gives it an hour, then walks.

The shelter is in the local hall, a shed beside the old stone church, built on the highest ground available. Jude's never been inside before. There's a woman at the desk who directs her, doesn't ask her name. The hall is full of camp cots, people. Along one wall, boxes of packaged food, a table piled with donated clothes. On the other, a list of people missing, notes with forwarding addresses that are just the names of towns. Jude reads the names. Behind her, Nikki and the kids are getting what they need from the boxes. She pretends she hasn't seen them. When she turns, they're heading out the door. She walks past the women in orange overalls, past the stacked loaves of sliced white bread. There are too many people at the urn, so she takes her tea and biscuit back to the board with the lost.

Elders, siblings, dogs. The sugar in her mouth doesn't feel right. She could be making herself useful.

She steps out into the daylight. The town below smells damp and soiled. More people milling around out here. A grey bird hovers over the grassy hillside, paused in a pocket of air. Jude stands watching, mesmerised.

'That bird's stuck,' she hears a child tell her father.

'It's a kite,' the father says. 'You watch.'

A moment later, the bird drops suddenly to its prey. The movement so precise, so clean and brutal, the lizard or mouse wouldn't have known it was over.

Inside, Jude finds dishes to do, clothes to fold. Stays the day, and then another.

After this, there are other disasters. Other towns to walk through, looking for survivors. Houses to clear of mud and silt, furniture to haul out onto the street and examine for damage, organisations to hassle and wait around for and get sick of. There are bodies, but more often there are survivors. Safe and grateful. Passing cats and dogs out windows, looking hollow-eyed over damp babies, laughing.

You have to find a way to live in it.

She climbs into the empty rooms of people who left before things got worse, left in a hurry, disappeared. There are lists of people who can't be found, who have chosen not to be found. She moves in a stream of them.

People always ask questions eventually, as the catastrophes are sorted out, in the quiet moments between with a cup of tea or a beer in some country town's shed or sports club. How she came to be there, volunteering. Where she's from, who her people are. How long she's planning to stick around. She registers herself under the name Jude Kite, when she has to, but often she doesn't have to. She finds out where they need people next, and goes there.

In every town, there are stories about what's happening up north. She's never paid much attention to politics, but she gathers that the Australian government's in retreat. Trading back the land in pieces. The border has been redrawn: that's why people are moving. There's a lot of talk about sovereignty, about treaties and reparations.

When people are missing, that's where they are said to have gone: up north, shot through. Jude feels the rumours draw her on.

37

SEPTEMBER

The minivan to take them to the worksite was parked up by the Common. Clint, the driver, beamed at her, but she ducked away from his greeting with only a murmur. The van was already half full of people, the humid air thick with chatter. She found an empty place, bundled the jacket on the seat beside her and rested her head against the glass. The sea looked calmer from this distance, but there was bad weather building.

She cracked the window open a few centimetres, put her nose to the cool air. Clint's driving was steady, careful. They passed a stretch of barren country where the mountainside had collapsed into rubble. Celeste had believed the world was dying, that it was too late. But here it was, still taking the damage.

Fry lied to them. In the end he didn't even go. But he hadn't forced Celeste to leave. She made that choice herself.

Jude sat up, blinked at the view, tried to clear her thoughts. The forest was healthier here, the trees thick with shadow. It was not a long drive; soon the work would fill her, tire her.

Clint pulled up at a clearing where the road ran alongside a narrow waterway. Summer rains had been heavy, and it was easy to see what had happened: the swollen creek had collapsed part of the retaining wall, taking a section of road down with it.

They got out of the van and stretched and got to work.

The task was demanding, but not complicated. Jude lifted heavy stones, moved them into a form that would hold back the river. Solving the puzzle of their erratic shapes gave her satisfaction.

When that was done, there was gravel to shovel into the gaps in the old road, a pile of sand to rake. Most of the party paused to rest, but Jude kept on. She wanted to wear herself out against the rock. The Freelands wasn't like the ships she'd been on, it wasn't polite to work yourself to exhaustion, but she didn't care. She hadn't felt so capable in weeks. She lifted a shovel, pushed it hard into the gravel, felt the satisfying give of broken stone. Let people look at her however they wanted. She needed to make herself useful, to swim the body out past thinking.

She swept and tamped the ground, tidied the edges. A discussion had been going back and forth about whether the whole stretch would need to be resealed, and a barrel of sealant was carried out and warmed. Old tyres and recycled plastics: it wasn't perfect, but it was what they had. With plenty of hands, the job went quickly.

Now and then, Nora's expression rose to the surface of Jude's mind, sometimes gently mocking, sometimes disappointed. She would not be sorry that Jude was gone. Relieved, more likely. Anyone could sit in that chair, do a better job. She wanted someone reliable. A new medic was supposed to arrive from Portosacre: Jude could extract herself then. And why should she care what Nora thought? They were practically strangers.

There was a house in the mountains, past the Fort, not far from here. She'd stayed there with Gloria once, on her own a few times, more often with Ali. It was isolated, an hour's walk from the road's end, and it was in some disrepair; they'd fixed the roof, cleaned out the chimney, but there was still a lot of work to do. She'd thought once that she might restore it. Gather stone and tin and timber. She could go there tonight, get away for a while, get her head straight.

Stopping, she felt how cool the air was, the season shifting. Half the trees on the slope beside her were dead or dying, but new saplings stretched up between them. She climbed into the van for her jacket, stuffed between the seats, a bundle that had lost its neat folds.

Jude sat, drank water, felt her shoulder muscles harden. The others were standing around outside, talking and laughing. The day's work already done. The river would keep its course, at least until another wave of damage came along. Most work was like this: maintenance, not making.

From inside the van she could hear the bells of cattle returning to their places, the chatter of roosting birds. It would soon be dark. The walk to the little house would be dangerous without a torch, and there would be nothing to eat when she got there. She had not checked the F to see that it was empty.

Jude yawned, waited for the others. She thought of the little bed in the room back at the Common, the room that was not really hers. Thought of Nora's steady observation. She rested her head against the glass, was asleep before Clint started the engine.

*

'Why should we help her? She chose to go.'

Jude was awake. Trees flashed past in the headlights, the road twisting. They hadn't travelled far. She'd only been asleep ten minutes, but the group's mood had shifted.

'They got what they deserved,' said someone up the front.

'That doesn't matter. If you can help, you must,' said a man behind her.

'But we don't have the resources. My brother needed the clinic yesterday, and they could only give him fifteen minutes.'

'They think she's more important. Worth something.'

'You know they're watching, don't you.'

Jude tensed, waited. They, they. But no-one explained.

'Well, we'll see what the new medic says.'

'For what that's worth.'

Jude straightened up in her seat, and the talk stopped quickly. Faces turned away in the dark. After a silence, the conversation began again, but it was only small talk: the meal that night, the state of the hotel repairs, the weather. She wrapped her jacket tightly, pushed the window closed.

The man behind her was right: the Freelands was supposed to welcome anyone in need, no matter where they came from. That was Nora's attitude. But the only people who had fetched up here had nothing and no-one, had nowhere else to go. It was easy to help people like that. When a billionaire fell to earth, who should take care of them?

Celeste might have done anything with her inheritance. She might have built a hospital. Brought water to cities cut off by storms and war. Given it back to the traditional owners. Instead she had spent every last cent to escape. To make herself safe. And now she was taking from people who had less than nothing.

They would send her away. Jude with her, if they knew. She'd never had a right to this place to begin with.

38

BEFORE

Hitching a ride north up the highway, she watches all the traffic going the other direction. A row of army trucks, the covered trays with personnel inside, and then a tank on the back of a transport, the dark green camouflage absurd against the pale red ground behind. The first driver who stops doesn't ask her any questions. He's only going as far as the border, to drop off supplies. Another company takes over on the other side; they might give her a lift, or they might not.

'It's haywire up there,' he says. 'A free-for-all.'

'Huh,' says Jude. They are wearing matching shirts, blue check. Seems that's enough to make him comfortable.

'Fuel stop,' is the next thing he says, an hour later. When they pull up at the roadhouse, she follows him in, needing to piss. There's a key; she has to wait in line for it, and he stands behind her, watching the screen above the counter play a slideshow of missing people.

'You're not on there, are ya?' he asks, his breath stale.

She shakes her head. There are whole families on the list. Unaccompanied children. A few men look rough, like wanted criminals. But the vast majority are women on their own.

'I didn't know there were so many,' Jude says.

'Oh, most of 'em are just up north somewhere,' the cashier

says; she obviously has this conversation several times a day. 'We get all sorts in here. I tell the department, I tell the families, we can't keep track of them. We're not the police.'

She leans in. 'Not that the police are doing anything much about it.'

The boss comes in from the back room, carrying an archive box. 'That's the last of it,' he says, and with a cursory wave walks out, pointing his keys at a new-looking SUV, huge caravan on the back. He cuts out in a trail of dust, heading south. Two emus stand at the front of their enclosure watching, sleepy in the heat.

The cashier sighs. 'You can't blame 'em, can you.' It isn't clear if she means the boss or the missing people, or maybe the emus. By the time Jude gets back from the toilet, the truck driver has left without her.

She stands in the shade of the roadhouse sign for an hour, watching vehicles turn in and pull out. Most are heading south, but a few go the other direction. Full cars that look lived in, pillows jammed against the rear windscreen, no room for a guest; she doesn't bother asking. Across the road, the horizon dips and shimmers. She must be close to the launch site, though here, in the centre of the country, close is still a long way.

A few black kites dip and reel in the afternoon sky, their voices piercing. Jude watches, wants that soaring. The longer she stands there, though, the more she feels like the prey in the grass.

Just as dusk is beginning to colour the sky, Jude gets a ride. A woman with two kids in the back, faces glued to their screens. The kids seem excited, the woman nervous. She half-whispers hello. They reach the new border before dark. There's a checkpoint, but no fence, just a temporary marquee. A couple of guys sitting in the glow of an LED beneath it, insects swarming round. They wave them through without speaking.

The woman breathes out. Winds down the window.

'Here we go, kids!' she calls out. 'Home!' She gives the desert a wave, the highway behind her the finger. Then she winds the window up, relaxes back into her quiet. The teenagers smirk, but not without affection.

'Where you from, anyway?' she asks, an hour later.

Ordinarily, Jude would be evasive. *Out west*, she'd say, or *All over*. But something about this woman, crossing the new border together, makes her want to say the name.

'Endurance,' Jude answers. She reaches into her pocket, feels for the stone. Solid and real.

'Never heard of it,' the woman says.

*

Despite the flow of cars moving south, there seem to be twice as many people arriving in Darwin as leaving it. Everyone she speaks to has just got there. Jude spends a week in a city hostel in exchange for cleaning work, then a friend of the manager tells her about a job out of town that 'might be more your style', and she takes the hint.

She catches a bus to a small town outside the city that she's learning not to call by its old name. Half the signs are already changed to Larrakia. The town is dominated by huge fig trees in a small park that is always dark and damp, even in the brightest part of the day. The water looks peaceful but it can be deadly. There's always something here trying to kill you: crocs, jellyfish. Most people swim in it anyway.

The family that runs the caravan park welcome her without

asking for ID. Maybe that's what the hostel owner's friend meant when he said that this job would suit her. Maybe her disappearance, her membership of the lost, is obvious to everyone.

Two days in, she decides it's nothing like that. It's just the quiet of it. The chitter of bats in the park opposite, the gentle wash of the sea.

*

Hope shows up a few weeks after Jude, with a bruise the size and colour of a passionfruit on her upper arm, her face unblemished but nervous. She rents one of the sites that used to belong to the old permanents, most of whom left in the land handover.

Hope tells her most of the traffic coming across from Queensland was headed back east. She says it's lucky her car, a station wagon older than she is, made the journey.

'Overheating.' Hope fans herself with an old map.

Jude signs her in and fixes her radiator. For three days they smile at each other on the gravel pathways. On her third night, Hope comes to the caretaker's hut with a plastic container of biscuits, sits herself on the top step of the deck, and pats the empty place beside her.

'I don't bite,' she says.

Jude wanders over, stands beside her, not too close. The sky is hazy from fires; she can't see the stars.

'Made these for my kids, but I won't get to see them yet,' she says, clicking the lid off. 'Might as well, eh?'

And just like that, Jude falls for her.

*

It's easy for Jude to say she's from down south and wave a hand. People here are used to gesturing at the past like it's a pile of unwashed dishes. But for the first time in years, she feels like she *might* talk. Hope talks like talk will do some good.

Jude mentions Endurance once, just as a story, not her own, but the Prospect River disaster has faded from popular memory. There are a thousand stories like it, even just in this caravan park.

Hope tells her about stealing baby clothes from the op shop. Her kids, six and three, are at her sister's in Ipswich. She thinks they're safe enough, but she wants to get them over. Lots of women fleeing for a chance at safety, but the rules are vague. Police do nothing, or they do their worst. She left the ex-husband, his violence, thinking she could get a place, but there was no housing after the cyclone. The department won't let her take the kids over the border, not yet.

'Because it's overseas,' she says. 'Even though it isn't.'

'Out of the country now,' Jude says.

Every week Hope is on the phone to the lawyer, and almost every day she speaks with the children on screen. Jude lets her use the office wi-fi, even though she's supposed to charge a fee. The wi-fi is better near her unit, so Hope comes over every evening.

Hope isn't much older than she is, a couple of years, but it feels like more. She checks in on the elders in the caravan park, gets supplies for residents without transport. Jude wants to look after her, but knows she's clumsy at it. She listens, cooks. Makes sure Hope gets her sleep, some nights. Sometimes they wake, watching each other in the dark, and it's as if the universe shrinks itself around them, everything else – planets, trees, bats – just decoration.

In that dark embrace, in the dense foliage, Jude can pretend the launch isn't happening. People here are building a new world of their own, rich in other ways. They're not giving up on it. They're looking for their place in it, a way to live.

For a while, Jude thinks she can be one of them.

She skips the residents' meetings at the holiday park, even though it's part of her job to go. She skips the card games and pot lucks. So she doesn't hear the way they talk about the Endeavour. It's been on the news, the launch date approaching at last.

The residents decide to throw a party. Wave the rocket off. There will be a barbecue, and dress-ups for the kids. The launch is funny to them, and also perhaps awe-inspiring, that people would do it. Go all that way. When you could stay and find out.

There are paper astronauts on the laundry windows. A string of moons hangs from the carob tree out front. A kind of festival, a magic to it. The Endeavour still speaks to some human dream. At the very least, it's a distraction.

When Hope says they have to watch it – the kids will kill her if she doesn't – Jude reluctantly agrees. But she doesn't want to be at a party. Her neighbours will let off fireworks and drink wine in deckchairs, watching the sky. She can't sit with them and pretend, go through the motions of enjoying the spectacle or laughing at the folly of it. So she convinces Hope that it will be romantic to walk up the hill behind the park, and watch from there.

She just wants it to be done. When her sister's gone, she'll be able to start over.

39

STATION

Celeste opens her eyes, then closes them. Her head hurts. Light hurts. She thinks she might have fallen. She forces herself to look, to focus. There is a single, huge eye floating above her head. A circle inside a circle. The pattern is fuzzy, a form that refuses to resolve. Then it goes dark.

She is in her room. The house is quiet, a giant asleep, a ruined city. Jude has gone. She took a car. Celeste only has to wait. She will come back: she has to. She already has, because Jude is here, on the Station. Her voice is here. This is real. She blinks awake.

The circle is the hatch at the top of the ladder. The hatch is open. The back of her head aches, the soft place where the skull joins the neck. She feels dizzy when she lifts it. Must have climbed up there and fallen. The mask has already retracted, the instruments folded away. She moves carefully, lets her mind catch up as she goes. It takes time to clamber up the rungs, to push her head from the hole, to look along the corridor to either side. It is hard to see. The air is like fog or smoke. It feels different. Smells different.

The gravity is stronger, or her muscles have weakened. Neither possibility is real. When she pushes her feet into the slippers, they stick. Her legs feel numb; she can walk only with one hand against the wall beside her. The corridor is dim. The curve is unsettling, her brain still expecting flatness after all this time. How much time? Eight days, nine? After a few steps, she pushes the slippers off and slides along barefoot. Feels easier. Half walking, half dragging herself along the scratchy surface. Unstuck.

The Station is changed. Each time she wakes, she is different. Remembers differently. Needs to remember with, to be known, it is work. But the Station helps. Her sister is here somewhere. One of these rooms. Has to be close.

Now a hole in the floor ahead. Dark circle, open. She falls to her knees beside it, leans over. No light inside. The light from the corridor gives a dim impression: a room like her own. The bed is empty, its upholstery sprung back, stretched new. The mask in the wall, a dim beetle-gleam, waiting. No-one in the corridor. Has she turned by accident, returned to her own empty place? No, there are her slippers in the hall behind her, there is the hole from which she emerged, she has only come a little way.

The headache makes her think slowly, makes her queasy. Jude was always carsick. She has to wait before she can stand. She has to wait. How much time is left? There are no days, no nights, no months here. Time is something the machines keep track of. She doesn't need to know. She should go back to her room.

She crawls along the floor to the next hatch. Seems to take forever. When she gets there, she is sweating. The hatch is closed and the circle beside it is a dull grey. Celeste puts her hand against the sensor, her palm, her thumb. It doesn't react. A ghost haunting the corridor. She sits a while, concentrating on the sound of her breathing until she is sure she is alive. She crawls on. The breaths are not deep enough. The next hatch further than the last, and further. They are all the same distance apart. Twelve marks on a clock. An hour away, a year. *Happy birthday.*

This hatch is open, this hole as dark as the last. The same empty hollow, like an abandoned chrysalis. She puts her head down, expecting the pattern to repeat. Here is the pale shape of the bed, the mask put away. But inside that paleness there is a darker shape. It is a body, curled on its side.

Celeste climbs down. She is dizzy, but she needs to see. There is no odour. The instruments are not attached, they have retracted, their work is done. There is no room for her except on the bed, beside the body. It is curled and small. It is mostly skeleton. Up close, it seems to have deflated: the bones are prominent, the skin stretched. There is hair, still life-coloured, long and blonde. She takes it between her fingertips. Not Jude.

Celeste breathes out. She reaches for the ladder. Maja is dead, she remembers this, they told her, she knew, that's why it is not a shock. The solid Swede, she seemed the healthiest of them, she seemed the most alive. A headache, a few days ago, however many meaningless months ago, or mummifying years.

Is that all it takes?

Celeste has a headache. She has always had a headache. She pulls herself up the ladder. Her hands are leaden, clumsy. Some of them will not be strong enough. He warned her.

Jude is here somewhere. She must be asleep. Celeste would know if she was gone. She would feel it in her bones. Her bones are brittle. She will crawl the whole circle, open every door. Wake whoever she can wake, whoever is left. She will begin in a moment. She will gather her strength.

They are eating together at the huge table. Her small, hopeful, earnest face. This is all she has. *I promise you*, she says. But who is promising? Who refuses? The garden so overgrown, the fires. They have not spoken in days. The house gathers memory, sucks at its prey. Jude is her evidence, her sustenance. She must live.

It's cold. She can't remember being aware of cold before. But that doesn't mean anything. Memory is changeable: it adapts. The Station is the same. There is the hatch with the grey circle, closed and unresponsive. Here is the corridor. She will not look down; she will go on. The next room is closed. The next is empty. Ahead, the hatch to the cupola is already open. Jude will be waiting there for her. She must keep moving.

When she climbs down, there's no-one else there. Only her body and the stars in the bowl at her feet. It isn't a bowl but an eye. It isn't an eye but a navel. She is in a womb, looking out, waiting to be born. Her feet are purple with cold. That's not right. She feels sick, puts her hands down, lowers her body, curls on her side. Can't feel much. The press of linen into bone.

The Station preserves them. It is still spinning. It will hold. The stars are turning. She waits there, curled against the rim of the universe, but Jude does not come. No ruined Earth passes below her eye. No cool Moon appears.

She is in the car on the way to the launch. Last one. Spence driving. When they arrive, he will be let go, walk free. The country is on fire, drowning, split across the middle, there is war everywhere. No-one knows how much longer any of it will last. She can't see Jude in the mirror. Jude always lies down in the car to watch the stars, to settle the sickness in her stomach. Celeste won't turn to look at her. It is enough to know that she is there.

The cold wakes her. Her teeth have been chattering; her jaw feels bruised. She climbs the rungs with frozen hands. Her skin is loose. She pulls herself out of the hole, then lies on her back in the corridor, exhausted. The lights twinkle and go dim. There are others: there must be others. When the lights grow steady, she rolls onto her stomach and begins to crawl.

They are there for months, preparing. Getting the interface put in. The mesh. The way the Station reads them, keeps them safe. No pain. Torpor will suspend them. They will wake up unchanged and ageless, healed and ready. While the world. While the world goes dark below, they will be saved.

She is still crawling when she wakes. Sweat in the corners of her eyes. Two dull shapes on the floor ahead. It takes an age to reach them, but at last her hand makes contact. The soft fur of an animal, the warmth of life in the dark.

Synthetic. The slippers. The open hatch. The room below must be her own.

Jude will be waiting.

40

SEPTEMBER

Jude pushed her way through the gathering crowd in the hall, joined the people at the front stacking chairs and lifting them, passing the stacks into waiting hands.

There were eight or nine musicians on stage; two sets of keyboards, a trumpet, and a complicated percussion setup, mostly old PVC pipes. When the person in the jumpsuit moved one end of it, Jude heard the familiar tones of mountain cowbells.

'We picked them up at the Fort,' Solare said, appearing beside her. She looked pleased with herself. 'I hope you don't mind,' she added.

How quickly she had become a Freelander.

'Of course I don't mind,' Jude said, careful to keep her voice light.

'Alosh wants to move up there,' she said. Solare had more or less adopted the pair of teenagers that had arrived soon after Celeste. The boy's leg was healing quickly; he was getting round with crutches now. The other one was standing by the door, watchful, their injuries interior. Solare followed her gaze. 'I don't think Tik will go. Too isolated.'

Tik saw them, gave an anxious wave. Jude raised a hand and let it fall as Nora appeared in the doorway, laughing with Ramon at some private joke. She had changed into black pants and a grey-green shirt that hung loosely from her shoulders. Her glasses were pushed up on her forehead, pressing the spiked hair askew.

Jude steeled herself, but Nora smiled as she approached them. 'So good about the Fort,' she said to Solare. 'Alosh will love it up there.' Jude tuned out, looked past her at the exit. It should be easy to make an excuse, to slip away.

'Jude?' The others were staring at her.

'How was your work crew?' Nora asked, a little tersely.

'Fine. Tiring,' Jude said. There was a black mark on the floor beside her boots. She scraped one toe against the boards and made another. 'I guess I needed a break.' She tried to rub the mark away, made it worse.

'You must be exhausted,' Nora said. 'Your hours are way over.'

In the eyes, there was that gentle mockery. Jude hadn't been logging the clinic time on the F. She didn't think Nora would notice, but then, not much got past her. The medic held her gaze, her expression hard to read.

After a moment, Solare squeezed Jude's wrist and left. Jude leaned back against the wall, the silence growing awkward.

'Hard to believe they just got here, isn't it?' Nora said. She was watching Solare and Tik, the older woman showing the kid something on stage. 'Thick as thieves.'

She was standing close, their shirtsleeves touching. Jude had to summon courage sometime.

'Sorry about today.' Her voice was low. For a minute it was as though Nora hadn't heard her, then she moved to face her, leaning against the wall.

'Don't be,' she said. 'It's a lot for anyone.'

She sounded tired. She'd attended that birth half the night, had probably been at the clinic since.

Nora cleared her throat. 'I never really asked you. I just

wanted – I was being selfish,' she said. The warmth of the crowd had flushed her skin. 'I should be the one to apologise,' she said.

'Please don't,' was all Jude managed.

There was another long minute. On stage, one keyboard tinkled, then the other blared like a ship's horn.

'How was she today?' Jude asked.

'No change,' Nora said. The stage lights playing in her hair. She seemed relieved that the conversation had turned to work. 'She asked where you were. I think she likes having you around.'

Jude could not tell her. Not yet, not here. The look of horror in her sister's face.

'I'm getting a beer,' she said, and pushed away from the wall. The crowd parted around her.

*

When she came back with two bottles, Ramon had taken her place. He shuffled over, making space beside Nora. She refused the drink with a wave, but he took it gratefully.

'Who's at the clinic?' Jude asked. Nora and Ramon exchanged a look.

'We got some extra help today.' Ramon was watching the stage, where the band were still tinkering. 'There's a new medic up from Portosacre.'

'I heard,' said Jude.

Nora's eyes were lowered. The music started up in earnest, and conversation vanished. There was no cause to be uneasy. They needed help, skilled help. Were probably just tired.

It was stuffy in the room, too crowded. Jude separated herself, stood by the door where the outside air could reach her. Nora appeared beside her for a while, moved away again, circled back. It was too noisy to speak.

The band were leaving the stage now, the singer attempting to dismiss complaints about their finishing good-humouredly. Ali was talking with the long-legged bass player. Jude watched him flop an arm around a shoulder, laugh, so easy.

'Before,' said Jude.

Nora touched her wrist, and the whole room paused.

'I meant to say,' she began. Then Ramon, an apologetic look on his face, called her over. Nora was needed.

The scene suddenly felt distant, colourless. Jude went to find more chairs to stack.

41

BEFORE

Jude watches the launch from the bonnet of a rusty sedan, abandoned halfway up a small hill not far from the caravan park. A few weeks ago, she and Hope decided to keep a blanket in an old suitcase in the front seat. Jude spreads the blanket out over the bonnet to cover the rust. She circles the vehicle, clearing its spiderwebs. No engine, no back wheels, but it has a good view of the stars. They can see a long way south, sitting up away from the three-corner jacks and dust.

Not to mention the snakes. Hope has a thing about snakes, a kind of nervous obsession. Jude has a similar thing about Hope, just as unreasonable and just as hard to shake. It could be love, but no-one's said the word. The moment hasn't been right. Jude likes being around her, though. Hope cares about the world, about her kids. Hope gives a shit about things, including Jude.

It's still light when they climb up. Jude's brought a flask of gin, a bag of chips. They sit and watch the light change, the smoke from fires in the surrounding country turning gold, then crimson. It cools a bit when the sun goes, but the bonnet stays warm. The moon's a sliver. Stars appearing one by one, like they're shy.

'Venus,' Hope says to the first and clearest. She was teaching her eldest the constellations when she had to leave.

They open the gin too early, and Jude drinks too fast. She's glad of Hope's company, but neither one is fully present. Hope's with her kids, and Jude's with everything she hasn't told her.

She remembers watching the International Space Station go over the compound when she was a child. Celeste walked out into the grounds with her, switched off all the lights. It appeared just where it was supposed to, at the right angle, a few seconds late. They lay on their backs and watched it sail overhead. A little star with people in it. Something they shared. Before the accident, when there was still order in the world.

Jude liked the idea that you could cut yourself off like that, from everything you depended on, from the air. Turn loops out there, and look down, and know that you were coming home again.

And then the ISS was decommissioned, sold off in pieces. Private interests stepped in. Now there are so many satellites in the sky, more moving lights than stars. Half of it's space junk.

Hope still finds the stars romantic. Loves the thought that there is something beyond her own little life, beyond the fragile bubble of the Earth's breath. Puts things in perspective, she says.

After so many false starts, so many test launches, Jude thinks she'll feel relief when it's over. Even if it blows up on the way out, she will be free. They will be free of each other. Life can begin: a life she's chosen.

At half-past nine, a notification on her watch startles her, even though she set it herself. No clouds, but the southern horizon carries a smoky haze, the stars brittle and motionless overhead. She's a little drunk. Can't see much.

'You okay?' Hope leans her head against her arm. Jude feels her muscle tense beneath the weight, and touches Hope's hair.

'It's nothing,' she says.

They sit and wait, close and distant.

Maybe it's the haze, and maybe they're too far away, but for whatever reason, they don't see it. Hope falls asleep. Jude's vision blurs. The sky taunts her with an archive of dead stars, old launches, junk. So many specks out there, like insects lit up by a campfire.

She gets her phone out with her free hand, looks for footage on the cracked screen. The livestream was subscriber-only, but the replay is everywhere. She can tell from the tone of the posts that it's been a success. No slow-motion explosions this time. There is the countdown, a silver line in the air, and the commentary falls silent. They have gone.

She flicks back.

Footage of the pods loaded onto the rocket. A nest of eyes set into the head. The footage blurs and skips, reception is poor here, but Jude knows what is happening. At the edge of the atmosphere, they jettison the engines that got them that far. Most of the weight is the fuel they need to get out of the air. Earth's atmosphere doesn't want them to leave, but they do, passing the Kármán line, the beginning of space, a hundred kilometres out. Escape velocity. It will take a few days to get to their Lagrange point, where the arm of the Station will reach out and pluck them from their trajectory, carry them into its mouth.

She goes back to the start, to the faces.

There are eight of them now. There were supposed to be twelve. Two pulled out, changed their minds about it. One overdosed. And Nick Fry.

All his idea, his dream, but he isn't with them. Last year they found something wrong with his heart. All that money, and some quirk of the body could drop him in an instant. He was far too important to risk.

And then there's Jude. She should be out there, on her way. Instead she's here, lying on a car bonnet on a hill in the dirt and weeds, the heat of the Earth against her back, the weight of another human being against her arm. The weight of her betrayal.

She swallows gin, scrunches her face against its sharpness.

When she plays the next part of the footage, there is a close-up, and a familiar flash: Celeste's wide grin, her face fresh and happy. No trace of grief, regret, no sadness about what she's leaving behind. Only that pure excitement.

The flask is empty. Jude's teeth ache. The video cuts again to the rocket, a minute before lift-off. White vapour pours out of it like smoke from a burning building. She's seen this part already, but she watches it again, lets repetition strip the air from her. The images already stale, nostalgic.

The smoke is in Jude's lungs. She wants to touch the rocket, burn her hand against its heat. Wants to be the one to set the fire, to kick it into the sky. Instead she scrolls back again, lets it repeat on the screen. Celeste's head is fitted into a tiny enclosure, her body strapped into its narrow nest. So vulnerable, and so complete.

She mutes the ads: fried chicken, fireproof bunkers, disaster insurance, holiday ships. Millions, maybe a billion people are watching. Few can afford these offers of escape. She shuts it down.

Hope doesn't wake. Jude's arm has gone numb. The gin has balled to a tight knot in her stomach. She can still see it: Celeste in her bundle, the rocket ascending. Jude waits for the relief to hit.

'That's that,' she says, trying to force it. But Jude is no lighter without her sister. She feels heavier, too heavy for the car bonnet. She wants to reach down and put her fingers in the dirt. Sink into the soil, disappear.

Hope stirs, and Jude takes the chance to slip the other woman's weight from her shoulder.

'I fell asleep,' Hope says, sitting up. She looks up at the sky, scanning for a marvel. 'Did I miss it?'

Jude's already slipping from the rusted wreck. She's on her knees, hands in the sand and stones. She wants to press her face into the dust, to lie against the rock and roots and grasses, to pour herself into the dear crushed bones of the world and dissolve.

It is no different.

She puts her head down, but it won't stop. The face wrapped in padding. The way the part pulled away and fell against the edge of atmosphere. The cluster sailing towards the Station. It waits for them, arms folded above the sky. It will reach out, devour them. She is so heavy.

Jude turns her head and retches. The contents of her stomach are mostly gin. The acid burns her mouth. When she lifts herself up, first on all fours and then kneeling, the stars above are spinning; the satellites among them carve unsteady courses through the darkness. There is no way of knowing which speck is her sister. Which points are suns and which are machinery.

Somewhere up there, eight people are flying. They will unbuckle their harnesses, open silver-foil packets of gel flavoured with the good champagne. Laugh as it escapes their mouths. They will not spare a thought for what they are leaving: they are ascending, beyond human limitation.

Hope is beside her, a hand on her back. Jude rests her head against her lover's thigh.

'Sorry,' she says. 'Something I ate.'

'You've eaten nothing all day,' Hope says. 'Here.' She passes her a bottle of water.

Jude drinks steadily, her eyes cast down. She has never been so thirsty. Hope's shadow in the dim bit of moon and her own, conjoined a moment. She knows she has spoiled this, that it will not last. The tracks of a lizard planted in a line between two tree roots, the glitter in the stones. Jude loves this woman. Her kindness is profound and impersonal. She does not know the first thing about Jude.

'Finish it,' she says, and passes back the bottle, struggling unaided to her feet.

42

SEPTEMBER

Jude was so tired that she barely noticed Nora's knock at the door to her room. The medic perched on the bed and watched while she kicked off her boots and moved around, vaguely tidying. Eventually, Jude ran out of tasks. When she turned, she was surprised by Nora's vulnerable expression.

Nora pushed her hair back with a hand, then left the hand there for longer than she needed to, as if it might order her thoughts.

'Jude,' she said, and let the hand move to her side.

'Nora.' Jude couldn't stop a smile forming, but she quashed it. There was a long quiet, Nora squeezing the edge of the blanket. Jude picked at a splinter in her thumb.

'How are you?' A little of the professional composure had returned, but Nora's voice was softer than usual.

'I'm fine. You don't need to doctor me.' She meant it to sound casual, but it must have come across as defensive; Nora flinched very slightly, addressed her next words to the door.

'I'm asking as a friend.'

The tenderness surprised Jude. She sank onto the bed beside the medic.

'Actually, I'm fucking tired,' she said.

They were sitting a small distance apart, but the mattress

tilted them closer. Nora had to steady herself, one hand between them.

'Me too,' she said.

'That's my fault.' Jude should not have left that morning without a word. She waited for anger, but Nora only looked at her in surprise.

'No, it isn't. We're dealing with a complex problem, completely unprecedented, and we don't have the people, we don't have the equipment. The new medic is supposed to help, but –'

Jude found that she had closed her eyes. When Nora stopped speaking, she opened them. Old pain in her expression, but she blinked and it was gone, back below the surface like a fish. Something plain and open in its place.

'Do you want to talk about this now?'

Jude shook her head. She was acutely aware of the warmth of this body beside her own, of the hand pressed into the bed between them. Jude opened her mouth to speak, and the hand moved, and whatever words she'd thought to say were lost.

*

Jude woke stiffly. Looked at the ceiling, the door, then the body beside her own. Nora was facing the other way. Jude watched her breathing, her back move very slightly, the curve of a hip beneath the sheet. There was a tattoo of a wren on one shoulder blade, life-size, its single ink eye direct.

They had both been tired, too tired to think clearly. The medic would realise this when she woke, so the polite thing to do would be to go before the awkwardness had a chance to descend. Give her an easy way out, time to gather herself. Jude sat up as slowly as she could, dressed silently, carried her boots out in one hand.

She padded down the hallway, pulled her boots on at the top of the stairs. She found her way to the kitchen, exchanging basic greetings, feeling the press of community expectation all around her. By the time she extracted a cup of coffee, Freddie was rounding everyone up for a meeting. Nora would no doubt attend; Solare was already there, looking serious, and Tik with her. Jude took one look at them all and walked away.

*

The sun stretched along the coastline like a cat. A luxury of colour, this time of year. Jude walked slowly, drawing at the sea air for sustenance. It was gentle today, a muddy shade of blue, the little waves almost conversational.

Things could not go on as they had. Probably they should not go on at all. A friend, Nora had said. They hardly knew each other. It was all a mistake, a moment's weakness. Jude needed to think. It was hard to concentrate out here, the light distracting, the restless dance of the sea.

There were three strangers at the desk when she entered the clinic. A tall man, grey-haired, was examining her through thin-rimmed glasses. The new medic. Seated with him were two nurses she didn't know, one dark and friendly, the other fair and suspicious.

'You're Jude,' the tall man said. His tone was curt.

Jude nodded. All those years working in kitchens had taught her not to buy into other people's bullshit. She didn't hold out a hand: didn't want to give him an opportunity to slight her.

'And who are you?'

'We're from the hospital in Portosacre,' he said. 'We're here to help.'

She waited for a name, but it didn't appear. The darker nurse, his long hair piled into a high bun, gave her a sympathetic look. Jude peered past them, but from this angle all she could see was glass and machines.

'How is she?'

'Awake,' said the nurse. 'Lucid, but . . .' He looked up at the medic.

'This place is clearly inadequate for her needs,' said the tall man.

Jude shot him an irritated look. 'She's been doing well,' she said. 'Improving.'

The man's lip curled. 'The neural mesh alone is well beyond your capabilities,' he said.

'The what?' Jude's face was hot. She wished Nora was here, and then was glad she wasn't.

'The device in her brain,' the nurse said. 'We're pretty sure it's some kind of interface.' He moved a hand to the back of his own neck, fingers spidered, and turned the wrist.

Jude screwed up her face. 'Nora would have said something.'

'Nora didn't know,' the new medic said. 'In Portosacre, we are more familiar with this technique. Though it isn't something we would ever *use*.' He looked around with an air of distaste.

'Whatever it is, we're dealing with it,' Jude said. 'I'm going in.' She moved calmly, careful not to let her fury show, though it felt like mice were running laps around the inside of her skull. Her hands shook as she donned the mask, and she wiped them against her jeans. She pushed the door open, stepped inside, and was surprised to feel, on seeing Celeste, a kind of relief. The routine of coming here had become a comfort.

She sat in the office chair, the one Nora had found for her, and set her hands in her lap. Celeste was asleep, of course; she was almost always asleep. Was it the device in her brain? The equipment looked shabby, the monitors out of date. An interface, a technique, whatever. It wasn't what kept her living, breathing, present. People did. The company, the voices. Nora.

'Inadequate,' Jude said, and her sister opened her eyes.

For a moment, there seemed to be a kind of recognition. The glassy blue was looking into her, alight with knowing. But then she frowned, and the illusion withdrew.

'Where are the others?' Celeste whispered.

'Just me,' said Jude, a knot in her throat.

Celeste turned her head to the wall. 'You went away,' she murmured. 'You weren't there.'

'I had other work yesterday,' Jude said. No need to feel guilty about that, but she did. This room was not a comfort but a duty. She sat in silence, the machines marking steady time around them. Celeste blinked at the ceiling.

Jude cleared her throat. 'You met the new guy?'

The eyes scanned distantly. They seemed empty, like a tide had gone out. She was disappearing.

'He says you have a neural mesh,' Jude tried.

A minute passed. Celeste's expression may have subtly clouded, or it may have been a trick of the light. Her mouth had fallen open. Jude could see her rotten teeth, her gums drawn back.

'You don't remember,' Jude said.

The mouth closed, seemed about to smile with an old charm, but the expression never formed. Celeste drifted away.

The machines showed the pace of her breath, the heart rate slowing. How small it was, this flickering existence. A device in her brain, beyond their capabilities. She was never going to get well.

*

Later, the tall man came in, typed a few notes into his tablet, fiddled with a machine, cleared his throat and went out again, all without looking once at Jude. Celeste slept on, and the minutes slipped away, and Jude waited for some certainty to form, for the mess that surrounded her to resolve into a pattern.

Jude was faintly aware of movement on the other side of the glass. She looked up, hoping to see Nora, afraid to see her watching.

Nora deserved to know who Jude was. What she had done, how she had failed. For a moment, Jude felt she might have the courage to tell her. But it was only the pale nurse, tapping away at her screen.

43

BEFORE

The party is still raging when they come back down the hill. People are setting off fireworks in the driveway, shouting 'Lift-off!' with each burst of light. Hope wants to stay and watch but Jude is tired, as tired as she has ever been.

She sends Hope away and goes to her small room, closes the curtain. Along the edge of the fabric, the coloured lights of cheap pyrotechnics flare in a line. The walls are thin; she can hear conversations outside. Hope's voice, the hurt not hidden in its laughter. Jude buries herself in the blankets, covers her head with the pillow.

They are mocking the launch, the rich idiots just versions of the other rich idiots who still dock superyachts at Cullen Bay. But she can hear their desire, too. They want the door left open, the possibility of escape – even Hope. Jude lies awake until the fireworks run out, the air sulphurous and silent.

When Hope comes to bed, she slides a warm hand around Jude's ribs. Tugs the covers over them both. Jude slows her breathing, pretends to be asleep. When the dawn comes she regrets her distance. Hope's phone rings early; she is up and moving quickly. By the time she shakes Jude awake, the decision's been made. It was made before this, Jude knows, before they even met, but it still stings.

'My kids,' Hope says.

There's a week-long window for entry back into south-east Queensland, an amnesty before they formalise the border. If she moves now, she has a chance at full custody. After that, she'd be entering as a foreigner.

'You could come with me,' she says shyly, addressing the view from Jude's window. Bougainvillea tumbles down the front office wall, the colour of bull's blood.

Hope is a good person. Her kids need her. Family means everything to her. When she turns, Jude shakes her head, just slightly. Hope doesn't ask again.

*

After Hope leaves, the world is smaller. The caravan park is full, and Jude is aware it's overcrowded, especially when she's cleaning the toilets. At the same time it feels deserted. She hasn't bothered getting to know that many of the new residents. She's always been aware that she wasn't staying, that the hospitality here won't last. The longer she remains in one place, the more she risks being recognised, named. She's seen photos of herself in the newsfeeds, with all the attention on the launch. A kid who disappeared years ago. She looks different, but still. They would hate her for who she is, for where she's come from.

Black kites circle over the tip where she takes the caravan park's rubbish once a week. She sits in the one-tonne truck and watches them. Scavengers, carrion-eaters. They've adapted well.

Jude wants to fly away as much as anyone does, only there's nowhere to go. She got as far north as this, hit the edge of the continent. Doesn't have the paperwork she'd need to get overseas; won't be let back into Australia, either. Or only under her old name. The longer she stays, the more she feels it closing in, the lack of options.

She is digging a trench for the water pipe with the help of one of the residents when he tells her about a mate of his who runs a charter between here and Rubibi, over west. Rich tourists, mostly. He needs staff desperately enough to ask no questions. It's good pay, in the old money, for what that's worth up here.

'Might stop your pining,' he says, and prods her with an elbow. He's right: it would get her away from crawling memories. She doesn't tell him it's not just Hope.

It shouldn't hurt so much, this heartbreak won on false pretences. Hope didn't really know her, didn't see her for who she was. And she had her kids, her family – was always going to go back. Jude knows how uneven it was, how unfair.

When they've laid the pipe and tested it, she rides one of the shared bikes down to the marina and asks around. Speaks with a woman in a yellow skiff, a grinning border collie under one hand, *Shearwater* painted across the hull in cursive script. The other hand points across the dock at a floating block of flats made of white angles and black glass. 'That monster,' she says.

The guy in charge sees her coming, looks her up and down. Scruffy, unshaven, his grey hair in long wisps under a cap that's done nothing to keep the sun off.

'Can you cook?' he asks her.

'Sure,' says Jude.

'Great. A week's trial, across and back. Full pay. If it doesn't work out, you're back where you started. Take it or leave it.'

'I'll take it,' she says.

'You got any gear?'

She shakes her head, and lifts the small bag on her shoulder. He nods and shows her around. The yacht is even bigger than it looks from the outside. The customers aren't strictly tourists, not anymore; some of them are working remotely from the boat. He shows Jude down to the kitchen, her bunk in an alcove beside it, her locker. How simple it all is, how contained.

'Keep everything latched,' he says.

She stashes her bag in the locker: a change of clothes, headphones, bundled socks with a small chunk of stone pushed in between. There isn't much back in her room at the caravan park. A toasted-sandwich maker, a couple of blankets, cups. Jude was there almost a year, and will hardly leave a footprint.

They leave the next morning, but there's a pile of dishes already waiting when she steps into the kitchen.

The scruffy man knocks on the door a moment later, clipboard in hand. 'What did you say your last name was?'

'Shearwater,' she says, without hesitation. She likes the sound of it, a boat slicing through the waves. Later one of the crew will tell her it's a bird, a long-distance flyer, hardly ever lands.

*

The galley has no windows, and time passes quickly. The next day, after she's made breakfast, cleaned up, prepped the lunch platters, she ducks out onto the deck for a moment to find that they have left the harbour, are tracing the shoreline. There was no-one to wave her off, anyway.

She can still see the coast, a cliff line crumbled by the tide. Above it, a row of trees, and between the trees, bright colours.

Flags, she thinks, a protest, like Holly and Rachel all those years ago. But it's tents, displaced people, all the way along the edge of the country. She's got no right to feel anything but lucky. She gets to work.

44

SEPTEMBER

It was dark by the time Nora reached the clinic. Jude happened to be standing outside: the new medic had sent her away while they set up equipment brought from Portosacre in Celeste's room. Storm clouds were collecting over the water, an electric charge building in the atmosphere.

'You're here,' said Nora, with apparent delight. Jude stepped back to let her in, annoyed by the note of surprise she thought she detected. Nora hesitated, her face half-shadowed. Lightning flashed into the sea behind her. Too far away for thunder. Jude counted anyway, then felt the cool shift in the air as Nora went inside, realising too late that she might have greeted her more warmly.

'How is she today?' Nora spoke without turning as Jude followed her to the desk.

Jude busied herself with her mask for a moment before answering.

'She talks. It's hard to tell where her mind's at.'

She had sat with Celeste all day, but the few moments of wakefulness had been brief. It was hard to gather meaning from her murmured words. Something about a headache, the light. A room that may or may not be this one.

'Of course,' Nora said, attending to her screen. 'It will take time.'

The words seemed to admonish Jude, but she lingered,

waiting for more. The others were still in there with Celeste; Jude could see the tall man gesturing impatiently at one of the nurses, a bundle of cable under his arm.

'That new medic,' Jude said.

'Grecu. He's a specialist,' Nora said. Her glasses reflected her screen.

'In what?'

Nora looked up but didn't answer. Her expression seemed pained.

'What's a neural mesh?'

It was Grecu who answered, emerging from Celeste's room and snapping off his gloves. 'It's a device in the brain, in this case the parietal and occipital regions.' He pressed a palm to the back of his skull, cupping the nape of his neck. 'It allows for an interface with external technology.' He was already leaning over Nora's shoulder, reading her screen.

'What technology?'

He tapped at something on the terminal and sighed.

'We don't know,' Nora said eventually. 'Research was halted a long time ago. Too dangerous.'

Grecu cleared his throat and stalked across to the window, peering in. The two nurses were making signs at him from beside the machines.

'Is that why he's here? To study her?'

'We asked for help,' Nora said, calm. 'She needs support. We are limited in what we can manage.'

'I know that,' Jude said, irritated.

'It's not your fault,' Nora said. 'It's just life here. There aren't enough of us. I need to rest sometimes, you know.'

Jude felt her skin flush, glad that Grecu's back was turned.

'You should go, try to sleep,' Nora said. 'We'll still be here in the morning.'

Jude tried to catch her gaze, but her eyes were cloaked now, professional; she only nodded, and Jude was dismissed.

*

She found Ali in the hall, but he was sitting with the musicians, one hand on the bass player's back, the other raised mid-story. He waved her over, but she shook her head and crossed the room. Better to catch him later, on his own.

It rained heavily all night. Jude lay awake, thinking about the roof, the road repairs, how easily it would all be washed away. It would be worse in the mountains; summer storms always caused flash flooding.

She must have slept a little because she dreamed of struggling through the dense undergrowth of a forest, carrying a punctured tyre in her arms. Nowhere to repair it. When she woke it was sunrise, the storm had passed, she carried nothing. Jude paused at Ali's door on her way out, but it was too early to wake him, and he probably wouldn't be alone. She went downstairs, waited for the coffee to brew, then drank it standing in the street, watching a few dogs sniffing at whatever scents the rain had woken, the light sparkling around them.

At the clinic, Ramon waved her in. 'Nora's back at nine,' he said, dismissing the burden of rest and Jude in one gesture. Jude returned to the room.

She shifted in her seat, uncomfortably aware of the mesh in Celeste's brain, of what it might be doing to her thoughts, her memory. Whether it held some version of her history, a life discarded, a burden dragged behind.

When she glanced up, Nora was watching through the glass, her expression ambiguous. She was listening intently to Grecu, who stood just behind her – no, *loomed*. The conversation looked tense. Jude didn't like the man, didn't like how close he stood to Nora, using his size to try to diminish her, the way he pursed his lips when he spoke.

'You're still here,' came a voice, small and frail.

Jude had almost forgotten Celeste was there.

'Yep.'

Her sister's eyes on the ceiling, fixed on that distance. She seemed afraid.

'Where.' The lips barely moved.

'A medical clinic. They're taking care of you.' Jude heard the impatience in her voice, regretted it. This was perhaps the fiftieth time she had said a version of these words; for Celeste, each time might be the first. Jude looked down at her, studied the expression. It didn't seem like distress, but it wasn't comfort either. She leaned close to listen.

'I'm so sorry,' Celeste said. Her voice was barely a whisper, but the tone was formal, the sound of an old self held below the surface. For a moment, Jude felt her sister might be in reach.

The mining word was *stope*. It was the space left underground when all the ore had been removed, a kind of void. If it wasn't supported properly, a stope could collapse, becoming a deadly sinkhole. The hungry earth opened its mouth and swallowed men, cars, sheds, whatever was there.

Jude's eyes were dry. She lifted them to the machines.

'Go on,' she said, breath close, watching for a change.

For a while, nothing. Then a quiver.

'An accident,' Celeste said, and Jude understood.

'We'll sort it out,' she said.

Celeste was already gone, adrift at the edge of sleep. Jude left the room to find a fresh bed pad.

Nora met her at the door, wielding one. They turned her, cleaned her, changed the pad in silence. The body was easy. It was retrievable. This was how it would be, this quiet pragmatism, until the end.

When they were finished, washing their hands, Nora stood beside her at the sink.

'Are you okay?'

'Are you?' Jude asked, wiping her eye with a sleeve. Nora only looked over her shoulder.

'Can I talk to you outside for a minute?' There was something forced in her brightness. Jude followed her out through the clinic, Grecu nowhere to be seen.

Outside, the light was gentle, the water still as glass. There were days like this sometimes. If you didn't look at the buildings too carefully, just saw the shapes and colours at rest on the cliffs, you could pretend that the sea hadn't reached their lower floors, that the rise hadn't crumbled homes like old bread. You could pretend it was beautiful, a life you chose, and not the rubble that was all you had left.

'Let's walk a minute,' Nora said. At the water's edge they watched the reflection of the little town move gently on the surface.

'So calm now,' said Nora. She waved at the sheds, the Common, the buildings beyond. 'You wouldn't know.'

Jude could feel the movement of waves in her body, as if she was at sea. She missed the water, maybe. A land-sickness, a longing that still sang in her bones after all this time.

Oh, no. This feeling was not the sea. It was much worse than that.

'You wanted to tell me something?'

It was like motion sickness. If she looked at the horizon, she could manage it. The air was clear. In the middle distance two birds were bobbing on the surface, enviably calm.

'Ali said you wouldn't mind.' Nora had been speaking for a minute or so. Something about the band needing to get home, and Tik and Solare going with them for a break.

'Mind what?'

'Driving them up to the Fort when the road's cleared. Stay a few days up there, if you want. I have help here now.'

She was asking her to leave. To drive off into the mountains. Of course, Jude was a driver. It made sense. It was an ordinary work request. It definitely shouldn't sting.

'You don't need me,' Jude said softly. The clinic was work she hadn't ever wanted. She should feel released.

'I don't want to burden you.' Nora would only face the water.

'You could come,' said Jude, before she could stop herself. A shiver of nervous energy ran through her, and she waited for the blow.

Nora reacted slowly. A glance inside, towards the clinic. She would measure her words. It was her profession: she wouldn't want to injure.

'I'll think about it,' she said at last. Her smile was brief, perhaps a little sad. A hand brushed Jude's hip. 'I'm sorry. I'll be needed in there. Can we talk later?'

She turned without waiting for an answer, and Jude could only watch her go.

45

BEFORE

Jude gets used to the life quickly, finds she does not look forward to her breaks. The days on shore are long. The charter trips are sparser in the wet season. On her days off, in another stuffy donga by another creek, sleeplessness sticks to her. The earth seems too still, a damp sponge sucking at her feet, and it's too hot to breathe. The moon's gaze is unforgiving. She covers the louvres with a blanket, keeps whisky by the bed.

There are people who live on the water year-round. Whole cities on the move, luxury flotillas crossing the oceans, docking only for repairs. In the galleys, in the makeshift bars in back lanes, warm beers on milk crates, acquaintances tell her they are desperate for staff out there, pay well, ask few questions. Someone warns her that you work for days on end without seeing the sky.

She asks around, cobbles together a brief, half-factual CV. Hopes they won't call to check, or run her paperwork. She thinks Jude Shearwater has enough of a trail to pass. A woman who carries her own good knives in a canvas roll, and little else.

But when she goes down to the marina, those in charge shake their heads at her. Wary of undocumented people, criminals in flight. Most of the ships that wait here are too small to go far, anyway.

Jude's ready to give up when a bigger cruise ship docks. She stands at the gangplank, hand up against the reflected glare of its white walls. An officer passes back her papers, shakes her head, eyes hidden behind sunglasses. A few white faces, pink really, peer down at her from an upper deck. When Jude looks up, they disappear.

The thought of going back to another sleepless night in the donga makes her stand there too long, paralysed. A deckhand walks past with a hose, sprays down the windows. Walks past again, squeegee in hand, swiping until they gleam. On his third pass he looks both ways before he calls out to tell her:

'Don't ask. Step on. Past that headland, papers don't matter.'

She hesitates, but not for long. When he reaches out a long brown arm, she takes it, steps over the gap, lets her flimsy paper existence fall into the sea. The little gate is only waist-high. He shows her to a bench nearby, opens it to reveal a messy pile of life jackets.

'Six hours,' he says. 'Safest if you wait til morning.'

She gives him a look of such gratitude that he waves his hand in her face and laughs.

'Better to ask forgiveness, not permission,' he says. 'Sweet dreams.'

As the ship leaves the harbour, Jude is stretched out on the life jackets in the dark, the knife roll heavy against her chest, peering through a strip of scratched glass. The docks are breaking away behind them, lots of black spaces between the lights. Fancy developments a few decades old, falling like matchsticks.

This is the most comfortable bed she'll have on board, but she doesn't know that yet. For hours, she can't sleep. It's too exciting to be leaving. The big old continent has carried her weight for long enough. It's changing; they both are.

When she wakes, she knows they are safely out of sight of land. The long, slow waves tell her, and the silence. She lifts the lid of the bench and daylight hits her with a blinding force. She stacks the life jackets neatly, walks out onto the deck.

A blue horizon dips and sways. She will present herself to the first person she sees, take her chances. She knows how to work hard. She will pay her way to another life, go anywhere she has to.

*

She lasts a season on that first boat. Six cooks in the galley at once is harder than working by herself. It's not long before people start asking where she's from, who her people are. Jude knows they are just being friendly, but as soon as she gets the chance she joins a bigger ship, trading places with a kitchen hand who can't believe his luck. The money's worse but the operation suits her, its noise and crowded nature, even the yelling. By the end of every evening she is steamed to exhaustion, the smell of dishwater in her hair.

In all the kitchens after that, she keeps her distance. It's easy to get lost in the floatels, with their long corridors and complex stacked decks. The workers live below, come up to the lower decks to socialise away from the guests and residents. Easy to avoid those occasions or hide in a crowd. Floatel guests tend to be long-termers; they last a year or two, sometimes up to ten, like the caravan-park permanents.

The crew have a much higher turnover. In the kitchens she finds herself part of a free, transient population, young and adventurous, international; Jude's in her mid-twenties but she's often the oldest one there. She's not a total loner, but her few encounters are no-strings affairs, happen furtively in laundries, bunks, or in the rooms that are being stripped and cleaned between uses. She moves on before she gets too close to anyone. They all do it.

There are more ships than she imagined. Ships designed for the pleasure of thousands of guests. Floating tax havens, belching unregulated emissions. Guests' needs are met by a vast staff who remain, for the most part, invisible. Sometimes there's a research project aboard, artists, orchestras, awkward groups of conservationists, but these tend to be decorative additions. The main purpose is to live on, unattached. Working the other side of it feels like paying her dues.

Her legs adapt to the roll of water, her mind to the routines of the kitchens, her sleep to harsh physical and temporal constraints. She works harder than she has to, but not as hard as she did at first; co-workers call her out when they think she's setting unreasonable expectations for the rest of them. She learns to pace herself, but often covers shifts for others.

Menus change based on what can be bought or caught or faked, rare meats treated more preciously than any animal that still lives. Tonnes of food are brought on at a time and frozen. They deal with an absurdity of tastes, intolerances, limitations, complaints. Failure's not catastrophic; there's always someone below who will eat whatever's sent back. Complaints are the main source of entertainment.

When they do tie up, Jude doesn't go on shore and party with her co-workers. She stays with the guests and works. Losing touch with the world is the point.

Some news is unavoidable. She catches occasional reports about the Endeavour's progress, knows when the Station completes its first year in orbit, successfully trailing along behind the moon. There are several lunar bases under construction, a number of companies offering recreational trips to the Kármán line and back. More than once, she overhears a guest who has been up there bragging about the experience. It's a badge of honour, being capable of such excess.

In the kitchens, people are more ambivalent. It's just another way to waste money and resources. Even some guests begin to cultivate an air of superiority about *not* going into space, especially aboard the eco-cruisers: the kind of guests with impact investment portfolios and start-ups for robots that will clean up the oceans.

On the ships you don't notice the water rising. On shore it is impossible to ignore. When they near the coast, Jude can see the damage from storm surges, cyclones, conflict. They keep their distance. After a couple of years, even calm seas make her nervous. Ships have cured her of motion sickness. The movement underfoot feels natural to her now. She sleeps better on the water, comforted by the starless drift below.

The seasons pass. She learns that there's usually a library on board, rarely used, and she can spend her free hours reading history or natural science. She is on the system, has accumulated evidence of her existence, a reputation, the bones of an official story. So long as she keeps working, remains consistent, no-one needs to know where she came from.

At the end of each night, they mock the sustainability declarations on the walls as they crack the unshelled crabs and pick at the untouched salads. The world is ending, but they laugh and they eat well, and that counts for something.

Meals are when the stories come out. Some workers have come from deep poverty. Many are paying off a debt, or sending all their wages to their families. People talk about their hopes for the future. This is where Jude first hears of a place called the Freelands. A house for anyone who wants it, no need to work. She decides it is a fantasy, invented by people in need of an exit. Anyway, she likes work.

Though the pay is not as good as she expected, Jude finds that she is saving. She has few needs and nowhere to spend her money except the onboard shops and casinos. She changes ships every season, accepting the increasingly common quarantines between them. Sometimes she'll spend a week in perfect isolation, with only books for company. There's always more work waiting when she gets out. She doesn't need to think about the future; she can go on like this indefinitely, a permanent escape.

*

At night, when she can't sleep, she steps out onto the upper deck.

She sits back on the bench and rests her head against a pipe. Her body feels sore, strong, capable. Air or fluids are passing in the vessel, the enormous engines belching like an animal. She's bacteria in its stomach. A microscopic function, essential but unseen.

The night is clear; the stars are unavoidable. Streams of satellites cross the sky. She's read that someone is working on a machine that will retrieve orbital junk, but she doesn't believe it any more than the ocean-cleaning robots.

Somewhere out there, one of those specks is her sister. It's been a while since Jude has seen any news. The longer they stay out there, the stranger it seems. They drift in their sleep, waiting for something. The end of the world, or another escape. But the world is still here. There's no escaping it.

The water rises, falls.

46

STATION

The house takes care of them. With the camp cleared away, they are safe for a time. But nowhere is safe anymore, nowhere on Earth. At two degrees, things are falling apart. There are fires up and down the coast; there are floods. There are attacks on people like them. They must stay together, stay close. Plan their escape before it's too late.

Nick calls often. Strange hours. He tells her things no-one else knows. Research projects. A line in predictive surveillance that reads body language, anticipates decisions. The idea is to be there even before the consumer is aware that they are going to make a purchase. To read the desire before it forms as thought. There are security applications. Not his goal, of course, but a lucrative market. He sends her beta versions, pre-release. All she has to do is grant access. The house takes care of the rest.

None of it matters. Only the Endeavour matters. On the Station, they will be safely out of reach.

But look: these are her slippers in the middle of the hallway. She kicks them in frustration, and they barely move. Her limbs are like tree branches caught in sand. Her body doesn't work right.

It's cold. She has a headache again, or it's the same headache. She doesn't remember.

Celeste doesn't want to sleep forever. Her body rolls forward, searching. Jude is lost; she is here in one of these empty cells. She is on Earth, smothered in a blanket of atmosphere, and she is safe. Jude says: *Okay. We'll go.* And it's a promise.

What has she done?

She sees Jude walking towards her now, hands in her pockets. Still walking. Still walking. No closer. This headache makes it hard to think. The implant at her neck, the mesh in her brain like a spider's web, catching her thoughts, arranging memories. *She will be with me always.* A version of her, like a saved game. One that the Station can play. All she has to do is grant acccss.

She puts her hand to the nape of her neck, and calls a name. Any name. It doesn't matter whose, but of course it is her sister's. There is no-one ahead and no-one behind her. The curved corridor is empty, disappears into darkness. She was right here a moment ago.

There were trees, floods. Reptiles. Branches. Silt. Rain. Rats. All the weathers. Air. Mud. Mould. Birdsong. It has been a long time. The earth was dying; it was already too late. People were angry; she had no choice. The Station preserves them. They will outlive it all. They will be ready.

The Station is so quiet. Should be someone else around. Two at a time, no conflict. *Not just conflict.* They're losing contact. Days ago, maybe years. Ready for nothing.

Celeste can remember them leaving. Smile for the cameras. Three heads stacked closely in the capsule, like batteries in a torch. It's not what you leave, it's what you aim for. There's no need to carry a thing. The body, the memory, the name you bring. Nothing else. *I don't want to sleep through it.* Walking in the ruined town, showing her the ending. Jude is the thread that attaches her, umbilical, stretched thin as kite string. Sleep is the thread. How far it stretches. Jude, and Nick, and all these empty rooms.

She dreams about the bodies of the others. Flesh held in the Station's casing, drained of life. She dreams that the Station is dying, that it has cut them loose. There are two pods gone, two grey arrows in the corridor at her feet. Only one green light remains. One place. *So bring her with you.*

When Celeste wakes, she is lying in the corridor. It is dark. She makes a sound. Nothing changes. The pain is in her hip, her legs, her shoulders, her neck. She does not remember arriving, but she will remember this. A version of this. The empty trapdoors, the headache, the lights flickering. Her choice. She is lying on something hard, something uneven. The last closed door under her skin, the press of the weave between. Too cold. Hard to breathe. You cannot outlive life. The Station is failing.

She puts her hand to the arrow, and the hatch slides open. A brief burst of stale air.

Judith, she says. There is no answer. Not here. But they found her, didn't they? She came home.

Jude tumbles out of the car into the crowd. For a long moment, Celeste is frozen. A white-out: everything is light. Her mind won't connect to her body. When it does, she is surprised that she is shaking with hurt, like something has been torn away. The hands hammer at the car windows, leave marks. They are filthy. She tells the driver to keep moving, get away. Run them over if he has to.

In that moment, she thinks only of herself. Her own safety. There isn't time for anything else.

One place. All you have to do is get in.

She turns and lowers herself into the hole.

47

OCTOBER

The trip to the Fort had to be delayed: storm damage had made the road impassable. The longer they waited, the more substance the trip took on in Jude's mind. Nora hadn't said no. Jude could take her to the mountain house. A couple of days would be perfect. Tucked away down a trail, not far from the Fort but far enough from other people. Up there, they would have space and time to speak honestly.

She couldn't do it here. They were too caught up in the daily business of the clinic, or else tangled in the wordless intimacy of her room. Jude would not ruin that with confessions. There was no talking to Ali; he was spending every spare minute with the bass player, Konstantin. As the days turned into a week, and then another, she grew anxious to leave. October and its shadows stretched.

Celeste was getting stronger, physically at least. With help, she could stand and move briefly around the room, her fingers clutching Jude's upper arm for balance, holding on tightly as though she might float away. Each day, Celeste made it a little further, then would let Jude fold her back into bed, exhausted. But she barely recognised her, and when she did, it was only as one of the people that attended her sickbed. As though Jude was staff.

Grecu made it clear that Jude was doing nothing of worth. He said Celeste would not recover, not under these conditions. Any attempt to remove the neural mesh would kill her. Sitting there no longer felt like a vigil to Jude. It was more like waiting for a cyclone to land, for the walls to fall down around her.

'Time for a walk,' Jude said, and gruffly helped her sister to her feet. The swelling in her hands and feet had gone, but there was nerve damage. The legs were discoloured, starvation-thin. Celeste looked down gravely as Jude pushed her feet into flimsy slippers.

Celeste made it out the door. A few steps into the main clinic. Then the outside of the chalet window, the furthest she had come so far. She stood looking in to the room, her hands on the glass for balance.

'There you are,' Jude said, rubbing at the soft flesh above her own elbow where Celeste had clutched it.

'There . . .' Celeste looked puzzled, gazing in at the equipment, the empty bed. She turned to Jude, her eyes decisive.

'The Station,' she said.

Jude inhaled patiently. 'That's right,' she said. *They left you for dead*, she wanted to add. *We all did. We might do so again.*

Celeste was looking over the equipment thoughtfully. She was no longer attached to much of it. There was still a drip in her arm, the catheter. The neural mesh in her head, doing who knew what.

'She won't be coming,' she said.

'Who?' Jude asked.

'Jude.'

Celeste nodded her little bird head, opened her mouth and closed it. Torpor was meant to preserve, but it had aged her.

It was more pronounced when she was standing, her back bent, her movements weak. Her mouth formed a thin line.

'Room,' she said. Her manner suddenly ordinary, a woman addressing a waiter. All the old entitlement was still there, the expectation of service.

'Actually, you're on Earth,' Jude said.

Celeste didn't hear, or didn't understand, or chose to ignore this.

'Room,' she said again.

Jude sighed and helped her back along the wall, into the room and onto the bed, reattaching the drip to its stand, the catheter bag to its clip on the frame. Celeste gazed at the equipment with disdain.

'I don't remember arriving,' she said.

'The capsule,' Jude replied. It was still in the shed across the street, its section cordoned off and shut away.

Celeste was losing focus. Her eyes shifted from Jude to the window, now curious, now imperious, now afraid. She was often like this, as if reacting to things that were not there. Jude sometimes wondered if she could see this place at all.

'Still here,' she said, to draw her back.

Celeste shook her head against the pillow, and the material rustled beneath her. 'Nick will fix it,' she said.

'Of course,' Jude said.

As far as she knew, nothing had been heard from Fry for years. There had been rumours of his death, but Jude hadn't believed them. Rich people had ways of disappearing, along with their wealth. He'd be on a ship, an island, in a bunker. Somewhere comfortable.

'Happy birthday,' Celeste whispered.

It was all nonsense.

'Shh,' Jude said, 'sleep now,' and Celeste's head shook like a child refusing, but like a child she slipped quickly back into slumber. It always seemed a more natural state for her than waking. She belonged there like a fish belonged to water.

Jude could still feel the cold of it on her skin, the release of its offer, the sea's desire. The stone had fallen from her pocket. Then the hand of an unknown friend was reaching. She was lucky. Plucked from catastrophe, lifted to safety. Returning, impossibly, from the dead. *We were never meant to survive.*

That stone had fallen in her place.

Jude moved the hair from Celeste's forehead. Didn't feel the change in the air behind her.

'You're safe here,' she said. A soft lie to offer comfort. Celeste couldn't hear her: she was too far gone. When Jude turned, Nora was standing in the doorway, smiling at them.

*

The next day, when they reached the door, Nora had a wheelchair waiting. 'Come on,' she said. 'Let's go outside.'

Helping Celeste into it, lifting from the hip and shoulder, Jude was shocked anew by the weightlessness. She was shorter than she used to be. Her hair wasn't growing back, the pink scalp beneath as grotesque as a baby bird's. Jude's throat ached.

The sea was murky, dashed with foam, and the wind felt threatening. Remnant buildings toppled against the hills, a slow calamity unfolding. Autumn had burnished the afternoon light.

They moved together to the water's edge, Jude behind the chair, Nora beside her. Gulls were screaming in the east, trying to chase back the gusts. Nora bent to set the brake and stayed on one knee a moment, her hand on Jude's hand on the chair's handle, watching Celeste's face. 'There,' she said gently, and pulled herself up. 'Look.'

Jude looked down at Celeste. Her face was wet. Maybe the wind was in her eyes, or maybe she was seeing the world as it was. She'd been protected from it all her life. Here was the damaged planet, aching with all that was lost and all that there was still to lose. Her lips moved, and Jude bent to listen.

'Beautiful,' she said.

The hand that clutched Jude's leg was ice cold. Jude shivered.

'Enough?' Nora asked, glancing behind her.

Jude nodded, followed quickly. At the door, Nora took the chair. Her face close, she whispered: 'We should talk.'

*

Celeste was asleep before they got her back into the bed. Jude must have dozed as well, because she woke to raised voices on the other side of the glass. Nora and Ramon, Grecu and his team. The five of them were in some kind of meeting, clustered over the central desk. It was the new medic whose voice was raised. Nora was probably getting in trouble for taking the patient outside.

She found that she could not sit still, so opened the door and stuck her head out. They all fell silent, looking at her. The air seemed to have been sucked from the room.

'Just getting some water,' said Jude. She hurried across to the sink, filled a glass. No-one spoke. She retreated into the room. Celeste's eyes were open, but distant.

'It's time,' Celeste whispered.

'Time for what?' Jude's voice did not hide its irritation.

'We have to leave,' said Celeste. The pupils darted rapidly from side to side. 'It's all collapsing.'

There was a time, when she was a child, when Jude would have leapt to her sister's command. Done whatever she was told without question. Even now, the papery voice had such authority, such entitlement. It would not be contradicted.

'Okay,' said Jude.

Celeste calmed, and sank back into sleep.

Jude waited until Nora was alone to go back out.

'What was that about?' She leaned on the desk.

Nora took a moment before looking up.

'That's what I wanted to talk to you about. Some people are coming from the Alliance. Doctors,' she said.

'The Alliance?' There was no official recognition of the Freelands, just fragile tolerance and minimal trade. This was unprecedented, as far as Jude knew.

'Don't mention it to anyone,' Nora said. 'It's sensitive.' She busied herself with papers on the desk.

'What do they want?'

'To assess her. We think they might understand the neural mesh. How to deal with it.'

Jude couldn't speak.

'It means I can come to the mountains with you,' Nora said. 'Just for a day or two.'

It was all she had been hoping for, but Jude felt a knot of fear forming in her chest.

'Don't you need to stay here and observe, or something?'

Nora shook her head. 'Out of my hands,' she said.

She put a hand on Jude's forearm, pale skin paler against the dark green check of the shirt. Her fingers danced a little, then withdrew. The electricity travelled up Jude's arm, but when she met Nora's eyes they had a nervous expression.

'That road must be fixed by now. Let's go soon. Tomorrow, even. Make the most of it.'

48

BEFORE

'The Endeavour's gone dark,' Clarice says to Fernao and Jude over the clatter of the galley. Her expression is indifferent, like she's reporting a distant flood.

'What do you mean?' Jude's aware of a gruffness in her manner, but no-one else notices. She's always like this. Makes no effort towards friendship.

'You know. That space station. They lost contact with it,' Clarice says, turning away to stack the dishwasher. 'No-one knows what's happening up there.'

'And no-one cares, either,' Fernao adds, squeezing past with half a ham tucked between chest and elbow. He mutters something into the freezer, but Jude can't hear it.

It's been one bad year, and then another. Fires visible down the coast, smoke that reaches them out in the Pacific. A cyclone too close, out of its range and out of season. The tone of kitchen conversations has changed. There's an edge of fear, of restless anger.

'They won't last long,' Clarice says. 'Might be dead already.'

The knife is still in Jude's hand, its meditative rhythm forgotten. There is nothing before her but the airless void. Her own hands, numb and pale. She would know in her body if Celeste was gone, wouldn't she? But her body doesn't know anything. Time has stopped, and movement. The knife hangs wetly in the air.

Someone jostles her elbow, restarts the clock. There is no time to waste in the kitchen.

Jude hurries to finish slicing the vegetables, scrapes them into a container, slides it into place for the next person to assemble. Beautifully crafted salads will be delivered, still crisp, many floors above them. Most of them will come back uneaten.

She cleans her knife with a soft cloth, returns it to its holder. Wipes the sweat from her face and centres herself for the next task. The hands move automatically. Behind her, Fernao is laughing again, dancing on his feet. Still hours to get through.

When she finally climbs into her bunk at the end of the shift, Jude is exhausted. Tonight, sleep eludes her. Why this ache against her ribs, in her throat, these thoughts rushing skyward? Celeste chose her path. That was not Jude's responsibility. This is not her catastrophe.

*

There's been no signal from the Station for days. Jude pauses in the kitchen, catches fragments on the screen in the corner. The Endeavour has crept to the top of the news broadcasts, briefly hovering above the climate summit and the ongoing war.

No fresh images, so here's an artist's impression: bodies floating in miniature circles, clustered to the bigger circle of the Station's wheel. A segment of the diagram flashes: life support. The Station's AI should alert a ground crew to any errors. But who is listening? The Station has been spinning out at its Lagrange point for years now, much longer than was promised. Fry is described as *eccentric, reclusive*. He can't be reached for comment. They list the people's names, mention their families. Experts discuss the likelihood of their survival in weeks, days, hours. Sooner than some projections suggest, they begin to be described in the past tense.

An image of their shining, hopeful faces, taken years ago. White helmets under their arms, white teeth. The whites of eyes cast skyward. And now, the latest from the crisis in Europe, where the war has buried thousands of civilians in the rubble of their homes. No-one is timing their deaths, very possibly no-one is recording their names.

Jude stumbles forward, and a warped reflection bounces off the stainless steel. Bells clang, doors swing, the news is replaced with advertisements, the kitchen's rhythms drown out both, and time upends into demand like always.

Every night, the job is the same. Only the menu changes. There's a clarity of purpose to it. She will exhaust herself, stop thinking. This has always worked.

It has stopped working. Jude no longer sleeps at all.

At sea, she can't feel the earth's rotation. Only the driving engines, and beneath them, the unevenness of ocean. A living body that tips and churns, heaving with its massive power. She can feel her own body moving in answer, subtly tuning itself to the water. She is only a drifting weed caught in a current. No solid ground under her, no roof overhead. This ship isn't even a place. Celeste is lost, and Jude is nothing, nowhere. She does not have a right to grieve.

49

OCTOBER

In the hills beyond the town, the high trees were already turning. The autumn colours were a transient flare at altitude. The season had changed without Jude's noticing. Maybe its timing was off, or hers was.

The truck was filled and charged. She tidied the interior, wiped down the dash, did her best to make it look presentable before she went looking for something to eat. She could smell something delicious before she reached the Common.

Inside, the kitchen was full of voices. Someone had been gathering mushrooms. She found Ali tipping wine into a pan, and he squinted at her, faking suspicion.

'I'm not avoiding you,' she said.

He shrugged, lifted a wooden spoon to her mouth. 'Try this.'

She sniffed uncertainly.

Ali bumped his hip against hers, and said: 'Go on. It's good.'

Jude opened her mouth. She had once taken great pleasure in preparing food, taken pride in it. But life on the ships had soured, and she'd lost the knack of cooking for people.

'Needs salt,' she said. This life, too, might soon dissolve. 'We'll go tomorrow,' she said. 'The mountain house. Nora's coming.'

'Good for you,' he said, looking over her shoulder.

When she turned, Nora was at the door. How long had she

been watching? The expression on her face was ambiguous. Ali was already sauntering over to the pantry, making room. Jude wondered if they were conspiring.

Nora wiped her hands on her jeans, wafted a little steam from the pan into her face and sighed. 'Do you want to go for a walk after you finish up in here?'

'She's finished,' Ali called out. 'She's not even helping.' That got a few laughs.

'Let me get my jacket,' said Jude, heat rising at her throat. There was no privacy here.

'I'll come with you,' Nora said.

Jude was tired, her legs felt heavy, but her mind was racing as they walked side by side across the Common. She supposed the fresh air would do her good.

While Jude dragged her jacket on, Nora looked over the items that lay on the crate by her bedside. She picked up the packet of herbs from Gloria and sniffed it.

'It's just tea,' Jude said. 'Herbs. For the insomnia.'

Nora scanned the contents scientifically. 'Do they work?'

'Haven't tried 'em, to be honest.'

'What about the pills I gave you?'

Aside from one or two, they were still in the bottle. Jude buttoned a sleeve. 'Took the edge off a bit.'

'It's still bad, then.'

'I'm used to it.' She took the packet from Nora, dropped it in the crate. Gloria was a helper, had always wanted to talk, but talk did nothing.

Nora lay back, propped her head up on one elbow. 'There's no honour in it, you know.'

'In what?'

'Suffering.'

The light was dull, but Jude thought she caught a look of disappointment in Nora's expression. She nodded at the door.

'That walk.'

Nora stood, resumed a practical manner. 'Yes. Let's go before it's dark.'

They followed the shore past the clinic, hands in pockets, the sea breeze cool. Jude took a path that led to a shack of sorts, half-rotted into the earth. The place had drowned a dozen times, been stripped bare, but it had a stillness about it she liked. She often visited in spring, when the wildflowers were abundant.

Now the path was overgrown, still muddy from the storms. She held back branches, trampled fronds to bend them down. The scrub grabbed at her with its wet tendrils, clinging to her clothes. Jude forced her way through rusting blackberries.

She heard a voice behind her, turned and saw that she was some distance ahead of Nora, who moved more cautiously through the scrub.

'Jude, wait,' she said, sounding more than a little annoyed.

Jude sank onto a fallen log to wait, not caring when the damp seeped into her jeans. Nora picked her way over the brambles, her pants stained dark with water at the ankles, feet only in sneakers. She stopped to untangle a branch from her shoelaces.

Jude scratched at the bark beside her. 'Sorry. I'm used to being on my own.'

'It shows.'

There was a grave in a bend of the trail ahead, a memorial to a drowned teenager, his likeness carved into stone a century ago.

Jude would have showed it to her. They were almost there. The chestnut trees, and then the shack. Unreachable now.

'In the clinic, you know, it can be hard sometimes to figure out what people need,' Nora said. 'Sometimes they can't tell you. Quite often they just need first aid, someone to listen to their pain.' She spoke gently, as if preparing Jude for bad news. 'But Celeste . . .'

'Celeste is complicated,' Jude said.

Nora's head tilted, the eyes curious, uncertain. It was like a gap of species between them sometimes: Jude could only guess at the shape of her thinking.

'She needs specialist care. I just want you to know that we are doing our best to help her.'

There were a thousand things Jude might have said. She listened to small birds arguing in the vines above their heads, scrambling for position. A mosquito buzzed at her ear.

Nora sighed. 'Come on. It's getting dark,' she said. 'We'll have to come back this way in the spring.'

Jude stood without a word. By spring, she would be long gone.

*

Jude woke after a couple of hours of sleep, thoughts racing through the dark. She ran through a list of what she had to take with her, then all the tasks the truck required. The list became a loop, a knot of anxieties, hard to untangle into separate strands.

Nora's shape in the cling of blackberries. Her own aloofness, stupid. She could not go on like this. She would make things right when they reached the mountains. Explain where she had come from, what she had done, what she had failed to do.

But how could she say it to Nora's face? Nora, whose work

was to care for others, who always had such moral clarity. Jude had been willing to let her sister die out there. So far from home, so alone, as profoundly alone as any person had ever been.

She would let Nora see it. How selfish, how cold she was. And she would let her go.

When she opened her eyes again, it was growing light. She pulled on her jacket, boots, stuffed a few things into a backpack, and went down to the kitchen to make coffee. A strong pot today, a large mug.

It was hours before they were due to leave. She took her coffee to the harbour. It was still and cool out. She stood a moment, watching the sky turn peach-pink and pastel blue, before heading to the truck.

She started with the rear tyres and worked her way to the front, began to relax in the simple processes, checking and rechecking the list in her head. This was care, this meticulous attention.

When Jude looked up, the light in the sky made her squint. There was a drone hovering around, its buzz fading in and out. The barge bobbed idly at the harbour's edge; the wind-churned sea was rimmed with dirty foam.

Ten minutes early, Nora emerged from the glass doors of the clinic, her face flushed, her arms full of packages. 'Help,' she said, and as Jude took the weight, she turned towards the sea and inhaled deeply.

'How did you sleep?'

'Pretty well,' Jude lied.

Nora looked her over, patted her on the shoulder, began to strap the cardboard boxes down.

Salvage

Soon the others appeared in the road, Ali wheeling a sack truck stacked with amps and instruments, Kon and the other musicians carrying more instruments, blankets, their clothes. Solare and Tik walking behind, smirking at some private joke.

'I was going to drive up,' Jude said, but the musicians only waved her help away.

Jude secured the load, folded down one of the benches, stepped back to wipe a bead of sweat from her temple, and found the others standing in a clump, faces to the sky. The drone was still hovering high overhead.

'What is that doing here?' Tik asked, anxious.

'Oh, it's Jude,' said Ali. 'Those things love her.'

Sol looked at him uncertainly. Jude shrugged and held the door open. It was sort of a joke, because they did seem to follow her, always had. 'It's probably nothing,' she said.

They would go first to the Fort, drop off the musicians and their equipment; Nora would deliver medicines, check on Alosh, see how that leg was healing. Then they would go on to the house. Maybe the others would come with them. Probably there would be no chance to talk until the next day.

Jude started the engine and heard the radio come alive. Sol must have left it on. It was playing an old folk song, and Ali and Sol sang along in the back of the cab, so badly that Tik began singing just to mock them, and it became impossible to think or talk. She drove past the Common, the hotel, the houses. Turned left at the road to the mountains. They were capped with white now, almost sparkling. This should be a holiday, a few days' reprieve.

The music became static after half an hour, and Jude switched it off. Nora hadn't spoken for a while. She seemed withdrawn, worried.

'They'll manage without you,' Jude said. 'It's only a couple of days.'

'I know,' said Nora, but she did not sound reassured.

*

The Fort loomed in the middle distance, a subtle geometry among the jagged slopes. It had acquired a new mural, colours ribboning along one stone wall, an array of flags waving from its entrance.

Jude cut the engine. Ali and Solare helped Kon and the rest with the gear. Tik went looking for Alosh, and Nora disappeared inside the Fort after them, and Jude had nothing to do. She stood by the wall for a moment, then wandered around the building.

There was a vegetable garden all along one side of the grassed-over roof where it met the hill. Fenced off from raiding animals. A row of walnut trees beyond. Apples, too, laden with green fruit. The orchard at least must predate the war. The apples weren't ripe yet. Jude knelt to inspect the emergence of a young sapling, grown perhaps from fallen seed. When she stood, Nora was watching her from just inside the gate.

'Whenever I come to the mountains, I remember how much I like it.' Nora's expression seemed to contradict her words. A sadness swam below the surface. It was probably the work she did, the grief in it.

'Me too,' Jude said.

A group of ringneck parrots rose chattering from the trees, happy migrants from another world. They watched in silence as the birds swooped through the sunlit valley.

50

STATION

The capsule has no window, only screens. At the centre, there are little lights, the operations, still live and calculating. She doesn't know what to touch and not to touch, so touches nothing. She concentrates on where she is going, and all she can think of is her sister's face, Jude's hand in her own, her trust. Here and not here. No distance between. She remembers what they showed her, the others, when they left. *The Station will calculate the way.* She has to trust it, even now. The capsule will not wake her. Will not let her sleep.

Calvin, Carolyn, Arvind. Gone. The body decaying in a room. Not her own, but the same as her own. Maja, looking for her wife. Perhaps she found her.

There's no-one there. It's just the Station.

She does not feel the capsule detach from its coupling, doesn't feel it move. With her eyes closed she might still be in the room. Its surfaces stripped, no longer soft. The mask descending, bringing air. She might be dreaming.

Hui, Jun-Sang. *Where do you go?*

First there is the sound of machinery. Then it is only the rattle of her breath. The pain finds ways into her body like water. The chest aches, the knuckles, the back of the eye. The heart is enormous, exhausted, working so hard to accomplish so little. She sleeps or wakes. There is less and less space between these two states. It is the distance between life and death, between the Earth and the Moon; it is no distance at all.

There is no power. No acceleration. Only decoupling and drift.

Jude is here, keeping her company. The body is only a shell. It is not too late. The mesh will outlive her. It will be floating out here like a message when she's gone. Something will remember. Something will be saved.

The Station has failed. Jude knows: she has always known this would happen. Celeste has failed them both. You can't save everything.

One place.

No. Jude is here, safe beside her. She is safe. Celeste can feel her hand here, closed around her own. The younger sister, reassuring. So caring. Still feels like a child's hand. She can't see it. So dark here. Can't feel it. Hands numb, cold. Movement slowing. But there is life left. A desire like water, greater than the body but beholden to it. Held within its limits.

Impossible to think with this headache.

All the others. Nick. *If you must die, make it spectacular.*

Eight rooms. Eight passengers. Celeste is going under, but her thoughts are swimming clear. How many days awake, in how many years? How much time spent, how much left? Numbers are meaningless. Time is meaningless, away from the Earth. Oxygen ticks away. The body becomes insubstantial, fallen away from the body of the world.

No windows. Won't see the Station move away. But in her head, this tearing, the slow sticky ripping of a bandage, the pulling away, the image dissolving, the body terribly awake and the pain in her skull suddenly everywhere. Her hands are empty. Jude is not here.

Jude was never here.

What has she done?

51

BEFORE

The ship stalls somewhere in the eastern Mediterranean. At first, she doesn't bother to find out why. Disruptions are normal: it will be the war, a virus, some other disaster. They are well stocked, can go many months without docking anywhere. Jude hasn't been on shore in years.

Passing a door out to the lower deck, she hears what she thinks are fireworks. She steps out into the warm evening air. Above her, glasses clinking, music, a woman's howling laugh. The parties all sound the same. Something lands at her feet and she bends to pick it up. Fine linen, unsoiled, soaking up the sea water. She stuffs it in a nearby laundry bag.

A few stars are out. There's a sliver of a moon. She looks across to the distant shore of a country she's never visited. Small lights swell and fade and swell again. It looks pretty, until she realises what the lights are. Not fireworks. She can't hear planes. Must be drone strikes.

People are dying over there. Buildings collapsing. Jude isn't even sure what country it is, or what they're fighting over. She has whittled herself down to this slim existence, as though the purpose of life is simply to grow lighter, to retreat. She's almost thirty, and she's done nothing good. All she's ever done is leave.

A tinkle of laughter upstairs. The yapping of a small dog. Some little pet that lives in luxury.

She'll be late for her shift.

*

The battle keeps them out at sea, away from harm. It's the eastern border of the Alliance, which stretches over most of Europe now, a local rebellion flaring. The captain's announcement says five days at most, then a fortnight. The meals go on, the entertainments, but the mood becomes strained.

Over the years, Jude has had to take part in drills and role plays for every kind of emergency: people overboard, fires, quarantines, an active-shooter homicide, pirates. When they looked at what would happen for a nearby vessel in distress, they stayed in the presentation room, watching a series of slides. It's something best left to the experts, they were told. The seas are patrolled by international organisations, the Med heavily. Commercial shipping still relies on the old trade routes. Unofficial vessels are dealt with swiftly and efficiently.

Jude accepts this gladly. One less thing to worry about.

She is pacing on the lower deck when it happens. It's overcast. The low sky seems to glow, an illusory reflection of ships and cities and bombs. When she pauses at the end of her row, she hears unexpected sounds. Just a child, she thinks, or a cat, on the loose past bedtime.

It *is* a child's voice, twisting in the wind. She walks on, but can't pinpoint the source. Goes on looking into entrances, glancing up and down the levels, taking stairs. Eventually she understands that the sound is not on board.

She's several storeys above the water line. Looking down is

like looking out from a tall building. The water is black, striped by the occasional lighted window from the crew cabins below. She watches until she sees them: shapes moving in the lighted parts. There is more than one. The voice she can hear is definitely human, definitely distressed.

Jude runs inside and hurries down the stairs.

There are others coming and going, even at this hour. No-one is moving particularly urgently, and there are no alarms. It's possible they haven't noticed. That the accident and rescue crew haven't been alerted.

She glances at the red alarm panels on every floor, their glass unbroken. No, of course, it was in the training: someone will already have alerted whoever is in charge of this.

Almost at the water line. Below: storage, supply, the engines. There is a narrow deck that runs along the starboard side of the prow; the door says *MAINTENANCE ACCESS ONLY*, but she knows that people use this deck to smoke and get some air. She pushes through, lets the door latch behind her. The wind is easier lower down, but there's spray in her face and the railing is wet. She can't hear the voices anymore. For a moment she thinks she was mistaken. Then she hears a splash, the gasp of breathing.

She looks up, but the bellies of the lifeboats remain in position. She has a memory of orange jackets in a box, her body curled against them. A stranger looked out for her. There are international organisations. They must be on their way.

The only lights on the horizon are from distant explosions.

There are six life-preserving rings along this deck. Jude takes one and throws it into the water. The light is shuttering: it's hard to see down there. She takes the rest across, two and then three in her arms. Opens a storage bench, then another, and finds only three old life vests. The good gear will be upstairs, for the guests.

She pulls off her anorak and slips two of the vests over her head, carries the third under an arm. Then she climbs over the rail and onto the ladder. She's moving automatically, unafraid.

Later, Jude will wonder if she'd already made a decision, had been waiting for a way out. If this was something that had been growing under the surface, like mould or mycelium, feeding on her. Maybe it was just sleep deprivation.

At the time, she doesn't think. Doesn't feel anything. Just steps off steel and into falling.

A brief exhilaration, then the cold swallows. Does she have time to welcome this, to wish for sinking? Hardly. Her head surfaces, and her legs are treading in the living water's body. Salt in her mouth. Voices rising and falling around her. She's clinging to something. Someone clinging back. Feels life working in their movements, the struggle for buoyancy, for air. Then very close, the face of a woman. Her child in her arms, her mouth below the surface.

Jude reaches for her, tries to push one of the vests across, but the woman won't let go of the child to put it on. Jude takes her elbows, tries to hold them both up. They tread water, faces close and desperate, legs knocking in the blood of the world.

The child looks cold. Too cold. Jude tugs a vest over them both and holds on. 'Okay?' she manages to croak. The woman doesn't answer. All her force is in her body.

Celeste's body, cold and distant. Everything she might have done. The water in her ears, her eyes. She should have stayed.

Jude will die with this stranger, with this lesson in her mouth.

She kicks her legs, aware of the pull of deep water below. The stone slips from her pocket, plummets to her grave. What the water wants, it will have.

She is not a strong swimmer: she won't last long. The ship is a skyscraper, a wall of light and comfort. When the water lifts her, she can see the silhouettes of spectators in windows. Rows and rows of witnesses.

Jude spits out salt as someone on the ship throws down a life preserver. The tiny ring barely makes a splash. She realises there are several other people in the water nearby, hears a grunt as they try to reach it. They call out to each other. She will die with these people, and she doesn't even understand their language.

On board, there are twelve lifeboats. There is a medical unit, staffed around the clock. There are hundreds of comfortable beds, many of them empty. A ballroom and an infinity pool. And so much wasted food.

On the lower decks, workers crowd to the windows. Some are waving, others filming. A few are on the deck, trying to help. Only a few. There is always someone lower.

Her legs are past aching now. Soon she won't be able to move them. She whispers an apology into the woman's hair, uncertain if she's still alive. She whispers the name of her sister.

The light changes. Jude turns, blinded by torchlight. An inflatable dinghy, shouts. She feels the woman decide with her body, feels it choose for both of them. They swim together for the light, a last attempt. The child slumped against the woman's shoulder, its eyes gone.

A long-haired man is reaching down from the dinghy, brings

the child up, then the woman. His arm is slender, covered in fine dark hair. The open hand insists. The simplest offering, and all she has to do is accept it. She reaches, and he pulls her out of the water. She falls into the little boat, her debt unpaid.

52

OCTOBER

A short drive from the Fort, they began the hour's hike along the farm track that banded the low slopes. Tik and Sol followed at a steady pace, while Ali and Kon chattered away up ahead. Jude was glad that the others had decided to come and see the house. Nora seemed caught up in her own thoughts. No matter; it would be easier to speak when they got there.

The track was muddy but they covered the distance quickly, the stone walls appearing out of the hillside before Jude was ready.

It was only four square rooms inside, a central fireplace, a basic pantry dug into the hill. There was no-one else staying in it now, but people had been up recently: the woodpile was stocked, the floors were tidy, and there were tins of food in the pantry. A handprinted flyer listing the Fort's events sat under a jar of dead wildflowers on the kitchen table.

Jude went outside to inspect the garden. No sign of the deer she and Ali had found when they first came, a few years earlier. The vegetable crop was overgrown, most of it eaten by slugs and rabbits, the fence in need of repair.

It was late by the time they were sitting around the fire after a simple meal. Ali had opened a bottle of wine, one of a dozen or so that he'd found in the pantry labelled only with a scrawl.

Jude busied herself tidying a bookshelf, filling the quiet with the solid, reassuring sound of books on timber.

'We used to talk about moving here,' Ali was telling Kon. He turned to Jude. 'Remember?'

They'd talked about planting an orchard, getting the solar working. The garden could be revived with a bit of work. Jude tried to think as she used to, but it felt flimsy, was only ever a fantasy.

She glanced around the room. Nora sat in a chair that faced the fire, silently absorbed in her own thoughts. On the couch opposite, Tik was asleep in Solare's lap, the older woman absently stroking their hair.

'Do you have children?' Nora asked.

Jude straightened the picture on top of the bookshelf, a simple watercolour landscape, the blues of moonlight. She had never asked Solare about her family. Never thought of asking.

'Three sons. I lost one before the war. My war, I mean. The other two during the fighting. They are all home in the village, together now.' Her voice was low. She was trying not to wake the teenager.

She looked up, her gaze finding Jude. 'What about you?'

'Never,' said Jude, just as Nora scraped her chair back, stood. The fire flared, flushing the room with heat.

'I'm sorry,' said Nora, and walked into the kitchen. Jude moved two taller books to the bottom shelf, crouching until Nora came back with a glass of water. She knelt before the fire, her profile flickering.

After a moment Solare yawned and patted Tik's arm. 'Come on. Time for bed.'

'Yes,' Ali said. 'We'll leave you to it.' He shot Jude a weighted glance and disappeared into one of the bedrooms, tugging Kon along behind him.

Jude went to the couch, and Nora sat beside her. They said nothing for a while, just watched the fire burn down. Ali had left the wine, but Jude found she had no taste for it.

She had to begin her story. There was no avoiding it. She inhaled deeply, set her glass down on the table, and smoothed her hands on her jeans.

'So,' Nora said.

She would begin, and all this would begin to unravel: the firelight, the cool clean air in their lungs, the freedom and the closeness. The house would sink back into the mountain, the roads unlace from their maps.

Jude put her hand to Nora's lips, saw the light dance in her eyes. There was still time.

'Not now,' Jude said. 'Let's just go to bed.'

*

The view of the mountains at dawn was breathtaking. Their tips pinkish, the high snow a distant gleam. The sections of slopes below that were still forested, or had been reforested, were bright gold. Jude stood at the window until Nora joined her, put an arm around her waist. When the colours began to fade, Jude went to make coffee.

The others were awake already, and there was no room for private conversation in the small kitchen. They would stay another night, walk together into the village and see what they might forage. They were on the track before Jude was ready, but it was still early, there would be time later to talk.

The village wasn't much, just a few houses beaded along the

trail, then a cluster of them set around a little church. Most of it was in ruins. The only living things they saw were birds, squirrels, and wild goats that stared at them through the trees before bolting away up the slope. They went into the houses and called out, but no-one appeared. In what was left of the church, Ali found a small pile of books, sat studying the decaying pages.

The morning sun was high before they were walking back to the house, hungry. The air was warm, the silence almost comfortable. When she saw that Nora was trailing behind, Jude paused and waited for her. As soon as they were side by side, Nora cleared her throat.

'Hey, so. Celeste might be leaving us,' she said.

'What do you mean?'

'The Alliance doctors could take her back with them,' Nora went on. 'She'll have better facilities there. They can understand the mesh – maybe they'll even be able to remove it.'

Jude tried to hide her expression, but her face felt cold.

'It's good news. We can't give her the level of care she needs, as you know.' Nora stopped to look down over the valley, not hiding the frustration in her voice.

Jude stood stiffly beside her.

'When,' she managed.

'I don't know. They should be there already.' Below, the Fort was a toy dropped by a giant's child, the road out of the valley spooling. The others had disappeared on the path ahead. Nora's voice was hushed.

'I'm not supposed to say anything, but I think you have a right to know. You've done so much for her, it's only fair,' Nora said. 'And now you'll have your life back.' She smiled firmly.

Jude remained silent.

Nora turned to her, eyes dark.

'What is it?'

'My life,' Jude said.

*

There were the words she rushed out on the track as they caught up to the others, stumbling and struggling with half-sentences. There were the parts of it she told as they all hurried around closing shutters, packing bags. There were the parts Ali already knew, that she went over, and there were answers to his questions, to the questions from the others. But it wasn't all of it, and it wasn't a life. It was a series of fragments snatched on the run: escapes, rescues and near misses. It was not fabric, and it would not hold for long.

She had to go back. Jude insisted on driving, despite Sol's offers. They stopped only to leave Kon at the Fort, just in time for Halloween festivities. The rest of the trip was a blur of road and voices, Jude's heart in her chest, the rumble of the engine. Nora's dismayed expression beside her, the headlights paging through trees, the light failing.

It was after midnight when they got there. She pulled up at the Common, waited for the others to get out, engine running.

She drove on to the harbour. Red light spilled over wet concrete. It must have rained; Jude hadn't noticed it on the road. Her chest ached; her eyes were burning. When she raised the handbrake, Nora's hand was on hers, light as a moth.

'I'll go in,' she said. 'You wait here, and I'll tell them. They won't try to take her, once they know.'

Jude only stared at the water on the road, the illusion of depth in its surface.

Nora said her name, and Jude looked over. That reticence in her expression. The distance already lengthening between them.

'If I had known,' she said.

'Go on,' Jude said.

Nora hesitated for a fraction of a second, then climbed down and left her.

Jude sat in the dark of the truck. She unclenched her hand from the handbrake. Cleared her throat. Watched the clinic doors, unmoving. Listened to the click of the motor cooling.

You've done so much. But Jude had done nothing.

A seagull cried out over the harbour, a frightened sound at this hour. Jude watched the insomniac creature settle on the post of a dead lamp. No people around, no other vehicles. Northport was a junkyard, nothing more. The bird groomed its grubby chest and eyed the harbour. The moon hung suspended over the water, its shattered twin floating below.

She climbed down from the driver's seat, swung closed the door, and headed for the clinic.

The doors slid open. Inside: bright lights, raised voices. The room through glass, stripped of its equipment. There was Grecu, and the two nurses, and Nora with her hands on the desk in front of her like a barricade, shaking her head. There was no-one else.

Nora looked up, her expression tight. 'I'm sorry,' she said. 'We're just too late.'

Jude went past her to the room, looked in at the window as though the image there might change under her gaze. Inside, the space was bare. It could have been any room in any clinic or hospital, prepared for the next person that might require it, each fresh guest erasing the presence of the last. A space for waiting, purified of any memory.

Nora was beside her.

'It wasn't supposed to happen so quickly,' she said. Her voice was very quiet. 'I thought we had more time.'

'Where have they taken her,' Jude growled.

Grecu was only too happy to explain.

They had come for her the day before. The extraction – the word he used – had been organised quickly; the Alliance people were incredibly efficient. She would already be across the border. In a proper hospital, getting the help she needed. It was where she belonged. In return, they had received vaccines, essential medications and equipment that would help hundreds of people. He waved at a stack of green plastic crates that were set against one wall, proud of his achievement.

Jude listened, her face hot with shame and fury. They had traded her sister away. This was Celeste's worth, this sprinkle of charity.

'We didn't know,' Nora was saying. Her voice seemed to come through water. Jude turned on her. Nora had known about this for days. She had known last night, and known as they were driving to the mountains. She had wanted Jude out of the way.

Grecu's expression did not falter. Jude could not breathe. She backed out the doors, not listening, refusing to hear the words spoken behind her, glad when the glass slid silence between.

The sea shimmered. Salt water calling. Her sister gone, her chance.

Jude returned to the truck, touched its fender, tried to think.

*

She went to her room in the Common, even lay down a moment, but could not close her eyes. Her mind raced on a loop, kept coming up with the same answer. There was nothing to do but to go after her. They all knew who she was, where she had come from. She could not stay.

At two or three in the morning there was a knock at her door, but she ignored it. A second tap, a small voice. Then footsteps, walking away.

She had passed Ali's door on her way back to her room. A light on behind it. She knew that she should go and speak to him, knew that she owed him a proper goodbye. But that would only make things hard for him. He had Kon now, and his work. Jude's story would slip into his history like all the rest. A few stitches, a few scraps.

She got up, found the bag she'd taken to the mountains, and began to shove a few more things into it: another change of clothes, her headphones. It was still a few hours until dawn. She cleaned the room, wiping dust from the furniture and the windowsill. Erasing her presence, making room for whoever came next.

She hesitated on the landing. Ali's door was right there, but there was no light on anymore. She hurried down the stairs to prepare coffee before anyone else got up. Jude dropped her bag in the free box on the way out. Anything she carried now would only weigh her down.

Her boots fell easily on the cracked ground, a steady rhythm. The lights were working: the depths of the shed were empty. They had taken the capsule with them.

Jude refuelled quickly. Her hands shook; the water churned behind her. The sheds smelled of rust and salt and rotten timber. She could barely taste the tears that slid past the corner of her mouth, just licked them away and kept working.

Frost patterned the outside of the windscreen. Her heart was hammering. She pushed the mug of coffee into the centre console, wiped the glass with her sleeve, and then her face. She needed to focus.

The truck didn't start at first, and then it did. She sat waiting for the motor to find its rhythm. Remembering the camp, her trust in this improvised machine, her foolish hope. Ali running in the mirror, shadowed by children.

That was the past, and she had to drop it. She'd let herself go still here: that was her mistake. This banging of her heart inside her chest, ready for an exit. A forgotten music.

That sound was not her heart, and not the engine. It was the sound of hands beating on the passenger-side door.

53

STATION

The next time she wakes, Celeste can't open her eyes. Pain at her throat. She can't swallow. Can't move. This must be death. It's smaller than she thought.

She was in the capsule. She felt the thread pull tight and thin, felt it fray and snap. The Station let her go. She was free, then. Lighter than air. She would not wake again.

But she wakes again, and there is the smell of her own body, the inside of her mouth as it rots away. Of oranges and cinnamon and disinfectant. Under this, what must be an invention, the Station's gift to her imagination. The smell of the sea.

In this dream, there is still a voice. Jude's voice, which has been with her all along. So the Station still has hold of her. She never left its cradle.

She dreams she is in a room. There are machines, too many of them. There is pain.

Jude is still here.

You're still here, she says, speaking the words to test the world, waiting for the image to tremble and fade as they all do. But the image persists. The Station knows.

There are others; they come and go. The Station is clever, constructing them from nothing. It feels so real. The smell of diesel, of coffee. She can't get up: the gravity is much too strong. Under all of it, the sea endures. Not a scent or a sound but a presence. The ghost of all that's lost.

She walks a little. The Station insists. The other still signifies. No conflict, no friction. The body takes hold. It takes all she has to accomplish this much. She is not herself in these dreams. There are no slippers. No engineers. What remains? Jude's help, the details persisting. She thought for a moment that she could get away. Get free.

Time spools quickly, returns in great loops that can't be gathered. Not a life, only these knots that refuse to untangle, these hands that refuse to work.

She dreams that they take her to look at the sea. It seems so real. Tugging at the feet of these hills, these buildings. The little towns that barely exist at its edges, so ready to sink. Drowning in the pretty light.

Jude's voice is here. Changed and constant. There is kindness in it, and old promises. But it isn't real. It's all in her head.

Salvage

The Station still has hold of her. The artifice persists. There is no escape. Has never been any escape.

54

NOVEMBER

Jude wakes from a deep and dreamless sleep feeling calm, rested. She sits up and begins to untangle her thoughts. A moment later, there is a knock at the door.

When she answers, the General's round face greets her with that same warmth. 'Dinner will be ready in the meeting room at seven – we're not set up for VIPs,' she says, with an apologetic tone. She looks Jude up and down, seems pleased with herself. Jude can only wait for her to turn away. A few minutes to get ready. She was asleep less than an hour. She splashes water on her face, avoids the mirror.

There's a soldier waiting in the corridor when she steps out. She follows him to the meeting room at the end of the hall. The others are already there: the General is seated at the far end, facing the door, and beside her is a person of indeterminate gender who could be an assistant, could be a bodyguard. She introduces them as Lieutenant Dennis, and they nod blankly.

It's a kind of boardroom, blank screens and a large rectangular table, but there are proper napkins, folded and ironed, and cutlery that has been well polished. Jude notes all this work, wonders who has done it. She sits beside Ali on one side of the table. Nora on her right, in the corner of her eye, head bowed. Sol and Tik sitting close, watchful, across from her.

The food is delicate, varied, and keeps arriving in small courses. There's fish, ocean fish, that must have cost a fortune. Jude understands that this is part of the performance, but since they seem to be its only audience she also understands that the impression they're being given, that they're important, is not a complete falsehood. They are here because they are useful. She doesn't know what the rules are. Needs to stay on guard, not eat too much, hold to this alertness.

When dessert arrives, Jude takes a slice of blueberry pie and thanks the server, who does not even glance her way. Eventually the General puts her napkin to her mouth and sits back in her seat. She waits for everyone to make room for her to speak. That softness in her is not a yielding.

'Well, once you're all cleared, I can let you proceed with your journey,' she says. 'We have taken the liberty of organising your onward travel to Newbank tomorrow. The Health Minister will meet you there. I understand that's in accordance with your wishes?'

Jude swallows blueberries and drops the tiny fork on her plate. 'You know why we're here,' she says.

It's not a question, but the General nods solemnly. 'We have been expecting you since the patient was transferred,' she says.

'Abducted,' Jude says, before she can stop herself. She sees Ali shoot her a glance in the corner of her eye.

The General's expression doesn't change. 'I understand there was some internal disagreement about the extraction. That's not our concern.'

'Not disagreement, exactly,' Nora says. 'The decision was rushed. Without the proper processes.'

The General looks up at her, the orange in her eyes aglow.

Jude thinks of an enormous tabby cat. She wipes icing sugar from her lip before speaking.

'The Alliance made an agreement with your central medical committee,' the General says. 'A contract, setting out the terms of the exchange.'

'There are circumstances they weren't aware of. We're hoping the agreement can be amended.' Nora avoids glancing at Jude when she speaks, but Jude can sense the question in her statement, a river running under sand.

The General nods at the server bringing coffee to their table, waits until the tiny cup in front of her is filled. Porcelain, and dainty little spoons. More dishes for someone to clean. The server withdraws.

'You will have to talk to the Health Minister about that. It's not my area,' she says, in a tone that suggests the attempt is probably hopeless. 'I've arranged for a driver to take you to the Airail in the morning. From there, you'll travel on to Newbank. I trust you will all sleep comfortably here for the night. As our guests.'

Jude catches Nora's eye in time to see the concern flash across it. Sol is staring into her coffee, Tik at their own reflection in a spoon. Even Ali looks a little pale. None of them should be here; she shouldn't be putting them at risk like this. But selfishly, she's very glad she's not alone.

*

When Jude gets back to the room, escorted by the silent Lieutenant Dennis this time, her mind's racing. Celeste is worth something; the neural mesh alone is worth something. But what can the Alliance want with the rest of them? She's staring out the window, still trying to puzzle it out, when she's startled by a small sound at the door.

'I can't sleep,' Nora says. 'Can we talk for a minute?' Her hair on one side has escaped, curved from habitual tucking behind an ear. The corridor is dark and silent, no trace of a guard. They wouldn't need one, with all these cameras.

'They let you leave your room,' Jude says.

Nora glances at the open curtains, the big window. There is a soft chair at a small desk, but she sits on the bed.

'This is all so weird,' she says.

'Thanks for talking before,' Jude says, deflecting. 'With the General.'

Nora pauses before speaking. 'I don't know what they're up to, and I'm not used to all this – ' Her hand takes in the room, its sterile luxury.

'Yeah,' Jude says. 'They're being too nice to us.'

'I have some theories,' Nora says.

Jude wants to hear these theories, but she also wants Nora to understand that she has not forgiven her yet. Celeste was sold to these people, sold cheap.

'The mesh,' she says.

'Yes,' Nora says. 'But there's something else going on. It seems personal.'

'Of course it's personal,' she says. The urge to make Nora feel bad is evaporating. If Jude had told her sooner, maybe they wouldn't be here.

'We asked her, if it makes you feel any better,' Nora says. 'She wanted to go.'

'She doesn't know what she's saying,' says Jude. 'Doesn't even know where she is.'

Nora is infuriatingly calm. 'She has a chance at life here, Jude. I couldn't help her. You don't know what that's like.'

Jude puts a hand to the back of her skull. Her fingers are cold. 'Why do you care?' she asks, her voice hoarse.

Nora shivers as though she feels this chill in her own body too. She doesn't answer for a minute.

'I had a family before,' she says, in a small but steady voice. 'A partner, Rania. Her child, Callie, who was three. TB. Rania got it first, but Callie died quickly. After that, it was harder for her to be alive.'

Jude had heard of TB outbreaks, resistant strains. It hadn't reached the ships, had been contained.

'The embargoes. It was hard to get medicine. I did my best.' Nora's voice wavers. She moves to the window. 'It's easy enough to treat, you know. Antibiotics.'

Jude has never heard her sound so bitter. She switches off the light and stands beside Nora. Her chest feels empty, her anger turned to vapour. Before them, the floodlit expanse of the border station. Beyond this patch of light, the world is dark. Above it, the flow of satellites. Watching their every move, or just circling pointlessly, dumped like the wrecks of cars beside a highway. She thinks of the sickness that tore through the camp, how easily she left all that behind.

'I'm sorry,' Jude says at last. 'I wish you'd told me.'

'Me too,' Nora says, and blinks, and Jude understands something she should have seen before. Nora hasn't forgiven herself. They have recognised this in each other. An obligation unfulfilled, the burden of surviving.

'If they take that thing out, will it kill her?' Jude asks.

Maybe they already have, and it's too late to save her, all this effort meaningless, another missed chance.

She reaches for the curtains, ready to shut out the world.

'We won't let that happen,' Nora says.

Jude catches her kelp-brown eyes, fierce in the darkness. Then there is hot breath against her skin, and no more words.

55

BEFORE

Jude takes off her uniform and changes into the T-shirt and tracksuit pants she has been given, then slips on a pair of the kind of plastic shoes people used to take on holidays, that used to wash up on the beach in Larrakia country. Her skin still feels waterlogged. They are supposed to hang their other clothes from the fence between the rows of tents, but Jude sees the logo on the polo shirt, the floatel's brand sewn into the pants, and bundles hers into a knot. Later, she takes them to the southern edge of the camp where the rubbish has collected, forming small hills, and buries the uniform in the nearest pile.

When she comes back, a tall, slender man with long hair is moving between the tents, taking names, checking for injuries. He calls out questions in one language, then another, then a third. When he gets to her, he looks at her face for a moment longer than is comfortable. Kind brown eyes. She feels her heart sink. Here is the arm that lifted her from the water, reaching to shake her hand.

'Ali,' he says, touching his collar. 'English?'

She nods.

'Your name?' Just a hint of amusement in his expression.

'Jude,' says Jude.

'Last name?' He's recording details in a form on his tablet.

The information will go into a database, connect to a map of her existence, identify her whereabouts. She shakes her head. Shearwater has drowned, another version cast off like clothing.

Jude's legs are weak, her head tilts with the water. She sinks to the ground.

He squats in front of her and points to a badge on his chest, under the name tag. A humanitarian organisation, international, as promised. Beside it, another badge for pronouns, he/him. She thinks suddenly of Holly and Rachel, of her childhood. But she will not dissolve into self-pity. It is just exhaustion, dehydration.

'Are you hurt, Jude?' he asks gently.

She blinks, the dizziness already passing. 'How many survived?'

'Nineteen.'

She doesn't know how many were there to start with. 'The woman, the child,' she asks, her eyes on the dusty ground.

'I'll find out for you. Do you know her name?'

Jude lifts her head slowly. Somewhere nearby, a baby is crying.

'Any relatives on board, friends? Anyone missing?' He means the boat that capsized.

'No.' She is a fraud: she has stowed away on someone else's catastrophe.

'Will anyone be looking for you?'

'No-one on Earth,' she answers.

He rests his hand over the screen. 'They will need a last name to process you,' he says. 'Just pick something. It doesn't matter what it is.' He looks her in the eye, and she understands that this is not a test or a threat. It's a gift.

She can't go back to the ships. They would make her pay for the ruined uniform out of her wages, for a start. She sifts the ground between her fingers. Small stones in the fine sand.

Oh. Her money's all gone. Her card, her pager. All those lost hours of labour. That life is sunk.

She needs to start from zero. Put her feet on the ground, return to land. She looks out through a row of tents and washing. In the fields beyond, a dark flock lifts in unison. Their bodies glitter in the light.

'Starling?' she asks.

The man puts a hand on her shoulder, gives it an almost imperceptible squeeze while he helps himself up. 'That will do nicely,' he says. 'Go well, Jude Starling.' In his kind voice, the name seems to belong to someone worthy, someone good. He whistles as he moves along the row.

There was a meeting when they first arrived, where they were sorted and collected by the humanitarian organisation, given packages of ill-fitting donated clothes, thin blankets, toys for the children, and told about the rules. Women here, men there, families in the family section. Meals here, one a day; showers there, twice a week maximum. No violence, no exit.

There is the meeting when they organise the bodies of the dead. Identify them. An impossible task, since so many are unknown and unconnected, and no-one was carrying papers. Eight of the nineteen survivors enter the morgue and leave, some shaking their heads, others crying.

There are meetings where they make lists of who is missing, checking and crosschecking names, descriptions. There are rule changes and meetings about the rule changes. There are meetings where they talk about the procedure for beginning an application to leave the camp. All of these meetings are really lectures; one or two people from the humanitarian organisation tells them things, and they can sometimes ask questions afterwards, but hardly anyone does.

Nobody leaves unless they have papers. Nobody arrives with papers. The process of applying for papers is entirely obscure, at least to Jude. She supposes it will become clear. They are the newest people here. There is a long wait.

Jude shares a tent with three other women. She learns not to go to the meetings, to pick up information as it falls, in pieces.

There are twenty thousand people in the camp, in a space intended to house three thousand. It was made – not built, but claimed and cleared – by another humanitarian organisation, early in the war. The war has been going for five years. The humanitarians have been made illegal and the camp is illegal too, but it is still here. There are hundreds like it. This is one of the smallest.

There is not much to do except live. Craft dwellings and repair them, from whatever materials are lying around. Carry water when the water is delivered. Line up for the meal once a day and the shower every few days and the bathroom when you can no longer deny that you need it. Clean as you can; sleep if you can. It isn't hard to know what to do in a day, but when she thinks about the weeks ahead, it all clouds up.

*

Every few days, Ali comes past on his rounds. Sometimes he just waves, and sometimes he stops to sit with her. He tells her that the woman who swam beside her made it, is doing well. The child? He shakes his head.

Jude knew, but she bows her head a moment anyway.

They are in the waiting place now. It is a kind of living. There is a square of cardboard to sit on, and a shaft of morning sun. Ali's company is easy, calming. There are thousands of people he could sit with, each of them worth more than she is, but he stays a long time.

'I could use a coffee,' Jude says.

He tips his face towards the sun.

'I could use a day at the beach.'

'How long have you been here?' She isn't sure if he works for the humanitarian organisation, or if he helps out while he's stuck here like everyone else.

He thinks. 'Two years. A bit longer. You lose track.'

'Two *years*?'

He lifts a hand to shield his eyes. It's going to be another hot day, forty degrees at least. The warm wind comes up from the south and smells of decomposing garbage from the tip, which she has learned predates the camp by many years. Jude has a dim sense that she should apologise.

'It's not so long,' he says, but she can hear the dissatisfaction in his voice.

'You ever try to get out of here?'

He frowns. 'Where would I go?'

'I don't know. The Freelands?' It's sort of a joke and sort of a question.

He lifts the hand from his eyes and waves it evasively. His expression seems pained.

'What is it?' Jude asks.

He looks past her. Three teenage girls are peering out from the next tent, made of a banner that once advertised a mobile phone. *BEYOND*, it says.

'Come with me,' says Ali.

56

NOVEMBER

The General shakes their hands, warmly taking each in both of hers. They are driven to the station by Lieutenant Dennis, who barely speaks at first but seems courteous enough. The car is silent, air-conditioned, spacious. The land ahead flattens itself away from the mountains like a fearful animal. Dennis answers Tik's questions in a clipped but friendly way. Points out wind farms, a distant hydro station, the wetlands where a group of them go some mornings to photograph birds. Jude thinks of the cranes, wonders where they might end up.

There is no town, just a huge terminus surrounded by its asphalt moat. The Airail station is white, formally elegant, new-looking, though the date on its lintel says it's been here a decade. Inside, there are none of the things she remembers about railway stations: ticket machines, shops, other passengers. Soldiers are posted evenly around the perimeter. There are multiple platforms, but only one seems to be open.

The train is a single car, smoothly rounded, with no visible engine. There are only twelve seats, facing forward in pairs. Jude takes a window at the front and the others settle behind her. No doubt they are all filled with regret. Jude wants to say something encouraging, but everything she thinks of sounds anxious or unconvincing in her head.

Back in soldier mode, Dennis hands them over to a man in a dark blue uniform, his grey hair trimmed close, his eyes mild but distant. He enters something on a console, and another soldier gets in, taking the front seat across from Jude. The doors close and the car begins to slip quietly along its track, quickly picking up speed.

They watch the Alliance take shape around them. Flat land gives way to rows of identical townhouses, then white warehouses, then rice fields, more warehouses, more homes. Jude sees few people in the fields. Groups walk along a road, carrying bundles. Soldiers are in the streets. Calm, organised, clean: it looks like the future.

Jude can read their speed on the display above the console. Two, three hundred, and it becomes harder to make out details outside. She can't help feeling a little exhilarated.

The Alliance had seemed dangerous when she crossed it with Ali. Now the predominant impression is of open spaces: long low buildings, wind and solar farms, all sparkling with the glint of reflected sunlight.

'How far is it?' Ali is leaning over Jude's shoulder, too close.

The soldier's expression doesn't change.

'Forty minutes,' he says.

'How many people live in Newbank?'

'Official population six point one four million,' he rattles off.

Ali can get no more out of him.

The outer suburbs of Newbank are, as expected, all similar: white and grey townhouses, then bigger buildings, large complexes of matching high-rises set in groups, many still unfinished, flashing by like cardboard cut-outs. Water between the buildings has been arranged into a canal system. The few people they see are well-dressed, riding other train lines or moving walkways between buildings.

It occurs to her how poor the five of them must seem, with their mended clothing, their scuffed boots. Like peasants from a past century. She looks down at her calloused hands, the skin softened by the gel from the shower she took that morning after Nora left. Hands that have known work and tenderness. She has been lucky, safe.

She has been selfish. Hadn't even thought to ask Nora about her history, or to consider what she'd lost. Now she doesn't know what to do with the information. It's embedded in her like a shard of glass.

The train releases them at one end of a grand piazza. All the buildings around it look official, but one is particularly imposing. A logo glimmers on its surface, animated in the smart glass; around it, human faces appear and disappear, smiling, caring. Jude stands watching the display, trying not to look impressed.

The soldier climbs out last, and the car slides away immediately. Somewhere there must be algorithms that send things wherever they are needed, like a much smarter version of the F. She thinks of the people she saw walking in the fields outside the city with their bundles, wonders if they get access to these miracles, what it costs. What the five of them will be expected to give the Alliance in return for its hospitality, when they have nothing to exchange.

They are herded by soldiers across the piazza to the building. Tik and Sol are whispering cautiously behind her. At the enormous doors, they are welcomed by Director Zhao, a pleasant older woman in an informal white garment. They follow her into the foyer, along white halls flanked by populated offices.

They go through three security doors. The route seems designed to reinforce the difficulty of escape. Probably Jude is just being paranoid. Opposite the last door there is a table covered in food; Jude notices Tik pause over it, but nobody takes anything.

Jude was expecting to arrive at a hospital or a holding facility. But they are led into another meeting room, surrounded by screens. Zhao turns to face them, joins her hands together in front of her chest, and smiles.

'She's not here,' Jude says.

The smile barely falters. 'We made her very welcome,' Zhao says. 'Offered her the best of care, of course, the best of everything. But yes, the Minister wishes to inform you that she has moved on.'

'Where is she?' Jude asks.

'Not far,' Zhao says. 'With Nicholas Fry.' The expression on her face could be hunger or triumph. She smooths it away.

'Fry's alive?' Jude asks. She can feel the others staring at her.

Zhao nods. 'We must defer. He does have – technically speaking – a prior claim on the situation, and so we find our hands are rather tied.'

'You let her go.'

Zhao looks offended. 'This is a research hospital, not a prison,' she says. 'Your sister was free to come and go.'

There is something she's not saying, Jude is certain. She has seen the soldiers at every gate, the reach of their surveillance. She has the sense that nothing unacceptable happens here. An arrangement would have been made with Fry, maybe even before they took her. What has he offered them for Celeste? What is she worth? Her mind hits the white walls all around and stops.

That thing in her head. Jude has an image of her sister on a slab, conscious as the man dissects her, his metallic-black hair glinting. But he'll be older now, and he wouldn't do this work himself. Wouldn't know how. Was just a showman, an overgrown child playing with toys.

'How do we get to her?' Jude asks.

'I will arrange your transport,' Zhao says, with the same calm as she has said everything else. There is a staged pause. 'I wonder if you might assist us in return?'

'With what,' Jude says flatly. Here it comes. She is thinking of the untouched food, the empty new buildings. The Alliance has everything, and it's never enough.

'I was hoping you might share what you learn with us.' Zhao is looking at Nora.

'You want the mesh,' says Sol quietly.

'Of course,' says Zhao. 'It's very important. She would not have survived without it. With it, we could help so many people.'

Nora steps forward. 'You can't –'

The Director raises a hand.

'Don't worry. We won't harm her. But you must understand the implications. We don't want this for ourselves, you know. We can study it. We have the best scientists here, the best facilities. We can make the most of this technology, share it with others beyond the Alliance,' Zhao says.

'She's not a technology,' Jude says.

'A miraculous recovery, wouldn't you say? Given what your clinics can do?'

Jude knows that Nora, the clinic, the Freelands is being insulted. She feels Ali move closer, probably to check her temper. But before she can compose a retort, Nora waves a hand to reassure her.

'It's okay,' she says, looking sideways at Jude. 'Just tell me what you need. I'll do my best to get it.'

'Please.' Zhao indicates another door. A guard Jude hadn't noticed moves away from the wall. It is not a request. Jude watches Nora walk into the room with Zhao, the guard following, and has a sense of the world slipping out of her reach, everything distant and unfamiliar. Nothing here seems real. No: it is all too real. It's the rest of it – the Freelands, her safety and autonomy – that was insubstantial.

A knee-high bot rolls out and escorts them to a table where they are offered refreshments: fruit again, delicate little cakes and, to Jude's dismay, coffee. She pours herself a cup and holds it to her mouth, inhaling the aroma. The bot rolls quietly beneath the table, dog-like.

'Where do they grow this stuff?' Jude wonders aloud. It tastes better than anything she's had in the Freelands. She can feel it charging through her bloodstream, poisoning her with want.

'It's synthesised,' the machine responds from below. 'Lower level 4, section H, lab 9.'

Tik kneels to look at it, fascinated. 'What is that?'

'Assistance bot,' Sol says, amused.

Jude wants to kick the little robot, send it wheeling into a corner. This is the future, but so are the camps like the one she and Ali were in: the tents made from advertising banners, the illness and garbage. It is all the one future, a jumble of bargains and chances, the safe and the lucky, the sick and the damned.

'I've never seen one in real life,' Tik says, kneeling back on their heels. 'Can I touch it?'

Solare begins to speak, but the bot replies first. 'Certainly.'

Tik pats the bot on the head and it rolls gently towards them, emitting a wordless purr.

'If I ask you something, do you have to answer truthfully?' Tik asks it.

'Ho,' says Ali, amused.

The bot seems to hesitate; it's probably been programmed not to think too fast. 'Yes,' it says, 'within certain limitations broadly regarding legality, probability, and security.'

'Is this place safe?'

'The Alliance protects and defends every one of its citizens,' the bot recites.

Tik recoils, stands and puts their half-eaten cake back on the counter. Solare lifts a hand to their arm, but they shrug it off.

'I don't like it.'

'We won't stay here,' Jude says, her blood restless, her voice uneven. She is deciding as she speaks. 'We'll keep moving. Find her.' Ali whispers her name, and when she looks up the door is swinging open.

Zhao and Nora step through it, returning from their private meeting. Nora won't meet her eye, but the Director's gaze is quietly triumphant. Whatever she needed, Nora has promised it to her. She has come all this way only to make another deal.

'Thanks for your patience,' Zhao says, flashing white teeth. 'Your onward transport will be waiting.'

57

BEFORE

She follows Ali to the southern edge of the camp, to the garbage tip. They climb a steep hill of decomposing clothes and bits of furniture and whitegoods. Crows and gulls and ibises ascend in front of them, swoop and settle, glaring, on the next pile over. There are more piles than Jude can count.

Ali balances on an old fridge, and Jude climbs up beside him. It's early, but she's sweating. The sun is powerful, the smell too.

He raises an arm to point out the road beyond the dump.

'People walk out all the time,' he says.

There's no gate across the road, no fence keeping everyone in. Jude assumed they were prisoners here, but now that she thinks about it, no-one has told her that she can't leave.

'Where do they go?'

Ali lets the arm fall. 'If they make it, we don't hear from them.'

The road stretches out into an arid landscape, distorted by heat. It reminds Jude of the launch site.

'Snipers,' he says. 'Drones. You only go that way if you carry a death wish.'

A sharp sound below interrupts him, and they both turn.

It's only a person salvaging metal poles from one of the piles nearby for their tent. When she looks carefully there are more people on other piles, dogs too, foraging for scraps.

Jude looks down at the vast tip face. The Freelands is probably like this anyway. A damaged place for damaged people. Or just a Big Rock Candy Mountain fantasy.

'You see how little security there is,' Ali says. 'They don't need much. Just take away the options.'

In flight, the ibises have a strange grace.

'Hot,' he says, and begins to climb down from his platform. It must be why his voice sounds rough.

Jude slips, grabs at a jagged piece of plywood, gets a splinter in the meat of her palm and swears. She scrambles off the pile and paces, putting the painful place to her mouth. When she stops he is waiting nearby, and behind him there are a few rusted vehicles: the shells of cars, an old truck that must have broken down out here and been abandoned. Its trailer has been stripped of anything useful, but the cab looks intact.

'You should take that to the clinic,' he says, but she is staring past him.

'I'll be right,' she says.

*

She does not plan to drive the truck, only to see if she can repair it. There are others that come by to help, some with skills she doesn't have. Tyres are found, fixed. Grease is concocted, spare parts improvised. A child presents her with a *Back in Five!* sign that somehow wound up here; she laughs and sticks it on the dash. It is winter before the engine turns over, and almost summer again before she can ease it out of its position. It moves for ten seconds, then sputters and dies.

Jude volunteers for long shifts in the kitchen. When she can, she collects oil in old plastic drinking bottles, bits of cleaning products. She needs lye and methanol. She finds an old hot-water heater, tries to make the oil into something the diesel engine can digest, but doesn't have much luck. Jude wishes Spence was here to look under the bonnet beside her. But she hopes that if he is still living, it is somewhere nicer than this. With the brother up north, maybe, a bunch of nieces and nephews, a garage of his own.

Ali knows nothing about engines, but he hangs around anyway. She collects his story like the oil, in little stolen pours. A world destroyed, a homeland razed while he was away at university. A friend – no, lover – here who tried to leave. Samir. He underestimated the Alliance. She learns that people from the camps, non-citizens, are rounded up and disappeared. Maybe they're in prisons, and maybe they're in graves. There are no records kept, no histories written. Ali seems almost as angry about this as he is about the deaths.

Hardly anyone gets to leave the camp, but people keep arriving. There are diggers in the eastern part, clearing the land for more tents, watched by security details. She's gotten used to sleeping in the heat of the day, but now the sound keeps her awake.

A strain of cholera tears through the population. Jude is under-slept, too thin and often dehydrated, but she's stronger than most. She tells the women in her tent, the teenage girls next door, to avoid going out, brings them food from the kitchen. She hoards milk powder for Mona, a young woman with a new baby on the other side, bringing her what she can until the camp runs out. Ali isn't seen for weeks because he's helping at the clinic, sorting people into categories: the dead, the dying, those able to be saved, and the vast majority who are unwell but strong enough to recover on their own.

She won't go near the clinic. In the tent at night, when she can't sleep, Jude is afraid. She will catch death, the way she almost caught her sister's; worse, she will carry it with her, deliver it to her neighbours.

Only leaving has ever saved her. One decision: getting in that car and driving away. She turns the truck over in her mind, like a jewel. Those diggers standing idle, full of diesel. She could steal what she needs when no-one's watching. But every morning, there is so much to do. She does not have the courage.

The days are getting shorter when the diggers start up again. They are digging graves. Officially, nobody says so. But everyone seems to know.

She will go from tent to tent, making the offer. She starts with Mona and the baby, then the teenagers. It spreads out from them like a tree, a root system and branches, the message travelling through the camp the way the sickness has. If and when she does leave, she realises, there could be thousands of people who want to come with her. She will have to sort them, the way that Ali sorts the living and the dying. She has no right to make choices like that.

Some people shake their heads and tell her it won't work. Once you're in the Alliance, you're taken straight to prison, or another hole in the ground. They have to maintain their borders, their integrity. They tolerate the camps, but only in their place. There are millions of people in need. Nothing about her is special.

Others say they will chance it. Dozens, a hundred people.

She tells them dawn, when the moon is full. Whoever gets there first. And that's what makes her brave enough to steal across to the edge of the hole and siphon away the diesel.

It's dark; there's a wall of soil around the excavation. She doesn't look in. But there's no disguising the smell. A death wish, Ali said. But death's right here. She covers her mouth with a sleeve, breathes.

Jude can't help them all. She can barely help herself. She will not think about the choices to come, the risk they tell her she is taking. She will do her work, watch the moon, and take her chances.

58

NOVEMBER

Director Zhao and her assistant walk them out to the piazza. She shakes each of their hands and thanks them; just like the General, she's most effusive when she's certain they are leaving. The glare of early afternoon filters between the high square columns, but there is very little warmth in it. Jude shivers as they cross the gleaming paving stones.

At the centre there's an abstract and almost featureless block of stone, with soldiers standing at intervals around it. A war memorial, Jude sees from the plaque. She wonders how they talk about the war here. Where this white stone came from, and who carried it into position.

Sol stops to speak with one of the soldiers, but he only stands blankly while her hands move, her voice a whisper. He seems terribly young, barely Tik's age, but he's already learned to be impervious.

'Come on,' Ali says, bouncing on his anxious leg.

The Airail car is waiting for them at the opposite end of the square. Jude climbs in after Nora. There is no escort this time, no driver. When Jude looks out, Zhao is standing between the enormous columns that flank the doors of the ministry, undiminished by their scale. She has told them they will travel to the southern edge of the Alliance, to the coast. She is not too busy to watch them leave.

The others climb into the car in silence. Jude is anxious to get going. The journey to the end of the line will take four hours. They will have to walk from there, cross the channel to the island. Past that point, the Alliance can't help them. Private domain, corporate jurisdiction. Zhao said they will be welcomed, safe, but Jude does not trust her.

She tries to picture Fry at the gate of a compound, waving them through. Celeste in the foyer, dressed and walking, right at home. A trophy, a success of his. Just as likely he has eaten her.

Jude will be at his mercy.

She thinks of herself as a survivor, but she has always lived at somebody's mercy. The Freelands is only a camp, just like the others. Its existence depends entirely on the Alliance's tolerance, its image of itself as a merciful state. As soon as that image is no longer needed, everything will change.

She turns to the others, about to speak this aloud. Realises it's probably always been obvious to everyone else how contingent their lives are.

'A countryman,' Sol explains to Ali as she takes the seat beside him. He gives her a sympathetic look. They are all aware of the cameras in the Airail car, and of Nora's silence. Whatever these people asked of her, she agreed so readily.

Jude tries to catch her eye, but Nora only folds her hands and gazes out at the hospital doors. After Nora gives them what they want, Jude thinks, she can go home again. Or be welcomed this side of the border, given work and proper resources, resettled in safety.

There will be time to argue later. Now the piazza shimmers, as if preparing to dissolve. The machine is vibrating, readying its charge. Soon they are moving.

There is no going back. This quiet machine will carry them to the end of the line. Whatever happens next will happen when they get there.

High-density housing is swiftly replaced by vast crops, tended by arachnoid machinery. The few people she sees are at the fringes of fields. The human form seems out of scale here, in these neat expanses given over to efficient productivity.

Gradually, the fields grow less orderly, the scale shrinks. There are weeds, streams instead of canals, old walls. Still very few people, but it all looks more human.

Tik cries out when they see three dogs, or wolves, running through the long grass in the distance. Ali observes that they have seen no other animals, no birds, in all this time.

The Airail slows to a stop in a field. There is an old tree, a cement platform. No signage. It reminds Jude of Australia, of the flat country that meets the Southern Ocean.

Jude climbs out and inhales the memory. This was a wheat field once, but it has been left to grow wild. A group of white ibis lift, disturbed, and she is in the camp with Ali, she is at the launch site, she is at a rundown bus stop, leaving home. Jude sees kangaroos raising their heads from the grass, feels the fear in her body as she stands in that rough shelter with a stranger. She blinks. Not kangaroos, just the stumps of dead trees.

No going back? There is only going back. That is the worst of it.

'You right?' Ali hovers.

Jude nods. In the distance beyond the field she can see smoke, and a long, low building. There are no other structures in view. They are still in the Alliance, but there's no fence in sight. Where the land meets the water, there is the border. Maybe a camp. Maybe a graveyard. Maybe just the edge of the dirt.

'They said to go south,' Sol says.

They stand in the lowering sun on the edge of the platform until the Airail slips politely away, and they watch until it is out of sight. The birds circle back to their positions in the field.

'This way, I guess,' Jude says. She begins to walk.

There is an old concrete road, broken and weedy but visible between the grasses. Sol leans down to touch the white substance gathered around the cracks, lifts the hand to her lips.

'Salt,' she says. That would be why these fields have been left untended. Jude remembers to watch for snakes, thinks of a shed skin scraped off against a fence, a dozen lifetimes ago, another planet. That country goes on without her. It isn't so clear where one world ends and another begins.

They have been walking for half an hour when they come across a rusted sign on its back in the grass. A giant outline of a boat, white on blue, and the word beneath repeated in six languages: *Ferry, traghetto, transbordador*, other scripts Jude doesn't recognise. She can't see the sea, but the road has been sloping gradually down. A darker hill looms over the pale land ahead. Jude nods towards it.

Soon after the sign there is a fence flat across the road, a steel net, soft coastal grasses growing through it. The road beneath the net has crumbled into salty sand.

'I expected more of a structure,' Ali says, kicking at the earth. A glitter of shells and broken glass.

Jude squints ahead. She can't see any watchtowers. No sign of a camp, either.

'This must be the way,' Sol says. Tik looks warily ahead.

The track takes them up a small hill, really just a pile of rocks that slide underfoot. From the top they can see the water. The darker hill ahead is the island, rising close. Jude's heart sinks. It is not a wide strait, but it looks rough and deep. There is no bridge. There seems to be a small harbour on this side, the remains of an old dock, a newer pier floating beside it. To its left stands a cement structure, the skeleton of the ferry terminal with its feet in the water. On the right a white shed, constructed more recently on higher ground.

From here the island seems a feral place, rocky and hostile.

If Fry is there, he will know that they are coming. He will be waiting. Jude's stomach churns with the dark waves below. The long shadows of her friends beside her branch out like a hand.

There is so much she hasn't told them. She should have explained in the Airail, or in the truck, or before they left the Freelands. Before Celeste appeared. Should have made herself known.

'Okay,' she says, turning in the dirt to face them. They stand in a row on the stony hill, so Jude has the sense they are looking down on her. 'You can all wait here.'

'Don't, Jude,' Ali says softly. 'We know what we're getting ourselves into.' He sounds tired.

'But you don't know,' Jude says. 'I was meant to go with her.' Her voice breaks, and she swallows.

'It's not your fault,' Ali says.

Sol is nodding beside him. Tik scratches a toe at the ground, and Nora reaches for their hand. Jude takes them in. Everything that they have lost. Sons, lovers, whole families. Home after home. A sensation, something like relief, lands low in her body.

The sun is warm against her neck, but it is sinking at last, turning the sand burnt orange. Her friends are leaving space for her, holding her silence. These are Freeland ways, carried with them to this rough, neglected place.

Jude looks to Nora. 'What did they ask you to do?'

She hesitates before speaking. 'They asked about the neural mesh, what we understand about it. I don't think I told them anything they didn't already know. They know we can't remove it. It turns out they can't either. But they think *he* can.' She lifts her head towards the island. A white mark is moving along the water, rounding the base. It disappears into the spray.

Jude catches sight of a kite in the air behind the others, hovering. She waits for it to drop and snatch its prey, but instead it rises steadily, swivels slowly. Not a bird but a small, silent drone.

'They want whatever we can get them,' Nora says. 'I haven't promised anything. But you know. If it will help.'

A low buzz as the boat moves towards them.

'We need to go,' Jude says. She looks down at the foam below. The craft approaches the pier, and there isn't time to think.

The track cuts sharply down over the stone. Jude goes first, testing loose stones with her boots, using tufts of grass as steps. She can't shake the feeling that she's missing something, that she hasn't thought the implications through. But her body's so tired, and it doesn't matter what she thinks or plans. If this is a trap, they are already in it. She has been in it all her life.

59

BEFORE

Jude can't sleep for brightness. Last month she got up early, went and sat by the truck and waited. She wondered if she might have got the day wrong, if the perfect round moon she watched setting over the piles of garbage wasn't quite full. It was too cold to sit out there for long, so she climbed up into the cab and got behind the wheel and waited some more, until all the stars disappeared and all the satellites, until it was daylight. She flipped the little sign to *OPEN*. No-one showed up.

This time she stays in her tent until it's almost dawn. If no-one comes, she will go on her own, take her chances. People say it's too risky to cross the Alliance without permission. People who got on leaky boats and were crushed in airless truck trailers and walked until their feet bled to get away from where they were. It can't be as bad as that, can it?

When the first grey light shows, she walks out of the tent and down the row. Other people are awake, nursing babies, in pain or just alert; a few nod to her but mostly they look away. Everyone knows where she is going. Whispers of it in her wake. She lifts her head and keeps on walking. The security lights make the sky a painted backdrop, the camp a stage. Cameras are watching, but who knows if they are even switched on. This place doesn't exist. That is its purpose.

They will shoot her, if she's lucky. If not, they will throw her in one of their jails. No-one will even know that she's gone. Jude decides she doesn't care. She has already drowned.

Ali told her what happened to Samir. How he saw him fall with his own eyes, hit while he was running so that his legs kept moving a pace or two before he fell. Ali likes to believe that he died in the air, flying, free.

'It's suicide,' he said, gesturing out at the land beyond the camp.

The truck is where she left it. No-one else is there. She gets in the cab and waits, her hands restless on the wheel, tidying the console, checking the mirrors. Through the windscreen, she watches stars go out, one by one. Probably this beast will break down half an hour away.

Sunlight emerges over the garbage piles, birds descend. Jude thinks of Hope, her scramble across the border to her kids. The moon has disappeared in the west; somewhere behind it, what's left of the Station is drifting, still in position. Celeste is out there, whatever is left of her.

She's about to climb down from the cab when she hears footsteps. In the mirror, there's a group of shadows running closer. Her heart rate rises.

'Papers,' Ali says when he opens the passenger door. He's breathless, pale in the early light. Behind him, the laughing children chasing him fall silent.

Jude waits for the rest of the joke. It isn't possible. Processing has always been a lie; the Alliance doesn't even acknowledge they exist.

He hands her a plastic card, marked with today's date. Her name printed there on the top: Jude Starling. Below that, a few rows of smaller text she has to squint to read in the dim light.

Days: 3

It isn't real.

No-one gets a pass like this, a card that gives her permission to cross the Alliance unharmed. It should not exist, and if it did, it should not be offered to Jude. Ali's done something brilliant, or something terrible, to get it. He's grinning like a maniac.

'I don't understand,' Jude says.

He slings a bag into the cab. He's been here long enough to have possessions. It's suicide to leave, she thinks, but maybe this card changes the odds.

'Someone up there watching over you,' he says. He's still breathless, hiding his fear.

Jude sees the Station's blinking eye. Bodies fall through space, crash and burn into the atmosphere.

The key is just a flathead screwdriver jammed in the ignition. The engine starts with its first turn.

'You don't have to come,' she says.

'I know,' he says. 'It's not for you.'

They watch the country scroll past, changing from flat and arid to a hazy green. Fields of wheat, of corn and sunflowers. Twenty thousand more deserving people behind them. The road skirts cities: white high-rise glimmers in the distance. The farmland between is depopulated, industrial. Jude is too ashamed to speak.

Ali talks now and then, but after a few hours he climbs into the back and sleeps. She drives, afraid to stop, afraid the truck will break down. When the tank is almost empty she pulls up at one of the smaller farms, thinking they will have to beg or steal.

Ali climbs down with the pass in his hand; he has the languages. She tries not to notice how much his hands shake.

'They're giving us their diesel,' he says when he comes back. He has a parcel in his arms, a plastic bag, which he sets between his feet.

'Why?'

He raises the card. 'She said they have to.' But it's a kindness: Jude can see it in the woman's face, framed by a practical headscarf. She raises her hand in thanks, but the woman turns and disappears.

Ali unpacks the plastic bag. It's full of day-old bread, and there's a crumbly white cheese, three shrivelled cucumbers, four tiny hard-boiled eggs.

The gift gives them a strange euphoria. With the tank full and the road unfurling ahead, it begins to feel possible that they will make it. Jude drives all night. Before dawn, Ali wakes and climbs through to the front to sit beside her. Not long to go.

'I still don't understand,' she says, when he stops yawning.

'What?'

'Why no-one else wanted to come. I mean, this truck is running beautifully.'

When Ali replies, his voice is gentle. 'It's not the truck, Jude. Not even the Alliance. It's you they found suspicious. Different.'

In the mirror, a thin line of daylight emerges behind them.

'It is strange, isn't it? The way that pass came through.'

'That wasn't you,' she says.

He shakes his head, gazes out the window.

'Someone watching over.'

*

At the border, a man in uniform looks lazily at their card, flips it over, sounds the text out. He calls to his colleague. Jude and Ali sit there for an age with the engine off, listening to the two men open the back of the truck and check that it is empty. Jude begins to wonder if her sense of good luck was delusional.

There is the Freelands, right through this fence. Last place, last chance. The country looks the same on either side: mostly flat, patchy fields, a vague horizon. The road isn't great on this side, but it's much worse on the other. Can't see any buildings to speak of. Maybe it's where she can begin from scratch, a person with no history. Maybe it's just another nowhere.

Other people must make this journey, cross this border. But they can see no other people except these soldiers. There are abandoned cars and vans lined up. Huge watchtowers on either side of the road, and the high fence ahead of them. Jude can hear a surveillance drone buzzing in the air, like a huge wasp. The border guards wear their semi-automatic weapons casually, though they must be heavy.

There will be a problem. The pass will be false, the truck faulty. The men are young: they will be trigger-happy. She will say the wrong thing, and they will make them step out of the vehicle and stand against that fence. Or shoot them while they run, like Samir.

Ali's fists are almost white, his leg shaking. Jude can smell her own body's animal fear. She is nothing special.

But the gates roll open, and the first young man waves them through without a word.

As soon as they're across, they're laughing. The laughter is too light to hold, lighter than air. When it lifts away and leaves them, Jude is hungry.

'I keep thinking of Audre Lorde,' Ali says.

'Who?'

He smiles patiently, exhales. '*We were never meant to survive.*'

60

NOVEMBER

The boat turns at the pier's end, its engine purring quietly as it comes alongside. It's like the boats they use to take small groups on day trips from the ships, only nicer: tinted windows, sleek white hull. Jude glances at the empty horizon. Out at sea, all those people working and complaining, serving guests their exquisite meals, watching from the deck as strangers drown.

The door slides open. They wait, but no-one steps out of the boat to greet them. The waves are amplified in the space between island and mainland, the wind gasping.

'None of you have to do this,' Jude says.

'Enough,' Ali rests his hand against her shoulder. 'Go on. You first.'

Soft lighting offsets the shaded interior. It smells like leather and varnish and cleaning products. Soft seating arranged in a curve, facing the prow, upholstered in a grey velvet. It reminds Jude of JB's vintage cars, which makes her think of Spence. She cuts the thought like an engine. Behind her, Ali sighs and tilts his head, despairing at all this luxury.

There's a control panel, but no seat, no captain. No-one else on board. Jude circles the vessel as the others board, checking the perimeter without knowing what she's looking for. Sol glances around, nods once and takes a seat on the plush fabric.

When they are all seated, Tik with their feet up on the small table, the door closes behind them, sealing the air. The sea sound suddenly diminishes, though its pulse beneath persists.

'Welcome,' a voice says. The voice is light, neutral, everywhere at once. The boat begins to move. 'Please make yourselves comfortable.'

Instead of travelling straight across the narrow channel, the vessel rounds the rocks to the side that faces the open sea. Jagged stone cliffs, charcoal in the fading light.

Tik gets up to watch the island pass, and when they point Jude bends her head to see a red building high on the clifftop, an old palace or mansion, its windows dark gaps. It looks abandoned. Then the boat curves sharply towards the cliff and increases its speed. Nora's hand grips her own, the knuckles hard. Tik has hold of a railing, points again, this time to a dark channel between the rocks. The stone expands and swallows them.

They are in a cave, a tunnel, reinforced with cement. A line of green lights along the centre of the roof. Jude feels sweat prickle against her sides.

'Well. This is a bit fucking theatrical.' Ali leans forward in his seat, his face pale.

'I don't think he's changed,' says Jude.

The tunnel widens out into a large, brightly lit chamber. The boat pulls up, turning effortlessly in a circular dock surrounded by a waist-high handrail. As Jude watches, the light changes colour, warming to welcome them. The rail breaks at the edge of a platform, where a figure waits. Jude is already at the door when it opens, Sol close behind her, her breath clipped. Jude's fists are clenched.

The person waiting is a woman. Blonde hair, slender figure flattered by a long green dress. Elegant hands poised against the rail. Jude goes still.

She looks just like her. But this is what Celeste looked like fifteen years ago, or twenty. Before she left, when she was well. This must be one of his assistants.

'Where is she?' Jude snaps. The woman doesn't answer. She reaches out and grasps Jude in a tight embrace.

'I'm so glad you're here,' the woman says, in her own voice. She has tears in her eyes. Jude steps back, sees the resemblance to Celeste is superficial, a type rather than a version. This person has another face, a stranger's. The emotion in it does not seem false.

'Eleanor Fry,' she says, placing one of her pale hands flat on her chest. 'Please. Welcome.'

Jude cannot stop staring.

Eleanor greets each of them in turn, taking their hands and saying their names.

'Come on in, please. I'm so glad you're finally here.' As though they have kept him waiting.

'Celeste is upstairs,' says Eleanor Fry, finally answering Jude's question. 'You can see her as soon as you get settled.'

'We're not staying,' Jude manages, but she allows herself to be led away. Into an elevator, then into a broad hallway, its glass walls shining. She catches sight of people working in the rooms to either side, cleaning or gazing into screens. There are dozens of them. As she follows Eleanor, it feels like she is walking back into Sovereign House. Like she never left.

'How is she?' Nora asks, her voice low and cautious. It's the question Jude should have asked, would have asked if she could think.

'Your patient's doing wonderfully, thank you,' Eleanor says. 'Thank you for all the care you gave her. All of you. I'm afraid she was a complicated burden on your – community.'

'It isn't like that,' Jude says, but her voice doesn't seem to penetrate the space. They have stepped into a large room, a table at its centre piled with food and drinks. The carpet is the soft green of desert plants, closer to grey.

'Please. You've all had a long journey,' she says. 'You must be hungry.' Her expression is strained.

Eleanor turns and moves to the other end of the room, where there's a glossy grand piano, a velvet chaise, and double doors panelled in reflective copper. The doors swing open, and she pauses to look back at them. Celeste would have done this, Jude thinks. Known when to move, to show herself at an advantage. She would have *worked* this.

'I'll leave you to it,' Eleanor says.

Jude is hungry, but she doesn't move. She can feel the weight of the stone around them, heavy and cool. A scent of earthy moisture, barely detectable. Sea water flickers darkly out the windows. Night is descending. No stars yet.

'I don't know if I want to eat anything. It feels too creepy,' Tik says, sniffing at the buffet.

'Persephone liked it in the end,' says Ali, lifting an apple to his nose.

'What?'

'The underworld.' He grins, takes a bite, turns to Jude. 'Come on. It's probably the least contaminated food you've touched for years.'

Tik nibbles on a pastry, pockets another quickly. Jude surrenders, takes one. They are warm. Somewhere there are kitchens, staff. People pouring flour into bowls, crumbing the butter, washing the dishes. Somewhere there are apple trees, somewhere fertile and far away. All this must have cost a fortune.

Jude remembers lining up for a meal package each day, smuggling water to the sick. Some of those people must have survived. Must still be there. Tolerated, even cared for, so long as they understand their place.

*

By the time Eleanor comes back, they have all eaten something. Jude is standing at the grand piano, looking at her reflection in the flawless black lacquer. She is thinking of the broken one in the Common. Every few months someone tries to fix it, but it has always refused to tune. Sea water has warped the timber. Still, people go on playing it. Children, with their sticky hands.

When Jude looks up, her friends are spread around the room, examining their surroundings. The Freelands is where they belong; this world has no claim on them. It is Jude's debt.

Her breath catches, but she steadies it. Can't think too far ahead, not yet.

'I'm no great shakes,' Eleanor says beside her. She has changed into a flowing pale shirt and trousers, a costume that suggests both bride and ghost. 'But I've had plenty of time to practise over the years.' Jude can see tired lines around her eyes, can see the sadness. She is older than she looks. Jude swallows her anger. Doesn't know what to say. She is acutely aware of the food going stale. Of Nick Fry in the building somewhere, orchestrating all of this.

Opposite the piano, an enormous telescope stands aimed at one of the windows, its barrel as wide as a cannon. It looks antique, but also brand new. Not a fingerprint on it. There is no dust on anything here.

'What was this place before?' Tik asks. They are gazing out one of the windows. The red building is visible from here, high on the rocks. Above it, and through its gaping windows, stars are emerging.

'It was a private estate, and then a hotel before the war,' Eleanor says. 'But the sea came up, and they moved on. Nick bought it for a song.' She leans on the piano, her cream-coloured sleeves falling daintily across the backs of her soft hands. Someone has done her nails. Someone has cleaned the shirt and polished the windows and presented them all with this immaculate silence. All this staging. Jude can't stand it for another second.

'Where is he?'

Eleanor's face falls, the sadness breaking out of its captivity. She recovers quickly, but Jude notices it. Celeste wouldn't have shown even that much weakness.

'Where is my sister?'

Eleanor puts a hand to her mouth, then lets it trace the collar of her blouse. 'It's easier to explain if I show you,' she says. 'Please, come with me.'

They pass through the copper doors and into another wide hallway. Above them, the roof is unsealed, hewn from stone. It smells damp.

'Are these natural caves?' Sol asks.

'Oh no, entirely artificial. We had to excavate the core, secure it. The system seals itself off in the event of an emergency.' Eleanor's smile is anxious; she looks away fast. Jude has to walk quickly to keep up with her.

'What kind of emergency are you expecting?' Sol asks, doing a decent job of seeming nonchalant.

'Oh, we're prepared for a range of eventualities. Terrorists, and so on.'

'How would you get out, in that case?'

'Helicopter,' she says, waving vaguely at the roof. 'Nick keeps a few. Would have sent one for you, but we know Jude doesn't like to fly.'

Jude flinches. He has retained these little details about her. Will deploy them like weaponry. She must be on guard against his artful manipulation.

The corridor ends at a double door, heavy steel set into a white wall. A hum of electricity can be felt as much as heard. Eleanor touches the back of her neck before turning. Beside the door, there's a sensor: an oval shape with a red circle inside.

'What does he want from us?' Nora asks. Her voice is hoarse.

'He needs your help,' Eleanor says. Her expression is distant. That sadness ripples just below the surface. 'You must understand. He only ever wanted to continue his research. It will change everything.'

'It could,' says Nora. 'If he can get something like this to work –'

'Why, he'd be rich,' Ali murmurs.

Nora doesn't smile.

'If he knows how to make it safe,' she says.

'I'll let him tell you all about it,' Eleanor says, and waves an arm at the sensor. The circle turns green and the doors slide open.

Jude looks up expectantly, braced against his presence. But

there's only a screen, a broad black rectangle as glossy as the untouched piano. Ali clears his throat behind her and she steps back a little, closer to his warmth. The stone gives this room a chill. It smells cold and sunless.

The man on the screen is older than she remembers, but not by much. The image is cropped, so they see his head and shoulders, part of his chest. He is set against a plain dark background. The image must be doctored: his skin is youthful, clear, his hair still glossy and dark.

Welcome. I'm sorry I can't be here in the flesh. The speakers are hidden in the walls, so the voice surrounds them. Smooth, flawless, unhesitating.

It's a fake, Jude thinks. He's too young, his movements too controlled. It's part of the performance.

When we lost contact with Endeavour Station, I was heartbroken, he says. He puts a hand to his chest. *I put everything I had into the project. I dedicated my life to its success.*

There's a good approximation of grief in his voice, but Jude baulks. Everything he had? This man took her sister from her. Left her to die out there, convinced she would be safe. And the seven who were with her, bodies still adrift or burned up in the atmosphere. He failed them, too. Those deaths were on his hands.

She glances at the others. Tik is watching open-mouthed, Sol beside them with a calculating look, Nora serious. Only Ali meets her eye, then glances quickly at Eleanor. When Jude follows his gaze, she is surprised to see tears streaming down the woman's face. Two small versions of the man on screen are reflected in her glistening eyes. Jude faces the screen again, though it's only another echo.

It was a technical error. There were failures, and I am sorry for that. I truly am. I want to take responsibility.

He is staking a claim for forgiveness, and Jude doesn't want to hear it. You can't argue with a recording. She looks for an exit, wanting to wrench open a door and be outside in the fresh air, to hear the rhythm of the sea up close. She can feel it beating against the rocks below, the blood in her body answering.

'Shh,' someone whispers near her. 'Listen.' Jude isn't aware that she has made a sound.

I didn't want their loss to be for nothing. We had the data, up until the moment we lost contact, so I knew that it was working.

He is pitching them now, the old salesman, the old evangelist.

It was working, he says. *So I had to try. We lost the Station, lost the mission, but there was still so much that I could save.*

He touches his hair and the gesture is so lifelike, so tender and real, that Jude finds she is mirroring his movement with her own hand. She forces it into a pocket.

So I rebuilt the Station. Here. A better version. And now it's up to you. I know that you are here to help. That is the work, after all. That is the Endeavour.

We will remember them.

He raises a fist. Jude hears Ali exhale sharply behind her. She waits for more from the man on the screen, but he is frozen, his jaw clenched. Then he is replaced by a grid of faces, the centre square the old Endeavour logo. Her sister's face is at bottom left, young and hopeful, smiling. Music is soaring: 'The Blue Danube', a seasick joke returning. Celeste was younger then than Jude is now. Her life was barely beginning.

'Where is he?' she asks again, turning on Eleanor.

'He's asleep,' Nora says.

'It isn't sleep,' Eleanor says. 'It's torpor.' She lifts her moist eyes to Jude, pleading.

The screen goes dark.

61

STATION

The next time Celeste wakes, her heart rate feels slow. Here is the strange weight of her body, a reluctance to move that sits in muscle and joint and bone, a syrup between thought and action. Pain at the nape of her neck, between the spine and the skull. Was it always like this? She can't remember.

There was her sister's voice. It is still here, just out of reach.

She is still here. The mask lifts, the air hisses. She sits up, opens her eyes. Puts her hand to the wall to steady herself. Soft, curved, just like before. The room is white and fuzzy. A shadow feeling in her body, an echo of purpose.

She has to get up and walk her circuit, make sure the body moves. The mind, too, sickens without company. So every cycle they have to walk around the wheel together. A different person each time, so there's no conflict. No friction. This time, it is Nick's turn.

She swings her feet over the edge of the bed. Her body is too heavy here: nausea flows up her thighs and into her chest. She sits and waits for the mask to retract, and when it does she feels better. There are six rungs in the wall when she looks for them. She climbs automatically. The body knows the way.

The circle turns green: the hatch opens like it always does. The corridor above is dark, except for a row of tiny green lights down the middle of the ceiling. Yes, she knows this, the lights coming on ahead as she moves. She looks for a pair of slippers in a niche beside the hatch, but they are missing. So is the niche. Perhaps she doesn't need them. She walks barefoot on the soft carpet. The hall gleams. Ahead, two copper mirrors swing open. She doesn't catch her own reflection in time.

Nick is standing in the centre of the corridor, the outline of his body traced in emerald light. Still a young man, still fit and handsome. He is looking at the floor. The linen pyjamas are too short on him, and his feet look pale and clumsy. No slippers. He's been waiting.

Hello, she says. He looks up. The green lights play in his hair.

Celeste. He sounds surprised to see her. Maybe he doesn't remember. A different person each time. She has a name and a purpose here: she has been sent to save him. Take him home.

He turns away from her voice. He begins to move down the corridor, walking slowly away. It's the wrong direction. She follows, she is faster, lighter, but she struggles to catch up. Can't seem to get enough air in her lungs. There was a problem with the resupply, with contact. Probably he has to go and fix it. Find the engineers, the astronauts. The others.

No. There is only the Station.

Up ahead, Nick is crouching. He folds down like a bird, all angles. Her eyesight is clearer than it was before, her body stronger. She sees his hand move, palm against the sensor. She keeps walking towards him, treading the curved corridor, her feet sinking. There is a rhythm in the distance, a rocking like waves. It's only the spin of the Station. She reaches for the wall. It is cool and damp as stone.

Her neck burns. There's no stone here, no soil. Twelve hatches. Eight passengers. The Station's graceful symmetry. Nick is right here, just in reach. She has to help him. Keep him awake, or wake him. Yes. Stop him from falling asleep. She watches him climb down into the hole he has made. She has to stop him before he falls.

When she gets to the open hatch, it isn't a sleeping place. It's the observation room, the great bowl below them. Inside the bowl, his shadow moves and covers her reflection. She blinks and lets her focus shift, won't look past what is there. She climbs down the rungs into the room and stands beside him.

It's so small, he says, looking down. His voice is small too. Barely a whisper.

Celeste looks with him, ready to steady herself against the universe. The wonder of distance. There are their feet, pale, naked and clean. There is the cupola, the curve of an eye. But there is nothing in it. Nothing past it. Only darkness, a blank screen.

It's dying, you know, he says. *We had to get away. Exceed our limits.*

He had a plan, she remembers it now. He told her by the water, the ice cream melting in its bowl on the table. Such heat. His sweet-tooth confession, his love of the place that should be drowning. They would visit the ruins one day. The man beside her is the same man. She has to help him. There is no-one here that can, except herself.

Where am I? he asks her. He sounds like a little child. She imagines picking him up and carrying him down the hallway, the weight of his body, its meaning against her own.

Lagrange point five, she says. But it doesn't sound right. When she looks down, the moon is nowhere to be found.

When she first saw the Earth from here, she felt so powerful. The wonder all her own. When she sees it again, maybe that feeling will come back. They have come so far. They are the first, the strongest. This is where the future begins to open, where humanity emerges from its larval stage. She will carry her sister with her. She will bear her away.

This is what it is to be saved. To be safe.

Celeste is unsteady on her feet. A rhythm rocking beyond these walls. A memory of disinfectant. Cinnamon. The ghost of the sea.

No. That's all gone, even the oceans. It's only her body, off balance from all that sleep. No up, no down; the wheel can't tilt. None of it is real.

Nick's hand reaches for hers. It's too soft, much too soft and swollen, and it slips out of her grasp. She keeps her eyes on the blankness below, waits for her vision to adjust, for stars and earth and moon to reappear. But the dark persists. There's nothing out there.

Stay with me, he says, in a voice that is barely present.

With a lurch, his legs give way and he falls back against the wall. There is a bench there now, soft, olive-green upholstery. There are details flashing on the wall behind him, patterns on screens that make no sense to her. The Station must be calculating their trajectory. Yes, the machine will know the way.

She slides around the hollow eye and sits beside him. Takes his hand, sets it in her lap and presses it between her own. His hand feels cold. It doesn't press back. She isn't doing this for him.

I can, she says. She peers at his face. He is fast asleep, his head tilted back, mouth open. He won't have heard her.

It's all she wanted. To be safe, away. So peaceful here, above the darkness. She rests her head against the wall of the enclosure. She closes her eyes and imagines she is home.

62

NOVEMBER

The facility feels familiar, and at first Jude's not sure why. It has a wide central corridor with rooms off to either side, uniformed staff moving quickly through the space. A mix of luxury, security and efficiency: more like a hotel than a hospital. Jude is unsteady on her feet for a moment, and that's when she realises it reminds her of the ships. Not the galleys and the narrow bunks below, but the guest quarters.

The staff make way for them, busy but subdued. Everything is neat and tidy, the workings and equipment hidden away. Jude looks for Nora, but her back is turned. Looks past her, through the wall of glass, and into the room beyond.

Celeste is lying on her back. She is wrapped in a white robe that covers most of her body, the feet protruding in clean white compression socks, her bare hands folded on her stomach. She looks like an exhibit in a museum, a treasure brought up from its tomb. She appears to be fast asleep, but there are electrodes on her face and head. They have shaved her hair to position them. There are two other women with her, wearing masks, watching closely. Data flickers on the screens above her head.

Eleanor stops outside the glass, arranges herself in front of this scene.

'She is making progress,' she says.

Celeste has gone backwards. She looks like she did months ago, before she could speak or walk. When she could not wake at all, and they thought she was dying. Slowly, patiently, with small acts of care and attention, with the thread of Jude's voice, she was making her way. Now they have dragged her back under.

Nora is stepping towards the door, but Eleanor raises a palm.

'You aren't going to take it out,' Nora says. Her shoulders have fallen, her hands hang at her sides.

'Not yet.' Eleanor's expression is clear and calm, all trace of emotion gone. 'She's the only one who can help him.'

'You sent her back,' Jude says, before she understands what she is saying. Then it becomes clear.

Her sister is still alive, only a pane of glass away. Her eyelids flicker with submerged intelligence. The body is present, but the mind is in a dream. Another version of the Station. A dream that exists just to hold one man. To keep him alive.

Jude touches the glass. They found her, and she's still so out of reach. As far as the moon, and farther still.

Eleanor is already moving away. Jude follows numbly, the others behind her, stitched into the shadows.

Their host leads them further down the corridor to a generous room with a high bed in it. The walls are upholstered in a soft olive-green fabric, the few fittings polished brass. A small row of upholstered seats, also olive, are set against one wall. It's lit subtly, a reverent light. Again, Jude lurches, has to steady herself with a hand on Ali's back. His whole body shifts as he inhales sharply. Jude catches Sol squinting up at the ceiling.

There is a body on this bed, too. It is also wearing a white robe, and its feet are in the same tight socks. The feet are bloated, bulging inside their casings; the belly rises like a mound in the centre of the room. The body's hands are swollen, tucked against its sides. The face obscured behind a mask. Jude sees grey hair, very thin. Tubes and wires connect the body to panels along one side of the room, and the wall above the panels flashes with graphs and numbers.

Three other people are in the room, taking notes, moving around with attentive deference. Without their presence, Jude might not have recognised him. Nicholas Fry looks nothing like he used to, nothing like he did on screen.

'How long has he been like this?' asks Nora. Her voice is calm, but Jude can hear the emotion swimming below the surface.

'Four years.' Eleanor's voice is clear. She is more comfortable here; it is a place where her work, her importance, is evident. 'For a long time, we woke him every month, as they did on the Station. Exercise, society. But it became too difficult.'

Jude watches the eyelids. They don't move.

'All this is keeping him alive,' Nora says.

The advanced technology and the support staff, the clean equipment and the undivided attention: what Nora could do with all these resources in the Freelands, Jude thinks.

What this could have done for her family.

Nora should be furious, but it's compassion that dominates her expression.

'He's dreaming,' says Eleanor, gesturing at the wall. 'That's good.' The attendants stand in a line behind the bed, looking up at the display. Eleanor doesn't take her eyes off her husband's body for more than a second. Perhaps an eyelid twitches, a corner of the mouth. Perhaps she's conjured it with the force of hope.

'Celeste should be with him now,' she says. 'There's nothing we can do but wait.'

*

It won't work, of course, it can't work, but at the same time, it has to work, or how will they get Celeste out of here, get her free? Jude paces between the two rooms, up and down the wide corridor. She has been told they are witnessing a great advance, witnessing history. It feels like a form of torture. She watches at Celeste's window, streaks it with her fingertips. They won't let any of them into her room. Too risky. Contamination. The screens play out traces of the absent scene, a language she can't read.

From here, her sister looks serene, maybe even happy. Sleep is home to her, a safe place. It's all she ever wanted.

'Four years,' says Nora. 'It shouldn't be possible.'

'I know.' Eleanor beams.

Jude gleans what she can from listening. The others are asking plenty of questions while she paces. The Alliance wants the neural mesh, but only if it works; it suits them for this to be happening outside their jurisdiction, in the realm of plausible deniability if things go wrong.

'They asked us to bring it to them,' Nora says. 'Whatever we can learn.'

'Of course. It will help so many people. Revolutionise medicine.' Eleanor waves a hand as though this has little relevance. Lately, she explains, the Alliance has been losing patience with troublemakers. Unrest at the margins. Unspecified attacks.

'The camps, you know,' Eleanor says. Her mouth twists in distaste, and for a moment she is Celeste's double again, transported through time. 'But if we can preserve life like this – beyond the body, beyond the Earth – imagine what we could save.'

Jude, furious, doesn't speak. She can see that Nora is already thinking it. People are dying because they don't have drinking water, working toilets, enough to eat. Antibiotics, for fuck's sake.

'Here.' Eleanor presents Nora with a silver box, barely the size of a mobile phone. 'Take it. It's the future. Everything that we have learned.'

Jude can't stay silent.

She wants to explain about being on the ships, in the kitchens, listening to people talk about the Endeavour in the steam of feeding and cleaning. She wants to say: when they died, we laughed at them. *Serves them right. A one-way ticket.* They were not extraordinary, not miraculous or heroic. They were just people who happened to be rich. Who thought they were worth more than others. Who had to believe they could exceed the earth, in order to harm it.

'They only wanted to save themselves,' she says at last.

'Then why take you with her?' Eleanor asks.

'She didn't.' Jude feels ghosted, split in two.

Eleanor touches the box in Nora's hands. 'She kept you with her. A version of you.'

'I don't understand,' says Jude.

Eleanor's smile is cool, controlled. 'You're what kept her alive out there. All that time she was on the Station. That's why you're here. All of you. So we can understand how that happened. Because it *worked*, Jude. Your presence, your voice. You saved her life.'

'That wasn't me,' Jude says. If it was true, it would be like the video of Fry that greeted them here. Her voice, her gestures. Her habits, her attitude. All fake.

A version of Jude had been there. Gone with her. Had cared for her, in a way. Not let her down.

The false Jude was a better person than she was.

She presses her forehead to the glass. Her sister's room, her closed-off world, its slender limits. The compound, the Station. Islands upon islands. Always mistaking separation for security. For a moment, Jude's mind goes dark.

Somewhere behind her, Tik yawns dramatically. Ali clears his throat. The room reappears, the map of their positions in it like stars returning.

'Is there somewhere we can rest?' Sol asks, directing her question not to Eleanor but to one of the members of staff that bustles past.

Eleanor answers anyway, standing to attention.

'Of course. I'm so sorry. It's very late. You must be exhausted. Please, be our guests. Your rooms are ready. Someone will show you to them.' She lifts a hand and a dark-haired young woman appears, wearing a neat blazer.

'I'll stay here,' Jude says, her hand still pressed to the glass. Her sister needs her.

'But there is nothing you can do,' Eleanor says.

Jude can feel the need tugging at her every muscle, like deep water. Her legs unsteady, right eye twitching. She hasn't slept more than a few hours since they left Northport.

Ali's voice is in her ear. 'You need to rest, Jude.'

'Please, let me show you to your rooms,' the woman in the blazer says. This is not hospitality. It will not be refused.

Jude's eyes fall closed a moment. When she opens them, Nora

is standing in front of her, an arm out ready to take her weight. 'We're going,' she says, and the hand grips Jude's shoulder. Her look is full of meaning. Jude is grateful, only grateful. She has sunk too far to think.

A blur of corridor, sensor, elevator, sensor, door. Little green lights in the ceiling, little red circles that turn green under their escort's hand. When they finally close the door behind them, Jude puts her back against it and sinks to the floor. She hasn't spoken much at all, but her throat feels raw.

The room is enormous. An entire apartment with grey linen bedding, soft lighting, fresh flowers. Jude sees eucalyptus leaves and wonders where they came from. No trees on this island. All the supplies brought here.

When Nora lies down on the bed, Jude crawls to the edge and puts her head against the softness of the mattress. Carpet under her hand. There are no windows in the room, and the air smells strange. She can feel the pressure of the island closing in around them, the air too thin.

'You're okay,' Nora says.

'Can't sleep,' Jude says.

'Just try.'

'I don't know what to do.' The admission burns in Jude's chest. She has brought them here, and now they are caught. She has nothing left to give.

'Wait,' says Nora. 'Rest, take care of the body. Sometimes that's all you can do.'

Jude climbs into bed beside her, stretches out. An arm wraps her at the waist. Fingertips slide gently to her spine. Jude waits, and Nora's breath slows.

The silence is different from any other silence Jude has experienced. They are insulated, completely isolated. If she concentrates, she thinks she can hear the sea at the edge of her awareness, but only just.

She rolls onto her back and something sharp digs into her. She pulls the box out from under her and opens it under the bedside lamp. The device inside is tiny, enclosed inside a small brick of glass. She has to bend her face close to see it. It glimmers like a flaw, its filament legs extending from a pinhead core. She slides it back into its silver box and sets it on the counter.

A little artificial habitat, for the mind to live in. A little tank of memory, a little cage for company. It doesn't seem worth it. She's never been sure if Celeste meant to die. If that's what she thought she deserved for surviving. Something in her must have wanted life, to try returning.

Jude tastes sweetness in her throat. She is back where she started, a useless kid caught in her sister's pain. Still grieving what is not yet lost, still powerless to save it. Surviving means nothing if it's all you can do. If you do it alone.

Beside her, Nora is deeply, peacefully asleep. Jude's eyes won't close. The same thoughts wash up over and over in her mind.

Enough. She gets up to have a shower, hoping the water will clear her head. In steam, she stares at a single speck of mould until her vision goes fuzzy. When she returns, she sits in the chair by the bed. The faint light only just tracing the outline of the door, the outline of the box on the counter, under the outlines of leaves.

Everything carries what is gone. Even people, she thinks, watching the rhythm of Nora's breathing. They become the shape of what they've lost.

When she finally climbs back into bed, it is almost morning. She pulls the covers over her head. In her sleep, Nora reaches across to cup Jude's hip bone. Jude surrenders, lets herself be held.

Quick dreams slip past her as she falls. Escape, entrapment. The Station. Her other version. Following her sister around endless corridors. Sovereign House. Celeste needs her; Jude can't reach her. She finds the deck, the open air, the open water. A life jacket, a life. She is falling. Water all around, pressing in. Kelp pulling at her feet. The walls are beginning to crack under the pressure. The Station is flimsy; it will disintegrate. The pieces breaking. She clings to something. A limb, a life. She fights for air.

They are flying over the border, following the fence line. She recognises the country's contours, the mountains in the distance. The Alliance is spread out beneath them: white buildings, laid out in rows. But the roads aren't empty. The ground is churning, moving in waves. People everywhere. The border is in chaos.

A watchtower has collapsed. Crowds of people pushing against the fence, heaving against it so that it rocks with the rhythm of many bodies acting in concert. Like the earth itself is shaking.

She can just make out the truck on the other side. They are almost home.

Then she is awake. Light pours in: warm sunlight. Earthlight breaking through. No windows in this room: daylight falls in shafts from tubes in the ceiling. Jude looks up, her eyes fuzzy. Distant rounds of sky at the end of each small tunnel. She is still here.

'Jude?' A warm whisper at her ear.

Nothing has resolved itself: no pattern, no plan. But there is the next step, and then the one after. And there is the shadow of a retreating dream. She is not alone. Jude swings her feet over the edge and touches solid ground.

63

STATION

Celeste must have fallen asleep. When she wakes, she is alone in the dark. She is sitting on the floor, her back to the wall, in the observation room. No displays here, no olive bench, no Nick. The door above her head is open, and the small green lights in the corridor up there make it possible to see the outlines of this room. The outline of her own body, of her feet against the cupola. She pushes. It feels flimsy, made of cheap plastic.

She finds the rungs in the wall and climbs them. They are made from a brittle material that creaks and threatens to snap under her weight. She is heavy here, but she is strong. She has a purpose.

Celeste walks barefoot to the next hatch, and the next. She reaches for the sensor, but it doesn't respond. At the third, the oval is refusal grey. This is the capsule. Some of them already left; she will remember their names in a moment. She was leaving with them, going after them. She woke on the capsule, the breaking of the Station's hold. That sudden awareness, a tearing, but then there was her sister's voice. She is still on the Station. She shakes her head and moves to the next trapdoor. The carpet is soft under her feet. It moves like seagrass in shallow water. Her neck hurts.

The hatch opens, and she looks down. There is the bed, waiting for her. The instruments, the mask. All that keeps her alive. So small and neat and orderly. But something's not right. There was a body, wasn't there? Her body, curled on its side.

She won't go back.

She crawls along the corridor, hands and feet tangling in the seagrass, until she reaches another hatch. She puts a hand to the sensor and it opens. This is his room. The piano and the telescope. He is sitting on a velvet chaise, face pressed to the eyepiece.

Please, he says, without looking up. He pats the seat. She climbs down, the rungs solid, made from polished brass. She sits beside him, and the springs creak.

Beautiful, isn't it? She follows his gaze. The telescope is pointed at a wall of stone. Maybe he can see stars there.

It's beautiful, she says. She licks salt from the corner of her mouth. It smells damp in here, a little mouldy.

Jude was just here. Her voice was here. There was water, a harbour, the light of evening. A hand on her shoulder, the weight of her body in the chair. Her head hurts. That was Earth; it was a long time ago. A dream she had.

She wants to go back there.

She puts her feet on the floor, presses them against it. She can feel the rhythm of the sea under the carpet. Tides, currents, winds; the dance of air and gravity. It's inside her, has been in her body all this time. In the limits of the body, infinite memory. The ground below trembles like a living creature. The Station is running out of air.

We have to go, she says, turning for the rungs. *We have to find Jude.*

She's not here, he says. He grunts and squints into the lens. *This is all mine.*

No, she says. *She's here.* She has always been here. It's Nick who is absent, left behind. He didn't come with them. The heart. He couldn't risk it.

The lights flicker.

He waves a hand at her. *That's just your imagination. The mesh perpetuates her image. That's what helps you to survive here. Just like you are my imagination.*

Celeste stands. She is steady on her feet, then unsteady, then steady again. She is here and not here. The Station is getting smaller. Even this room with the piano and the telescope is shrinking around her. It is smaller than the wardrobe where her sister used to hide.

I want to go home, she whispers.

In a minute she will go there. The smell of oranges and cinnamon and disinfectant, of oil and earth. Her sister's voice.

This is your home now. He doesn't lift his eyes from the telescope.

No. There is barely room to extend her arms, to reach for the wall. No rungs in the wet stone. Only cracks, old roots to grasp, the slime of living things. She needs air.

There is a trembling, a tilt in the machinery. She is unstable; it is all unstable. The air shimmers, but she is climbing. He grows smaller in her shadow, the stone cracking before her, the water seeping in. She can just see his outline below. The trace of purpose between her feet. At the top of the hatch, there is sunlight. It is all she needs.

Goodbye, Nick, she says. *Take care.*

She rises, falls.

64

NOVEMBER

The woman in the blazer is waiting by the door. She greets them coolly. Long-termers on the ships were like this, commanded respect. Jude always tried to emulate it. Now she asks for a name.

'Amina,' the woman says, with just the hint of a smile. She leads them to a large room at the end of the hall, a kind of meeting space. The table is a lovely timber, complex burls and knots preserved under the gloss. Screens on the wall, dark now.

'Will Eleanor be joining us?' Ali asks.

There are a dozen chairs around the table, but no-one sits.

'Any changes?' Nora asks.

'Please, make yourselves comfortable,' says Amina. 'I will escort you to the ward in just a moment. Do you want coffee? Breakfast?'

Jude shakes her head.

Amina disappears through the copper-panelled doors, and they swing closed silently behind her.

'We have been exploring,' Tik whispers.

'Careful,' Jude says, glancing for cameras.

Ali pulls his hair into a ponytail.

'What are they going to do? They already caught us.' He sets his hands on the table. His tone is light but his eyes are anxious.

'Shh,' says Nora.

There is a distant groaning. The table shudders, and Ali lifts his hands and peers at them, as though they are responsible.

The moment doesn't last long; Jude only understands it when it's over.

'Little quakes,' says Sol.

Amina reappears in the doorway, her hands folded in front of her, pale brown against the dark blazer. Her face is grave. 'Don't worry. We get them all the time.' She smiles tightly.

'Please come with me,' she says.

Behind her, the lights begin to flicker.

*

They follow Amina to the end of the corridor, into the elevator. The machine seems to hesitate before moving, then sinks smoothly. The doors spring open. There is another corridor, and they hurry down it, infected by an air of urgency. There are no windows down here. No sense of the outside world at all. Here are the double steel doors with the sensor to one side. Amina's hand extends gracefully, and the doors swing open. There is the screen, hanging blankly on the wall. A starless sky.

Jude opens her mouth to speak, and the ground moves.

Her brain takes a long moment to catch up with her body. Legs braced against the shifting floor. A hand on her elbow, someone – Nora? – tugging her into a doorway. The lights are flickering; she wasn't imagining that, before. The island is restless.

Much stronger this time.

When the shaking stops, there is a pause. Then the screen falls from the wall and smashes. Behind it, the plaster has cracked. It looks so flimsy. Amina is speaking softly into a device at her collar. Somewhere, a siren goes off, the sound dancing through the corridors.

'Evacuation,' she says. 'Are you sure?' It's not clear who she's speaking to on the other side, but her glance seems to include them.

The doors to the ward are in front of them. Nora reaches for the sensor, but it won't open. Amina steps in. There is a protocol for this, a plan. Below the sirens, there are voices in the hallways: *Remain calm, proceed to the assembly area.* Amina points behind them, back through the steel doors where the rest of the staff are beginning to gather. Jude and Nora move in the opposite direction, pushing through the tide and into the ward. There is no time to speak.

Eleanor Fry is standing in the centre of the room, wearing a grey suit. Broken glass at her feet. Behind her, a window has shattered. Workers are stepping across the glittering surface in their soft shoes, helping each other. Her eyes are wide and dark, two circles of deep space.

'She woke up,' Eleanor says. Her hands make fists at her sides, unmake them.

'Your husband?' Nora asks.

Jude is already pushing at the door of her sister's room.

'His heart,' Eleanor is saying.

'Aftershocks,' someone shouts. Then the door closes behind Jude, and they are alone.

No lights on the wall now. No devices, no people. The sirens pause. Celeste is lying there peacefully. Her expression distant, a little puzzled perhaps. The electrodes are still attached, but the screens aren't moving.

Jude waits for her to speak, for those eyes to open and swarm with clouds. To accuse her, be disappointed in her. 'Jude,' she will say. 'You're still here.'

She says nothing. The machines are quiet.

'Celeste?' Jude has drawn her sister back from the edge of death before. Kept her alive. She will reach for her now, take hold.

She is standing out in the overgrown garden. Celeste is watching from the house. She raises a hand, and her sister mirrors the movement. They are safely caught in each other's orbit, reaching through glass. There is still a chance.

Jude's touch meets a body gone still. She's too late.

The lights flicker again, and the ground moves below her feet, a living thing rumbling in anger. The tremor rises through her, fills her skin. Jude forgets to brace herself. She falls against her sister, an elbow connects with something unyielding. There is the sudden shock of unresponsiveness beneath her. And then it is over.

'I'm sorry,' she says, stepping back. The earthquake has stopped, but the floor cannot be trusted. There is a tearing sound outside, a magnificent creaking. Some lights stay dark.

'I couldn't stop it,' she says. Her voice is broken. She isn't sure she's spoken aloud.

Celeste is gone. Under the lifeless wires, Jude can see no pain in her face, no fear and no forgiveness. All her composure disarmed.

'We have to leave,' says a voice in the corridor. Nora, grasping Eleanor's arm. But the other woman won't move from her place. She is watching the emergency through broken glass.

Jude turns at a sound, a grinding like a skateboard's, to find that Tik is sailing down the corridor, using a gurney as a scooter. They see Jude's face and stop.

Salvage

'Hurry!' Ali says. He is at Jude's side. 'We need to move.' He shouts in her ear to be heard over the sirens. There are still sirens: Jude stopped hearing them. She feels the numbness seeping out of her, a wetness at her ear. A hand pushes her towards the door.

Sol looks her in the eye, then Nora. 'Roof. Quickly.'

*

The elevator is standing open. The walls inside are intact, but the buttons do nothing. Of course it's not working. Sol pulls her to the fire escape nearby, another heavy door, a few people shoving through ahead of them. The stairwell welcomes them with a warm-toned voice, a suggestion of human generosity. *Please proceed to the evacuation station,* it says. *Emergency procedures are in place.*

The steel door closes behind them with a bang.

Jude sees Amina on the first landing, giving directions. They follow the other staff. Jude's right arm feels like cold concrete. Friends and strangers reach and assist, pass and encourage. Without them, she would not move at all. She sees Nora up ahead, squeezed between people, glancing back, and keeps on climbing.

When they reach the roof, there are people everywhere. Some of them are shouting. Others speak into small radios, count heads, give directions. There are dozens of them. Maybe five helicopters. A group are throwing supplies out of the largest, making room. Fresh flowers tip absurdly onto concrete, crates of wine shatter. A fat tomato rolls at her feet, its green stem still attached.

Here is the authority of crisis. Jude's good arm is still of use. She steps in to help, assisting people into the machine.

The others are close by, she thinks, but when she looks up Sol has disappeared. Someone is bleeding, someone crying, Nora giving first aid. Everyone seems to know what to do.

Jude recognises a version of herself, from all the other emergencies. Taking up whatever work is needed in a swarm of necessary action. They all rush back as one of the helicopters takes off, pushing the air beneath it. Her boots in a dark stain, the glint of broken glass. The island groans.

When the noise subsides, someone is saying her name. Taking her side, leading her to the smallest helicopter. Jude's vision has blurred. She wipes at her eyes with her good arm, sees blood on her sleeve. A cut on her brow, pain she hasn't felt yet. She blinks it away.

The helicopter is grey and angular, with the bulbous eye of an insect. Nora is already inside, and half a dozen strangers, some injured. She is holding the box in her lap, the flaw suspended in its glass brick, the brick nested between her fingers.

Jude remembers she is afraid of flying. She holds her body in the door, braced between living and dying. All she can see is her sister's face, the image burning. So unguarded, almost amused by what she has done, or undone. Jude will never stop seeing it.

'I can't,' she says. Her good hand on the hatch, resisting. The broken one bent against her side and beginning to tingle.

'Stop it,' Ali says behind her, his arm on her back. 'You're not afraid of anything.'

The image resolves, and there's Sol, bent over the controls. So many screens. Jude hopes it's true that she can fly. She gets to her seat, finds the belt, can't manage it with one arm. Nora leans across to buckle her in, touches her forehead, brushes at the blood. Takes the hand that can still grip back.

Salvage

'It's not your fault,' she says. 'You did what you could.' A recitation.

'Where are we going?' Tik asks from the front.

'Home,' says Sol, as if it's obvious. 'There's work to be done.'

Her face is tight as she turns to flick at the controls. 'They'll follow us,' she says. And then the rotors spin, and it is too loud to speak.

Other helicopters are already in the sky, leaving the island. Jude twists in her seat but can see no-one left on the roof. Only whoever is inside. Celeste, Nick: this hollow he built around himself.

A part of Jude is still there with them.

The ground lifts away below, and they are in flight. Such an unfamiliar feeling in her body. But an echo, too; a memory. The lurch of a future brought up from the wreck. Tik screams, and Sol is laughing. Ali close, his eyes shining.

She can still feel Celeste leaning against her, the pain of her small weight. The arm is broken, but that doesn't matter. It wasn't enough. It wasn't ever going to be enough. Jude lives as she has always lived, in the wake of her sister. Nothing has changed. At least Nora got what she came for.

Jude turns to look at her. The little silver box clasped on her lap, her fingers tapping at its sides. A window still open, noisy with air. Her face unreadable.

Sol moves and the machine tilts around them, making the earth tip, making Jude's stomach lurch. Below, the sea is ferocious, pummelling the rock. The island seems to be collapsing. From this distance, its structure has no solidity at all. Nothing but a cracked shell breaking open. She catches a glimpse of the red building still standing on a shard of rock, the old ruin outliving the new. She watches as the rest slides into the water like leftovers scraped from a plate.

Celeste is swallowed by the waves, returned to the earth's care. There is no refusing it. She will be held in the shape of those rooms, the shape of his Station, a sunken wreck. The sea will take and take, and Jude is drowning.

The craft pitches as it rises and the ground expands below, the contours of the land becoming visible. She is held, in the air. And everything she sees is living.

Work to be done. Fences to be brought down.

They tilt again, and it's out of sight.

Beside her, Nora raises the silver box to her face. She holds it for a moment, then lifts it to the wind and lets it fall.

ACKNOWLEDGEMENTS

I began writing this book in Torino, Piemonte and finished it on unceded Kaurna land. I am grateful to these places, their movement histories and their many caretakers.

My thanks go to publisher Geordie Williamson, editors David Winter and Belinda Huang, the team at Picador Australia, and my agent Martin Shaw. I am so fortunate to be working with each of you and very grateful for your care.

The writing was sustained by grants from Creative Australia and Arts South Australia. Thank you to these organisations and to all those who work to support and restore public funding to the arts. Thanks to Jessica Alice, Sophie Cunningham, Leon Fernandes, Mathilda Imlah, Laura Kroetsch, Matthew Lamb, Kate Larsen, Fiona Kelly McGregor, Tara June Winch, and everyone at the ASA and MEAA. Thanks also to Emma Webb, Vitalstatistix and its extended community for the support of a long and fortifying residency in 2022.

I am indebted to many friends, colleagues, comrades and strangers who are working to change this world, as well as survive it. You have my respect and my solidarity.

My deepest thanks to Hannah May Caspar, always.

More fiction by Jennifer Mills

DYSCHRONIA

An electrifying novel about an oracle. A small town. And the end of the world as we know it . . .

One morning, the residents of a small coastal town somewhere in Australia wake to discover the sea has disappeared. One among them has been plagued by troubling visions of this cataclysm for years. Is she a prophet? Does she have a disorder that skews her perception of time? Or is she a gifted and compulsive liar?

Oscillating between the future and the past, *Dyschronia* is a novel that tantalises and dazzles, as one woman's prescient nightmares become entangled with her town's uncertain fate. Blazing with questions of consciousness, trust, and destiny, this is a wildly imaginative and extraordinary novel from award-winning author Jennifer Mills.

Finalist for the Aurealis Award for Best Science Fiction Novel 2018

Shortlisted for the Miles Franklin Literary Award 2019

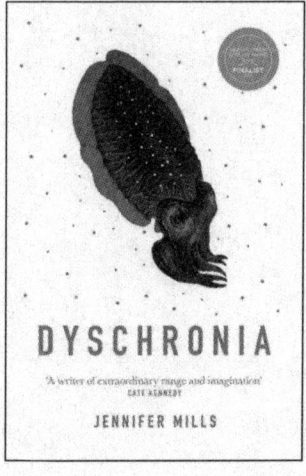

THE AIRWAYS

I had a body once before. I didn't always love it. I knew the skin as my limit, and there were times I longed to leave it.

I knew better than to wish for this.

*This is the story of Yun. It's the story of Adam.
Two young people. A familiar chase.*

*But this is not a love story.
It's a story of revenge, transformation, survival.*

*Feel something, the body commands. Feel this.
But it's a phantom . . . I go untouched.*

They want their body back.

*Who are we, if we lose hold of the body?
What might we become?*

The Airways shifts between Sydney and Beijing, unsettling the boundaries of gender and power, consent and rage, self and other, and even life and death.

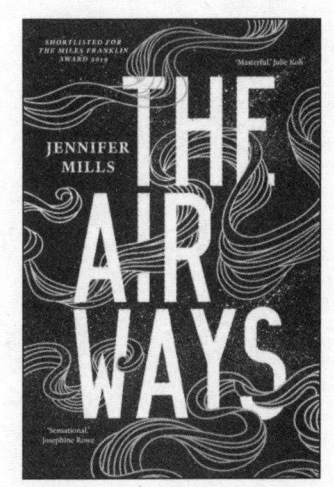

A powerful, inventive, and immersive novel from award-winning author Jennifer Mills.

Shortlisted for the Aurealis Award for Best Horror Novel 2021

Longlisted for the Miles Franklin Literary Award 2022